Susan Sallis is the number one bestselling author of over a dozen novels including *Daughters of the Moon*, *Sweeter Than Wine*, *Water Under the Bridge*, *Touched by Angels*, *Choices*, *Come Rain or Shine*, *The Keys to the Garden* and *The Apple Barrel*. She lives in Clevedon, Somerset.

SEA OF DREAMS

Susan Sallis

CORGI BOOKS

SEA OF DREAMS
A CORGI BOOK : 0 552 14867 9

Originally published in Great Britain by Bantam Press,
a division of Transworld Publishers

PRINTING HISTORY
Bantam Press edition published 2001
Corgi edition published 2001

1 3 5 7 9 10 8 6 4 2

Copyright © Susan Sallis 2001

Set in 11/13pt New Baskerville by
Kestrel Data, Exeter, Devon.

Corgi Books are published by Transworld Publishers,
61–63 Uxbridge Road, London W5 5SA,
a division of The Random House Group Ltd,
in Australia by Random House Australia (Pty) Ltd,
20 Alfred Street, Milsons Point, Sydney, NSW 2061, Australia,
in New Zealand by Random House New Zealand Ltd,
18 Poland Road, Glenfield, Auckland 10, New Zealand
and in South Africa by Random House (Pty) Ltd,
Endulini, 5a Jubilee Road, Parktown 2193, South Africa.

Printed and bound in Germany by
Elsnerdruck, Berlin.

For my family

Chalets and Residents

Bungalow:	Reg Jepson, Arthur and May Long, Mark and Holly Jepson
Linnet:	Paula and Dennis Chiverton
Magpie:	Ted Harris, Ivy Edwards, Tom, Adam, Gemma and Giles
Seagull:	Mavis Gentry, Pansy Pansetti, Bernice Smythe
Wren:	Cree and Cass Evans

One

Mark had his indulgently kind face on. Holly noticed the way the mouth lengthened in gentle amusement, the eyes creased with regret.

'No can do, Nunc,' he said and combed back his floppy brown hair with distrait fingers. 'Much as Holly and I would like to be with you as per usual over Christmas, it means taking time off from the garage and holiday periods are quite our busiest time.'

Holly felt a sudden pang of guilt; Mark would have liked to spend Christmas here in the holiday village with Reg just as they'd done ever since they were married. It was she who was desperate for a change. Then she swallowed her guilt: Mark was quite right, it was terribly difficult to get time off at Christmas. It was the same at the estate agent's where she worked. Come Boxing Day everyone thought it might be fun to move in the spring and they phoned the office and asked what was on the books. Most of them weren't serious but there was always a chance there would be a sale, so she'd meet them and show them round whatever was available. Hugo, the local manager, knew that she and Mark would be back home on Boxing Day.

Uncle Reg looked totally crestfallen.

'But you always come for Christmas dinner. It won't be the same without you. And Holly helps May. How is May going to cope? We've got ten bookings this year and that still leaves Magpie Cottage empty. Sure to get a last-minute enquiry. And Magpie is a six-berth job. So we could have sixteen on Christmas Day!'

Holly was practically certain he was lying; it was the second week in November and people had to be desperate to want to spend the last Christmas of the millennium in Reg's holiday village.

She said sarcastically, 'And with us that would be eighteen. My goodness, what fun that would be.'

Uncle Reg was impervious to sarcasm as well as to indulgent amusement.

'Listen. The garage has got to close on Christmas Day. Could you go back in the evening? Latish. We could bring lunch forward to half-past twelve perhaps, which would give us time to clear away, listen to the Queen, have a jolly good walk by the sea – kids could throw a few pebbles and so on—'

'Kids?' Holly's very clear blue gaze, which

Hugo said could sell a house at twenty paces, sharpened suddenly. 'Have you got a family coming this year then, Reg?'

He moved slightly and laid his arm along one of the radiators. The bungalow had every mod con imaginable.

'Not yet. But I'm expecting a family to take Magpie Cottage. It's big enough and it's got an open fire. Kids love to collect driftwood and keep that going.'

Holly said, 'This family – they've enquired, have they? You know there are children?'

'Not exactly. It's a feeling I have.' Uncle Reg thumped his chest. 'You know me and my feelings.' Holly and Mark nodded resignedly. 'They usually work out.'

'Well . . .' Mark glanced sideways and then strengthened his voice. 'That's all rather by-the-way, isn't it? The thing is, Nunc, we can't make it. You know we wouldn't let you down if we could possibly—'

'Not even for Christmas Day itself?'

Holly stood up and went to the window. Mark continued to make excuses in an apologetic voice and she stopped listening. Outside the enormous picture window, the field sloped down to a mini cliff, then grey shingle and seaweed and the metallic sea. It wasn't the kind of shore-line that attracted children. The sea was muddy and so were the pebbles; there wasn't a trace of sand and unless the Severn Bore pushed a big

tide up to Stonebench the waves were un-
exciting. In the eleven years she had been
married to Mark they had spent every Christmas
here at Uncle Reg's so-called holiday village,
and every Christmas she had imagined trawling
that muddy little beach for driftwood. At first
her dreams had centred around their own
children; now that had ceased to matter. Anybody's children would do.

Mark had started telling his uncle about
the new manager at the garage who wanted
to amalgamate the parts department and the
repair shop.

'He's barely out of short trousers. Pushy as
they come. That's the kind they like these days.
He simply cannot see that spare parts are just as
much a specialist area as the repair shop! I
mean, Nunc, I've been there sixteen years. What
I don't know about spare parts for all major
makes . . . well, not worth knowing. That's all I
can say.'

But it wouldn't be all Mark would say, unfortunately. Holly took a deep breath.

'We want to have a quiet Christmas, Reg,'
she said firmly. 'We don't want a turkey or
a pudding. We don't want to see one piece of
mistletoe. We don't want to get up until midday.
Then we want to go for a drive somewhere and
come back when it's dark and have poached eggs
on toast.'

There was a little silence then Mark laughed

uncomfortably. 'What Holly means, Nunc, is that we need a bit of a change from the usual routine.'

Holly turned and came back to her chair. She said, 'We're tired, Reg. And we're both discouraged. We're working our socks off and we don't know why any more. We need to have time together and talk about where we're going.' She leaned forward. 'It shouldn't be hard for you to understand. You had Maude and you loved her. We know that. But you were like us – no family. You must have felt . . . surely you wondered at times . . . what it was all for. Didn't you feel that, Reg? Be honest. Stop being bluff old Uncle Reg who opens up the holiday village at Christmas to give people a good time – a kind of latter-day St Nicholas—'

'Shut up, Holly,' Mark said.

But she couldn't. Somehow she couldn't. 'I'm surprised you don't dress up in a white beard and red dressing gown and go round with expensive presents—'

'Holly, for God's sake!'

Uncle Reg said easily, 'I don't mind. I know what she means.' He turned to face Holly and gave her a smile. She felt a very small lump in her throat. He had been seventy when they came here first, eleven – no, twelve – years ago. That made him eighty-two. He was old. And alone.

He said, 'Listen, Holly. It's because we didn't have any family that we took this place on. We knew we'd never lack company. And by gum, we haven't! And people come to have a good time – they're in a good mood – we see them at their very best.' The funny thing was, he might be old but he was right, he never seemed to be lonely. She stared down at him: the thick hair was so like Mark's except that it was snow-white; the craggy face was still so alive.

She said weakly, 'Reg, that might have been the case – might still be the case – in summer. But now . . . look!' She gestured helplessly at the window. 'Predominant colour, grey. Sea and sky and mud. Lots of rain. And what kind of people come at Christmas? People who are lonely and unhappy . . .'

'That's why I always insist on Christmas dinner here. Together.' He spread his hands with the kind of sweet reasonableness she had seen before. It usually served him well but this time she was not going to give in.

'Exactly what I meant just now. About you seeing yourself as a bountiful St Nicholas-type person.' She tried to take the sting out with a slight stammer and a smile. 'It's not for us this year, Reg. It's not the real world, you see. We need this little holiday to sort out what our real world is. And . . .' She glanced at Mark and then away. 'And whether we can bear it. Frankly.'

Reg turned and looked at Mark too. And, of course, as usual Mark looked away.

Reg took a deep breath. 'Well, I'm not going

to pretend it will be the same without you because it won't. You're my special family. I'm going to miss you. But . . .' He searched for one of his truisms and came up with 'What will be, will be.' He grinned suddenly. 'D'you remember that first year you came down as a couple? I don't think you were married then, were you? But Maude said, they can play at being house owners and what they get up to is none of our business, so you went into Magpie Cottage and, by gum, did you play! I can just see Holly going into the sea on Christmas Day – there was a bit of snow mixed with the rain and she screamed fit to bust but then she said it was warm! Warm, my foot!'

Mark said, 'I went in too!' He laughed. 'We came out covered in mud, didn't we?'

'You went in too, Mark? I don't remember that!'

'I didn't want to. But I couldn't let her go in that icy sea on her own.'

'No. You were very close.' There was a little pause then he went on, 'That was the year Maude said we'd have to have showers fitted in all the chalets.'

'You've had a lot done, Nunc. Can't be much profit to be had out of the place, surely?'

'Enough to keep me and Maude going. And now me. And in the lap of luxury.' He grinned at Holly. 'Might be grey outside, Holly, but look round this room.'

She did so. It was a hotch-potch of colours; chocolate-box pictures, brass ornaments; literally dozens of photographs cluttered several odd coffee tables; every chair was filled with piles of cushions mostly embroidered by Maude. Along each radiator shelf, lines of jet elephants marched; in the corners were padded stools made from elephants' feet. She shifted her gaze and saw the film of dust covering the top surface of each object. Last year she and May had given everything what May called a good going-over while the men went up to the Ship's Lantern for a Christmas Eve drink. The small lump in her throat made itself felt again. She said sincerely, 'It's lovely, Reg. Warm and homely. Lovely.'

He nodded. 'Every item in this room could tell a story. Every single item.'

Mark said jovially, 'We know. We've heard every one of them!' He glanced at his watch. 'It'll be dark in an hour, Reg. Don't want to be too late back home. Work in the morning. How about a stroll around the baronial estate?'

'Why not?' The old man levered himself out of his chair. 'Can you get my coat, Holly? And Mark – my stick's in the umbrella stand in the hall. And I'll have a hat too. I was reading in some paper that you lose most of your body heat through your head. Did you know that, Holly? You should take to wearing a hat. Well, both of you. But I suppose because you've got all that hair, Holl, you don't feel the cold so much as we poor men. But it said in this article—'

'I'll wrap my scarf over my head, Reg.'

'That's a good girl. Maude always said how lucky you were to have curly hair, Holl.' He huffed and puffed into his coat. 'Something to do with it being better insulated or something. She knew these things. She said you being fair was good too because the grey hair doesn't show up so much.' He hesitated, looking at her closely. 'She was right too. I hadn't noticed before. How old are you now, Holly?'

She answered very deliberately, 'Thirty-eight, Reg.'

'Sorry. Never ask a woman her age. Maude told me that too.'

She forced a grin. 'We're family, Reg. No secrets.'

He grinned too, pleased, and took his stick from Mark. They went outside and the grey, damp air wrapped them around. There was a short gravel path through Reg's little garden to the six-foot-wide concrete pathway that would just take a car. A few withered snapdragons struggled out of the borders and skeletal rose bushes made arthritic shapes under the windows of the bungalow. Mark led the way, walking sideways to keep an eye on Reg; Holly brought up the rear, locking the front door in spite of Reg's assurances that he never did. They took up formation on the concrete and walked down towards the sea. The road was steep, the chalets all stepped in on terraces so that each one could offer uninterrupted views of the sea and the distant misty hills of Wales. As usual Uncle Reg said, 'Easy going down, tough going back up.' And Mark said, 'Why don't you get one of those little electric chairs, Nunc? Be just the thing to get you up to the pub at nights.'

'Only chance for a bit of exercise, lad. While I can do it, I will.'

'Well, hang onto me with your free arm. Take a bit of help while you can.'

'Righty-ho. And Holly that side. Reminds me of the Gay Gordons. Maude used to love all those old dances. The Veleta and the Gay Gordons and the Dashing . . . what was it? . . . the Dashing—'

'White Sergeant,' Mark supplied

'White Sergeant. That was it. Maude wanted us to build a dance hall, you know. Lots of these holiday camps have a dance hall. Somewhere for people to go in the day too if it's raining. Play cards. Table tennis. Never got round to it.'

'Doesn't seem worth it now,' Holly said without thinking. And then could have bitten off her tongue. Because it was giving Uncle Reg an opening to ask them to keep the village going after he was gone.

There was a short, breathy silence while they negotiated the bend that led round to the

18

largest chalet, Magpie Cottage. Then all Reg said was, 'Yes. True.'

Holly thought gloomily that he had probably written something into his last will and testament.

It turned out that Reg had the key to Magpie Cottage with him, and he insisted on having a look inside. 'Haven't done an inspection since summer,' he said, pushing the key clumsily into the door. 'Could be a leak in that back porch. And if that family take it on . . .'

'What family might that be, Reg?' Holly asked.

'Not sure yet.' Reg was oblivious to her sarcasm. 'Can't say too much. Not my business really, is it? Families are families. That's all I know.'

Across his Russian-style fur hat which Maude had so lovingly chosen for him, Holly widened her eyes at Mark. He blinked and shrugged.

'Looks all right,' Reg panted, going straight through the living room to the kitchen and verandah. 'I had a builder look at that porch in the summer. After the Edwardses reported the leak.' He glanced around him and sniffed suspiciously. 'Smells a bit of damp, doesn't it?'

'What can you expect, Nunc? No-one's used the place since September, I suppose?'

'October actually. They came back. To try and patch things up.'

'So . . . this Mr Edwards was a builder?' Holly enquired.

19

'Oh no. I don't know what his job was. Patch up his marriage, I meant. Don't reckon it would work though. She used to go up to the dustbins sporting new bruises every morning. Couple of kids too. Always hard on the kids.' He pulled off a glove and put his hand flat on the wall. 'He said it was all right – no wet at all. But of course it didn't rain the week they came back so he didn't know whether the leak was still there. Or not.' Even Reg was getting confused.

Mark patted his arm reassuringly and pulled the sofa away from the wall. 'It's dry, Nunc. No need to worry. If you do get this family back again for Christmas, switch the heating on the day before and leave a couple of windows slightly open. That will do the trick. Frankly, they don't sound the sort you want here.'

Holly said, 'Might give those poor kids a break though. Next time we slip down, I'll bring some air freshener and pot-pourri.' Reg gave a tiny secret smile and she added sharply, 'Gesture of goodwill, Reg. As we're not spending Christmas here this time.'

'Nice of you, Holly,' he panted as he made for the door again.

She could barely wait to get up to the road and into the car before she started.

'What a dump! Honestly, Mark, we're well out of that! When I think of how we've slaved down there all those years – May and me in the kitchen, you in and out of the chalets trying to deal with the complaints. It's ridiculous to open the place up in the middle of winter. He's such a sentimental idiot—'

'Christmas is a time for sentiment, Holly. And he's always done his bit.'

'The St Nicholas bit, you mean?' She sighed with exasperation. 'Don't tell me you're going to miss it? That hideous room with the trestle tables down the middle and the tinsel falling into the gravy boats and the obligatory carol singing and the freezing walk after?'

He was laughing. 'Well, of course I'll miss it – so will you if you're honest. But the alternative is undeniably attractive.' He grinned at her. 'I shall expect at least six crime novels in my stocking and no talking while I'm reading—'

'I thought we decided to have a lovely country drive?' she protested.

'You can drive and I'll read.'

He was joking, of course, but she couldn't help saying, 'That just about sums up our marriage, doesn't it?'

And he stopped joking and was quiet as he negotiated the roundabout and got onto the M5 for Bristol.

Holly Farleigh was an only child of almost elderly parents. They could hardly believe it when she was born, and when she grew into a pretty little girl and then a stunning teenager they hardly knew how to cope with her and lived in perpetual fear that she would 'bring home trouble'. But Holly had common sense as well as beauty. At school she loved all kinds of craft work especially modelling with clay, but she knew she was not good enough to earn a living at a potter's wheel. Her friends thought she should become a model, and with her cascading fair hair and intensely blue eyes she might have stood a chance. But all she could find to say to the careers adviser was that she wanted to 'help people'. Much later she would remember that and cringe with embarrassment.

Nursing was suggested and turned down. Social work met the same fate. Holly had had enough of studies and lessons. Her school report stated that her ideals had no practical basis and perhaps some voluntary work for a charity organization would give her a better idea of her options.

Her mother's friend worked for a large firm which offered funding to worthy causes. Holly joined them as a junior in their charity office. She read some statistics and was amazed and delighted at the amount of help they dispensed. For five years she opened applications for funding and sorted them in all kinds of ways: local and not so local, from registered charities and from informal sources, for enormous amounts of money to pleas for payment of a three-month lease on industrial premises. She took tea into the meetings and learned how decisions were made. She took application forms to the printers and collected them; put them in envelopes with a standard letter and posted them. Sometimes she sat in on interviews and went home afterwards to cry because the deserving never seemed to get any money. And by the time she was twenty-one she was disenchanted with the whole business of charity funding and took a job stacking shelves in the local supermarket.

She worked all hours at KutPrice and when an elderly aunt left her a small legacy she was delighted to find she could afford to buy a flat in the Bedminster area of Bristol. It wasn't what her father called an upmarket venue but it suited her very well. It also gave her the opportunity to change her job. Hugo Venables ran the Bristol branch of Jamieson's, a reputable firm of auctioneers who had specialized in selling cattle in the first half of the century and turned their attention to houses after the war. It was so different from the charity office and yet, in a strange way, she felt she was really helping people when she guided them through the intricacies of buying a home. When she arranged a mortgage and saw the delight on the faces of the would-be house owners, she felt what Hugo called job satisfaction.

Hugo had needed office staff who 'had something about them' and it was obvious from the start that Holly Farleigh had quite a lot about her. She knew he fancied her but he was married and she was no longer a schoolgirl. She could cope with Hugo.

He suggested that, as she so often showed clients around properties, the firm should provide her with a car. And that was how she met Mark . . .

Mark Jepson was two years older than she was and lived with his mother in a tall old house on the Wells Road. He had rather wanted to be a farmer but, like Holly with her hazy notion of wishing to be a potter, he had been sensible and accepted that farming was not for him. He too had left school at sixteen, when his father died. He had quixotic ideas of becoming the sole breadwinner, but his mother had reapplied for her old job at Lewis's and was soon a buyer. They lived together comfortably but separately. Mark worked in the office at Minster Garages and was quite confident that one day he would run the spare parts department and then later be made manager.

When his mother brought a colleague home to tea, Mark liked him. Nevertheless it was a shock when they married and Mark could never quite rid himself of the feeling that his mother had betrayed his father. He still lived separately in the tall house but he did not feel comfortable there any more.

Hugo Venables took Holly in to look at a new Ford Fiesta in the showroom just as Mark was walking through to the storeroom. He assumed they were a couple and that she was therefore out of bounds, but he noted that she was the most beautiful girl he had ever seen. Her springy hair was gathered into a bunchy ponytail and her eyes seemed to light up when they met his.

'May I help you?' he asked.

'We'd like a test drive.' Hugo indicated the Fiesta.

'I think our salesman is out just now.' Mark smiled into Holly's blue eyes. 'I'll get the keys. If you and your wife would like to sit a moment?'

Hugo laughed, enjoying the mistake. It was Holly who said quickly, 'This is my boss. We're looking for a company car.'

Mark scooped his floppy brown hair away from his eyes and widened his smile. 'In that case, perhaps I can take you out?'

In those days she had loved the way he flipped his hair back, and she had never ceased to marvel at how he managed to exclude Hugo from the test drive and take her out himself.

The Bedminster flat was a temporary arrangement until they started a family. They talked over everything; they constantly exclaimed at how identical their feelings and experiences were. They were especially delighted to find that a family was top of the list of priorities.

'It's because we haven't got siblings,' Holly said wisely.

'Perhaps.' Mark took her hand. 'For me, it's something to do with my ma marrying again. I feel rotten about it – rotten that I resent it too. Why shouldn't she make her own life now? Dad died so long ago . . .'

'If I die will you marry again?' Holly asked.

'No.' He gripped her hand. 'What about you?'

'Never.'

They couldn't believe their luck in meeting each other. It was so obvious that there would never be anyone else. What if she hadn't gone into the car showroom that day? What if the salesman had been there and whisked her off before she set eyes on Mark? What if Hugo had turned down the suggestion of a test drive without him?

'You wouldn't have let that happen,' Holly said with complete certainty.

In those days she had thought him master of both their fates.

Everything went so well for such a long time. Her parents loved Mark and at last appeared to relax from worrying about their never-errant daughter. Mark's mother and her new husband moved to the south coast and bought a gift shop and Mark and Holly went regularly to stay with them. They also visited Mark's uncle, Reg Jepson, at his holiday village. Holly fell in love with Uncle Reg and Aunt Maude that first

Christmas. They insisted on their taking the large Magpie Cottage. 'When you have a family that will be the one for you. So you might as well get used to it straight away!' Reg said with meaningful looks at his nephew.

They had slept together before then but they hadn't kept house together. It was delightful, like a special game. They shared most meals with Reg and Maude up at the big bungalow and took long walks along the coastal path to Portishead and then to Clevedon and almost as far as Weston. Holly insisted on having a swim, so Mark had to go in with her. They romped in the brown water like seals and waded out through the mud, laughing helplessly. It took three baths full of water to clean them.

'Can we come next Christmas?' Holly asked as they said their grateful farewells.

'You've started so you have to go on,' Reg said, parodying a television quiz programme of the time. 'This is how you spend Christmas from now on!'

'Oh, wonderful!' said Holly.

It was. For the next three years, while Maude was alive, she could not imagine a better way of spending the Christmas break. They got extra time off from work and stayed until after New Year's Day. Reg would hug them both when they left and say, 'Maybe next year there will be three of you! Eh? What have you got to say to that?' It must have been Maude's last Christmas when she said sharply, 'Shut up, Reg, for goodness' sake! Of all people, you should know better.'

That year Holly was very quiet as they drove back to Bristol. Mark glanced at her several times and then took the bull by the horns.

'It will happen, darling. Exactly like Doc Whitman said. There's nothing wrong with either of us. All we need to do is relax.'

She said quietly, 'All that business. Taking my temperature and keeping a graph of fertile times and then . . . that wasn't exactly relaxing.'

He laughed. 'No.'

'It's not funny, Mark!' Her voice was unexpectedly sharp.

He gave her another quick look. 'No. But if we could see it as funny it might also become relaxing.' He took one hand from the steering wheel and put it on her knee. 'Listen, sweetheart. We've had a week in Magpie Cottage Very relaxed indeed. Let's wait and see, shall we?'

She should have put her own hand over his and said she was sorry. She was sorry; she had been sorry for so long because she did not conceive like normal women. She was sick of being constantly sorry.

After a while he removed his hand and they drove through Abbots Leigh in silence. There was very little traffic; it was not a day for a drive, the trees dripped from the last rainstorm and the sky was leaden. Mark changed gear and they began the long descent to the Cumberland Basin.

She said, 'Maude was annoyed with Reg, wasn't she? Teasing us about having kids. I hadn't thought of it before but they've never had a family.'

'No.' He negotiated a bend. 'I think that must be why they were always so close to May and Arthur's kids.'

'Oh? Have I met them? The kids, I mean.'

'No. They're grown-up now. Both went into the Forces, I think. They used to be a couple of tearaways. I was frightened to death of them.'

'May and Arthur are such a couple of softies too.' She tried to laugh.

He said quietly, 'It will be all right, Holly. Really.'

She wanted to believe him. But she was wondering whether sterility ran in the family.

They did not move out of the flat; after all, they were both working all day and sometimes late into the evenings and the flat was easy to maintain. So nothing changed. The next Christmas, without Maude, was not so much fun; Reg was very subdued and May needed help so Holly rolled up her sleeves and tried to take Maude's place in the kitchen. She wasn't that used to domesticity and this was catering on a large scale. There were twelve around the trestle tables that year, and eighteen for the next three years. She and Mark found it difficult to get away together for their long walks, and after that first year they stayed at the bungalow so that Reg could let a proper family have Magpie Cottage. It became less and less fun and more and more hard work.

Other things went horribly wrong. Mark's mother died and his stepfather almost immediately married a much younger woman. Within a year his new wife was pregnant. Mark was appalled and though Holly was sympathetic she felt bound to point out that second marriages often did bring second families.

'It's not only the sheer lack of loyalty,' Mark said, 'it's the fact that my mother's share of the money has gone. I don't want to sound grabbing, Holly, but that was ours. Ma would have wanted us to have something.'

Holly nodded. 'It's the luck of the draw, Mark,' she agreed sadly. 'Please don't be bitter about it. Your mother would certainly not have wanted that.'

She had almost given up on the idea of children. Talking to May as they worked in the kitchen at the bungalow, she had had to accept that – as May put it – it was the luck of the draw.

'Maude would have loved a family,' May said. 'We were best friends at school and stayed best friends until the day she died. She told me everything. Reg was very . . . well, you know . . . keen in that way. So it wasn't for want of trying.

But nothing happened.' She still wept at the mention of Maude's name and blew her nose with some violence as she straightened her back. 'No good crying over spilt milk,' she said briskly. 'Reg is always saying that to me. And he's right. What's done is done. We've got to accept it.'

Holly thought it was a strange way of dealing with both childlessness and bereavement. She said, 'Did they go for tests and things? I mean, were there tests in those days?'

'Of course there were!' May looked quite huffy. 'But I don't think . . . I don't really know.'

Holly concentrated on the sprouts; she must have done six pounds already. Christmases at the holiday village were rapidly losing their charm.

She blurted, 'Mark has had tests. We both have.'

'Oh!' May opened her grey eyes wide and then went back to rolling pastry. After a long pause she said, 'Test results aren't always right. I do know that.'

Holly cut a cross on three more sprouts then said, 'So you think it runs in the family? Reg couldn't have children and neither can Mark?'

May was shocked. 'I didn't say that, dear! All I'm saying is that at the end of the day tests don't prove anything. If you're both all right and there's no children, then what do the tests matter?'

Holly opened another net of sprouts and said grimly, 'Well, you're right there.'

'It's just the luck of the draw, dear. That's all.'

At the end of November, Hugo Venables threw a party. It was twenty years since Jamieson's had opened the Bristol branch and put him in charge of it and in that time they had gone from strength to strength. There were now six full-time members of staff and five part-timers. Hugo was determined this party would do him credit. He invited council members, members of the Chamber of Commerce, builders' representatives, developers, anyone he could think of who might be of help to the firm. 'This will be the biggest public relations job we've ever done!' he exulted to Holly.

'It's supposed to be a celebration of twenty years of business,' Holly reminded him. But she smiled because over the years they had become friends. The friendship was cautious on her side and familiar on his. He still congratulated her sales with a kiss which she always had to end; he could never stand by her desk without draping an arm around her shoulders. Mark called him a creep and she thought that was probably a good description of him. 'Job qualification,' she laughed.

In spite of all that, she found she was quite excited at the prospect of the party. She bought a full-length off-the-shoulder dress in a sea-green taffeta with long matching gloves. She tried it on for Mark, who had popped in for lunch though Saturday was his busiest day. He was almost startled.

'Is that kind of thing back in fashion? What about the short black strappy frock you usually wear?'

She was crestfallen. 'I thought, as this is really rather a grand occasion, I'd go for a traditional . . . well, ball gown, I suppose. Is it over the top?'

'It's wonderful. And you look absolutely stunning. You'll outshine Dinah Venables completely.'

'Ah.' She bit her lip. That probably wasn't a good move. Dinah would be the hostess after all.

Mark picked up her fingers and kissed them. 'Go for it, Holly. You've helped make Jamieson's what it is. In fact you've probably done more than the rest of them put together.' He smiled then spoiled it all by adding, 'All that overtime! You deserve to be the star of the show.'

She retrieved her hand and said sharply, 'You know why I've done the overtime. It all seems a bit of a waste now.'

He said tiredly, 'Holly, please. We've decided to talk it all over at Christmas. Change direction perhaps. Buy a house. Adopt.'

'We're too old to adopt. And anyway you never really wanted to—'

'What makes you say that? I thought it was you who was against it!'

33

She stared at him. Did he really think that? Was it true?

His voice dropped again. 'It's rather academic anyway, isn't it? Unless you really want us to hurl recriminations at each other?'

She said slowly, 'No. I don't want that.' She went to the window and looked out. The view was as bleak as it had been from Uncle Reg's but without the sea. She said, 'When I bought this flat, I thought it was great to look out on people hurrying in and out of shops. Delivery vans. The barber shop. Somehow . . . Dickensian.'

He stayed by the coffee table. It was Saturday afternoon and he had to go back to work. He stared at his wife's long slim form swathed in the green taffeta. With her blond hair she looked like a daffodil.

'And now . . .' he sighed, 'now you don't feel that way any more. Probably it is time for us to move then.'

'I don't want that either. I don't want to argue with you. I don't want to move. But I don't want . . .' She swept her hands around vaguely. 'I don't want any of this.'

He knew what she wanted. She wanted him to take command; to decide their future in positive terms. She wanted him to say, 'I've seen this old farmhouse in the Mendips. We can do it up. Live the simple life. I've worked it all out. You can make your pots again in the stable. I can run a smallholding.'

Or did she? Maybe it was him she was fed up with? And in any case it was probably years too late for him to stop being an underdog.

So he said, 'I know what you mean. I'm not that keen on moving either. We're in the doldrums, that's all it is.'

She said dully, 'Yes. That's all it is.'

He went to the door. It was late; if there were customers waiting it would be another excuse to amalgamate the departments.

He hovered helplessly and then said, 'Anyway, Holl, we haven't given up hope of starting a family, have we?'

She did not turn but shook her head. After the door had closed on him she went on weeping until she could no longer see him waving from below. The awful thing was, she really did not know any more why she wept.

Two

Hugo arranged a special line-up to greet the guests. Zeb Jamieson himself had put in an appearance; he was over retiring age and looked it with his full beard and scant white hair. His father had insisted on his learning the cattle business from slurry upwards, and he was known in the firm – with some affection – as Farmer Zeb. His wife had died some time ago so he had brought his sister with him. She and Holly were the only two women in the line-up who wore long dresses. Holly hoped very much she did not resemble Hannah Jamieson in any other way.

Hugo and Dinah Venables stood next to the sister. Hugo looked as impeccable as ever in his dinner suit. Dinah seemed to be in competition with Hannah for looking somehow entirely wrong. She was in a ballet-length dress with big puff sleeves. It was so completely out of date Holly could not think where she could have bought it. Holly and Mark stood next to her. By the time they had reached the Harbour Hotel, parked the car and got rid of their coats, Holly had been certain she too was in completely the wrong dress. Dinah's Snow White outfit did not help. Holly glanced sideways at Mark, who was leaning down to hear what Dinah was saying. He was smilingly attentive just as he had been with Uncle Reg. She hoped that Dinah – or Hugo – would not see him as condescendingly indulgent, in the way that she did.

She held out her hand to someone wearing a chain of office, then to an effusive lady in black – 'My dear, you look absolutely wonderful!' – and then to two girls, presumably their daughters, who giggled and blushed. It was becoming automatic. She leaned towards an elderly gentleman with a red shoulder sash who was saying something inaudible.

'Mrs Jepson? A message for your husband . . .' It was the master of ceremonies. She swayed back to make room for him to speak to Mark.

He spoke sonorously. 'Your uncle, sir. He's in Southmead Hospital. Orthopaedic. He fell and appears to have broken his hip.'

Mark said, 'Oh my God . . .'

'He's asking for you, sir. Perhaps you would like me to get a taxi?'

'I've got the car. Holly—'

She said swiftly, 'We can't go now, Mark. It's miles. And the weather—'

He said gently – she noticed he used the same tone on her as he used on Dinah Venables –

'Darling, I have to go. I'm his only relative.' He smiled and flipped back his hair. 'No need for you to come. It's your show after all.'

She knew he was right and that she was being unreasonable, but she could not help herself. 'Leave it for an hour – just an hour. Once the whole thing gets under way it won't matter half so much—'

'Holl . . .' He had already dropped back from the line-up. People were passing them by and Hugo was shooting his special look in her direction. 'I have to go. I'll be back to take you home – have the last dance or something.'

He seemed to melt away. She returned Hugo's look and immediately smiled at the chairman of the Chamber of Commerce.

'Good to see you and your wife. I think we met last Christmas? Carols in the Lord Mayor's Chapel?'

They obviously did not remember her. She stood next to Dinah and felt like the office junior again. After all, she had no actual standing in the firm. She was the complete and absolute spare part. Her smile became grim at that thought because Mark, who was an expert in spare parts, was no longer there. As she shook the next hand she caught a sideways glimpse of Hugo explaining who she was. People probably thought she was there because of her blond hair and blue eyes. When the hand-shaking had finished and Hugo ushered them into the dining room, she had to explain about Mark's sudden disappearance.

'His uncle? Oh well, that's a relief. I thought it might be something really awful.'

She said feebly, 'Mark is his only relative,' but Hugo was not listening. People were milling around the enormous room, finding their places. She was next to Hugo on the top table. Dinah was on his right. Mark would have been on the end, so she had no-one else to talk to. Hugo did not mind looking after her in the least; he had never made any pretence of being interested in his wife. He was already flushed and bright-eyed.

He said tensely, 'Well? What do you think?'

'I think you've had quite a lot to drink,' she said, smiling brightly. 'Dutch courage before you left home?'

'Don't start nagging me. I've had enough of that from Di.' He blinked as if dazzled. 'God, you're looking wonderful. Second thoughts, I don't mind you nagging me one bit. Shows you care.'

'Actually, I don't.'

'Don't what?'

'Care. I don't care.'

He grinned. 'You're mad with Mark and you're taking it out on me. That's OK too.' He jumped as Dinah dug him in the ribs. The soup had arrived in a tureen on a trolley. He leaned hard against Holly's shoulder while he was served. 'Looks good. Di-dear, let me introduce you to Councillor Stevens. Jack, is it? Jack, this is my wife, Dinah. And this is my partner, Holly Jepson.' He filled Holly's wine glass as he spoke and put his free hand on her arm. 'I couldn't manage without her.'

Dinah bridled. 'Or without me, Hugo.'

'Absolutely not, Di-dear. See if you can sell Jack a new house!' He laughed inordinately as he turned back to Holly. 'Holly, drink up. We're celebrating tonight, remember.'

She was stunned. 'Yes, I remember. Celebrating twenty years . . .'

He slid his hand from arm to shoulder and then to waist. 'And we're doing that by making you a partner in the firm. What do you think of that, Holly Jepson?'

She stared at him, then drank quickly. 'You're joking.'

'No. I talked it over with Farmer Zeb and he was all for it.' He refilled her glass. 'You've been depressed lately. It's because you felt unrecognized. I wanted to put that right.'

She was filled with gratitude. 'Oh Hugo.' She wished Mark could be there to enjoy this too. 'Wish you'd told me yesterday.'

'Only thought of it tonight. When you came in wearing that frock and looking like a million dollars, I thought, why not. If Dinah can be a partner with no hope of selling a house ever, then surely—'

40

'I thought you said you'd discussed it with Mr Jamieson?'

'I did. When we stood in that line-up I told him what a wonderful member of staff you'd always been and he said why not make it a threesome.'

'Threesome?'

'Me and Dinah. And now you.'

'I see.' She sipped her wine; was it her third glass? A third glass for a third director.

He said, 'Salmon. Isn't that an aphrodisiac?'

Zeb Jamieson leaned across Dinah. 'Don't think you need any of that newfangled nonsense, Venables.' He smiled at Holly. 'Welcome to the firm, my dear. Here's to the three of you.' He held up his glass. They all drank. Zeb patted Dinah's hand and she giggled; Hugo patted Holly and she heard herself giggle almost in unison.

The evening seemed to take flight after that. Holly knew she had had too much to drink but she wasn't driving and Mark wasn't there and unexpectedly she was having a good time and might even be happy. She wasn't quite sure about that; after all maybe it wasn't such a wonderful thing to be a co-director with Dinah Venables. But it must surely mean more money and that might mean she could leave work altogether in a year or two and they could buy a place in the country, and then she might even set up a pottery and a kiln. Poor Uncle Reg.

Hugo said, 'Poor Uncle who?'

'Reg. Did I say that out loud? He runs this grotty little holiday place on the coast and he opens for Christmas and we always go but we're not going this year because we've got to sort ourselves out.'

'Hang on. Which coast?'

'North of Clevedon. A few chalets. He lives in a bungalow – spacious. Lets the chalets. Magpie Cottage is quite big. We stayed there years ago. It was fun then. I went swimming on Christmas Day . . .'

'It's muddy down there, surely?'

'Oh yes. I got covered. Plastered.' She giggled. 'Mark came in with me and afterwards we had a bath together.'

'Ooooh.'

'Maude had showers put in after that. I think we must have bunged up the pipes or something.'

'Maude being . . . don't tell me, Uncle Reg's wife. A dragon. That's why you're not going down this year.'

She laughed; it seemed so funny. Hugo should surely know all this. After all, they worked together fairly closely and now they were on an equal footing professionally. Well, almost.

'Maude is dead. And Reg expects me to take over from her in the kitchen.'

'And you're rebelling. Well done. Let's get together and have a Christmas without kitchens.

What was that song about keeping out of the kitchen . . .' He tried an experimental melody between his teeth.

She said hurriedly, 'Nothing to do with kitchens. We want – we need – to talk about ourselves. Mark and me.' She shouldn't be saying this. But she was Hugo's partner and he had always been so . . . receptive.

Hugo stopped whistling and looked at her. 'Uh-oh. That's the sort of thing I say to Di-dear when I want a divorce.'

She felt her brows rise. 'I didn't realize—'

He glanced hastily over his shoulder and saw his wife deep in conversation with Zeb. 'She won't have it. At any price.' He giggled. 'Not that I've offered enormous amounts of spondulicks. Not worth it. Remember that, Holly. Separate lives and no nagging – go for that every time.'

'Oh, we're not talking divorce. Nothing like that. Just to see what our goals might be. Perhaps even move the goalposts.'

An enormous spun-sugar swan was placed on their table. Its back was scooped out and filled with fruits. Gentle applause rippled around the room. Holly smiled delightedly and Hugo blinked again.

'My God, you're gorgeous, Holl. I haven't seen you like this for ages. We must do it more often.'

Everyone was laughing and talking across the tables. Hannah Jamieson tipped her chair to ask

43

Holly whether Mark would be joining them later. Holly could not remember. 'Yes, I think he must be. Otherwise I've no way of getting home.'

'There are such things as taxis,' Hannah said repressively.

'Of course.'

'I will take you home, Holly.' Hugo was flushed with success. It was obvious everyone was enjoying themselves very much indeed. 'Di-dear doesn't drink so we shall be all right.'

Dinah said, 'Hugo, you've had enough. You've still got to make your speech.'

'I'm introducing Zeb. I can manage that.' He glanced at Holly and she choked back a laugh. This was the sort of fun she used to have with Mark. Ridiculous jokes that weren't amusing until they were shared.

The swan was emptied of its fruit and the master of ceremonies proposed the toast to the Queen and then Hugo stood up and welcomed everyone and talked rather ramblingly of the beginnings of the agency in Bristol, 'springing from the rootstock of the long-standing firm of auctioneers well known throughout Somerset and Wiltshire'. Holly nodded and stared down into her demitasse of black coffee and waited for him to mention the new partner. He left that to Zeb, who did it with old-fashioned charm and courtesy. She stood briefly and smiled and said she hoped the new millennium would be good for all of them. She had not had time to think of a speech and knew that she was barely making sense. Some of the women at the other tables exchanged glances. She suddenly wanted Mark by her side. These people were strangers and probably did not know she was married. Did they link her with Hugo?

The evening ended quite quickly after that. Zeb and Hannah Jamieson were staying in the hotel and made their departure as soon as they decently could; they were used to early nights. She found herself in the foyer with her coat and umbrella; people were milling around waiting for taxis and there was no sign of Hugo or Dinah. A woman she half recognized peered at her from beneath a rain hat.

'My dear, isn't this just awful? Everyone needing a taxi and only a few of us with the forethought to book one!' She laughed. 'It's going to be a long wait. Good job we're all in a party mood!'

Holly found she was no longer in a party mood. She wanted Mark to appear and whisk her home so that she could go to bed. When he didn't she felt angry with him. She should have been angry with Hugo, who had promised her a lift. She held her coat around her and tried to be sensible. Taxis eventually arrived and took people away. The night porter was arranging for all the cabs to return as soon as possible; every-one would have transport, he assured them.

She wasn't quite the last in the foyer when

45

Hugo appeared. She was so pleased to see him she could have wept.

'I thought you'd forgotten.'

He was over-gallant, opening the door in the pouring rain and gathering her skirt onto her lap.

'This is the best bit of the party – how could I possibly forget?'

'You're driving?' she asked as he settled beside her, much too close. 'But we've been drinking all evening.'

'You sound like Dinah. Did you hear that woman in the foyer? Thought we were . . . what's it called? A *ménage à trois*!' He laughed and pulled out from the kerb much too quickly. Luckily there was no traffic around.

'It's Mark's fault. Obviously they thought you and I were together.' She was vexed at first, then when he continued to laugh she had to join in. 'I know. It's just so silly.'

'Not at all! It's like I told you. Don't go for a divorce, go for separate lives. That way, you and I can make it a real partnership.'

She was horrified. She peered through the wiped cone of clear windscreen glass. 'What are you doing, Hugo? We're heading towards Clifton!'

'Oh damn.' He grinned. 'So we are. Better find a safe place to turn, eh?'

He twisted the steering wheel and they bumped over grass and then onto the Downs.

He switched off and reclined both their seats with grinding bumps.

She said, 'For God's sake! What are you doing? Hugo – stop – you can't do this! You know very well I'm married—'

'Don't be coy, darling. You know this has been boiling up for the whole of our time together. You're fed up with your marriage, no kids so it's obvious there's no danger there—'

She sobbed and hit out at him but he was amazingly strong. He was kissing her and tearing at her clothes and though she kept hitting him she could not free herself from the seat belt and roll out into the rain. She thought with a shock that this was it: she was being raped. And Hugo did not even realize it. She had been giving him false messages all evening – and apparently before that – and now she was trapped.

In the end she stopped fighting and tried to feign complete indifference. She remembered all the times she had been examined and one of the nurses had said to her, 'Pretend the lower half of your body does not belong to you.' She had perfected that technique and it stood her in good stead now. Her one fear was that she would be sick. When he rolled off her she had to stay very still, fighting nausea. He kept one hand on her abdomen as he fought for breath.

'All right?' he asked at last. She made a sound and he gasped a laugh. 'You can say that again.

47

Have you done it in a car before?' He assumed she had not. 'It's an acquired taste.' He laughed again and took his hand away to deal with his clothes. She reached for her seat belt and when she could not find it she sobbed aloud. He leaned over her and kissed her. 'It's all right, Holl. First time and all that. Don't worry.' He adjusted both the seats and immediately switched on. 'Better get you home in case Mark's there. You can pull yourself together as we go along. OK?'

She put her hand across her mouth as the car bucketed over the grass and back onto the road. Her one thought was that she must not be sick; somehow that would be the last indignity.

She scrambled out of the car as soon as it drew up outside the house. Hugo was saying something smug and awful which she did not hear because she was looking up at the first-floor windows. They were dark so Mark was not yet home. She did begin to weep then with sheer relief.

By the time Mark arrived she had had a bath, bundled her dress into a bag and the bag into the outside dustbin and faced the fact that she had not been raped at all. She could have flung herself over Hugo and leaned on the horn; she could have screamed at him to leave her alone; she could have . . . bitten his ear off. She had done none of those things. So she had been unfaithful to Mark.

When she first reached this conclusion it was one of the worst moments of her life. She had not expected guilt to have physical symptoms. She had only to think of Hugo, or the interior of his car, or even the sound of the rain on the roof, and she would feel the general ache of her body escalate into a sharp pain through her midriff. Deep shame became self-loathing. She hated herself.

She knew then without a doubt that she still loved Mark; she cared desperately how he felt; she did not care whether they changed their way of life or not. To be with him was enough. And if she told him about tonight, that would be the end of everything. He might have forgiven her for a momentary lapse but the utter sordidness of tonight was something no-one could begin to understand.

She put her hands over her face; she was red-hot with shame. She said aloud, 'What am I going to do . . . what am I going to *do*?'

She knew the answer but for a long time she searched for another one. To deceive Mark would be like a long-drawn-out betrayal. It would mean living with this shame for the rest of her life. Could she do that? Could she keep this secret and carry it by herself . . . always?

Very slowly she took her hands away from her face. She would have to.

Tortuously she worked out what she must do. She could never go back to work with Hugo;

she never wanted to see him again. On Monday morning she would leave as usual at the same time as Mark and go to the Jobcentre. She would continue to do that until she got another job, then she would tell Mark that she had left Jamieson's. And then she would work at her marriage.

It sounded simple enough. The main thing was that Mark must never know what had happened. There were all kinds of dangers about that; Hugo might ring when she wasn't there or he might call round. She would have to write to him and make sure he did not contact her again. Just at the moment she was too tired to work that out, but tomorrow was Sunday and Mark would probably go to see poor old Reg again and she would be able to think of something; settle down to a letter. She cut some sandwiches – Mark hadn't eaten – and switched on the kettle.

When she heard Mark's key in the door she knew a moment of sheer panic. All her logical plans were blown apart; she was convinced he would know that she had been unfaithful. He knew her so well; he would ask her about the evening and she couldn't remember anything. The swan . . . the spun-sugar swan filled with fruit . . . she hung onto the memory of that.

Mark came through the living room and stood in the doorway of the kitchen. She saw instantly that something was wrong but all she felt was relief.

'Mark? What is it?' She swallowed her guilt and said, 'Oh my God. Is Reg dead?'

He shook his head; he wore his hangdog look which normally irritated her. Now she felt a kind of yearning pity.

He said, 'He's broken his hip. They can replace it. But apparently he's got a dicky heart.'

She waited, knowing there was more.

He spread his hands. 'Darling, you're going to hate me. I didn't know what to say. He was so worried. OK, so he can put May and Arthur off. And apparently he met three old ducks on that cruise he took – he doesn't care about cancelling their booking either. But there's a honeymoon couple and a late booking for Magpie Cottage. A couple with four children. He says he can't put them off. Don't know why – special circumstances, he says.'

She knew what he was going to say. She closed her eyes; it was possibly the answer to an unknown prayer.

He sounded anguished. 'Darling, don't look like that. I know you hate it there. Listen, we've got the money – why don't you go to a nice hotel? I'll manage fine on my own—'

She went to him, put her arms around his waist and pressed her forehead into his plain white dinner shirt.

'I want to be with you. The holiday place . . . it

will be wonderful. We'll make it the sort of Christmas Reg would want.'

He held her gently, almost cautiously. 'What's happened? Why this sudden change?'

She could have sobbed it all out then and there. But she said very calmly, 'It was an awful evening without you. They knew I was fed up and they gave me a sort of token partnership. Didn't mean a thing. I made up my mind then that I'd leave and find somewhere else. And this is a chance to help Reg out too.'

'Is that why you've been so unsettled? Because of bloody Jamieson's?'

She lifted her head to look at him. It was only half a lie after all. She tried for a self-deprecating laugh. 'I don't know. I suppose I *have* been awful to live with. But . . . Mark, it will be different now. Whatever we do, it will be different.'

'He wants me to go down next week actually, Holl. Loads to do apparently.'

'What will you do about the garage?'

'Special leave, I suppose. By the time I get back in the New Year, they'll have done that amalgamation thing. Golden opportunity for them, with me out of the way.'

'Oh darling . . . do you mind?'

He pushed her hair behind her ears. 'I don't think I do. Let's just wait and see what happens.'

'Oh Mark.' She lowered her head again and sighed deeply into his shirt then straightened.

She had to live with this. Uncle Reg had provided a breathing space, but ultimately she had to live with it. She said, 'Come on. I'll make a pot of tea. I've done you some sandwiches. It's late.'

He looked wonderingly at his watch. 'You're right. It's almost two. The doctor came and had a look at him and they gave him something for the pain. He didn't want me to go so I waited till he went to sleep.'

She poured tea and said, 'You're a nice man, Mark Jepson.'

Later, lying sleepless next to him, she thought he deserved someone better than she was. She lay on her back and put the palms of her hands flat on her lower abdomen. She was aching from the waist down. She remembered how they had laughed at a melodrama they had seen on television where the heroine had said comically, 'Oh husband, I have been violated . . .' She had been violated and it was not something she would ever be able to laugh about.

Three

May Long glanced at herself in the mirror then quickly away. She looked like an old man with her straggly curls and two large hairs sprouting from her chin. She knew that lower down things did not get better; she had put on a lot of weight in the last two or three years. Reg had commented on it last time they'd gone to see him. Not nastily, of course. Reg wasn't like that. But obviously he remembered her when she had been practically sylphlike. Everyone changed but Reg seemed to have changed for the better. His hair was as thick as ever and even though he had to use a stick to walk, his body was still so . . . manly. And that twinkle in his eye . . .

Swiftly, without looking, she swept her wispy hair into a pathetic pleat on the back of her head, teased a few waves onto her forehead and grabbed the tweezers.

'You've been in here almost an hour!' she said as she went into the bathroom without knocking.

'I don't know what you get up to morning after morning.'

Arthur was sitting on the lavatory reading the paper. He looked up without pleasure. 'That's not a question to ask a bloke, May,' he remonstrated without humour. 'As a matter of fact I did think it was the one place in the house I could get some privacy. See how wrong I was.'

'You didn't lock the door.' She was already at the mirror thrusting out her chin and squinting at a space she'd cleared in the condensation. 'You know we've got to do it today. It's no good hanging about and getting tetchy. The sooner we make that phone call, the happier we shall be.'

Arthur went back to the paper. 'I'm quite happy,' he said mildly. 'It's you who's fed up with Christmases at the bay. Just because poor old Reg expects you to cook a meal – just one meal! He takes us out all the time, never accepts a penny in payment . . .'

'When I heard Mark and Holly had copped out, I knew it was time for us to go. You and Reg will be all the time up at the Lantern or talking about that ghastly society you both belong to—'

'If you mean the Ancient Order of Whelks, kindly say so!'

'. . . and I'll be expected to sit by myself with some knitting! At least if we're here we shall see our friends.'

'All right. I've agreed to it, you don't have to keep on.'

'I simply want you to understand my point of view! I'm not being unreasonable as you seem to think' – she twitched the tweezers and grimaced with pain – 'it's simply that, without Holly, I've got no female company whatsoever!'

'Fair enough. Now could I have just ten minutes to commune with nature, then I'll do the dirty deed before I have any breakfast. How's that?'

She tweaked out the second hair and for some reason snapped, 'Oh shut up, Art!' before slamming out of the bathroom. As she laid their breakfast in the kitchen she said aloud, 'I'm damned if I'll feel guilty! So there, Reg Jepson!'

The phone rang as if in reply to such defiance; she started on her cereal and let Arthur pick up the receiver because it would be something to do with the ridiculous Whelks.

He came into the kitchen before he could possibly have made the call to Reg. She did not even look up from her bowl.

Arthur said slowly, 'That was the hospital. Reg has had a fall. He's in orthopaedic waiting for a hip operation. They didn't want to say much because we're not related but they admitted he had had a bad night.'

She put a hand to her throat. 'Oh . . . God.'

'Yes. Bit of a bombshell, eh?'

'Oh Art. Poor old Reg. Oh dear.'

'We can visit. Any time.'

'We'll go now. This morning. Shall we?'

'Course. The old chap hasn't got anyone except Mark and he can't be very interested if he wasn't going down this year.'

She said, 'Well, we weren't either. And I don't know why you call him an old chap, Art. We're the same age.'

'Yeah. Makes you think, eh?'

'I feel terrible, Art. As if I'd wished it on him.'

'What are you talking about, woman?'

'Well, he'll have to cancel Christmas now, won't he?'

Arthur turned his mouth down. 'Suppose so. I hadn't thought of that.'

May said, 'Oh God. I'd better ring those women he met on the cruise. He was tickled pink when they booked – reckoned they were all after him!' She half smiled with nostalgia. 'He's been a lad in his time, has our Reg.'

Arthur said repressively, 'Not any more.'

May glanced at him. 'No. Not any more.' She rummaged in her bag. 'I've got everyone's address and number. Better let them all know, I suppose.'

'Sooner the better,' Arthur agreed.

She started to dial and lowered her voice mournfully. 'Last Christmas of the twentieth century. Everything is coming to an end, Art.'

'For Pete's sake, our May. Is that my tea? It's cold.'

'Serves you right for spending all that time in the bathroom.'

He drank it anyway and picked up a piece of toast as he went into the hall. 'Might as well put my shoes on and get the car out right away. And by the way, our May, you've still got a hair sprouting out of your chin. You trying to go into competition with Reg as Father Christmas?'

She opened her mouth to give him a withering reply but Mavis Gentry picked up her receiver and the moment had gone.

A few days later, Mavis Gentry was sitting up in bed with her first cup of tea of the day. Down in the hall she heard the post arrive. At least two letters. Could be three. Difficult to tell because sometimes the paper boy did not wait for the paper to drop through the box and the postman had to push it through himself. So three plops did not always mean three letters. She sighed, knowing she should get up anyway. It was eight forty-five by her bedside clock, which meant that actually it had just gone eight thirty because she kept all her clocks ten minutes or so fast and eight thirty was her time for getting up. She put her empty cup on the bedside table and began to take the pins out of her hair.

It wasn't that she felt old. Everyone said she did not look her age and that did not surprise her because she spent a lot of time and money on not looking her age, but she felt . . . languid.

She smiled, liking the word. Languid. It smacked of scented baths and lady's maids. She put the last of the pins in the small shell-encrusted box all ready for tonight and ran her hands through her hair, scribbling on her scalp with her fingertips just as the masseuse had told her to do. Apparently it stimulated the flow of blood to the roots of the hair. It also made her look like Shirley Temple. She scribbled for some time, then, exhausted, leaned back and surveyed the outside world through her net curtains. It was, as usual, grey. The wavering outline just above the roofs of the houses opposite could be the Malvern Hills but could be rainclouds too. She reached for her glasses and looked again. The Malverns. Oh God, how depressing. They were always there. You couldn't get away from them. If only they had been going to Somerset for Christmas . . . Reg had said that the sea was grey but at least it was uninterrupted by the Malverns. And Reg had also told them about the nice little pub called the Ship's Lantern, and the unrivalled views of the Somerset Levels with the Mendips and the Quantocks in the distance.

That was why she was languid, of course. Christmas – as irrevocable as the Malverns – was on her particular horizon and after the news of poor Reg Jepson it had lost its savour. In fact the three of them were left completely high and dry for Christmas and Bernice wanted them to try to book at a local hotel. Neither Mavis nor Pansy was keen on that. Reg had taken each one of them – separately, of course – onto the boat deck during the Mediterranean cruise and told them how much he was looking forward to spending Christmas with them. Bernice had taken this with a pinch of salt. 'For God's sake, girls! He's playing us off against each other – can't you see that? Wants our money as well as our bodies!' They'd laughed because they always did laugh at Bernice's jokes, but Mavis knew that Reg had a soft spot for her; nothing to do with money.

The downstairs clock struck a single note and she glanced at the bedside table again. Half-past nine, which meant quarter-past nine! What had happened to that three-quarters of an hour?

She scrambled out of bed and felt with her feet for slippers as she draped her dressing gown over her shoulders. Poor old Reg. Maybe she would send some flowers by Interflora. In case he planned on a cruise to convalesce. Yes, she would write a note and suggest it. It wouldn't be forward . . . well, not too forward anyway. People were always talking about self-assertion these days. And if she didn't do it, Pansy would get in first.

She went to the bathroom and then padded downstairs. Three letters, no newspaper. She made a sound of annoyance as she picked up two envelopes heavily embossed with the tell-tale logo 'Old Stagers'. She loved having all the special offers they advertised but objected to everyone knowing she was an old stager herself. She picked up the third envelope with a faint oooh of curiosity; it was handwritten in an unfamiliar script. She ripped it open on her way to the kitchen and looked at the signature. Holly Jepson. Who on earth could that be – surely Reg hadn't been married all the time?

She scanned the letter as the kettle reboiled. It seemed that Holly and Mark Jepson were Reg's family. Nephew and wife. Holly Jepson was writing to say that Mr Jepson had asked them to act as hosts at the holiday village over the Christmas weekend. They were used to doing the Christmas lunch because they always helped out, but would quite understand if Mrs Gentry wished to cancel the booking. They looked forward to hearing from her.

Mavis made toast and ate it behind another set of net curtains. It was raining now and must be windy because passers-by were holding their brollies like shields. Mavis smiled at her own thoughts; she had always been fanciful. It was because of her fancifulness that St John had loved her and married her and because of her fancifulness that he had left her.

She went into the hall, picked up the phone and hovered between dialling Pansy's number and Bernice's. She chose Pansy's and then wished she hadn't when Pansy immediately said, 'I knew you'd ring. As soon as I opened my letter

I knew you'd ring me. So I did a Bernice and sat and waited.'

'Clever,' Mavis said. 'You can ring Bernice then.' Pansy was such a cheapskate. Bernice wouldn't ring because she wanted to be in control; Pansy wouldn't ring because she was too mean.

'Yes. All right,' Pansy said equably. 'But let's make up our minds together then I can simply tell Bernice what we're going to do.'

Mavis bit her lip, cross with herself for her swift condemnation of Pansy. 'Good thinking,' she said. Though actually Pansy *could* be mean on occasion. 'But . . . it won't make much difference really, will it?'

'Well, I know what I'm going to do.' Pansy was unusually definite. 'I'm going. Full stop.'

'What? Even if Bernice and I don't come?'

'Yes. I'm going for Reg's sake. He was so keen about it all. Christmas lunch in his bungalow, walks by the sea, drinks in that pub, a trip to Weston-super-Mare to see the panto . . .'

'But he's in hospital!' Mavis reminded her.

'I shall do it for his sake. I shall do my best to add to the merriment. I thought he was a lovely man.' Her voice wobbled sentimentally. 'The least I can do is to try to make Christmas what he would have wanted.'

'For goodness' sake, Pansy, we knew him for two weeks! And like Bernice said, he was playing us off against each other.'

'Bernice actually said he wanted our money as well as our bodies. Well, if he's up to it, he can have my money and my body!' Pansy sounded loud and defiant.

Mavis was flabbergasted. 'What on earth's got into you? I'll ring Bernice. I don't want you talking like this to her – she won't speak to you again. Remember what she says about widows being independent.'

'I'm not a widow, I'm a divorcee. And so are you. Our husbands are living it up with other women. If I get half a chance I'm going to live it up with other men!'

'Men? In the plural? Unfaithful to Reg before you've even started!'

Pansy seemed to collapse. 'Oh Mave. Come with me. We can go into Bristol and visit Reg in hospital.'

'You're forgetting Bernice is the driver. We haven't got cars.'

'We can get a taxi. Oh please, Mavis. What else are we going to do? We're not hotel people, not really. And this young couple – they'll need our support. If Bernice won't come we can get a train to Bristol and a taxi from there.'

Mavis felt she was being swept away on a tidal wave. Pansy had never been so determined before. She deferred, as they both did, to Bernice. Bernice was always saying, 'Why do you leave everything to me? I have to make decisions, drive the car, buy the theatre tickets, call every damned shot!' But she liked it that way. She wouldn't like this new Pansy at all.

Mavis smiled into the receiver. 'Yes. All right. Why not? If Bernice doesn't like it, Bernice can lump it. Actually I will phone her, Pansy. And then . . . how about meeting in the Shakespeare Tea Rooms for lunch?'

'Fine. Bring some of your nice notepaper. We'll send just one letter from the three of us.'

'You think Bernice will come?'

Pansy giggled. 'She will when she knows we're both going. We're not allowed to do things on our own. Haven't you noticed?'

'Well . . . yes.'

And Mavis giggled too. She replaced the receiver and glanced again at the clock. She would phone Bernice immediately then she would go upstairs and choose a suitable outfit for lunch with the two of them. She was sure Bernice would join them and would be wearing her black slacks and that suede coat. So she herself would go for something bright. And not trousers. The red suit perhaps. With a plain sweater too because Pansy would wear a frilly blouse.

Bernice's voice said in her ear, 'Hello. Bernice Smythe speaking.' She always pronounced Smythe in that way. Mavis was convinced that she had started married life as plain Smith.

'Hello, Bernie darling. Have you had the letter?'

Mavis was delighted to feel full of energy. It was so much better than being languid.

Paula and Dennis Chiverton were absolutely delighted and very relieved to receive Holly's letter. They had been living together for the past two years and had married at the beginning of the month because Paula discovered she was pregnant and they both felt it was so much better for children to know their parents had a marriage certificate.

They had told no-one about the baby because Dennis's parents refused to believe that Paula and their son actually slept together and had sex. They raised their brows with amusement and told their friends that this flat-share arrangement was common to university students and was a true sign of sex equality. They were thrown completely when Dennis told them that he and Paula had decided to get married.

'But why? You've been friends for ages now. Why can't you leave it that way? At least until after you've both graduated and got jobs.' Helen Chiverton was genuinely bewildered, Walter a little less so. He took his son aside and said in his man-to-man voice, 'Have you got to marry her, son?'

Dennis wished that Paula could hear this. She was a natural mimic and she would exactly catch his mother's disbelief and his father's deep embarrassment and distaste.

'Of course not, Dad.' He smiled ingenuously. 'Can you honestly see Paula grappling me to the ground and demanding a wedding ring?' Paula was barely five foot tall and as thin as a rake.

Walter actually flushed. 'You know what I mean, Dennis. Is she in the family way?'

Dennis couldn't resist this. He opened his eyes wide. 'What are you saying, Dad? That would mean she – we – well, wouldn't we have had to sleep together?'

Walter backed down fumblingly and offered to pay for the wedding. Paula's parents were dead and she had been brought up by relatives, literally handed from one to another. No chance of any financial help there.

Dennis was going to refuse graciously, and then he thought of Paula back at the flat making a batch of scones for a 'real family tea'. She loved his parents; she wanted to be part of his family; she didn't care how stuffy they were. And she would look a dream in a white dress. He would bet his last penny she had never had a dressing-up box when she was a kid.

He said, 'Look, Dad, we don't want a splash. But . . . if you could run to a white dress for Paula, it would be great.'

Walter relaxed instantly. If it were to be a white wedding then obviously Paula was a virgin. He clapped Dennis on the shoulder. 'Your mother will love every minute of it.'

Of course Dennis being Dennis couldn't leave it there. 'Thanks, Dad. I've overextended myself a bit on the honeymoon. Coupla weeks in Tenerife.'

Walter was delighted at this further proof of conformity. 'Well done, lad! So you'll be back for Christmas? You can bring her home and show us the snaps.'

'Sorry, Dad. Couldn't take it during term time. We're going over the Christmas hols.' He was pleased with himself. It meant they wouldn't have to spend Christmas under the eagle eye of his mother. Paula might be showing a few symptoms by then.

Afterwards, Paula was doubtful. 'It's all a bit false pretences, isn't it, Chiv?'

'You mean not admitting we're looovers?' He sidled up to her with what she called that look in his eyes.

She slapped him away. Sometimes she lived up to her red hair and then he realized that her small frame was deceptive; she was as strong as a horse. She said, 'Just listen a minute. If we go along with this, we've got to keep Cherub One a secret.'

'We'd have to anyway, honeybun. By the time she's born, I'll have my degree and hopefully I'll be able to get a job.'

'Yes . . . I might be showing a bit at Christmas.'

'That's where my forethought came brilliantly

67

to the . . . well, fore!' He grinned. 'We're going to Tenerife for our honeymoon, honey!'

'Oh no. Sorry, love, but no. Your parents will get a kick out of a white wedding. I can see that. But a honeymoon . . . no. That's immoral.'

He shook his head. 'Don't be daft. We shall have a nice quiet Christmas here. In Bristol.' He managed to kiss her nose. 'I love it when you go all Victorian on me. Immoral indeed. What do you think has been happening these past two years?'

She was huffy at first, trying to explain to him the difference between doing your own thing and hurting no-one, and extracting money under false pretences. Eventually she gave up and they laughed and hugged and told each other that no-one in the whole wide world was quite as happy as they were.

However, after the wedding up in Leeds, it became obvious that Paula was less happy. For one thing Helen and Walter kept posting Christmas presents to them. Helen explained on the phone that as Dennis kept forgetting to forward the Tenerife address – and she understood that perfectly, because no-one had known where she and Daddy were going for their honeymoon – then they had to take Christmas with them.

Paula said, 'I feel so *guilty*, Chiv.'

'Why? My God, if we were going up there for Christmas we'd get twice as much as this!'

'Yes, but we're having to live that lie you told. It wouldn't be so bad if we were going anywhere. But just to be staying here . . . we're tricking them in some way.'

They were with their group playing skittles in a pub at the time, Paula religiously drinking orange juice. The other members of the group, who knew the whole thing, nodded sagely. 'She's got a point, Chiv.'

Dennis said, 'OK. I'll book us a bed and break-fast in . . .' He looked round at the others. 'Where? Where is cheap and nasty enough to quieten my wife's noisy conscience?'

Everyone came up with ridiculous ideas. It was pointed out that anywhere in England this last Christmas of the old millennium was going to be more expensive than a package in Tenerife.

Someone from the opposing team, who called themselves the Ancient Order of Whelks, sud-denly spoke up.

'I know somewhere you could go. The wife and I go every year. It's in Somerset. Only a few miles away. Summer holiday village. The owner opens it up for Christmas. Bit basic but cheap. You might even enjoy it.'

Dennis said, 'It's OK, honestly. We'll be fine right here in the city.'

Paula said, 'We're not mad on holiday camps. Is everybody happy . . . that kind of thing?'

'It's not like that. There are only six chalets.

You do your own thing. But on Christmas Day we all eat together. That's the rule. After that . . . it's up to you.'

'Well . . .' said Paula.

And Dennis said quickly, 'We're broke. Honestly. Sorry. It's good of you but we couldn't afford it.'

The old geezer shrugged. 'If you change your mind, let me know. Reg Jepson, who owns the place, has been a friend for years. He likes to have some young people for Christmas. He'd probably do you a really good deal.'

They never quite knew why they went along with it. Paula squared her conscience by telling Helen – confidentially – that the Tenerife trip had fallen through and the company had offered them an English hotel.

'Different lie?' Dennis asked sarcastically.

'Afterwards I shall tell her that it was a holiday village. And we loved every minute.'

'Brilliant,' he said even more sarcastically. He had looked forward to Christmas in Bristol.

Paula said, 'This is a proper honeymoon, Chiv. Something we'll never forget.' Her face shone. 'Darling, I've never been on holiday before! Isn't it wonderful?'

He stared at her and then gathered her into his arms. He was almost in tears.

So it was a terrible blow when Arthur Long's wife rang them to say Reg Jepson had broken his hip. Dennis had gone so far as to enquire about hotel prices in nearby Minehead. It was hopeless. Reg's 'deal' had made the honeymoon cheaper than staying in the flat.

Then came Holly's letter. Paula waved it ecstatically. 'D'you know, darling, I'd started to think we weren't meant to have a honeymoon! I know it's crazy – well, I'm allowed to be crazy now I'm pregnant – but you see, if we weren't meant to have a honeymoon then were we meant to be married at all?'

'Oh God!' he said. But then he hugged her. He had always known Paula was a complicated character, but since she became pregnant he had realized the extent of the complications. He thought each one made him love her more.

Luckily May had not telephoned the last two bookings on Reg's list but they still received letters from Holly telling them about the accident and slight change of plans. Ted Harris's letter, addressed to 'Mr and Mrs Edwards', was picked up by the babysitter after Ted had gone to work and placed on the mantelpiece with the gas bill.

Fortunately the childminder, who was aptly called Mrs Sitter, did not notice the mistake. 'Your poor daddy,' she commented to Gemma who was four and lived in a world of her own. 'Another bill. He's certainly having a rough time. Good job you're going away for Christmas.' She leaned over the pram and tickled Giles's tummy. 'Going away to see Father Christmas, aren't you?' She straightened her back and looked gloomily at Gemma. 'Though what kind of holiday it will be for him in a self-catering holiday village, I do not know!'

Gemma waited until the babysitter was in the bathroom then she pulled one of the dining chairs up to the fireplace, stood on it, reached both letters down and threw them on the fire. She was determined that her daddy was not going to be worried any more. He might decide they couldn't afford to go to Somerset for Christmas and they had to go because Father Christmas lived in Somerset. Anyway, once they got there Aunty Ivy would look after him. But it had to be a secret. Aunty Ivy's children did not even know they were all going away together. Daddy had told her about it because he knew she worried.

'Everyone thinks you don't know what's happening, don't they, my little petal?' He bounced her on his knee. 'They think you don't even realize that Mummy has gone.' He shook his head sadly.

Gemma said, 'With the window cleaner.'

Daddy looked a bit startled at that, then hugged her close. 'My God. Not much goes past you, does it, Gemma Harris?' He held her away from him, studying her. 'What else do you know?'

'I know Aunty Ivy is going to run away because

Uncle Stanley knocks her about something cruel.'

He looked slightly alarmed. 'Where did you get that from?'

'Mrs Sitter said to the postman that Mummy didn't know which side her bread was buttered on, going with the window cleaner when she could have stuck with a nice bloke like you.'

'Oh, she did, did she? And does she know about Aunty Ivy too?'

'No.' Gemma smiled. 'Course not. Everyone knows that Uncle Stanley knocks her about. They say the only way she can get away from him is to run off and take the boys with her. They talk about it all the time at playgroup when they're putting our coats on.'

Her father looked very serious then. 'Oh dear. I don't think you should listen to all that stuff, Gem.'

Gemma looked at his face and stopped smiling. 'Is she frightened of him, Daddy?'

'She might be.' He sounded wary.

'Why don't you put a stop to it, Daddy? Mrs Sitter says if you'd put a stop to the window cleaner, Mummy would have had to stay.'

Her father's jaw moved up and down twice before he spoke. 'The thing was, Gem . . . she didn't want to stay. I couldn't make her do something she didn't want to do, could I, petal?'

Gemma frowned. People were always making her do things she didn't want to do. But she knew that rules were not always rules. The difficult thing was to decide when they were and when they weren't.

She chewed her lip for a second then said, 'Why can't Aunty Ivy come with us to Somerset, Daddy? Tom and Adam would like it. And I would like it. And Giles won't mind.'

He looked so surprised she wondered if she had broken an important rule. He shifted her into a comfier position and took a deep breath. 'Actually, petal, that sounds like a good idea. A really good idea. It's quite a big cottage. There would be room for them.'

She spread her small, plump hands. 'Well then.'

'Yes. Well then.' He too chewed his lip and added quickly, 'But it would have to be a secret. We mustn't breathe a word of this. Not to Mrs Sitter nor at playgroup. Can you keep a secret?'

It was a silly question. Gemma rarely spoke to anyone except her father.

Cree Evans did not see his letter until midday. He got up at nine o'clock as usual and going into the studio realized that the pale grey light coming through the Velux windows was exactly right for finishing his latest portrait. He started immediately, working like a demon, oblivious of the fact that the studio was bone-cold and he was naked. Cass, drifting upstairs with the post, late as usual, and hung around with draperies like a

Roman goddess, stood in the doorway surveying him without pleasure.

'Just because one solitary human being thought you looked like Augustus John, there is absolutely no reason on God's good earth why you should make such a deliberate and conscious effort to behave like some crass eccentric!'

He said, 'Either shut up or strip off, Cass. I could do with having another stab at your leg. What d'you think?'

She drifted around the canvas and stared, distaste turning into disgust.

'If it weren't that you peddle your ghastly stuff as abstract-bloody-art, it would be not-so-abstract-bloody-porn!'

'Shut up again, woman. My stuff keeps us in bread and butter.'

'And not much else.' She came nearer, peering with disbelief. 'Why is my left breast over my right shoulder?'

'You probably flung it there in one of your tempers! How do I know? That's how the painting turned out, for crying out loud!'

She moved away and found a chair. She riffled through the letters. 'Bill, bill, double-glazing promotion, bill, Daniel Freedom's retrospective . . .' She paused to allow Cree to give his opinion of Daniel Freedom's work. 'And a letter from Bristol. God, it's about the Christmas holiday in that ghastly hole. What does it say . . . blah, blah, blah . . . sod it, it's still on. Thought your old boy might have dropped dead . . . oh, he's broken his hip—'

Cree snatched the letter from her and scanned it quickly.

'Poor old Reg.' He looked up and through the Velux at the sky. 'Wonder if this is the end? Broken hip . . . probably get pneumonia . . . oh God, it'll be me next. We're almost the same bloody age, d'you realize that, Cass? Then what will you do for bread and butter?'

She smiled. 'Sell my body?'

'Nobody would have it,' he said dourly.

She bridled. 'Well, you seem to approve of it!'

He lowered his head from the Velux's view of eternity and came back to the attic and Cass.

'Well,' he grinned, 'I'm an artist. Probably a great artist only no-one seems to realize it. And you pose for free. Can't afford to quibble about your body in those circs, can I?'

She picked up a cushion from the floor and threw it at him. He dodged then went back to the letter. 'Seriously, Cass, if old Reg isn't going to be there, do we still want to go?'

She pushed her lips forward consideringly. 'I think I'd prefer the hole without Reg Jepson around. Every time I get near him he tries to touch me up. Dirty old devil.'

'He thinks it's expected of him.' Cree pushed his lips forward too. 'We went for his sake, not our own. Without him . . . well, bit pointless, isn't it?'

76

She got up and snicked the letter from his fingers. 'Hmmm. Hmmm. I don't remember this Holly and Mark, do you?'

'Don't remember any Christmas Days and apparently that's when they were around. Reg and I usually got blotto on Christmas Eve and stayed that way till after Boxing Day. It's a nice enough letter. Probably a lovey-dovey pair – Reg was a bit soppy when Maude was alive. Runs in the family, I expect.'

'I don't remember Maude. I wasn't on the scene then.'

'No. Reg invited me because I was on my own. He used to ask lonely widows and hope I'd team up with them.' He grinned. 'Thanks for coming with me, Cass. You saved my honour!'

She said fondly, 'Silly old fool.' She handed the letter back to him. 'I'll go and make breakfast while you have a think about this. Remember, if we don't go there, I shall have to cook. And I don't cook.'

'True.' He tweaked aside her draperies and let his grin widen. 'Not a bad body for a fifty-year-old!'

She pretended outrage and marched to the door. 'Remember, if I'm fifty, then you're seventy-five! At least!' She looked over her shoulder. 'I see that this Holly Jepson makes no mention of me. Reg couldn't have said anything. You'd better let her know you have a daughter.'

'No-one will believe it,' he said, his black eyes

glinting lewdly. 'I look much too young to have a fifty-year-old daughter.' He began to advance on her, reaching for her coverings. She screamed and disappeared and he sat in the chair she had vacated, laughing inordinately. Then he stopped and looked through the skylight again. It was still grey.

'Infinity,' he murmured. 'It's impossible. Everything has to be finite.' He sighed deeply. 'Reg, you and me, we're too small for all this infinity malarkey. We still like our wine, women and song.' He tried to imagine whizzing through space for evermore on an endless journey of debauchery. It was simply not possible. He sighed again. 'Don't you dare bloody die, Reg Jepson! We're old soldiers. And we're not supposed to die!'

Four

Tom and Adam Edwards went everywhere together for the simple reason that Adam Edwards had not spoken since the age of seven and Tom spoke for him. After a lot of tests, the doctor had said it was psychosomatic and his voice would come back eventually and meanwhile Ivy should be thankful for a bit of peace and quiet. He had a son of nine himself and when the boy got home from school, peace and quiet went out of the window.

Adam was nine now and his brown eyes were expressionless. But somehow he did not generate peace with his silence. Tom, who was almost eleven, spent a lot of his school day dodging between his classroom and his brother's in an effort to block any suggestion that Adam ought to go to a special school. What would happen next September when Tom moved to the big school was anybody's guess. Ivy often said coaxingly, 'You will talk soon, won't you, Adam?' But she never knew whether the child understood the question. He just looked at her and then away. It was Tom who said, 'He'll be all right, Mum. Don't worry.'

They all arrived at Reg's luxury bungalow just before lunch. Ted's Ford was bursting with children and luggage; they had left Ted's house before it was light but had driven off the motorway at Worcester to stock up with shopping, eat breakfast and perform what Ted called 'ablutions'. For a split second, as he said the word, extending it to 'ablootions' and pursing his mouth ridiculously, Ted thought he saw a glimmer of a smile on Adam's face. He knew that if Adam spoke it would be the best Christmas present any of them could wish for. And then Ivy might find the courage to see a solicitor and start divorce proceedings and marry him. The thought of all of them in the house in Birmingham filled him with such joy he had to bite his lip to stop it trembling. They should have been together from the beginning; from schooldays. It had always been Ted and Ivy, Ivy and Ted; smiling at each other during assembly, meeting up in the playground. Later, when they both had jobs, they did everything by the book. They went to the pictures every Saturday and had a walk on a Sunday and saved money towards a deposit on a house. Then when Ivy was eighteen, her parents were killed on a works outing to Wales. The coach swerved and toppled off the road, down a bank; eight of the passengers were killed and two of those eight were Ivy's mum and dad.

Ivy was knocked sideways. She was an only child – like Ted – and had to cope with all the business of death and inheritance. Ted was eighteen too and did not know how to help her. His parents were both working and told Ivy that time would heal . . . just give it time. That nice cousin from Swansea would help her with everything that had to be signed, they said; she should take it easy and let him deal with it.

The nice cousin was Stanley Edwards. He was ten years older than Ivy and 'knew his way around'. He made Ivy pregnant and married her within six months of the double funeral.

Stanley was very possessive and Ted saw nothing much of Ivy after that. He heard the gossip, of course, but you couldn't take too much notice of gossip. He met Ivy one day in the supermarket and she looked thin everywhere except her middle part and she was very pale but, after all, she was expecting and women did sometimes look pale then. She told him she was fine; she smiled a lot as if he were a guest met at a party; she said she was so excited about the baby and if it was a boy she was going to call him Thomas after Stanley's father.

'Stanley wanted to pass on his own name.' Her smile died a little. 'But Stanley is right out of fashion, isn't it? He isn't close to his father but he agreed that Thomas Stanley sounded good.'

'What about if it's a girl?' Ted couldn't believe he was talking to Ivy like this. And something was not right.

'Well, certainly not Ivy!' She laughed. 'Ivy is *much* too old-fashioned. Stan likes Marilyn. He thinks she's still the most beautiful woman in the world.'

Ted tried not to look at Ivy's dark hair, her tiny frame. Anyone less like Marilyn Monroe was hard to imagine.

'What about your mum's name?'

'Hilda?' Ivy looked at him with her old mischievous smile and they both laughed.

'You could lop it about a bit. Hildie sounds nice.'

The baby was born too soon and died two days later. It was Marilyn. Ted's mother said that Ivy had fallen down the stairs. Apparently Stanley blamed her for being so careless. When the doctors said the baby would not live he had a full christening by the bedside and afterwards a proper knees-up at the pub. There was a fight outside afterwards; fortunately they kept Ivy in hospital and did not tell her about it. It was easy for people to forgive Stanley; after all, he was upset.

He was so upset that he lost his job and though there were others they never lasted long. Ivy went back to work at the local supermarket and Ted would drop in for a chat occasionally. But word got back to Stanley and Ivy appeared with a nasty bruise on her cheek, and every time she lifted a basket onto the conveyor belt she winced. 'Put my shoulder out when I fell,' she explained.

Ted stopped using the supermarket. Over the years he heard that Ivy had Thomas Stanley and then, very quickly, Adam Gervase. He wondered sourly where Stanley had found that name but he knew the babies would make Ivy happy whatever Stanley was like. He met Louise and she was so different from Ivy; she liked dancing and going to clubs and she was always happy and carefree. Ted longed to be like that. When he asked her to marry him he hoped she would share some of her *joie de vivre*. He desperately wanted to be happy again. He wanted a family like Ivy had. He wanted to look after a proper family.

They bought a brand-new house on a development at East Heath. Louise was delighted with it for exactly a year. Then she became pregnant and said she could no longer go out. 'People stare,' she said flatly.

'Enviously,' Ted reassured her. 'You look so beautiful, love.'

'Nothing fits me. And no-one wants to dance with someone who's pregnant.'

'I want to dance with you.'

She looked irritable. 'Well, you're my *husband*!' she said dismissively.

After Gemma was born she found Mrs Sitter

immediately and went back to how she had lived before Gemma's arrival, and the marriage limped on. When she discovered she was pregnant again, she was furious. She stayed at home long enough to have Giles and then she looked for a way out. The window cleaner was only the first stepping stone. There was a nightclub in the centre of Birmingham; she set her sights on the owner. The window cleaner happened to be a terrific dancer.

Now she had gone and Ted would be free quite soon and Ivy had almost agreed to come away with him for Christmas and see how it worked. It depended on Stanley: he went home to Swansea each Christmas to get away from what he called Ivy's constant nagging if he had a little Christmas drink. For some time Ivy had been thankful for this respite.

Crossing his fingers, Ted wrote off to the address Ivy had given him and booked Magpie Cottage in her name. She said it was lovely and big and would take all of them and because it had damp problems Mr Jepson had let them have it last summer for next to nothing.

Nevertheless Ted could not quite believe it would happen. She was so much under Stanley's thumb that sometimes he wondered whether she might actually love him still. When she had arrived late last night he had known immediately something really bad had happened. He had let her in and looked at her searchingly but there were no bruises. And then he had noticed Adam's neck.

'My God.' His voice sounded flat in the warmth of the living room. Mrs Sitter had left him a cottage pie and though he had eaten it two hours before, the smell lingered and somehow took him back to when he and Ivy had been friends. Before.

Tom said conversationally, 'Where's Gemma and Giles?'

Ted blinked and transferred his gaze to the boy. 'In bed. Why?'

Tom shrugged. 'They might be scared. Us turning up and all.'

'They know you. They like you. Well, Gemma does. Giles likes everyone.'

Tom did not smile. He said, 'Can Mum sit by the fire with Adam for a bit? I'll help you make tea.'

They went into the kitchen and Tom said, 'Mum can't talk about it. Dad tried to strangle Adam. He said he was going to examine his throat. His vocal cords or something. Mum started to scream and when Adam went blue I got my cricket bat out of the hall cupboard and hit Dad.'

Ted swallowed. He was law-abiding, a conformist. He was still trying to come to terms with his own broken marriage and two motherless children. He did not know what to do, what was expected of him. The kettle boiled and he poured water into the teapot.

'You forgot the teabags,' Tom said stolidly and passed him the caddy.

Ted mashed the bags against the side of the pot with a spoon. He cleared his throat. 'Did you . . . is he dead?'

Tom reached four mugs from the hooks beneath the dresser and put them on a tray. 'No. Wish he was. Mum rang 999 and they took him to hospital. They said Adam would be all right. I told them what had happened and they said we should stay quietly together until the social worker came.'

Ted said, 'Ah.' He poured milk into the mugs and then tea. He looked at Tom. 'What did the social worker say?'

'We left the house. Mum put a note on the door to say we'd gone to relatives. She said that would buy us some time. She said we'd got to have a few days to decide what to do.' Ted noticed for the first time that the boy was trembling. 'I think she's frightened they'll take me away,' he said matter-of-factly.

Again Ted said, 'Ah.' He picked up the tray. 'There are chocolate biscuits in that tin.' He jerked his head to the shelf. 'I'll go and get some fish and chips in a minute.'

He went back into the living room. Ivy was almost invisible beneath Adam, who was sitting on her lap. He was sobbing into her neck and

86

she was stroking back his unkempt hair and murmuring to him. She smiled up at Ted.

'This is the first time he's cried for . . . oh, ages,' she said. 'So good that he can let it all out.'

Ted wished that Tom could let it all out too. He stood by the fire holding the mantelpiece like people did in old films on the television.

Ted said, 'Come on, Adam old son. Chocolate biscuits here. And a nice hot cup of tea.' He poured a milky half-cup and noticed that now he was trembling too. Only Ivy seemed calm.

She said, 'We'll have to get away, Ted. Just until things cool down. Mr Jepson will let us move into the cottage early. I'm sure of it. He was such a nice man. He didn't even get cross with Stanley when Stanley kept complaining about the cottage being damp. He smiled at me and said he'd get it seen to.' She paused, propping Adam upright so that he could drink the tea. 'I think he knew. And he was sorry for me and the boys.'

Ted felt slightly better. He nodded and handed Tom a mug of tea. 'We'll talk it over after the boys are in bed. OK?'

'No, Ted. They understand. They want to go. They want to get away. We'll go as soon as it's light tomorrow.' She fished around in her pocket. 'Here's my house key. Can you go round now and put some stuff in a dustbin liner for us? I've been stacking all our underwear and other stuff in the airing cupboard. So he wouldn't

87

guess and start asking questions. Take it all out. Don't put it in a case. That way Stanley won't know we've gone for a while. No-one will. Our things will still be in the drawers and cupboards.'

It sounded really weak but if it was what she wanted . . . He said, 'I was going for fish and chips for the boys – and you, of course.'

'Have you got a tin of soup? I'll heat it for the boys and bed them down somewhere—'

'They can have my room. It's a double bed. You can probably fit in with them too.'

'Fine. Hurry, Ted. Please.'

'All right.' He looked at Tom. 'It's going to be all right, old son.'

Tom did not answer and Adam hiccoughed on his tea.

Ivy wanted to knock on the door of the bungalow because Mr Jepson would recognize her and there would be less explaining to do, but Ted felt that somewhere in this crazy adventure he had to take matters into his own hands. And Adam's half-smile encouraged him in this.

He prepared to introduce himself as Mrs Edwards's 'partner' and felt his tongue cleave to the roof of his mouth at the thought. So it was a relief when the door was opened by a woman, older than Ivy certainly, but . . . so different. It struck him suddenly that with that head of hair Stanley would probably think of her as his 'Marilyn'.

'Er . . . hello.' He couldn't tell this woman that he was Ivy's partner. He waved helplessly at the car. 'It's Mrs Ivy Edwards and family.'

She looked past him and he was surprised to see her amazing blue eyes light up. She said, 'D'you know, when Uncle Reg mentioned a large family I didn't really believe him. Four children. How absolutely lovely.' She held out her hand and he took it and felt his own hand warmly gripped. She laughed. 'You got my letter? It didn't put you off? When I didn't hear from you I wondered . . . but here you are in person which is probably much better!' She laughed again. She seemed absolutely delighted to see them. Ted felt his face split in a bewildered smile.

'We hoped you wouldn't mind us being early,' he began.

She was already walking down the path to the car, leaning through the window saying something. The next minute she had opened the doors and was helping Ivy to get the children out. Ivy raised her brows at him and he shook his head. The woman said, 'We might as well get to know one another straight away. Then I'll get the key and come down to Magpie with you. I've got some squash and biscuits too.' She looked at Adam. 'Would you like that? While Mummy and Daddy and I have a cup of tea?'

Adam gave another tiny smile and Tom said robustly, 'Actually we would like some tea too. We drink tea like – like . . . fish!'

Everyone laughed at that and Giles threw his curled fists into the air and gave a small scream of delight. Ted glanced at Gemma who did not like tea but she was smiling and obviously determined to be like everyone else. Suddenly his heart lifted. Everything was crazy and they would probably lose Tom and end up in clink but he didn't care. This was the best adventure he'd ever had.

They got inside the big room overlooking the sea and Ivy sat down with Giles on her lap. Unexpectedly, he began to grizzle. Ted and the other children crowded around the picture window exclaiming with delight. The woman said, 'Yes, I suppose it is rather good, isn't it? We tend to take it for granted. But with the sun on it, it looks lovely.'

Ivy said fervently above Giles's escalating cries, 'Oh it's heavenly. Just like paradise!'

The woman said, 'I'm Holly Jepson. I don't think we've met before because I'm only around at Christmas. But I know about you because Uncle Reg has told me. You're Ivy and Stanley Edwards and you had two weeks in the late summer.' She smiled right at Ted. 'He misled me actually. About you and about the children!' She let her smile widen as she turned to Ivy. 'He said two children, not four!' She waved a reassuring hand. 'It doesn't matter a bit. There are extra camp beds in the cottage and we've got loads of linen and blankets.'

Ivy glanced at Ted and said quickly, 'That's really nice of you, Miss Jepson. Is Mr Jepson all right?'

Holly turned her smile upside down. 'Not really. He's had his hip replaced, as I told you in my letter. He's learning to walk again and they're sending him home for Christmas.' She went towards the kitchen. 'I'm married to his nephew by the way. But do call me Holly. And I'll call you Stanley and Ivy if that's all right.'

She disappeared and they could hear her filling a kettle.

Tom said gruffly, 'Can't someone shut the baby up?'

Gemma looked shocked. 'He wants Daddy. That's why—'

Ted interrupted. 'My God. She wrote to us. Holly Jepson wrote to us. The letter must have gone astray. I must tell her—'

Ivy interrupted fiercely, 'No! She doesn't know us. Her husband won't know us either. They might not send the old man home. And anyway, he'll be too ill to remember what Stan looked like. Nobody need know! It's much easier that way. Tom, remember to call Ted Daddy.'

Holly returned with a biscuit tin which she opened and placed on the elephant coffee table. 'Help yourselves, children. Give one to Mummy and Daddy and the baby. I'll get the tea things.'

She left again and they all looked at one

another apprehensively. Gemma whispered, 'What's happening? Why are we frightened?'

Tom said in his gruff voice, 'We're not. We're not a bit frightened. It's like a game. You have to pretend my mother is your mother and me and Adam are your brothers.'

She said hopefully, 'Like a family?'

Ted laughed his relief. 'Just like a family, Gem. You've got it exactly!'

Holly returned laden with a full tray. 'This is nice,' she said contentedly. 'Listen, if you like, you children can stay here while Mummy and Daddy make up the beds and get the cottage ready.'

Nobody spoke for a moment. Tom was looking at his mother for guidance and getting none. Then Gemma said, 'I'draver stay with Mummy.' And Tom said quickly, 'I'll help Dad unload.' Adam nodded.

Holly said, 'Yes, of course. How thoughtless of me.'

Ivy smiled. 'Shall I be mother? And you can hold Giles.'

Holly relinquished the teapot immediately and sat on the sofa and Ivy gently placed Giles on her lap. He looked surprised and then stopped crying and smiled. Holly smiled back. Tom relaxed visibly and handed biscuits around. Ivy asked Holly about Reg and Ted said how concerned they had been. When they had drunk the tea and made the biscuit tin lighter, Giles stayed where he was while the others went off armed with a key to Magpie Cottage. They were all smiling, especially Holly.

The next few days were packed with delightful busy-ness. Holly and Mark Jepson took the three children on a beachcombing exercise and ended the day with a bonfire on the beach. Mark acquired a little rowing boat from someone in Clevedon and took the boys out fishing; meanwhile Holly looked after Gemma and Giles, while Ivy and Ted went into Weston to get a few Christmas presents for the children. Mark confided to Holly, 'I don't like to mention it to Stanley and Ivy but Adam said not one word the whole time we were out.'

'Perhaps he's scared of the water,' she suggested, still flushed with the sheer joy of having Gemma and Giles all afternoon.

'I don't think so. He kept grinning . . . well, sort of grinning. He caught an eel at one point and jumped up and down – nearly capsized the boat!'

'Just shy. Gemma doesn't have a lot to say either. Must run in the family.'

Mark said, 'They're nice kids, aren't they?'

'Yes. Giles is such a happy baby.'

Mark put an arm around her shoulders and hugged her to him. 'Don't worry, love. It will happen one day. I'm sure of it.'

At one time she would have snapped his head

off for that. Now she smiled at him, almost weeping, and said, 'Mark . . . if you're happy then I'm happy. We're together. That's all that matters really.'

He enfolded her properly and stroked her hair and kissed her face. She had been so different since poor old Reg had his accident. She said it had made her get her priorities right. He felt so full of love for her . . . so happy. He wished he could give her something really wonderful for Christmas.

May and Arthur arrived on Wednesday. Holly thought May looked rounder than ever and Arthur as dour. May bustled around exclaiming about everything and Arthur went immediately to the bottles on the sideboard.

The decorations, unearthed from the roof space, had been cleaned and renovated and hung up and the tree was waiting in the corner of the living room.

May pretended to be disappointed. 'Reg always let me put the trimmings up,' she said. 'You've done it different-like. I usually put those bells above the table with tinsel hanging from them.'

'We know.' Mark winked at Holly. 'We thought poor old Nunc might like a surprise for once.'

'Nothing in the hall?'

'The kids have gone to the woods to get some

holly and ivy and stuff.' Holly grinned. 'We're leaving the hall for them to do. Also the tree.'

May raised her brows. 'I thought the father was supposed to be a real stinker. Is he allowing those boys to enjoy themselves for once?'

'He's an absolute sweetie,' Holly said. 'She's a bit subdued but Stanley is going all out to make it a good Christmas. And there are four children. Three boys and a girl. One of the boys is a baby. He's gorgeous.'

May frowned. 'I must have got it wrong. Anyway . . . sounds as if it's all organized. You probably don't need us.'

'Of course we do! If you think I'm going to dish up a lunch on my own on Saturday—' But Holly was laughing. She put a hand on May's arm. 'Listen. Reg is coming home on Christmas Eve. They want to close the ward or something. He'll need looking after. That can be your special job.'

'Thanks a lot,' May said dryly. But later she said to Arthur, 'It's funny, she didn't want to come this year if you remember. But she seems to be full of it!'

Arthur looked at her, then said, 'It's those children, isn't it? She just loves children. Crying shame she can't seem to have 'em.'

She returned his look for a brief moment, then moved to the window and looked at the view. 'Yes,' she said.

*　　*　　*

95

People would begin to arrive on the Thursday. Mark and Arthur had checked all the chalets and Holly and May had turned mattresses and switched on electric blankets. Holly picked some of the twigs from the berried bushes along the coastal path and filled a vase for each of the kitchens. May put out cups and saucers ready for that first cup of tea or coffee.

'Why are we doing all this?' May asked, bewildered at how keen she had suddenly become. 'Is it some kind of challenge because Reg isn't around? Are we still doing it for him – or what?'

Holly looked around the living room of Seagull Cottage. 'It looks cosy, doesn't it? Does it make up for being so chilly?' She hooked back the winter curtains she had just hung.

May said, 'It's all right once the fires are switched on. And Reg always insists they all go on.' She sighed. 'Reg again. We're obviously doing it all for Reg.'

Holly grinned. 'Do we have to have a reason? There are a million reasons really. All right . . . Reg. Christmas. Reg again. And of course . . . Reg.' She laughed. 'But I suppose, if I'm honest, it's for me as well. It always comes down to that in the end, doesn't it? I want to be happy and I want everyone else to be happy and this seems a good way of . . . doing it.'

May said directly, 'Holly, are you pregnant?'

She immediately wished she had not asked.

The girl's face seemed to close in on itself. She added hurriedly, 'It's only that . . . well, this business of making little homes for people . . . like the nesting instinct. You know.'

Holly forced another laugh. 'Sorry, May. I wish I could say yes. But, as usual, it's no.'

'I'm a silly old fool. Sorry, my dear. I shouldn't have asked. I know it upsets you.'

'Not . . . so much. I think I've realized that the important person in my life is Mark.' Holly switched the electric fire off and picked up her gloves. 'Anyway, perhaps that's why I'm enjoying all this. The Edwards family are so generous. I've been invited into Magpie tonight to bath Giles.'

'Very generous,' May said dryly. She followed Holly outside and locked the door behind her. 'Pity you've got to hurry back after Christmas. We could have extended the jollities until New Year for once. Reg would have liked that.'

'We're not in any hurry,' Holly replied, pulling on hat and gloves and taking great breaths of the damp, seaweed-smelling air. 'Mark has told them about Reg back at the garage. If they decide to oust him from his job while he's away I don't think Mark will care much. It might be a good thing, actually. He's really fed up with the new management.'

'What about you? You'll have to get back, won't you?'

Holly said briefly, 'I've packed it in.'

They were walking down the concrete path

towards Wren Cottage and May stopped in her tracks with sheer astonishment.

'What?'

'I thought Mark would have mentioned it. I left at the beginning of the month.'

'My God, I thought you'd end up managing that place. What happened? Was there a row?' May was onto it like a ferret. 'You've been there for years! My God, Holly. If you leave there's no golden handshake. Nothing.'

Holly shrugged. 'I wouldn't say nothing. A lot of experience.' She turned into the next pathway. 'I like this chalet. It's more like a studio, isn't it? Just the one big room. And it's got a different view. I see that artist chap has got it again. Cree Evans. He seems to come every year. Last two or three his daughter's come with him. Someone from Reg's army days.'

May made a snorting noise. 'Daughter, my foot! Fancy piece, more like.'

'But he must be well into his seventies.'

'And you think there's a deadline for that sort of thing, do you?'

They both laughed as they went inside but May had not given up. She seemed strangely on edge and Holly was aware of it.

They took off hats and gloves and began their usual round with dusters and brushes. May switched on the heating and Holly wiped the windows. There were just two armchairs next to the fire, a bar and stools separating the galley kitchen from the big room and a double bed which pulled out of the wall. The tiny bathroom had been added as an afterthought and was no more than a lean-to.

'It's pretty basic,' Holly said doubtfully. 'We've got Robin and Sparrow empty. What do you think?'

May said briefly, 'He always has this one.'

'But . . . double bed? I mean, it's possible that the woman is his daughter.'

'You've never met him.' May finished dusting the stools and tucked them under the bar. 'Anyway, you might need Robin. And we always have Sparrow.'

Holly said, 'You know very well we're all staying with Reg. Company for him.' She reached for cups and saucers and arranged them on a tray. 'We'll offer the artist a choice when he arrives. Perhaps that's best.'

'He wants the northern light apparently. And he likes to look down into St Margaret's Bay. He won't change.' May went to the window. She said suddenly, 'I thought I was in love with him years ago. Handsome devil. But . . . what's the word? Feckless. He was – and is – completely feckless.'

Holly was surprised and came to stand by the older woman. She could see that May must have been a pretty girl. But she had never thought of her without Arthur's name attached. May and Arthur. Arthur and May.

She said, 'Oh May. And you wanted a husband and a home and children.'

'I was married to Arthur already.' May sighed deeply. 'No children, of course. I thought Cree would give me children. But he wouldn't.' She turned sharply and began to pack up her cleaning materials. 'That's why I know his daughter isn't his daughter. He always said he'd never father a child.'

Holly tried not to feel shocked. May and . . . who? Arthur? Or Cree Evans? She said hesitantly, 'What about your boys? You and Arthur had them afterwards?'

May rammed on her hat and picked up her gloves. 'I shouldn't tell you this, Holly. But . . . well, I think you might be pregnant. And if you're not, then I don't want you blaming the Jepson side any more.'

Holly said quickly, 'We had this conversation before, May. The children thing. I don't mind any more. Really.'

May shrugged. 'You still need to know. My two sons are not Arthur's sons. He doesn't know. I'm sure of it. Almost.' She stopped, pursed her lips and drew a breath through her nose. Then she went on, 'I was like you. Desperate. Only I knew Arthur couldn't because . . . well, he couldn't anyway. So I thought I would leave him. Live with Cree Evans and have children and be Bohemian. Hippie. You know.'

Holly stayed very still by the window.

May said, 'We were happy. Deliriously. I used to slip down here when Art and Reg went fishing. Maude covered for me. I posed for him.' She smiled wryly. 'Yes. In the nude. And then I let slip that I wanted to leave Arthur and set up home with Cree. He couldn't stop laughing.' She fished for a hanky and blew her nose fiercely. 'I remember I tried to hit him and he held my wrists and I just cried and cried. He was sorry then.'

Holly said softly, 'Oh May. Oh May.'

'I know. It's awful, isn't it? And the worst part was that he told Reg. He didn't know what to do about me and he told Reg.' She looked at Holly. 'That's why I've got to tell you all this . . . rubbish. Because Reg was kind. And loving. And within a few months I was pregnant.'

Holly put her hand to her mouth and said again, 'Oh May!'

'Reg didn't want to hurt Art, you see. He put it to me that as Maude couldn't have kids and Art couldn't have kids, we might be able to do something about it without hurting anyone. So we did.' She stood in front of Holly as if waiting for judgement. 'Do you think that was so bad, Holly? The twins were a handful and Art was a wonderful father to them. When they come home on leave it's always Art they want to be with. I made sure of that. They've brought nothing but happiness to us.'

Holly moistened her lips. 'Of course . . . of course . . .'

'Perhaps I shouldn't have told you. But I wanted you to know that there's no history of sterility in the family. And they're – they're lovely men.' She began to cry. 'Oh Holly, I think I've always loved Reg. But then I love Art as well. And I might even still love bloody Cree Evans!' She covered her face with her hands. 'Oh Holly, what does that make me?'

Holly went to her and folded her against her shoulder. In spite of her girth, May was so vulnerable.

She said, 'It makes you a woman who is full of love, May.' She tried to look into the faded blue eyes and smile reassuringly. 'Is that so bad?'

And, for a while, they both wept.

Five

Christmas Eve dawned greyly, yet with a sense of anticipation that hummed through Magpie Cottage in time with the fridge. Tom rolled over in the double bed and stared at Adam through the gloom.

'It's Christmas tomorrow,' he whispered.

Adam had been awake for almost an hour. He was so pleased to know that Tom was too that he smiled.

'Excited?' Tom breathed. And Adam nodded vigorously. 'Throat OK now?' Tom went on. Adam nodded again, smile still in place. 'Brill.' Tom allowed himself a smile too. 'Look, I'm not shaking any more.' He held one arm straight up in the air and it stayed there, rock steady. He tucked it back under the bedclothes quickly because it was cold. 'They'll never find us here,' he whispered contentedly. 'And once Ted marries Mum, we'll be safe. He's going to adopt us.' His smile widened. 'It'll be great, Addie. Did you know that Ted and Mum were sweethearts at school?' Surprisingly, Adam nodded. Tom snorted a tiny laugh. 'Yeah, I bet you did. Just 'cos you don't say anything doesn't mean you've gone deaf! Funny, that. No-one seems to realize you listen twice as much.' He humped the bedclothes over one shoulder. 'I like Ted. He's ordinary. And he's good. Like Mum.' The pillow moved as Adam nodded again. Tom went on musingly, 'I like Gemma too. She isn't all yappy like most girls. She's a bit like you. Listens a lot.' He burrowed deeper still. 'And Giles is OK. For a baby.' And then he was asleep. And Adam lay beside him very quietly and listened to the high, violin note of Christmas coming very close.

Next door, Ivy woke in her narrow camp bed and lay just as quietly savouring her happiness. She and Gemma had chosen the camp beds in the second bedroom because they were the smallest. They had made a game of measuring up against the kitchen door and Adam had topped his mother by what she called a microcentimetre. So the two boys had gone in the double room and she'd joined Ted and his children in the room with the bunk beds. They'd made a little nest for Giles on the lower bunk and Ted slept above him and, sometimes, with him. Gemma and Ivy had put their beds close together so that they could hold hands in the night if they needed to. Just for a moment last Sunday when they settled themselves in, Ted had caught Ivy's eye and asked a silent question about the double bed. She had smiled back and he had known what she meant. Not for a while.

She swivelled her head and looked across the grey-lit room. There was Gemma, her hair all over the pillow, her lips slightly apart, smelling of the talcum powder given to her by Holly during a riotous bath time last night. Then there was a space and the tall bunk beds reared darkly up the wall, Giles invisible in the bottom one, and Ted . . . She realized suddenly that Ted was awake and looking down at her. She raised a hand and the next minute he was sitting up and very gently sliding to the floor. He knelt by the camp bed.

'Happy Christmas Eve,' he whispered.

'Oh Ted.' Quite naturally she reached up and put the palm of her hand to his cheek. 'How lovely this is. How simply lovely.'

He clutched her hand and turned his face to kiss it. She felt dampness and reared up to hold him.

'It's all right,' she murmured in his ear. 'Everything will be all right.'

When he could speak he breathed, 'I know. It's just . . . you're real. You're so real, Ivy. You've always been there . . . in my head. But now you're here. Really here. And you're real.'

She said nothing. Just for a moment she had recalled Stanley; the way he had kissed her and punched her and then kissed her again, weeping and begging forgiveness. Until the next time. But Ted was not Stanley.

'Let's get up and have a cup of tea.'

He said ardently, 'I'll get you a cup of tea. In bed.'

'No. Let's sit at the kitchen table together. You and me. Without the children.'

They crept out of the bedroom and across the little hall. The kitchen was big and square with an old-fashioned deal table set right in the middle. Between them they filled the kettle, lined up enough mugs for everyone together with Giles's feeder cup and made the first pot of tea of the day. They were always making tea; it was a symbol of their new family status. Gemma drank it, sipping fastidiously and watching everyone through the steam. Tom cupped his mug in two hands exactly like Ted. Even Giles drank a weak, milky mixture, banging his feeder cup delightedly on the table and laughing heartily when Adam did the same.

Ted lit the oven while Ivy poured the tea then they both sat with their feet on a stool in front of the open oven door. Neither of them had packed slippers or a dressing gown and they wore their anoraks and thick socks. 'We must look like refugees,' Ted laughed.

'That's what we are, I suppose.' Ivy breathed in the steam from her cup and closed her eyes ecstatically. 'Oh, that first cup of tea . . . oh Ted.'

'The little pleasures are the best,' he pontificated, mimicking her father from long ago. 'A perfect sunset. A good night's sleep. God's free fresh air—'

She was laughing. 'And wasn't he absolutely right? D'you realize that last night was a perfect sunset. We've all had a good night's sleep. And' – she looked at the door curtain stirring in the draught – 'there's plenty of God's free fresh air about. Oh, my dear old dad was right. No doubt about that.'

Ted felt his eyes filling again and controlled himself sternly because he had sensed Ivy's momentary withdrawal back there in the bedroom.

'Ivy. You know I love you,' he said huskily. 'Is it . . . are we . . . ?'

'Yes. We are.' She put her cup and feet down and stood up. 'I'm going to kiss you, Ted. Just an ordinary kiss. Like we used to in the pictures.' She leaned over him and pecked him experimentally, then confidently. Then she straightened. 'You see, Ted, we've got to start again. Where we were before I made a complete fool of myself and let Stanley . . . well, let him take over. Can you manage . . . to wait?'

His voice shook almost uncontrollably and he gave up trying to speak and nodded.

She was very serious. 'I think I might be . . . you know . . . a bit funny about some things. I know I love you very much. And I trust you completely. But . . . now and then . . . I can't explain it, Ted. I'm frightened. More than frightened. Sort of, well, terrified really. But not of you. Of . . . something else. I don't know what.' She sat down. 'I'm sorry, Ted. It might be difficult for you. Perhaps you won't want to try even.'

He made a gargling sound and she smiled. 'Yes. All right. I know.' She put her hand over his. 'I'm just so happy. Now. At this moment. I don't want to think about what will happen. I just want to be happy. It's been so long since I've been happy. I can't believe it will stay. So . . .'

He found his voice. 'Ivy. I am the same. I promise you that we won't talk about what might – or what might not – happen. I'm happy too. I promise you that is enough.'

She smiled at him. He was crying. Yes. But he did not try to take her in his arms and he did not apologize. He smiled back at her. It was a very wobbly, comical smile.

She said, 'Oh, my dear Ted. Shall we have another cup of tea?'

In Seagull Cottage, Pansy and Bernice were already up, showered and dressed.

'I've just looked in on Mavis. Dead to the world.' Bernice spoke with some disgust. They planned to drive into Weston-super-Mare that morning and get last-minute presents. Apparently Reg Jepson was coming home today.

They wanted him to be greeted by an enormous bouquet. Then there were the four children in Magpie Cottage and really they couldn't sit around the table tomorrow and share a meal with them and not give gifts. 'Just because we haven't had children doesn't mean we can't remember the sheer joy of Christmas,' Pansy had said yesterday when Mavis made a face at the prospect of sticky fingers and probably lots of loud crying.

She said now, 'I don't think Mavis was very keen on coming shopping. Perhaps we should just have breakfast and get on our way.'

Bernice thinned her lips. 'She simply wants to be here when Holly and Mark fetch Reg from hospital. I can just see her announcing herself as the advance welcoming committee!'

'But, Bernie, if we go now . . . well, in the next half hour . . . we shall be back with the flowers. That was the whole idea surely? To get the flowers before he returned.'

Bernice sat down and sipped her fruit juice judiciously. It was a special sort of fruit juice to help her colon. She knew she must not get in a stew about Mavis otherwise she'd be in and out of the loo all day long. Actually, annoying though Mavis's motives were, it would be much easier if she wasn't with them on the shopping expedition. Pansy would be guided entirely by Bernice whereas Mavis would argue.

Bernice said, 'You're quite right, Pansy. Yes.

That's what we'll do. A coffee and a bit of toast and we'll be ready to go.'

Pansy smiled, well pleased. There had been a dress in the Worcester branch of C and A's which she had decided was too décolleté at her age. But yesterday, on their arrival, Arthur Long had mentioned an artist and his daughter who had taken the little studio on the cliff edge, Wren Cottage. There had been an artist on a cruise several years ago who had admired Pansy's cleavage. If that dress was at the Weston branch of C and A's she would get it.

So it was that when Mavis surfaced at nine o'clock she found a note from Bernice telling her that she was on her own for the morning and how about decorating the cottage for Christmas. Mavis felt strangely let down. The first morning of the holiday and the others had deserted her.

She wrapped her dressing gown around her tightly because there was no central heating in the chalet and wondered what on earth she would do with herself all morning. Obviously she would shower and have some breakfast but then it would probably be only ten o'clock and they wouldn't be back till lunchtime. She glanced again at the note. Bernice said they'd be just over an hour. Of course, Bernice had no idea what Weston-super-Mare would be like on Christmas Eve; probably she was still driving around looking for a parking space. Pansy would be no help at all; she was the sort of passenger who always said, 'Oh, there was a space there but you were going too fast.'

Mavis stood by the window looking at the view and trying to find the resolution for a shower or breakfast, neither of which she felt like. She noted that the sea was grey, likewise the sky. The copse to her right, which presumably screened the small studio chalet on the edge of the cliff, all grew one way as if brushed by the constant south-westerlies coming up the Bristol Channel from the Atlantic. Beyond the concrete driveway, the land dropped away to a large shingly beach. Reg's nephew, Mark – nice boy, good-looking, with Reg's kind eyes – had told them that the other cottages, Linnet and Magpie, were over there. Apparently, from Magpie Cottage you could run straight into the sea. If you were mad enough.

Mavis sighed. It wasn't what she had imagined at all. Really, what on earth were they going to do with themselves for three whole days? Mark had said something about them being welcome to stay on for the New Year if they felt like it. She puffed a little laugh. Not very likely. The general grey drabness was un-utterably depressing. The only bright spot was the thought of Reg arriving today. She hoped the girls would remember to get him something nice. They'd give it to him today; as soon as he arrived. She smiled reminiscently, remembering Reg wearing an enormous panama hat under the Mediterranean sun. Surely Reg's appearance would brighten up this place just a little bit?

As if in response to this sliver of optimism a watery sun suddenly lit up the sea. It was like striking a match: a flare across the top of the water revealed that, far from being flat and calm, there was quite a swell. At the same time Mavis noted that the beaten trees were full of red berries. And something else . . . She peered, frowning slightly. Something white and fluttering. And a sound too: a shout. She said aloud, 'Oh my God! Surely no-one's fallen off the cliff!'

She ran to the door and flung it open. Nothing. The cold was intense and she immediately started to close it. But then came another distant shout. She said, 'Oh my God,' again and plunged into the great outdoors as if into a swimming bath, rushing down the short path to the ridiculous little gate. From the direction of the cliff there came a sort of gurgling scream and yet another loud shout. She ignored the path that led to the concrete drive and made for the trees. Her dressing gown caught on thorns, her slippers flapped hopelessly among the fallen leaves; she knew she should have gone for help to the bungalow. Mark or that nice Arthur Long . . . there was probably a boat . . . oh God, there it was again. A woman's screams, a man's shouts.

She broke through the thicket at last and

there was another chalet, the gate painted with the words Wren Cottage and a path leading from it to the cliff edge. The door was wide open; she peered inside. 'Anyone there?' No-one was. So it was them; they were in trouble. The artist and his so-called daughter.

She controlled her breathing with difficulty and began to negotiate the path to the edge of the cliff. It was not made up and was very muddy. She almost slipped over several times. Her dressing gown was filthy, her slippers done for. Her mind leaped from one thought to another. Was it an accident – a fall over the edge? Or was it a suicide attempt? 'Oh God,' she moaned.

She reached a cluster of bushes marking the edge and there, caught in the brambles, was some kind of garment. It could have been a Roman toga thing except that people did not wear them any more. Her mind clawed at other possibilities. Was it a sort of dressing gown? Or one of the sheets from the bed?

Then she saw that it wasn't actually caught in the bushes; it was hung over the end of a rusty handrail which ran above a flight of rough muddy steps leading down to a rocky beach. She clung onto it, gasping for breath, staring down incredulously. Because below, highlighted in the single ray from the winter sun, two people, apparently completely naked, were disporting themselves gaspingly in the grey sea.

They spotted her almost immediately and waved. The man called up – he had a voice like a foghorn – 'My dear lady! You look like a pink angel! Are you off a Christmas cake? Come and join us – please! It's worth it! Five minutes of hell – I defy you not to scream the place down – and then . . . oh my God . . . it's a rebirth!'

Mavis stared, still speechless. They were obviously the couple from Wren Cottage. The artist and his so-called daughter. Bernice's words. Mark had given them thumbnail sketches of the other visitors and as soon as they had got inside Seagull Cottage, Bernice had said, 'Daughter, forsooth! Model, more like. An old man and a young model. Disgusting.'

Pansy had said, 'Rather like Picasso. I read an article in a magazine about him and his models.' She had giggled. 'It's rather fun, isn't it, girls?'

Mavis, staring, couldn't see the fun in this particular situation. She had a chronic stitch, her dressing gown and slippers were ruined and she felt that somehow she had made a complete ass of herself. To make matters infinitely worse, for some ridiculous reason she started to cry. She clung to the rail and the Roman toga with one hand while the other went up to her shaking mouth and she let out a kind of wail.

The man and woman looked at each other, startled, concerned. The woman began to walk out of the water. She had enormous breasts

114

which made Mavis wail even louder. She slipped on an invisible muddy rock and went down. The man ignored her and waded vigorously to the shore and then almost ran over the pebbles to the base of the steps and started taking them two at a time.

He was completely naked. Mavis closed her eyes and wailed louder than ever. Her husband, St John, had always switched off the light before undressing.

By the time this completely uninhibited person had reached the top of the cliff she was almost hysterical. He wasted no energy on words, he simply clasped her in his wet arms and held her tightly to his wet body. Very tightly. Her wails were cut off at the source. She had to concentrate on getting enough air into her lungs to survive. She breathed in shallow gasps, her hands trying hard not to touch his bare back, her face definitely touching the strong muscles in his neck. She opened her eyes and saw the woman stumbling up the steps. She closed her eyes again.

The woman arrived next to them; Mavis could hear her panting less than a yard away. And then laughing. Mavis opened one eye; the woman – thank goodness – was wrapped in the toga. She met Mavis's Cyclops gaze and stopped laughing long enough to gasp, 'You two look as if you're in the throes of an orgasm!'

The man immediately slackened his grasp

though luckily did not back off sufficiently to permit Mavis to see his whole nakedness.

'God, Cass! Trust you!' he said in that foghorn voice. 'This poor distraught soul doesn't know whether she is coming or going and you have to reduce the whole situation to orgasms!'

The woman – Cass – choked back another laugh. 'Hardly a reduction, would you say? Here, you impossible old reprobate, put your sheet on! Pull yourself together. If you have to see yourself as a knight rescuing a damsel in distress, at least do it with some modesty.' She lifted another toga from the handrail and wound it around the man. She looked up from beneath his arm. 'This is Cree Evans, by the way. The artist. And I am Cassandra Evans. His daughter.'

Mavis said in a high, wobbly voice, 'And these are your sheets? From your bed?' It was a trick question, of course. If they were father and daughter they would hardly share a bed.

Cassandra Evans nodded. 'We didn't bother with bathrobes or anything—'

'Actually,' Cree Evans interrupted, 'we haven't got any bathrobes.'

'Exactly. And the sheets will dry by tonight.'

'Top and bottom sheets?' Mavis pursued doggedly.

Cassandra grinned. 'Absolutely. One from beneath us. And one from above.'

Mavis began to feel she was living inside a dream. She looked down at her own ruined bedwear and said, 'I heard you, you see. I thought you had fallen down the cliff. Or you were drowning. Or something.' She looked up and met Cree Evans's piercing blue eyes. She sobbed, 'I don't usually look like this. I came to rescue you.'

He looked stunned. 'How wonderful! Nobody has ever come to rescue me before. Cass, did you hear that? This pink angel came to rescue us.'

'Obviously I heard,' Cass replied dryly. 'I am standing here, next to you.' She shook her head at Mavis. 'We're awfully sorry to have worried you. How selfish. Cree was sketching me, you see. And I got cold and fed up and put my sheet on and just ran and he chased me . . . and we got in the sea.'

'Oh,' Mavis said faintly.

Cree clapped his hands suddenly and his toga slipped to his waist.

'I've got a simply splendid idea! Have you had breakfast, pink angel?'

'No,' Mavis whimpered.

'Then let us return immediately to Christopher's Cottage and cook up the most splendid army breakfast you have ever seen! You can shower and borrow a sheet from the airing cupboard and we will all sit around and talk the day away.'

'Christopher's Cottage?' Mavis sounded as if she might collapse at any moment.

'Christopher Wren, my angel! Wren Cottage. Don't you see?' And suddenly he scooped her up, mud and all. Her slippers finally fell off, her dressing gown gaped hideously, but she didn't care. She remembered years ago reading the most wonderful romantic novel where exactly this kind of thing had happened. The heroine in the novel had 'surrendered herself'. Suddenly Mavis knew that was what she had to do. She put her newly permed hair against a very hairy chest and surrendered herself completely.

Paula and Dennis had been unable to borrow a car as they had planned. They took a bus to Portishead and walked two of the four miles to the village before a passing car took pity on them and pulled up.

A woman wound down her window and looked through. She was probably about sixty but she was darkly handsome. The woman sitting beside her was younger, blond, more cautious. Dennis heard her say, 'Don't unlock the doors until we're sure they're all right.'

The dark woman ignored her. 'We're only going as far as the holiday village,' she called. 'But there's a bus stop at the top of the road.'

Dennis grinned his relief. 'We're going to the holiday village too,' he said. 'Mr and Mrs Jepson told us the bus went right through but actually it didn't today.'

Paula joined them. 'This is so good of you. We quite enjoy walking but we've brought a lot of luggage.'

The driver of the car flicked a switch and the boot opened.

'Watch our parcels,' she warned. 'We've been to Weston to get a few gifts. Some of them are fragile.'

Dennis stacked the two rucksacks in the corner of the boot and settled himself next to Paula in the back of the Jaguar. The car, the contents of the boot, even the two women, all smelled of money. He wondered what the hell they were doing at a place like this.

The blond woman tittered. 'We'd better introduce ourselves if we're spending Christmas together. I'm Mrs Pansetti. This is Mrs Smythe. And we're in Seagull Cottage with another friend, Mrs Gentry.'

Paula said politely, 'Pleased to meet you. We're the Chivertons. Paula and Dennis.'

Bernice said, 'No formality, Pansy.' She half turned her head and said, 'This is Pansy – obviously because of her surname. I'm Bernice. And our other friend is Mavis. We're pleased to meet you too, Paula. And Dennis.'

Paula was delighted. 'What a stroke of luck, meeting you like this. I've never been to the seaside like this – and at Christmas too – it's so exciting!'

Bernice glanced in her mirror. Paula had

the face of a happy schoolgirl; Dennis a sulky schoolboy.

She said bracingly, 'Holidays are what you make them, don't you think? We booked because we'd already met the owner when we went on a cruise last summer. And then when he had an accident we couldn't seem to make any other plans in time. But I have to admit the chalet is very comfortable, and Holly and Mark Jepson are charming and determined we should enjoy ourselves. And though the parking in Weston was atrocious, I've thoroughly enjoyed our morning's shopping. Haven't you, Pansy?' She darted a commanding look sideways and Pansy nodded vigorously.

'I just hope Mavis hasn't been lonely,' she said.

'Well, if she has it serves her right for sleeping so long. It was nine o'clock when we left. I call that sloth.'

Dennis and Paula exchanged glances; Paula grinned and, after a small hesitation, so did Dennis. He reached for her hand and moved so that his jeaned thigh touched hers.

Pansy slewed in her seat but appeared not to notice their connections.

'We haven't met anyone yet except Holly and Mark and the Longs. They're all living in Reg's bungalow which is really big and quite luxurious. I mean, there's room for the four of them plus Reg when he gets back—'

'Which I expect he has already,' Bernice put in.

'Probably because we're much later than we thought and we had lunch in Weston. Which was naughty' – Pansy giggled – 'but nice.'

'We know Arthur Long, actually,' Dennis volunteered. 'We met him at a skittles match at the Union and he told us about the Christmas thing. Sounds as though Reg Jepson is a bit of a philanthropist.'

'I wouldn't say that,' Bernice said. 'He certainly charged us the full price. But then, why not? He knows we can afford it.'

Paula squeezed Dennis's hand warningly. 'And are there many other people staying?' she asked Pansy.

'There's a big family in Magpie Cottage,' Pansy volunteered. 'Four children, I believe Holly mentioned. She adores them. They came early and she has been looking after them and helping with baths and things. Mark took the boys out fishing. They're having a whale of a time.'

'And there's the artist and his daughter,' Bernice said with heavy sarcasm.

'Really?' Paula looked intrigued. 'D'you mean a real artist?'

'Well, we've never heard of him. But yes, I think so. He's one of Reg's old army cronies. His name is Cree Evans.'

'Gosh. Quite a mixture,' Paula commented.

Dennis said, 'I've heard of him. He's an abstract painter. He did a portrait of a man opened up down the middle.'

'Chiv!' Paula remonstrated.

'No, seriously. It was called "External Internal". Everything was meticulously painted, colon, liver, kidneys, even—'

'Well!' Paula glared at him. 'Fascinating!'

Bernice smiled grimly. 'So. The girl might be his daughter.' She glanced at Pansy. 'He's hardly likely to need a model for those kind of paintings, is he? More likely a book with anatomical drawings.'

Pansy giggled. 'Oh Bernie, you are awful,' she said.

Paula went into the shop at the top of the road while Dennis collected the key from the bungalow. Reg was indeed back from the hospital and was sitting in his favourite armchair by the radiator, admiring the unusual Christmas decorations, while Pansy crouched by his side telling him over and over again how fit and well he looked, leaving Bernice to bring in the enormous flower arrangement and the fruit basket and the chocolates and cigars.

'He's not allowed to smoke!' May whipped the sandalwood box from the pile of goodies and swept into the kitchen to make tea. Holly and Mark were taking Dennis and Paula down to Linnet Cottage and Arthur had decided to go with them as he knew them. That left May to do the honours for these two women who obviously thought Reg was the bee's knees. She banged cups onto a tray and indulged in a fit of self-pity. She knew that Reg had slept with her out of sheer kindness all those years ago. And she knew that, even when Maude was still alive, he would oblige anyone who was interested. Except her. And damn it all, she was the mother of his sons! And now Arthur had gone off with the Chivertons, looking at the girl with the sort of moon-faced idiocy he had used on May once.

Reg shifted his leg slightly and Pansy noticed.

'Reggie darling. Does it hurt? Shall I put a cushion on the footstool? I think the frame is just catching your poor ankle.'

'Not at all, Pan, old girl. Matter of fact, it's the hospital stockings. They go right up to here' – he indicated his crutch – 'and I'm itching to glory.'

Pansy dissolved completely, eyes watering. Reg took the opportunity to ask Bernice how she was feeling.

'Fine, thank you, Reg,' she said briskly. 'And it's obvious you're all right in spite of being unable to stay upright. What was it? One whisky too many?'

'Bernie, how could you?' He grinned up at her, that blasted grin that seemed to her to say she was the only woman he was really interested in.

She said as coolly as she could, 'Remember, I know you, Reg Jepson.'

Pansy was still laughing and dabbing her eyes with a tiny hanky so that he could say, 'You're always using biblical language, Bernie. Remember, I know you too.'

It took her breath away. The sheer effrontery of it. Even Robert, darling, darling Robert, had never spoken to her so openly like that. And he had known her much better than Reg Jepson. He had said once, in the privacy of their bedroom, that she was a deeply passionate woman. He had been the only person in the world to know that. Until that cruise and Reg Jepson. She stared down into the grinning face for a long moment and then went into the kitchen.

'Let me help you, May. I'm sorry about the cigars. We just didn't think.'

May, slightly mollified, pushed the breadboard across the table. 'You can cut some bread and butter for him if you like. As thin as possible.'

Darkness came early to the little holiday village. The electric fires glowed and simulated logs fairly successfully, and the fairy lights came on around the bungalow. Dennis and Paula unpacked and ate the fish and chips brought to them by Holly, who then went over to Magpie Cottage to read a story to the children while Ivy cooked supper. It was Christmas Day tomorrow.

The children deployed their stockings. Paula and Dennis put a pillowcase at the end of their bed for their baby and began to fill it with rattles and a soft toy and a rag book. It took a long time because between each deposit they had to stop and kiss each other and make love. Bernice and Pansy finally managed to tear themselves away from Reg and take the car on down the concrete drive and turn right into their own parking space.

Pansy looked apprehensively at the dark windows of Seagull Cottage.

'She's not there, Bernie. Oh my God. What's happened?'

'She's sitting in the dark, sulking,' Bernice said crisply. 'She'll soon relent when she sees the wine and the caviare. Bring those packets of biscuits, can you? And the tree – don't forget the tree!'

'Ridiculous of us to buy a tree,' Pansy said breathlessly from behind its branches. 'And as for those baubles . . .'

Bernice pushed at the door with her right hip. 'Yes, she's in. Door's not even closed, let alone locked.' She barged into the kitchen and flicked the light switch with her elbow. 'Have you gone to bed, Mavis? Come and see what we've bought!'

Pansy followed, shivering. 'I say, it's cold in here. We'd better put all the heaters on. What shall I do with the tree?'

'Put it in the living room. By the window,

125

Pansy, where those children will be able to see it.' She lifted her voice again. 'Mavis! Come on, stop showing off and give us a hand.'

They offloaded all the shopping and put the kettle on before they went into Mavis's room and saw she was not there. Pansy was immediately panic-stricken.

'My God, Bernie. She's wandered off somewhere while we've been enjoying ourselves. Oh my God, if she's had an accident I'll never forgive—'

'Shut up, Pansy! For crying out loud! She couldn't have wandered off – look, here are her clothes. She's in her dressing gown.' Bernice sat down suddenly. 'Let's work this out sensibly. She had an early bath. Got ready for bed . . .' She looked up at Pansy. 'And then what?'

Pansy swallowed. 'She wanted to start a meal. So she . . . she went to the next chalet to borrow some – some sugar. Or bread. Yes, bread. She thought she would make some toast. D'you remember her saying how much she loved making toast by a fire? And there's a toasting fork in the hearth. That's what she's done. She's gone next door.'

Bernice too swallowed. 'Which would be—?'

'Wren Cottage. Where that artist chap is. It's the other side of the trees.' Pansy was already at the door. 'Come on, let's go and see. They probably asked her in and she's having a nice chat and finding out just what's going on. You know, whether the daughter is really a daughter or – or a model.'

They left all the lights on and ran back down the path to the drive, turned right and right again. Wren Cottage was tucked in the trees and beyond it the sea heaved a shoulder silently, powerfully.

Pansy groaned. 'Oh my God . . .'

Bernice rapped on the door. 'Pull yourself together. Mavis isn't going to be stumbling around in her dressing gown! There's got to be some perfectly ordinary explanation.'

The door opened suddenly and widely. Cree Evans stood there, wrapped in a sheet, his beard and wild hair making him look like a devil. He smiled and his beard tipped forward.

'Ah, ladies! How delightful. I cannot believe there are three of you! Amazing, absolutely amazing!' He stepped back. 'Come in! Come in and see what we have been up to for most of the day.'

Neither Pansy nor Bernice moved an inch. Because they could see perfectly well from where they were standing. At the end of the long room, Mavis was reclining on a mound of cushions. She too was swathed in a sheet. Standing above her was a woman similarly sheeted, presumably Evans's daughter. She was leaning slightly towards Mavis and in her hand was a bunch of grapes. Mavis's lips were parted as if to take a grape.

Pansy breathed, 'It's an orgy! Bernie – Mavis is having an orgy!'

Six

The bickering went on long after the actual row had finished.

Bernice snapped, 'You could have washed the damned dressing gown and had it dried by now. Look at it!' She surveyed the muddy, crumpled heap on the floor of the bathroom. 'We shall have to soak it overnight and then see if Holly will let you use her washing machine. It's too bad, Mavis!'

Pansy mourned, 'We could have bought you one in Weston if we'd known. It would have been such a lovely surprise.'

Mavis, who seemed to have lost all her niggling worries during the day, said, 'Girls, what does it matter? There are plenty of spare sheets and blankets. I can wrap myself up warmly—'

'Like you did over there?' Bernice said sarcastically, laying the table for supper with unnecessary vigour. 'I've never seen anything like it. You were as good as nude, for God's sake.

And at your age that is not something you should make a habit of! Just cast an eye at that woman – his model or whatever she is.'

'Yes.' Mavis nodded judiciously. 'I think she is his model. And of course he sleeps with her – I found that out almost straight away. But you see, girls, he's an artist. He's not bound by all the petty restrictions and conventions that bind us. He's the most amazing person I have ever met – and I mean person, not man. He's not even bound by the restrictions of sex – I mean gender, not sex as in—'

'For Christ's sake, shut up!' Bernice exploded. 'If you go into all that free spirit stuff again I shall be sick, and that's a promise.'

Pansy propitiated as best she could. 'Can't we talk about something else? Let's all sit down and eat this delicious food and we'll take it in turns. How does that sound? And I think I'd prefer coffee to wine. Will anyone join me?'

Mavis said blithely, 'Me. I've done nothing but drink wine all day.'

Bernice made a sound in her throat and Pansy said quickly, 'We met a very nice young couple on the way home, Mavis. Paula and Dennis Chiverton. As a matter of fact, from something May said up at the bungalow I've a feeling this is a delayed honeymoon for them. Isn't that romantic?'

Mavis was ecstatic. 'That makes it perfect! The whole place is so romantic, I can't believe it.

Honestly, girls, I know you're fed up with me going on about it, but I just wish you could have seen me this morning. It was like Cathy and Heathcliff. Tearing my way through the brambles thinking I was going to have to rescue someone and then nearly fainting and then Cree and Cass coming up those steps to *my* rescue and carrying me back to Christopher Cottage—'

'It's called Wren Cottage,' Bernice said icily.

'That's too twee for Cree. It's a pun on Christopher Wren. D'you see?'

Bernice remained silent and Pansy giggled. 'You're a poet, Mavis. Twee and Cree and see.'

Mavis laughed, a big open laugh, nothing like her usual titter. 'So I am! See what my day has done for me, girls!'

Bernice poured herself some wine and drank it like lemonade.

'Pansy, tell me about Reg. How was he? You had quite a heart-to-heart with him back there.'

'Yes. Sorry. I did rather hog him, I know. But you were helping May Long and everyone else went off with Paula and Dennis.' Pansy smiled beatifically. 'He's the same. He hasn't let the accident change him one bit – the only thing that worried him was that this Christmas would be cancelled. As soon as his nephew – Mark is such a nice boy – told him that he and Holly would take over . . . well, Reg was all right.'

'Good old Reg,' Mavis commented.

'Is he in any pain, d'you think?' Bernice asked, digging into the caviare with a will.

Pansy shook her curls. 'I don't think so. He doesn't sleep very well. But he thinks that will improve now he's home again.' She looked across the table. 'He was anxious about you, Bernie. D'you know what he said? He asked me whether you had found anyone yet. I laughed. I told you were much too independent to be considering that sort of thing.'

Bernice laughed dismissively. 'I don't need anyone else. Robert and I were all in all to each other and I could never look at another man.'

Pansy smiled slyly. 'Except Reg, of course.'

'Don't be ridiculous, Pansy! It was you and Mavis who made complete idiots of yourself over Reg.'

Pansy stood up and removed the plates, ostentatiously silent. Mavis drew a deep breath, half closed her eyes and said, 'It was strange about Reg. I felt so close to him. Attracted. Terribly attracted. But I couldn't have ever . . . done anything. Now . . . now I'm different. If he wanted me to, I'd go to bed with him. I'm a different person. It wouldn't seem such an enormous thing to do. Can you imagine that, girls?'

Bernice said bitterly, 'Only too well, thank you, Mavis.'

Pansy giggled and brought the sherry trifle to

the table. 'I think so. But it's one thing to have a little kiss and cuddle on the boat deck. It's another to – you know – actually *do* it.'

There was a small silence while the other two considered the absolute truth of that. Then Pansy said unexpectedly, 'I don't think I ever could actually. I know dear Luigi left me and I ought to hate him, but I don't. He was unfaithful to me but I don't think I could be unfaithful to him.' She paused in spooning out the trifle and looked at the Christmas tree. 'Isn't that the strangest thing, girls? I went to Rome for a holiday and did what all the silly young things did – fell in love with an Italian. I just assumed we would be married – I'm sure poor Luigi was so surprised to find himself in Worcestershire waiting for an English girl he hardly knew to walk up the aisle of a village church! He did his best – we had twenty years, after all – but his heart wasn't here. It was back in Rome with all the other girls.' She recollected herself and tittered as she offered Bernice the sherry trifle. 'Must be confession time tonight. All I'm trying to say, Mavis, is that, no, I couldn't go to bed with anyone. Not even dear Reg who is so sweet and kind I could almost cry at the thought of him sitting there in those awful white stockings being brave and cheerful . . .' She put down the spoon and felt up her sleeve for a hanky.

Mavis and Bernice tried to enfold her at the same moment. By the time they had assured one another that they each understood everything the others meant, they felt very much better.

'This trifle is manna from heaven!' Mavis said in her extravagant way.

Bernice smiled, well satisfied. 'Marks always do nice food. Have some more, Mavis. No point in keeping it. We're eating at the bungalow tomorrow and we'll take Reg to a nice hotel somewhere on Boxing Day.'

'Wonderful!' said Pansy. She smiled warmly at Mavis. 'Perhaps your Welsh artist will come too, Mavis? He and Reg were in the army together after all.'

'We'll see.' Mavis smiled back. 'As long as we're together, I don't care.'

Bernice let her smile deepen with satisfaction. The status quo was definitely back on course. She said, 'Shall I wash up while you two open up those boxes and get started on the tree?'

Mavis exclaimed delightedly at the ruby-red baubles. 'I love red on a Christmas tree. Green and red. Like the trees outside in that copse.'

Pansy hung an experimental bell and stepped back to admire it. 'My new dress is that colour,' she said. 'I hope the neck isn't too low. I was so pleased to find it in my size. Did I tell you, there was one back home and I didn't get it and I regretted it so much.'

'You told us several times, Pansy,' Bernice said. But she smiled as she ran hot water into the sink.

Holly finished the story about Santa Claus and closed the book quietly. Gemma was asleep in the big armchair and the two boys were heavy-lidded.

'Thank you, Holly,' Tom said, trained by the heavy hand of his father but meaning it. He had always been told that Marilyn Monroe was the epitome of female beauty – had not his dead sister been called Marilyn? And Holly Jepson was blond and blue-eyed and though she wore jeans and sweaters, he could see she wasn't skinny like his mother or fat like Mrs Dyson at school.

'A pleasure, Tom,' Holly said, not smiling, very serious. 'Have you got the strength to go and say goodnight to Mum and Dad? I'll carry Gemma in.'

But the dead weight was too much for her and Ted hoisted the small girl into his arms and put her in the camp bed. If Holly had not wanted the bathroom urgently she might have been surprised to see the boys go into the double room.

She locked the door and leaned over the lavatory. And after a while she straightened her back and looked at herself in the mirror above the basin. Her face stared back, strangely familiar. What on earth did she expect – a ghostly reflection?

She washed her hands and splashed cold water onto her eyes, looked at herself again and forced a smile. Better. Much better. She went into the kitchen where Ivy was laying the breakfast.

'You are well organized.' She sounded inadequate. 'I mean . . . May and I realized quite late this afternoon that we hadn't got a single Christmassy paper napkin. If only we'd made proper lists a bit earlier, the wicked widows could have got some nice ones from Weston. As it is, we had to have ordinary white ones and I'm going back to draw holly leaves in each corner!'

'Leave that till tomorrow. We've got presents to open in the morning and then we're taking the children to church. But after that they will be at a loose end. Adam is marvellous with felt tips. How many are you doing?'

'Well . . . eighteen of us, so I suppose a couple of dozen. Probably more.'

'The boys will want to do masses once they get started.' Ivy looked up. 'Oh Holly, I can't tell you what all this means to me. To be happy . . . like this. Without thinking. Just to be happy. It's – it's so marvellous!'

Holly tried to smile but she was feeling sick again. Ivy looked at her sharply.

'What did the boys say?'

'The boys?' The nausea was mounting into faintness.

'All right, not Adam. But Tom. Did Tom . . . tell you anything? When you were reading to them?'

'Tom? No. What would he tell me?' Holly held the back of one of the kitchen chairs. The mugs were different colours, six of them. What must it be like to have four children? She said, 'Were you sick when you were pregnant, Ivy?'

'No. Well, I was with Marilyn. But everything went wrong with her. And there were other pregnancies. They didn't last because I was ill. I don't remember being sick with Tom and Adam.'

Holly was startled out of her faintness. 'Oh . . . oh my God. What about Gemma and Giles?'

Ivy opened her eyes wide. 'Ah. Yes. Of course. Gemma and Giles. No, I wasn't sick with Gemma and Giles.'

Holly said, 'I didn't realize there were other children. In between. You must have been very happy to have Gemma.'

Ivy nodded then walked round the table and into the little hall. 'I'll send the boys up then, shall I, after lunch? Is that all right?'

Holly knew she was being packed off. She hovered by the front door wondering whether to ask Ivy's advice. From the double bedroom she could hear Stanley teasing the boys about getting to sleep so that Father Christmas could come. She frowned as the front door closed on her: she had thought Stanley such a considerate man but all those children . . . and Ivy so thin and frail. And the way she had spoken of happiness, as if it were a stranger to her.

Holly switched on her torch and walked along the garden path to the gate with its wrought-iron magpie. The air was cold and smelled of seaweed; she breathed it in hungrily and almost immediately felt better. On the other side of the concrete drive, lights twinkled among the stunted, sea-slanted trees. Wren Cottage was invisible from here, so they must be coming from Seagull. The thought of the three women vying for Reg's attention made her smile at last. She switched off the torch and stood still, breathing slowly and regularly, thinking about Reg who had insisted on being wheelchaired up to the Ship's Lantern by Arthur to meet Cree Evans. What sort of charm did he exert to win all these female hearts? She was still reeling after May's confession, yet in a way that was so understandable; but Mavis Gentry and Pansy Pansetti? And even more unlikely, Bernice Smythe with her stern good looks and common sense. According to May, Pansy had literally sat at Reg's feet most of the afternoon, and Bernice's nose had been so put out of joint that she had joined May in the kitchen.

Holly shook her head and began to walk back to the bungalow. She had made soup from the turkey giblets which she and May and Mark could have for supper, then there were carols from somewhere on the telly and then they could go to bed. She wished Mark had gone for a pub supper with Reg so that she wouldn't have to pretend to enjoy the soup, but he had escaped from that with positive joy. 'Early night, Holl?' He had kissed her nose and rolled his eyes suggestively and she had laughed. It was amazing that since that dreadful night of the party they had rediscovered their sex life. For so long it had been governed by thermometers, graphs, dates. Now it was as wonderful as it had been at the beginning of their marriage. More wonderful perhaps because, for Holly, there was something else, an aching tenderness, almost a nostalgia.

On her right, the lights from Linnet were all on and she went automatically up their path and knocked. There was a long pause then Dennis Chiverton answered, looking like a schoolboy with his hair tousled and his shirt hanging outside his trousers. Holly blushed with embarrassment.

'Sorry to disturb you . . .' Hadn't someone suggested the Chivertons were taking a delayed honeymoon? 'I'm not exactly doing the rounds but as you arrived just this afternoon I thought I'd ask whether there's anything you need in the way of milk, bread, basics. We've got quite a stock.'

He appeared delighted to see her. 'Come on in. Please. No, we were filling a pillowslip with some odds and ends we bought and I'm afraid Paula attacked me! No provocation, I do assure you.' He was grinning like a Cheshire cat and called over his shoulder, 'Paula, get dressed immediately! Mrs Jepson is here with complaints from the neighbours.'

The girl appeared, fully clothed and unruffled. 'Take no notice of him, Mrs Jepson. He imagines he's being funny.'

Holly actually laughed; they were so young, so completely carefree.

'Please, call me Holly. I was on my way home from Magpie Cottage, saw your lights and thought I'd drop by. Is everything all right?'

'Apart from the fact that the sea is grey and it's not Tenerife—'

'Shut up, Chiv!' Paula said swiftly. 'Everything is fine, Holly. Thank you for popping in. Dennis here is the original anti-Christmas man.' She shook her head at him. 'Listen, we've got some ginger wine – will you have some? In a real effort to put Dennis in a Christmas mood?' She looked almost pleadingly over her husband's shoulder and Holly got the impression she wasn't joking.

'Well . . . I would love some but actually I'm not feeling a hundred per cent—'

'In other words, everyone else has plied you with decent drink and the thought of ginger wine makes you want to puke.' Dennis spoke light-heartedly but Paula flushed.

Holly said quickly, 'It might settle my heartburn or whatever it is. Let's give it a go.' She went to the electric fire. 'Of course, to be honest, the chalets are summer accommodation but they're very well equipped. This will go the whole two thousand watts and it's included in the rent, so shall we turn it up for a while?' She smiled right at Dennis with her very blue eyes. 'Make it slightly more Tenerife?'

He blinked as so many of her clients had done when she turned her full beam on them. 'Sorry.' He made an apologetic face. 'I have to tell you though. When we made the deal originally with Mr Jepson, the rent was practically non-existent. I imagine that won't extend to electricity charges.'

Holly accepted a glass of wine from Paula. 'Reg likes to see young people around the place, so I don't see why not. Anyway . . .' She lifted her glass. 'Happy Christmas. To you both.'

Paula glanced at Dennis, then said, 'Well . . . to the three of us.' She blushed deeper still. 'I'm pregnant, you see. Three months.' At the sight of Holly's beaming face she confided, 'That's why we were filling a pillowcase. For the baby.' She reached behind the sofa. 'See? A rattle. Teething ring. Squashy Thomas the Tank Engine, in case it's a girl. Squashy doll in case it's a boy—'

'No gender discrimination,' Dennis put in.

'Vest. Matching hat and scarf—'

'How perfectly lovely,' Holly said. 'What about names?'

'Ebenezer if it's a boy. Jezebel if it's a girl.'

'Stop it, Chiv!' Her blush was nearing hectic.

She turned a shoulder on her husband. 'I never knew my mother, but apparently her name was Rose. I'd like that.'

Dennis said, 'I must have names with z's in them. I insist on names with z's in them. It isn't much to ask in this female-dominated world. Just a z. Like a bee. A buzzing bee.'

Holly wondered how much ginger wine they'd had before she arrived.

'That's easily solved,' she said. 'You can spell Rose with a z. No problem there. And how about fiddling around a bit with your name and making it Denzil?'

They both stared at her then Dennis said with awe, 'Paula, this woman is wonderful. She is a paragon among women. I want to fall at her feet.'

'Please don't do that!'

'In fact I would like her to stay for an hour with you, my dearest dear, while I walk up to the road and try to find that pub we passed in the car this very afternoon—'

'You're drunk, Chiv. And you don't have to make excuses to go out on your own. Please feel free. Immediately.'

Holly tried to keep things civilized. She said, 'Actually, most of the men have gone to the pub. Reg is up there – Arthur wheeled him up earlier on.' Dennis was already shrugging into his coat. 'You turn left at the top of the drive and it's about a hundred yards on your left.' He was through the door. She called after him, 'Perhaps you'd help with the wheelchair on the way home? Arthur has a bad back.'

Dennis called back, 'Not when he's playing skittles, he doesn't!' And then he was gone into the darkness. Holly turned back and found Paula still red-faced and very apologetic.

'I'm so sorry. He's not usually like this. His father gave him a flask – a full flask – for Christmas and he's managed to get through most of it since we arrived.'

Holly came back in and sat down near the fire. She wondered whether she might have the beginnings of flu. 'It's all right. I can understand he finds it a bit dull. Perhaps after he's met everyone tomorrow . . .'

'Yes.' Paula took a deep breath. 'I'm beginning to wonder whether he feels I trapped him into getting married. We were fine before. And we could have gone on being fine but he said if we had a baby we must get married. Make everything legal and above board. But somehow that's led into a lot of . . . well, sort of lying. Not really *lying* but almost lying.' She ran out of breath and stared at Holly. 'I say, are you all right? You're looking a bit green.'

Holly said, 'Bathroom,' and made a swift exit. When she came back in she looked better. 'Yes. The ginger wine was a piece of bravado, I think.'

'Are you pregnant too?' Paula asked on a note of excitement. Holly could almost hear her announcing it at the dinner table tomorrow night: I say, everyone, isn't it marvellous that Holly and I are both expecting . . .

She forced a laugh. 'No. I've been preparing vegetables and stuffing and bread sauce . . . oh, just the thought of it all.'

'What a shame! It would have been marvellous to have shared symptoms. I mean, I'm three months and I'm hardly showing at all and I thought I'd be the size of a house by now! I could have spent Christmas with the in-laws after all – they'd never have guessed.'

'Don't they know?' Holly asked.

'Not yet. They're a bit strait-laced – or so Dennis says. I'm not sure any more. I'm not sure of anything much any more.'

'Listen, you can be sure of one thing. A man who will fill a pillowcase for a baby that's not yet born is a man who wants the baby very much indeed.'

Paula brightened. 'It was his idea actually. And when we got here he was full of our little house on the prairie – that's what he called it. But then we went for a walk along the beach and he got muddy and then it was dark and grey and . . .'

'You must get to know Ivy and Stanley Edwards. They've got a baby. A boy, Giles. He's about a year old and he's really sweet. They've let me have a go at bathing him and putting him to bed and they'd let you do it too.'

Paula said, 'Are you sure you're not pregnant?'

Holly laughed. 'Sure. Yes, I'm sure.' She stood up. 'I think I'd better go. Why don't you walk up to the bungalow with me? You could try out my mince pies. Mark will walk you back.'

So they left Linnet and trudged up the steep drive to Reg's bungalow and spent a pleasant hour with Mark and May. Paula forgot all about Holly's sickness and Holly herself almost did. But afterwards, when Mark took Paula back, she had another attack and crept into bed before he returned and then lay sleepless and terrified. Why was she being sick all the time? May had suspected she was pregnant. Surely, surely she was not carrying Hugo Venables's child?

Cree left the Lantern before the others. Dennis, the young chap who seemed to have spent a lot of his time playing skittles with Arthur Long, had promised he would help get Reg back to the bungalow and though he was definitely the worse for drink, he was strong and willing. He also appeared delighted to be in male company. He had propounded a theory that the world was now run by women. 'Suits me,' Cree had said, looking at the barmaid through his glass and wondering whether he should suggest painting Cass through a glass of water. Distended, distorted. Christ, did all this mean that sub-consciously he hated women? Never. Never, never, never. He loved every one of them, fat or thin, tall or short.

Reg said, 'You OK, old man? You look a bit upset.'

'I love women,' Cree announced solemnly. He lifted his glass again and stared through it. 'What I see when I abstract my stuff is their souls.' He transferred his piercing gaze to the young man. 'Even their bloody souls are beautiful. Did you know that?'

'I'm not sure.' Dennis felt exhilarated. He was usually the oddball in any company. But this bloke was odder than he could ever be. Maybe Christmas wasn't going to be such a dead loss after all.

Reg said, '*I* know that, old man. I know it well. Mind you, Maude was the most beautiful of all. She had a soul like an angel.'

Cree remembered Maude. Four-square. A heart of gold but definitely four-square. 'I think we might be drunk, Reg,' he said.

'I'm not.' Reg was quite sure of that. 'I mustn't drink. Alcohol and painkillers don't mix.'

That was when Cree thought he should get back to Cass. 'My little girl. All on her own.' He looked sternly at Reg. 'And you *have* been drinking, Reg. I order you to go home. Arthur!' He projected his voice towards the dartboard where Arthur was playing a solo game. 'You'll see this gentleman back to his bed, I'm sure. And this amiable and affable young man will help you both.' He stared again at Reg. 'You're thin,' he said accusingly. 'You haven't been eating.'

'Hospital food. How is Cass?'

'Glorious. Fifty if she's a day. Glorious.' And he left.

Reg frowned up at Arthur and Dennis. 'I've never discovered who she is. She appeared a few years back. Long-lost daughter, he reckoned. I wonder.'

Now, after stumbling into several trees, Cree let himself into his personalized Christopher Cottage and flicked on the light. The enormous room stretched before him satisfyingly; it made a brilliant studio, and in any case Cree did not like small spaces. The cosiness of the pub bar had irritated him. This place though; this was good. And the big flat grey sea outside was even better. And seeing Reg was reassuring; he wasn't going to shuffle off his mortal coil just yet; life in the old dog—

There was a groan from his right and he realized that the double bed was down and Cass was humped on it inside a shroud of sheets and duvet.

'Sorry, baby,' he whispered hoarsely and flicked off the light.

'Coffee on hob,' she muttered.

'Right. Thanks. Dear woman. Dear, dear woman.'

Another groan, then she said, 'Sounds as if you bloody need it. Silly old fool.'

He grinned in the darkness and stood still, waiting for his pupils to dilate. He imagined them doing so; the messages going back and forth, brain to muscles. He tried whispering them aloud: 'Dark. Pupils not letting enough light in. Stretch . . .' Cass heard and snorted a protest. He chuckled and waited and at last the message got through and he saw the studio by the light of the moon.

He drew in a sharp breath and went to the big windows. The moon had been fleeting when he walked back down the drive, so it was no wonder he'd almost taken a toss several times: nothing to do with being drunk. He'd have to be careful though; didn't want to end up like poor old Reg.

A cloud moved and with horrible suddenness the moon went out like the light when he had flicked the switch. He stared blindly at where the sea had been; it was all complete blackness and the messages he sent to his eyes did not work any more. He tried to control an incipient panic attack but it was as if the darkness entered his soul. He drew another breath, this time of fear. Eternity was out there. In the sea and the sky and the bloody everlasting universe. Where was God in all this? And where was Cree Evans? Nowhere. That was the answer. No bloody where at all. It had all been for nothing; the constant hope that around the corner would come enough talent for him to paint something half decent, something that meant some-thing to every man and woman . . . it was all self-delusion. He was a man who had killed other men, who had eaten and drunk too much and slept with too many women. And soon he would die. And that would be that.

He must have sobbed out loud because from the bed Cass said very clearly, 'Stop thinking and come here.'

He stumbled over her clothes and fell onto the bed and into her arms. She pushed some bedding across him and then held his head into her shoulder. Within five minutes he was asleep, fully clothed, smelling of stale beer and cigarette smoke.

She sighed heavily and settled him on his side of the bed before sliding out and padding over to the galley kitchen to switch off the hob. She poured some of the coffee into a cup and carried it to the windows where he had been standing. The moon was now clear of cloud, full and piercing. It turned the sea silver and the rocks ebony black. It did not speak to her of eternity but of tomorrow morning when she would scream her way into its iciness again and thump it with the palms of her hands so that it splashed into her face. Perhaps Mavis Gentry would find the nerve to join her. Or perhaps her sense of propriety would rear its head again and they wouldn't see her until the evening.

Cass smiled wryly, wondering whether she would turn into a Mavis Gentry quite soon. Like Mavis she'd done nothing very much with her life except live it. And like Mavis she'd ended up alone: no husband, no children, no career.

She sipped the coffee and in the face of everything she felt her usual surge of energy. Dammit, it was the way you lived life that counted. And she looked forward to each day, helping Cree with his horrible pictures, getting meals, going to the theatre, talking to people on buses and trains. She had so rarely said no to anything or anyone. Surely that must count for something?

She finished the coffee and sat the cup in the sink before tucking the sheet more firmly around her full body and snuggling back up to Cree. For some reason she thought of Reg Jepson. She'd have to see him tomorrow. He'd start his usual tricks, smacking her rear every time she passed him, making his stupid jokes.

She put her arms around Cree's leonine head and kissed his ear and then grinned into the darkness. After all, if she couldn't let Cree's old mate touch her up, it was a poor show. Tomorrow she would be really nice to Reg.

Mark opened the door of Linnet Cottage and held it with one hand while Paula went inside. She had to turn sideways and knew then that her bump was most definitely a bump because although she shrank away from Mark it brushed against him.

She said, 'Dennis isn't back yet.' She switched

on the light. 'Would you like a coffee? Or some ginger wine?'

'Neither, thanks.' But he followed her in and switched on the electric fire. 'It's quite chilly tonight and you should keep warm.' He plumped the cushions in the easy chair. 'Come on. Sit down and put your feet up and I'll make you a drink. Hot milk?'

'Listen, I'm OK. Honestly.' But she sat down anyway and let him lift her feet onto a stool. 'This is nice. Really cosy.'

'Holly and I stayed at Magpie when we were first married. It was like playing house. We thought we'd come back year after year and bring our kids—' He stopped speaking and smiled down at her. 'Perhaps you'll do that. You and Dennis and your baby.'

'I'd love that. Oh, I'd really love that.' Paula clasped her hands. 'We've got a student flat in Bristol, not very homey. I'm no housewife – never had a home. My gran brought me up and then died and I was passed around like a parcel. I feel – here – as if I'm practising!' She laughed. 'Sorry to sound so idiotic.'

'Don't apologize. Everyone has to learn. And then learn again.'

She held out her clasped hands, almost as if she were praying.

'Give me a lesson! Now! Off the top of your head. What can I do tomorrow to make this holiday chalet into a home?'

Mark laughed. He thought she was probably twenty years old and he was forty, so if he'd started early she could have been his daughter. He frowned, tightened his lips and took up what he thought was an avuncular stance in front of the fire.

'We-e-ll. I suggest you and your husband . . .' He cleared his throat portentously then laughed and sat down. 'For goodness' sake. Go out and pick some of the holly. It's not real holly but it's berried and it's pretty and there's masses of it. Ivy, too, along the coastal path. Bring it back here and fill this room with it. There. First lesson done.'

She was delighted. 'It sounds such fun! I do hope Dennis will agree. He didn't like his first exploration one bit.' She smiled. 'It would be such a nice thing to do on Christmas morning, wouldn't it? Put us in touch with . . . you know, the whole meaning of everything.'

'Yes.' He looked into the fire and remembered Holly swimming in the iron-cold sea and yelling, 'Come on in, Mark! It's where life started after all!'

He said, 'I'd better go. What about the hot milk?'

'We haven't got any milk. But it was a lovely thought. Thank you, Mark. You and Holly . . . you're really nice.'

'Thanks.' He felt his face warm, probably from the fire. 'Well . . . sleep tight.'

'Oh, I will. I know it. I feel pretty good.'

He closed the door gently after him and made his way back to the drive. Down in the copse he heard someone crashing about, then a loud curse floated back in Cree's unmistakable voice. Mark waited and the crashing resumed reassuringly. Mark plodded back up to the bungalow. He wondered how Holly was feeling now; she hadn't been too good today. Was it something to do with her getting so involved down at Magpie Cottage? And now with the Chivertons? He had felt, tonight, a very definite pang every time he looked at Paula. He had imagined he did not care about children. He had told Holly so often that it didn't matter he almost believed it himself. But this young couple, these silly students, who were too young to have children, were reminding him, poignantly, that he and Holly had planned on a family. Had they ever hopefully filled a pillowcase like Paula and Dennis had?

He did not remember. It didn't matter anyway. It really did not matter.

Seven

It was Holly who had suggested that the traditional Christmas dinner should be an evening one. Reg had said, 'But we've always eaten at midday and then had a sleep before going up to the Lantern . . .'

May had proved unexpectedly supportive. 'That means Holly and me getting up at the crack of dawn to start laying up and everything.'

Holly nodded. 'Then afterwards it will be such an anti-climax for the children. If we say five, or even half-past . . .'

'They can have the morning opening their presents,' May took over. 'Then a nice light lunch and a walk in the afternoon and they'll be ready to eat properly.'

Reg opened his mouth and Holly said, 'That will apply to all of us, Reg.'

'But—'

'I'll wheel you up to the Lantern for a midday drink, Nunc. How's that?' Mark put in swiftly.

'All right, I suppose.'

153

Everyone accepted that as wholehearted agreement. It meant that on Christmas morning Holly was able to take her time about getting up and using the bathroom. She showered and washed her hair and decided she was feeling better today. Mark stayed asleep too, which helped. She crept around the bed pulling on a warm sweater and trousers and then let herself out of the front door as quietly as possible.

The weather was awful, grey and drizzly, but at least there was no wind. She stood looking out at the shrouded sea and, just for a moment, confronted the misery of what might be happening. All right, it wasn't the end of the world, of course it wasn't. She could have an abortion and she and Mark would be the same. But it was another thing to keep from him; a much more important thing. He must never ever know the sheer irony of what had happened. And she must not think about the baby; that was very important.

She straightened her shoulders as if settling a load; and then from across the road there came a sound: a giggling scream . . . a screaming giggle? She turned and faced that way and listened hard. Could it be Tom and Adam? Wrong side of the bay and anyway neither Tom nor Adam was a giggler; or a screamer, come to that. She heard it again and this time it sounded like a name. It sounded like Mavis.

Holly glanced at her watch. It was just gone

nine and any minute now Mark would appear. She ran down the path and crossed the driveway, heading for Seagull Cottage, and then as there was another scream she diverted through to Wren and followed the muddy path to the steps which led down to St Margaret's Bay. And there the most amazing sight met her eyes. Reg's friend, the artist, Cree Evans, was cavorting madly in the water, Cassandra, the daughter, was splashing around on her back and at the edge, slipping and sliding on the pebbles and screaming helplessly, was Mavis Gentry! Mavis was wearing a bra and what she would doubtless have called French knickers; it was all too obvious that Cree and Cassandra were naked.

Cassandra, laughing and helpless on her back, spotted Holly immediately.

'Come on!' she yelled. 'Come on down and join us! Mavis might just risk life and limb and get into the water if you show her the way!'

Holly felt a bubble of laughter in her throat. It was the most wonderful feeling after her recent incipient despair. She began to run down the steps.

'You won't get me in there!' she called back.

Cree bawled, 'Well, give my angel a bit of a shove then, will you?'

Mavis screamed again and tried to back up the muddy beach, slipped on a pebble and sat down abruptly. Holly arrived in time to haul her up.

'I'm all right,' Mavis panted. 'I want to get in.

I do really. It's just . . . I don't like the water and I can't swim!'

Holly was amazed. 'You must be mad. Oh God, you're covered in mud.'

'I was yesterday. And Cree said I might as well get properly muddy. But it's just that . . .' Mavis was petite and with her curly hair she looked to Holly like an elderly Shirley Temple. 'They're sure to duck me, you see. And I'm frightened of the water.'

Holly glanced at the two swimmers who were acting like maniacs, shouting and slapping the water and jumping up and down. She said, 'Does it matter, this morning swim? I mean, why do you want to do it?'

'I don't know. But I must.' Mavis looked out into the misty sea and sighed. 'I want to be like them. They – they're marvellous, aren't they? Other beings. Quite different from anyone I've ever met before. I mean . . . I'm so surprised they even tolerate me, let alone *like* me!'

Holly found that the laughter in her throat was near tears. She said, 'Oh Mavis . . . Yes, I do know what you mean. Listen. I'll come in with you and I won't let them duck you and you can grab onto me if you're scared.'

Mavis stared up as if Holly too had become an angel. 'Oh . . . oh, would you? Really?' Holly began to remove her clothes. 'Oh Holly. You are so kind. You and Mark and Reg . . . and now Cree and Cass. I can't believe this is happening to me.' She gave another very Mavis-like giggle. 'You've got such blue eyes too. I've never seen such blue eyes.' She glanced seawards again. 'Cree has got blue eyes. Have you noticed?'

Holly nodded and said dryly, 'Oh yes. I've noticed.'

The water was icy. For an instant she wondered whether it was the sort of thing she should do if she were pregnant and then she thought that it didn't matter. She jumped up and down frantically until she could bear it and then waded back to the shore and held out her hands to Mavis. There were more screams; alternating shouts of encouragement and derision from Cree and Cass; then Mavis slipped again and was up to her neck, gasping and hanging onto Holly's hands literally for dear life. There was a vortex of splashing and laughing and near-weeping but quite suddenly it was all right. Mavis was in the water, up to her waist, still gasping, holding her hands high, and Holly was swimming around her always within reach, smiling encouragement, keeping the other two at bay, waiting until Mavis gained enough confidence to submerge her arms and hands and push herself down until the water reached her chin.

Cree bawled, 'Get your head under, angel! Go on – give yourself a baptism in the mud!'

'No – no!' screamed Mavis, and Holly said,

'Leave her alone, the pair of you. She's doing fine.'

There was another shout; this time from the top of the cliff. It was Mark and he was already taking the big steps two at a time.

'Wait for me!' He pulled his sweatshirt over his head and threw it by Holly's discarded clothes. 'You did this before, my girl!' He pretended to be annoyed, splashing into the freezing water without flinching, throwing himself onto Holly, surfacing with her in his arms. She put the palms of her hands on his shoulders and lifted her face to the grey sky. Then he let her slither down and her toe touched the seabed and she kissed his muddy wet face and, for a moment, clung desperately and then leaned backwards and floated away, laughing, apologetic. 'I didn't mean to . . . Mavis needed encouragement.'

'I'm all right!' Mavis was panting, bobbing like a cork. 'Look . . . I'm all right!'

Cree swam up to her and picked her up as if she were a precious gift.

'You are that, my angel, my Mavis-thrush, my rescuer . . . you are that.'

He waded ashore with her in his arms and set her down by her pile of clothes. Holly watched, smiling, still exhilarated, almost unbearably moved by Mark's sudden presence. He raised his brows at her and as Cass splashed by, Holly said, 'Mavis wants to be like them. But she can't. Look. She has to turn away while he swathes himself in that sheet.' She frowned. 'My God, he's got a nerve. That's the linen from the cottage!'

Mark started to laugh helplessly.

Cass had a nerve too though she had an excuse for it as she had spent a restless night next to Cree. 'Listen, Mavis. If you're going to get into trouble again anyway with your so-called friends, how about inviting us to your cottage for breakfast? If we're not eating dinner until late, we could manage a good old-fashioned cooked breakfast. Eggs. Bacon. A tin of tomatoes. Fried bread.'

If they had asked her for her divorce settlement she could not have refused them. She smiled blissfully as she struggled into a sensible towelling robe borrowed from Bernice; she had never felt so happy in her life before. She allowed herself a glance at Cree, who was towelling himself vigorously on the sheet. He had the large barrel chest that so many elderly men have and with his hair wetly on end he looked . . . well, elderly. She felt a little quake of fear for him. He was Reg's contemporary and there was no way she could imagine Reg – even before his hip replacement – swimming in this icy sea and charging up the slippery steps yelling, 'The troops are coming!' at the top of his voice. She nodded at Cass and said, 'Is it all right for Cree to be so . . . so energetic?'

Cass tied her sheet in a huge knot and grinned. 'I haven't got the faintest idea. But nothing you or I can say will stop him. So let's join him, shall we?'

They waved at Holly and Mark, who were having difficulty getting their wet bodies into dry clothes, and went up the steps. Mavis found she loved the feeling of the mud between her bare toes. She loved the damp air on her face, chilling her wet hair, numbing her fingers. She panted, 'It's Christmas Day! I'm so excited!'

Cass, bringing up the rear, grinning at Cree's flapping sheet, holding onto her own, said, 'Steady on there, Mave. Tears before bedtime if you're not careful.'

Tom and Adam had collected enough driftwood to last for days. It was piled up just outside the kitchen door, the dry stuff around the fireplace in the living room. They lit the fire at six o'clock, Ted stacking the kindling in a wigwam shape, Gemma having the honour of lighting the newspaper with a long spill, Tom lugging the knobbly stockings out of the bedroom where Giles still slept blissfully. Reg had told them sternly that they must keep all the electric radiators going day and night and not to worry about the cost, so the cottage was delightfully warm and there was no need to switch on the oven when they sat around the table with that first magical cup of tea. Ted looked at them and felt the usual rush of love that threatened to spill into tears. Adam seemed to wear a permanent grin now and Gemma had picked up Tom's habit of talking for him as if he were her alter ego. For once she was not keen on the cup-of-tea ritual and wanted to start opening the presents.

'Addie. Addie. Addie . . .' She got his attention and changed her tone to one of sympathetic understanding. 'Yes, I know you want to look in your stocking. And you don't have to finish your drink if you don't want it. See – I haven't even started mine.'

Tom said sternly, 'For goodness' sake, Gemma! Leave him alone for a bit, will you? In any case, we can't start unwrapping until Giles is with us.'

'He's too little to know about Father Christmas,' Gemma protested. But Adam was lifting his mug of tea and after a moment's hesitation she did the same, and as if by magic Giles's voice echoed from the bedroom.

Ted and Ivy had done well on their forays into Weston. Both boys had radio-controlled cars as well as fishing nets, tool sets, gloves, hats and scarves. Gemma had the very doll she had admired in a shop window when Mrs Sitter took her out for a walk with Giles. There was a real wooden wardrobe too and inside a complete outfit for the doll. 'I shall call her Reg,' she crooned, rocking the doll jerkily as she sat cross-legged in front of the fire. Ivy forestalled Tom's protests. 'That's short for Regina. A lovely name, Gem. I think it's what they call the Queen.'

'It means . . .' Gemma looked deep into the caverns of the fire. 'It means being kind. Like Mr Jepson. He said we could call him Reg but I shall call him Regina.'

Tom rolled on his back; Giles clasped his new teddy bear and guffawed shrilly and Adam . . . Adam put his arm around Gemma and held her to him. Above the heads of the children, Ivy looked at Ted and Ted looked back at her.

By eight thirty they had eaten boiled eggs and toast soldiers, played with their new toys and banked the fire with its own ash. Ivy was wearing her silver chain and cross, Ted his new shirt and matching tie and the children were kitted out in their various matching clothes. Ivy wrapped the mince pies she had made into four packets of half a dozen and they set out for Linnet Cottage and the Chivertons.

Paula had slept like a top and woke with a sense of well-being that she knew was down to Mark Jepson and his visit last night. Beside her, Dennis snored, choked, breathed, snored again. She had not heard him come in or get into bed so he must have been quiet, which probably meant he had not been too drunk either, but the awful sounds coming from his side of the bed did not augur well. She lay on her back, very still, smiling into the grey half-light and planning their morning's expedition to fetch holly and ivy to decorate the little chalet. It amused her to realize that she was exhibiting a nesting instinct. She thought that if only she did not have to deceive Walter and Helen, it would be great fun to ask Helen to come with her to the January sales and buy a . . . what was it called? A layette. Lovely old-fashioned word. A layette.

Thoughts of Helen and Walter and how they would take the news of the coming baby were worrying to say the least, so she pushed them away and went back to planning how they would attach the holly to the thin walls of the chalet. And then perhaps they would empty the pillow-case they had so carefully filled last night, then they could have a sandwich and maybe a walk along the shore and then . . . She stopped and listened. Between Dennis's choking snores there were other sounds. Scuffles. Outside the kitchen door. She propped herself on one elbow and looked at her watch. Not yet nine o'clock. Early. Could it be a fox or a badger or some other kind of wildlife? She felt a mixture of excitement and fear. She was a city girl; every-thing down here on this ancient shoreline was different. Almost foreign.

And then someone coughed; definitely a human cough. And the next minute, hoarsely, came a song.

' "We–e–e–e . . . *wish* you a merry Christmas, we wish you a merry—" '

Someone had a drum and banged it at that point and someone else said, 'Shut up, Gem! Not yet!' And the old jingle continued, louder, full of laughter when it came to figgy puddings and the demand to bring one out here.

Dennis woke with a terrible groan as she was getting out of bed and wrapping her dressing gown around her nightie.

'What the hell—'

She hissed, 'Shut up, Chiv! It's the family the Jepsons told us about, from Magpie Cottage. They've come to wish us a merry Christmas. Get up and smile, for God's sake! It's Christmas morning!'

She ran into the kitchen and flung open the door. There seemed to be hordes of them standing there: a stocky, fairish man carrying a gorgeous baby; a diminutive woman peering from beneath an obviously new knitted hat; three children similarly hatted and muffled and gloved and carrying toys of one sort or another. And they all shouted in unison, 'Happy Christmas!' and then burst out laughing so that she had to laugh as well, clutching her dressing gown with one hand and hanging onto the open door with the other.

She said, 'Come in, come in.'

But the man said, 'No, we'd better not, thanks, as you're the first on our list. We have to do Seagull and Wren and then go up to Mr Jepson's.'

The woman said, 'We're the Edwardses. From Magpie Cottage. You came yesterday, didn't you? And you're having a lie-in. Sorry to wake you.' She leaned over one of the children. A girl with long blond hair: beautiful.

The girl said, 'These are for you. Mince pies. We made them yesterday. I cut out the tops.'

Paula was overwhelmed. 'How marvellous! I didn't think to make any – or to buy some. Oh how lovely – thank you so much! Listen, will you come in later? For a coffee or something? Oh . . . we haven't got any milk . . . oh dear.'

'Come to us instead,' the man said. 'We usually have tea but I think there's some coffee.'

'We'd love tea. We're going to collect some holly and decorate the chalet and then we'll come down. Will that be all right? Really?'

'Of course. The children are helping Holly later.'

They left in a flurry of goodwill and Paula went back into the bedroom. Dennis was sitting on the side of the bed with his head in his hands.

'I heard. I heard. Do we have to?'

'Chiv, it's Christmas! And they're a proper family. And they've asked us to join them.'

'OK, OK, don't make a big thing of it.' He glanced up at her. 'Come back to bed, Polly. We don't need to go and see them for at least another two hours. Come back to bed with me.'

'Darling, I want to go out and pick some holly and ivy and stuff. Mark told me how to do it last

165

night. Come on. We've got time to decorate the living room before eleven. Come *on.*'

'You must be joking.' He rolled back under the covers and closed his eyes. 'You carry on. Wake me at ten thirty. With a black coffee.'

'Chiv! It's something we should do together!'

He put the pillow over his head by way of reply.

Ted and Ivy and the children carried on across the road to Seagull Cottage and found Bernice and Pansy sitting over tea and toast in the kitchen. They had not met previously either, but Bernice, with her usual briskness, introduced everyone, thanked Gemma for the mince pies and informed her that though there were presents in return, they would not be handed over until this afternoon when they met for Christmas dinner.

'You will have quite enough to do this morning with all these lovely things,' she said, examining the drum without enthusiasm. 'And anyway, Mrs Pansetti chose something for the whole family, which, as it has turned out, is quite inappropriate so it might be better to keep it until tomorrow.'

Pansy, joggling the baby on her knee, was chanting, '". . . as the dog went to Dover/When it got to a stile up it went over."' She interrupted herself to say, 'I might as well tell you. I couldn't resist it. I always wanted one when I was a child

166

and after that snow we had last week I thought . . . well anyway, my dears, it's a sledge!'

Everyone was unprepared for the yell of delight from Tom. And . . . perhaps . . . from Adam too. It was hard to say because Gemma was clapping her hands and Giles was crowing as he always did when he felt joy around him and Ted and Ivy were laughing.

Bernice said, 'Well! I gather it's a popular choice?' She smiled widely at Pansy. 'You know children better than I do, Pan. Or maybe you're still a child yourself.' Unexpectedly, she hugged her friend. Pansy flushed. Bernice went on, 'Would you like it now? And save the individual presents until our meal?'

Gemma said, 'What's indy-thing?' And Tom said, 'Our special presents. The sledge is for all of us. And yes please. Can we have it now?'

Bernice went to fetch it. It was a small red moulded-plastic coracle. Tom breathed, 'It couldn't be better.' He looked up. 'Mum . . .' Then sideways. 'Dad . . . Can we put our trunks on and take it on the mud when the tide goes out? Like those skimming boards. It'll whizz over the mud. Addie, I'll pull you first if you like. Then we can pull Gem and Giles—'

Ivy said, 'We'll see.' And Ted said, 'Why not?' And everyone laughed again and suddenly the door opened on the crowded little kitchen and there stood a very muddy Mavis flanked by two sheeted figures. And mayhem ensued.

At one thirty, after what Cree called a fry-up and Bernice called a brunch, nearly everyone congregated on the long shallow beach below Magpie Cottage. Their garments were varied and they looked a motley crew. Cree had gone to the Lantern with Reg and Mark for a 'swift half' just before the fry-up at Seagull, so the three men were dressed fairly conventionally, though Bernice informed Cree crisply that his trousers could doubtless have wheeled Reg and his chair to the cove on their own. Cree had replied that she was dressed for the two of them and he regretted that she was the type that invariably wore sensible knickers as he had always had a penchant for thongs. She said she hadn't thought of him as a cross-dresser but would try to find him something he'd like. They eyed each other like a couple of prizefighters and then, suddenly and unexpectedly, they both burst out laughing.

Bernice of course was wearing a Burberry and wellingtons but her hat was fetchingly nineteen-twenties and tendrils of greying hair curled from beneath it to give her a look of secret naughtiness. Mavis and Pansy appeared to be dressed for golf in immaculate checked trews and chunky sweaters with matching knitted gloves and hats. Ted and Ivy were almost lost in huge sweaters; even their jeans, rolled up to the knees, were almost invisible beneath their bulky tops. The three children wore sweaters over their swimsuits. Giles had been left at the bungalow with May and Holly. The Chivertons arrived late wearing the jeans and tops they had arrived in yesterday. Dennis was white and unkempt; Paula determinedly joyful. Cass was decidedly the odd one out; after a quick consultation with Reg, she had rummaged around in a cupboard full of odds and ends in the bungalow and discovered an ancient wetsuit left there by some enthusiastic water-skier many years ago. Held together in its rubber grip and with her hair cascading down her back, she was revealed as a startlingly handsome woman. Reg looked up at Cree.

'What a figure! You should get her out of all those flippy-floppy things she wears—'

'I do that on a regular basis,' Cree put in.

'And into some decent clothes. She's a real stunner.'

Cree sobered. 'Like her mother. Except her mother hated me, and Cass . . . dammit, she must love me otherwise she wouldn't be here.'

'Mark's enjoying himself. He's like his father. My baby brother, you know. Died young and when he was still needed. Should have been me.'

'None of that, young Reginald! I'm not staying here if you're going to talk about death. It's a subject I avoid.'

Reg said nothing and they watched in silence as Mark and Cass between them launched the toboggan onto the mud. It skimmed satisfyingly and they drew it back in and loaded it with children. Everyone was making a lot of noise.

Cree said, 'How's May these days? I see Arthur is trying to cheer up that student bloke. Dennis whatever. Got drunk last night – and, before you say a word, not happily drunk like me. What a fool. To deliberately make himself miserable when he's got a wife like that girl there. He must be mad.'

'Arthur met them. Last autumn. Skittles match with the Whelks. They needed a holiday and couldn't afford it. You know what Arthur's like.'

'I know what you're like. Freebies all round. See yourself as a latter-day St Nicholas.'

Reg remembered Holly's scathing tone when she had accused him of trying to do a Father Christmas act. He murmured, 'She wasn't herself then. Lost something. Reckon she's found it again now. Whatever it was.'

'What?' Cree leaned over the chair. 'Talking to yourself, old man?'

'I was. Sign of it. So they say. I don't believe that. I reckon it's a progression of logical think-ing.'

Cree pretended astonishment. 'Didn't know you had it in you, Reginald! Been reading up on Jung, have you?' He squatted down. 'That's a lie. I've always known Reg Jepson ran dark and deep. And now he's putting me off the scent. I asked him how May was.'

Reg smiled. 'She's all right, is our May.'

'Our May? Mine, I know that. Arthur's, I suppose. But yours?'

Reg ignored that. 'She's mixed up. The boys have been gone for a few years now and they were her . . .'

'*Raison d'être*,' Cree supplied.

'Reason for being. Yes. And she's had time to think. She misses Maude. She knows she's always got me and Arthur. But she misses you, Cree.' Reg looked round and right into Cree's blue eyes. 'You broke her heart. Did you realize that?'

Cree was startled. 'I wish I hadn't asked about her now. For Christ's sake, Reg! We had a fling. And when it was flung, that was it.'

'For you. It's always like that for you. And it still is, isn't it? You're not much younger than me but you're still doing it.'

'What are you talking about? You told me yourself about those three women in Seagull and how they fell for you on that cruise! And you've got the gall to talk to me as if I'm the oldest seducer in town—'

'Mavis Gentry would die for you, Cree. And you know it. And I saw the way you fenced with Bernie just now.'

Cree stared. 'I do not believe this! Mavis is the perfect model—'

'Because she is free and because if you asked her to, she'd stand on her head all day.'

'I have not seduced her, Reg. And I do not plan to seduce her. All right?'

'She's too prim anyway. Bernie is different.' Reg sighed. 'Bernie is a passionate and wonderful woman. Don't hurt her, Cree. I'm asking you that as a personal favour.'

'For crying out loud, Reg! She was flirting with me! Surely you still know the difference between flirting and – and—'

'One step away, Cree. Just one step away.'

A scream came from the shore. Cass had been towing the sledge of children towards the distant sea and had fallen flat on her face. Gallantly, Mark rolled his jeans still higher and waded out to help her. The children, who had been bickering, began to laugh helplessly and it was obvious Cass had fallen down on purpose.

Cree sighed deeply. 'It's not only your hip you've lost, Reg, it's your sense of humour. But the last thing I want is for us to be bad friends. So . . . no flirting, Reg. I promise you, your Bernie – I gather she is your Bernie? – is safe from me.'

Reg said quietly, 'Thanks, Cree.'

Arthur Long said, 'Not going so well, old man? Why don't you roll up your trousers and get stuck in with Mark and the kids?'

''Cos if I did that my head might fall off,' Dennis replied without a smile.

'Come on. Last night is a long time off. You

didn't come up with us to the Lantern at mid-day. So what's wrong?'

'Nothing's wrong, for God's sake.' Dennis looked dourly at where Paula was cavorting on the edge of the mud with Pansy and Mavis. 'It's just that . . . nothing is right.'

'Same difference, old man.'

Dennis acknowledged this silently and Arthur waited by his side.

'It's just . . . I hate this place. It's a hole and a half. We could be in the city with stuff going on and we've chosen to come here.'

'Nobody's making you stay. Why don't you go back to Bristol?'

Dennis exploded. 'She likes it here! She *likes* it! She's made the place look like a bloody fairy grotto and she was playing with those boys and their cars and borrowing stuff off the woman so that she could make her own mince pies!'

'And you didn't enjoy any of this?'

'Listen, Art. You know how we live. Back in the flat we'd have stayed in bed till midday . . . you know. Doing stuff. Then we'd have gone to the pub and had a sandwich and played darts. Then someone would have been throwing a party and we'd have gone there. And she wants to stay here till the New Year. We'll miss the fireworks – everything!'

'We'll get our own fireworks, I expect.'

'Don't make me laugh!'

'Not many probably. But when they're let off

173

on the beach they reflect in the water so they double up. And we have a bonfire – a huge bonfire – and cook sausages. Reg plays the accordion, you know, and that little girl has got a drum.' He laughed as Dennis groaned. 'It sounds a bit homespun, I grant you. But you'd be surprised how much fun we have. Reg makes fun. He's always been like that.'

Dennis said, 'Who does he think he is – Father Christmas?'

Arthur thought about it. 'Probably. I could have Father Christmassed him many a time. But when I think about it . . . I realize that in the end he makes people happy.'

'Oh God . . .' Dennis looked again at Paula. She had taken off her shoes and was wading into the mud. 'I don't think I can stand it.'

Arthur said briskly, 'I know exactly what you mean. Your wife is having a great time and it's nothing to do with you. But you can't spoil it for her, can you? She's playing at house and mothers and fathers. What's wrong with that? She won't be playing at it for much longer – it's real life for you two, isn't it? Getting a home together and painting out a nursery.'

'But we're all right as we are,' Dennis bleated.

'Well, that's fine then. But let her play while she can.' Arthur looked down towards the darkening sea. It was starting to rain. Paula was reaching towards Mark and he was taking her hand to lead her to the waiting sledge. Arthur spoke urgently. 'Don't be a fool! Get your trousers rolled up and go on down! Now.'

Dennis looked at him in surprise and then kicked off his trainers and leaned down to his jeans. But by the time he had stumbled over the pebbles to the shoreline, Mark had settled Paula on the sledge and Cass was taking the strain on the rope.

'Polly!' he called as if he would never see her again.

'Chiv!' She waved her hand. 'Your turn next!' and she went skimming over the wet mud screaming like the kids had screamed and then laughing as Cass purposely went down again and let the sledge go flying off on its own. Quite suddenly Dennis was terrified. He tried to run after her and plunged knee deep in the soft mud. The sledge was describing an enormous parabola as Cass righted herself like some ghastly sea-monster and pulled on the rope and Dennis was certain that Paula would fall sideways into that deep and suffocating mud. It was like a nightmare; his legs moved in slow motion and with gasping sucking noises, yet he could not shorten the distance between them. Paula was still laughing helplessly and the sledge was whirling faster and faster and he realized that it was bound to come to him as it finished its circle. He stopped and waited, practically sobbing with relief, and then, just as Paula was almost within reach, he lost his balance, tried to move his left leg to right himself, could not and slowly, very slowly, collapsed backwards into the mud.

Everyone seemed to think he had done it deliberately to make them laugh. The kids clapped delightedly and Paula screamed – almost in his ear – 'Oh Chiv, you are the giddy limit! We only brought one change of clothes!' He said, 'Polly, don't leave me – help!' and grabbed the edge of the red plastic sledge, tipped it towards him and she slid gracefully on top of him.

Between them Mark and Cass got them both out and back up to Seagull Cottage and under the shower, clothes and all. Paula was still laughing and tears were running down Dennis's face too. When they were alone and naked and clean once again, Paula put her arms around him and said, 'Poor darling. Did you think I was leaving you for Mark Jepson? Silly boy . . .' She kissed him and they made love and she thought everything was all right. But, for Dennis, somehow, it was not. He hadn't even thought about Mark Jepson until she said his name.

The long trestle table, running the width of the picture window, looked wonderful. Gemma clasped her hands and sighed a long 'Oooh'; Tom said, 'Gosh'; Adam's grin nearly split his face in half and Giles jumped up and down in Ivy's arms and lifted his clenched fists to the ceiling. Mark carried in a high chair – 'I borrowed it from the landlord's daughter at the Lantern and we can have it for as long as we like' – and Giles settled his fat bottom into its security with obvious pleasure. He and Gemma had both had a rest in front of the fire and had got a second wind. Tom had the still, dreamy expression of one sated with contentment. 'Great afternoon,' he commented to Mark as he sat next to Giles. 'Ted's great. The girls are great—'

'The girls?' Mark queried.

Tom smiled indulgently. 'Pansy and Mavis and Bernice. They said to call them the girls.'

Mark coughed back a laugh. 'And Ted?' he asked.

Tom smiled sleepily. 'I meant Dad. That's his name. Ted. Ted Harris.'

The 'girls' arrived at that moment so Tom did not realize his mistake. There was the usual fuss about hanging up their coats and getting them a sherry. Pansy sat by Reg and asked him what he thought of her dress.

'Beautiful, Pansy. You have a wonderful throat, such milky skin.'

Pansy told him roguishly about the artist who had admired her cleavage.

'That too,' Reg said, smiling.

'And how are those itchy legs?' Pansy put her hand on his thigh. 'Have you got your stockings on?'

'All the time.' He sighed. 'They are very inhibiting.'

'You mean—?' Pansy flushed suddenly. 'Oh dear. How . . . awkward.'

He laughed. 'I was joking, Pansy dear. I'm doing fine. I walk to the bathroom. I can get under the shower. Put myself to bed . . . I'm doing fine.'

Pansy tightened her mouth against sudden tears. 'Oh Reg, I'm so glad,' she managed.

Arthur said loudly, 'Has everyone got a sherry?'

'No,' Tom said, holding up his glass, giggling like any normal ten-year-old.

Arthur advanced with a bottle of Coke. 'I do apologize, sir. The service in this restaurant is really bad . . .'

Adam's grin exploded into a laugh and Gemma widened her eyes and then joined in. Giles banged his spoon on the tray of the high chair. Cree and Cass were ushered in, Cree demanding to know what the joke was. Reg looked up and smiled at Cass. She was wearing what seemed to be a black satin nightdress. She looked magnificent. As soon as he could, he told her so and kissed her hand.

She sighed and kissed the top of his head. 'Why do I always attract older men who should know better?' she asked him.

'Because they've lived long enough to appreciate you to the full,' he said. And for once he did not speak with provocative gallantry and he hung onto her hand so that she looked sharply down at him and then blinked and looked away.

Cree said, 'Angel-Mavis. Did you enjoy your afternoon in the mud?'

She was still giggling at Arthur's ridiculous waiter-impression. 'Oh, I did, I did!' she gushed. 'It was all so . . . what was it you said this morning about the sea?'

'Primeval,' he supplied. 'Primeval mud. We came from it.' He sighed deeply. 'And we shall eventually go back to it.'

'Primeval. That was it. The earliest age of all. I looked it up.'

'Dear angel,' he murmured, turning to Arthur for his drink and brushing against Bernice. She smiled at him and he too, like Cass, blinked and looked away. They were standing much too close.

Bernice said, 'I don't think I like that idea. I stayed well away from the mud. And, I noticed, so did you.'

'Er . . . yes, I did, didn't I?' His gaze was on Reg, who apparently was still fully engaged with Cass. Yes. He registered that Reg was absolutely engaged with Cass. He relaxed and turned back to Bernice. 'Actually, no bamming now. I try to avoid thoughts of either past or future. They're part of that eternity bit. I can't somehow deal with eternity. The mud represents all that stuff . . . eternity.'

Bernice stared at him, fascinated. But all she

179

said, eventually, was, 'Bamming? What the hell is bamming?'

'You've not heard it before?' Cree sighed deeply. 'Shows my age. I think it's Shakespeare actually. It means . . . mucking about.'

Her face was lightened by a smile. Cree thought she was beautiful. Elegant; real in the way that Cass was real, beautiful in the way that Cass was beautiful. She was so comfortable in her own space, her own clothes, her own being.

She said in a low amused voice, 'So you're the same age as Shakespeare? How very interesting.'

He could not help smiling at her. 'It makes me very wise. All-knowing. I think I can see into your head. Into your soul.'

Her hackles rose. 'I do hope not. I would not wish to hurt your feelings,' she said.

He said, 'You're very honest. I think – I'm almost certain – that I could not be hurt by your honesty.'

'Not even if you discovered that I thought you were the most self-centred human being I have met in a long time?'

His smile widened. 'Tell me – be honest again – are you flirting with me?'

'Is that the stuff of flirtation? Why on earth would I flirt with you?'

'Reg thought I was flirting with *you*. He warned me off. But if *you* are flirting with *me* . . . well, surely I'm entitled to reciprocate?'

She stared at him and a flush slowly crept from her neck into her face.

He said quickly, 'Forget I said that. It didn't mean a thing.'

She said quietly, tightly, 'What else did he tell you? That I'm an easy lay?'

He drew in his breath. 'Bernie! Of course not! My God, what do you think we are? Yes – all right, all right! A couple of silly old codgers – we both know that. But we don't talk about friends . . . in that way. I can assure you that Reg . . .'

But Bernice had turned and moved along the table to a line of empty seats and luckily for her the Chivertons arrived at that moment and everyone sat down except Holly and May who raised their glasses and looked towards Reg. Reg raised his too and then announced, 'Happy Christmas, everyone. Happy Christmas!'

And Mark put in quickly, 'Here's to our host. Here's to Reg and a speedy recovery!'

To Reg . . . happy Christmas . . . Holly and May went to the kitchen and wheeled in the trolley and there were the two turkeys side by side on their meat dishes and then the dishes of vegetables and sauces, hot rolls, hot plates; everyone was flushed and no one noticed Bernice Smythe after all.

It was a very successful meal; Reg said it was the best one of all and Holly and May had excelled themselves. Mark, carving at the sideboard, grabbed Holly as she passed him and kissed her and Arthur then had to kiss May and unexpectedly Adam leaned forward and kissed Gemma. Everyone said how sweet that was except Tom who dug his brother in the ribs and told him to shut up. Then everyone laughed because Adam said equably, 'All right.' Tom looked across the table at Ted and Ivy and they looked back at him. When conversation started again, Tom whispered, 'He said all right.' He knew his mother was going to cry so he turned to Adam and hissed, 'Say it again.'

But Adam had shot his bolt and just nodded and smiled at his mother. She used her napkin to dab at her eyes and smiled back. When people began to pull their crackers she whispered to Ted, 'It's going to be all right, Ted. It's going to be all right!' He nodded, unable to speak. He felt that he and Ivy had been turning back the clock since they got here. Today they had been children again, playing with other children. And now . . . Adam was starting to speak again. They were all happy. Of course it was going to be all right. Quite soon now, Ivy would stop being frightened and they would sleep together. And somehow all the business with the authorities would be sorted out and they could get married and live like a normal family.

Arthur Long was refilling the glasses and Ivy shook her head gratefully. Ted knew that because of Stanley Edwards she was terrified of drunkenness and he too shook his head at Arthur. Holly followed after him and leaned down to Ivy.

'Someone on the phone for you, Ivy,' she said.

Ivy's eyes distended with fear. She looked from Holly to Ted.

'Not me. It can't be me. Nobody knows I'm here. It can't be me.'

Holly was mildly surprised. 'He's asking for Mrs Ivy Edwards.' She looked at Ted. 'Shall I tell him it's a mistake?'

Ted forced his mouth to work. 'Him. It's a man, is it?'

'Yes. Slight Welsh accent. I assumed it was one of your family.'

Ted swallowed. 'There has been someone . . . makes a bit of a nuisance of himself. Perhaps it would be better if you said there's no-one here . . .'

'I'm sorry, Stanley.' Holly imagined what it would be like if Hugo rang her. 'I'm really sorry. I didn't think. I just said I would fetch Ivy to the phone.' She put a hand on Ivy's shoulder. 'I'll tell him you're not available, shall I?'

Ivy shook her head violently. 'No! He knows we're here now. He'll come after us and there will be a terrible scene! I'll have to speak to him.' She half stood and looked down at Ted. 'I knew it was too good to be true. I'll have to go back. I'll have to—'

Ted knew he had to do something. He controlled the tremor in his voice with sheer will-power. 'Sit down, Ivy. I'll talk to him. Don't worry, my dear. I'll put him off.' He shifted his position to make room for Holly. 'Would you take my place? Talk to Ivy. Just' – he waved his hands – 'be with her. The children mustn't know.'

Holly slipped into his chair. It was obvious that Ivy and Stanley were in trouble. And she knew about trouble. She said, 'Ivy, it's all right. We're all here and we can help.' Beneath the tablecloth she took Ivy's hand; it was ice cold. From across the table Tom said, 'Mum. Where's Ted going?' And, like Mark, Holly noted the boy's use of the name.

She spoke for Ivy. 'Dad's just gone to help Mark sort out the puddings. Can you put Gemma's hat on for her? It keeps slipping into her eyes.' Both Tom and Adam turned to Gemma and Holly said in a low voice, 'Don't let them see that you're rattled.'

Ivy widened her mouth into a rictus and then said tensely, 'You see, Holly, you can't help. No-one can help. He'll make a bargain. We go back and he won't report Tom. We stay here and he will.'

'Tom?' Holly frowned. 'What on earth has Tom done that is so awful?'

Ivy said dully, 'He tried to kill his father.' She saw Holly's complete disbelief and went on, 'I'll tell you about it. Before we go back home, I'll tell you.'

And in the hall that was so liberally decked with holly and ivy, Ted had his face to the wall and the telephone receiver tight to his ear.

'How did you know? How did you know we were here?' he asked once Stanley had delivered his bargain.

'She loved it there. Last summer and again in the autumn when we were supposed to be patching up our marriage . . . She thought it was wonderful. It's a little hell-hole, isn't it, Ted? Go on, admit it. She's a whining, whingeing apology for a woman and the place itself is full of mud.'

Ted felt his face go hot with anger. 'Don't speak of Ivy in that way! She never whines or whinges! And anyway, if that's what you think of her, why do you want her back?'

'Because she belongs to me, that's why! And you've taken her away and no-one takes any-thing that belongs to me!'

'Well, she's not coming back. Your so-called bargain is a dead duck, Stanley Edwards! Report Tom to whoever you like and see what comes out of it! You'll end up in prison for assault of a child – that's what!'

Stanley started to laugh. 'My God, Ted. You don't know her, do you? She'll come back of her own accord. If I was there now, I'd just have to crook my finger. That's all. She does what I tell her, Ted. She's been doing what I tell her for so many years she can't really exist without me.'

'She wouldn't even come to the phone to talk to you! That's how much she can exist without you!' Ted was so hot he ripped at his tie.

'Oh Ted . . . Ted. By the time you get back to her she'll be wanting to pack. You're all up at the bungalow, are you? Well, she won't want to stop a minute longer. And as soon as you get back to Magpie – by the way, has it still got that leak on the verandah? I know it better than you, Ted. Been there twice, remember – as soon as you get back there, she'll be getting the dustbin liners out to pack her stuff. She packed in a hurry, didn't she? Only one nightie. And those knickers from Woolworth's – hideous, aren't they, Ted—'

'Shut up!' Ted snapped. 'Just leave us alone! You're sick, that's your trouble. My God, no wonder she's been unhappy! She could take you to court for what you've done—'

'But she never has, has she? Never complained – not about me.' Stanley's laugh came insidiously across the wires. 'Ted. Tell me the truth now. Have you slept with her?' He waited and when there was no immediate reply his laugh increased and almost burst Ted's eardrum. 'You see?' he crowed triumphantly. 'She knows she belongs to me! I knew she wouldn't sleep with you! She can't help herself, Ted. She's mine and she knows it!' He stopped laughing abruptly and then said in a hard voice, 'If you're not home by tomorrow afternoon, Ted, I'm coming for you. You needn't bother to tell her that because she'll know.'

And the line went dead.

Eight

Ted stood in the hall for some time, facing the line of pegs hung with coats and hats and umbrellas. The aura they gave off was of seaweed and mud, the same scent that had been with them all through the afternoon. It seemed to give Ted strength and he breathed it in deeply, fighting off nausea and fear. He had always known he was a coward; he should have done something for Ivy years ago and he had not. He should never have fallen for Louise and had his two children with her but he had. But this time . . . this time he had to find the courage somehow to rescue Ivy and Tom and Adam. His mind spun crazily around the problem: Adam and Stanley, Tom and Stanley, Ivy and Stanley. There seemed no way out of it because it always came back to Tom and Adam and because of them he knew that Stanley was right and that Ivy would go back to him. He made a dry, sobbing noise in his throat and consciously took another breath.

Arthur Long came out of the living room wheeling a trolley full of glasses and crockery towards the kitchen. He glanced at Ted and said, 'All right, old man?' Ted did not answer and Arthur opened the kitchen door with one foot and began to back inside. 'Go outside and get some air – too much wine, I expect.'

Ted breathed in the aroma from the assembled coats and took Arthur's advice. Outside it was dark but the clouds were moving and here and there the moon and stars appeared fitfully. He stood on the verandah and looked across the drive towards St Margaret's Bay. Holly had told them about the morning's dip, the icy water and Mavis's courage. And he and Ivy and the kids had been with Pansy and Bernice when the others had arrived for breakfast all wrapped in sheets. Later, Ivy had described the 'girls' as three widow ladies and Gemma had thought she said window ladies and that they must be female window cleaners which had caused much mirth. What a day it had been; the best Christmas he could remember. And now this. Spoiling it. And though the window ladies had such guts, he had none.

He took some more deep breaths, emptying his lungs and then sucking in the damp air. He told himself, 'You're *not* going to let it be spoiled for Ivy and the kids. This is something you can carry on your own, so that's what you're going to do. Tomorrow you can tell her. Tomorrow we'll decide what to do. Not tonight. Not Christmas night.' He turned and went back inside.

The games were well under way; Mark had one of Reg's big-band tapes on the deck and almost everyone had moved their chairs into a circle and was picking out hats from a big bag and ramming them on one another until the music stopped. Ivy, wearing a bowler, looked up as the door opened. Her face was wide and questioning. Ted grinned reassuringly and put one thumb up. He was delighted that she was still here and playing games with the children. Stanley was wrong about that, anyway.

Cree Evans glanced at Reg, who was wearing one of Maude's old sunhats and singing along with the record, 'In The Mood'. Cree moved over to where Bernice was stacking the dirty crockery.

'Are you going to join in this game?' he enquired.

'Not at this precise moment.' She glanced at him. 'Perhaps you haven't noticed. I'm helping May and Arthur to clear up.'

He said, 'Listen. Will you just listen a moment? I know I open my mouth and put my size elevens right inside it, but I do assure you that Reg and I have not discussed you in . . . that way. Not at all. Reg thought I was flirting with you and he asked me not to. That was all.'

She was still, her hands, long and bonily beautiful, holding a bundle of cutlery. After a while she said, 'Why would he do that, d'you think?'

Cree said, 'He felt – feels – protective towards you?'

The tiny beginnings of a smile curved her mouth. 'Perhaps.' She put the cutlery on a tray and rubbed her hands together. 'Did he make the same request on behalf of Mavis?'

'No.'

'How strange.'

'Perhaps he thinks Mavis can look after herself.'

'And I cannot?'

'Bernice, I didn't mean that! For God's sake—'

'It's all right.' She was smiling openly now. 'I think I must be getting used to you putting your foot in it.' She looked over to where Reg was now wearing a Turkish fez. 'Dear Reg,' she said. She picked up the tray and moved past Cree. 'Anyway, I don't think you were flirting with me at all. Flirting entails giving compliments – usually false. Like calling Mavis your pink angel.' Her smile widened into a grin. 'I don't remember one compliment paid to me. Not one.'

Cree opened the door for her and followed her into the kitchen.

'Exactly,' he said, well satisfied. 'Absolutely exactly. Our exchanges are . . . well, fairly acerbic.' He watched as she ran water into a bowl and added washing-up liquid. 'D'you want me to dry those? I think you're supposed to do them straight away, aren't you? And give them a really good polish?'

'If you're trying to impress me with your domestic skills, please don't bother. I wouldn't dream of asking you to polish Reg's precious silver.' She saw his look of relief and grinned again as she turned off the tap. 'That's my job. You wash them. Here's the brush. Be sure to get it well between the tines of each fork.'

When Giles fell asleep, Holly lifted him onto her lap and held him gently while Ted took her place in the game. Mark, fiddling with the tape deck, watched her covertly. She looked up suddenly and gave a small upside-down smile; he could have wept. She knew it and stood up with some difficulty to join him.

'It's all right,' she said as he tried to help her with Giles. 'I'm going to put him in our bed and suggest to Ivy that the others stay as well.' She saw his surprise and said in a low voice, 'Something's really wrong, Mark. Stanley isn't Stanley at all. He's Ted. And the boys aren't his, they're Stanley's. And Tom tried to kill his father.'

Mark stared at her and then remembered. 'Of course! Tom called him Ted. But . . . why? And how will it help if we have the children here?'

'I'm not sure. Perhaps it won't. Ivy has said she'll explain everything properly. But I think she needs some time with Ted. To sort things out. That was Stanley on the phone. He's got some sort of hold over her.'

Mark said, 'Well, of course, if you think it would help. Anyway it's no problem, is it? Reg will be delighted. And it's a four-bedroomed bungalow.' He held out his arms. 'Let me take Giles. Then I'll put Nunc to bed and I'll ask him.' He smiled. 'Oh Holly . . . I do love you.'

She stepped back and looked at him holding the sleeping child. 'Will you always?' she asked unexpectedly.

'Of course. I couldn't live without you – you know that.'

'But if I did something awful – something really stupid and wicked and awful . . . ?'

'You're thinking of Tom trying to kill his own father.' He leaned across Giles to kiss her forehead. 'Darling, if you went for me with an axe, I would still love you.'

They edged around the group of chairs, and Mark leaned over Dennis Chiverton and asked him to take on the business of the tape deck; then, nodding at Ivy and Ted, they made for the bedroom. And Holly felt as if her heart might break.

Tom was sleepily amenable to staying in the spare room with Adam and Gemma; Adam smiled and nodded; Gemma was already curled into Cass's black satin curves, thumb in mouth. With the children's departure the party began to break up. Mavis went to look for Bernice and gather up their coats, Dennis and Paula said their goodbyes and Paula leaned over Reg's wheelchair and kissed him. 'It's been the best Christmas of my whole life,' she said extravagantly. 'Say goodbye to Mark for me, will you Reg? I think you and Mark are so nice – really, really, really nice. I don't think I've ever met two men who were so—'

Dennis said, 'Come along, Polly. I had too much to drink last night and you've definitely had too much to drink tonight.'

'Not a bit.' She straightened and leaned against him and looked into his eyes in the special way she had. 'You're jealous, that's all. But you can't help not being nice, Chiv. It's not your fault, is it? I mean . . . you've had it so easy all your life. I love you just the same, so don't worry. Prob'ly you'll get nicer as you get older. I didn't realize how young you were till we came here. You are really young, aren't you, Chiv? Really, really—'

He stopped her words with a kiss and she laughed into his mouth, which always drove him crazy. He laughed too and zipped up her jacket and rammed on her woolly hat as if she were a child. He couldn't wait to get back to the chalet. It was still early, not ten o'clock yet, and they could make love for hours before they fell asleep.

*   *   *

Cass knelt by the wheelchair. 'I'll say goodnight too, Reg. Mavis has gone to collect Bernice and Cree. It's been two long days. But splendid. Really splendid.'

'Dear and beautiful Cass.' Reg smiled tiredly. 'You've spent quite a few years now looking after that father of yours. D'you regret coming back to him?'

'No.' Cass shrugged her wide shoulders. 'I wasn't leaving anything behind, Reg. Half a dozen failed relationships. No husband, no children. I take after Cree. We won't be leaving much behind us.'

'What a depressing attitude.' Reg leaned back and looked at her severely. 'You could say that you had made half a dozen men extremely happy. That you are now making it possible for Cree to paint what he wants to instead of what he has to.'

'Silly old fool is stuck in that commercial rut. Reckons he can't afford to do anything else. What he needs is to meet someone with money. Someone who won't let him get away with things like I do.'

'Someone who will go crazy with him? Swim in winter seas? Pose for hour upon hour?'

'Yes. Probably.'

Reg said definitely, 'Not Mavis Gentry, then. That's for sure.'

'You don't think so?'

'Perhaps for the rest of this holiday. No longer.'

Cass sighed deeply. 'You're probably right. She might not be able to hold him when he gets nightmares . . . 'slap him hard when he gets too randy—'

'Randy?' Reg looked horrified. 'Not with you? Christ, you're his daughter! Bad enough that you have to sleep in the same bed with him because he gets bloody nightmares! But randy?'

Cass grinned. 'Funnily enough, it's only with me now. And not very often, I can assure you. Once I've whacked someone down, they tend to stay down. I'm very strong, Reg.'

He continued to stare at her, amazed. 'You're the most unusual woman I've met in a long, long time, Cass Evans. I wish I were younger.'

'Don't think I haven't noticed your wandering hands.'

'Sounds as if I'm lucky to have got away with it!'

They both laughed and then Reg said seriously, 'Listen, Cass. If Cree ever finds anyone who will do what you do – and make him feel randy into the bargain – come to me. I'll need looking after now until I climb into my wooden box. And I can help you.'

It was her turn to be astonished. 'How?' she asked directly.

'Well, for one thing, I can appreciate you to the full. I would never ever take you for granted. And for another . . . we could be married, Cass. And then you'd have money when I'm gone.'

Her astonishment made her sit back on her heels and the black satin nightdress creaked a protest. He laughed and said, 'Steady there,' and she said, 'My God! What kind of a bargain is that? What about Mark and Holly?'

'They've got the village. I've sorted all that out. They could sell for building land. Or they can run it like Maude and I did.'

'Reg, I can't believe you're saying this. How much have you had to drink?'

'Nothing. I'm on drugs from the hospital. Can't drink.'

She stared at him. 'I don't know how to react to this. Of course the answer's no. You know that. I can't leave Cree. But . . . it's the thought. And I don't know whether I should slap your face or be grateful.'

'Neither. Just keep it in mind.' He put a gnarled hand to her cheek. 'It's a bit one-sided, Cass. Completely one-sided in fact. Since you came back from the States I've thought you were a marvellous girl. I tell myself you're the right age to be my daughter, but I still fancy you like mad. To end my days with you sounds like heaven.'

She squatted there in front of him, holding the arms of his chair to keep her balance, his hand still on her face. They stayed like that for what seemed a long time. Then she whispered, 'I want to cry.'

'Don't be silly. Other men have said better things—'

'They haven't meant them. I think you do.'

'I do. And other things as well. About your beauty which is so bountiful and generous . . . I won't say them. I just want you to remember . . . to keep this in mind.'

'I will. I will, Reg. The answer will always be no, but I will keep it in my mind until I die.' She pulled herself up and leaned over him, taking him in her arms. He closed his eyes, consciously registering her smell and the voluptuous touch of her bare shoulders and the weight of her breasts.

She said, 'Would you like me to take you into your room now? Help you get into bed?'

He smiled. 'Very much. But I want Stanley Edwards to do that. As soon as he gets back from putting his children to bed, I'm going to ask him to do the same for me.' He leaned back and looked into her face. 'He needs to talk to someone, Cass. It should be you, but he won't be able to talk to another woman because he can only see his Ivy. So it will have to be me.'

'Oh Reg.' She spoke his name with great tenderness. 'I used to think you were an insensitive old buffer.'

He grinned. 'I am. Now go. Take that old reprobate of a father and put him to bed instead. And enjoy your swim tomorrow morning. Enjoy everything, Cass.'

'I will.' It sounded such a solemn promise but she grinned as she moved away. 'I will.' She stopped by the door and looked back. Pansy, shrugging into the coat that Mavis was holding for her, said, 'Reggie darling, we've got to go,' and Cass's voice slipped beneath her higher pitch. 'Thank you, Reg.'

'Yes. Thank you, Reg.' Pansy leaned over and kissed his cheek and immediately straightened. 'It's been lovely. The whole day has been lovely. I think Mavis and Bernice would like to stay till New Year, if that's all right?'

'Of course. Of course.' Reg was already regretting making that 'bargain' with Cass. There was no need for it. As soon as business opened next week, he'd contact his solicitor and change his will anyway.

Mavis said, 'Well, I never thought I'd see you washing up, Cree!' She took his hands from the suds and held them to the light. 'The hands of an artist! You shouldn't have them in that hot soapy water!'

Cree said pathetically, 'Bernice made me. I offered to dry but she insisted that I should wash.'

Bernice smiled, gave an extra rub to the last spoon and laid it neatly in the cutlery drawer. Mavis said, 'You should know better, Bernie! These hands are insured, you know. Did you know that? They are the hands of a genius!'

'Hardly that, dear lady,' Cree said, smirking nonetheless.

'I agree,' Bernice said, picking up her coat and pushing her arms into the sleeves. 'I saw nothing in Wren Cottage that gave a hint of genius. I think I might call what I saw . . . pretentious porn.'

Mavis was shocked and horrified but Cree burst out laughing. And then so did Bernice. Mavis couldn't get over it.

'I expect the unexpected from you, Cree. But Bernice? Honestly, how you could – could – *denigrate* – Cree's work in that way and then laugh, I will never know!'

'Sorry . . . sorry,' Bernice spluttered. 'It just sort of popped out – so alliterative and – and—'

'*True!*' Cree supplied. 'I get commissions for that sort of stuff. We're in an age of analysis and people love to see human beings opened up for viewing. If customers in a bank have to stand in line and look at a wall of dissected women, it makes them think twice about asking for a loan!'

Bernice practically wept with laughter at that and Mavis had to smile, though she said doubtfully, 'What about the painting of me? Is that destined for the wall of a bank? You haven't let me see anything yet, but you keep referring to me as your pink angel, so I rather hoped . . .'

'It will be called "Pink Angel",' Cree promised. 'But it may well not look quite as you imagine. I paint abstracts, as you know.'

Mavis looked at Bernice, who was holding her side in obvious pain. She said doubtfully,

'The pink . . . that part of it . . . won't be blood, will it?'

Bernice gave a small sound between a whoop and a scream and Cree said, 'Shut up, Bernie, you're completely heartless!' He turned to Mavis and took both her hands in his again. 'I promise you faithfully, there will be no blood.'

'Only I've got a thing about blood,' she confessed. 'When Pansy cut her thumb that time . . . d'you remember, Bernie? It was when we did that cookery course and had to chop all those vegetables. Pansy should not be allowed within a mile of a knife. Anyway, I took one look at her thumb and fainted away.'

Cree looked into her eyes. 'That's because you are so sensitive, my angel.' He drew her to him. 'I am painting you being fed with grapes, remember. I want to convey warmth and luxury; good food; maybe just a hint of decadence.'

She gasped, closed her eyes for a moment then moved away.

'I think you're trying to hypnotize me into agreeing to discard my sheet,' she said breathlessly. 'I told you, Cree, I cannot pose nude.'

'You were practically there when Pansy and I arrived last night,' Bernice put in, controlling her laughter with difficulty. She buttoned her coat and turned to Cree. 'Just stop tormenting Mavis, please.'

He turned his intense blue gaze onto her. 'Why?' he asked challengingly. 'Are you jealous?'

She stopped laughing and said very steadily, 'Because she is my best friend and I won't stand by and see her baited.'

He widened his eyes and then relaxed and smiled again. 'Sorry. Sorry, my angel. Sorry, Bernice. I'm old and senile, you must forgive me.'

Mavis was instantly attentive again but Bernice made a sound of extreme impatience and brushed past him. The door opened, almost hitting her in the face, and Pansy said, 'Reg is going to bed now. Come and say goodnight and thank him. It's been wonderful, hasn't it?'

Cree said, 'Oh yes. It certainly has.' And as the five of them walked down the drive together, he lifted his considerable voice and sang, ' "It came upon the midnight clear . . ." ' Mavis and Pansy added their sopranos rather tremulously, but Bernice and Cass were silent.

Ted was used to caring for people and he undressed Reg tenderly and put his clothes on hangers while the old man settled himself on the pillows.

'One of the hardest things, Stanley, is having to sleep on my back,' Reg said. 'I long to roll over.' He sighed. 'But then I roll into Maude's place. And she's not there any more.'

Ted looked at the empty space and felt the old man's sadness. He spoke rallyingly. 'You need a few more pillows. Prop you up. And one under

your knees like that . . .' He made Reg comfortable and then said, 'I'm not Stanley. I'm Ted
Harris. I didn't mean to lie to you, but Holly just
assumed . . . it seemed easier at the time.'

'Of course it did.' Reg smiled. 'I knew.
Remember I've had to deal with Stanley and he
was a nasty piece of work. He knocked Ivy about,
didn't he?'

Ted swallowed. 'Yes. And the boys. That's why
we're here.' He tried to smile. 'We're on the
run.'

Reg patted the old-fashioned quilt. 'Sit in
Maude's place. Tell me about it,' he invited. So
Ted did. And Reg nodded and listened and
nodded again. When Ted had finished he said,
'Poor Ivy. So much unhappiness. But now . . .
things will change. You're both young. You
probably love each other more now than when
you were younger. Those boys think the world of
you, Ted. And your little girl thinks the world
of them.' Reg was sounding sleepy. 'You're a
lucky man. You've got so much to look forward
to. We need that. We all need something to look
forward to.'

Ted had been hoping for help and advice. He
said desperately, 'But what if Stanley is right and
Ivy just packs up tomorrow and goes back to
him?'

'She won't do that.'

'She might.' Ted closed his eyes for a moment.
'Oh God. She will. He's browbeaten her into a

kind of terrified submission. And now, with this hold he's got over Tom . . . he hasn't said anything about Tom hitting him. But she knows he will if he doesn't get his way.'

'Tom is his son as well as Ivy's,' Reg murmured.

'That makes no difference to Stanley. He's vicious – I expect you think I'm exaggerating—'

'No. No, I don't think that at all.' Reg made an effort. 'Listen, my boy. If Stanley Edwards had stuck to what he knew, then he might have got away with it. Ivy is married to him and probably thinks being knocked about is part of her wedding vows. But Stanley turned his attentions elsewhere. He went for Adam. Poor defenceless Adam, who has given up talking because he doesn't know what to say any more. And now he is threatening Tom, who did what he did to protect his brother and his mother. Ivy won't go back to him now. Not now. She'll fight tooth and nail to keep Tom and Adam. If he brings a case against the boy – says she is not a fit mother – she'll take it through every court in the land.'

Ted stared, surprised by the old man's conviction. He said, 'She's not like that, Reg. She's quiet and shy and never says boo to a goose.'

'She left her home in the middle of the night. She thought it all through, Ted. Note on the door to mislead the social worker. Coming down here early – escaping for a bit. She's finally turned, Ted. Stanley doesn't know what he's taking on.' Reg turned his head into the pillow. 'Sorry, my boy. I'm dropping off. Have faith in Ivy . . . have faith.'

Ted sat there on Maude's side of the bed and thought about it again. Ivy had appeared to enjoy playing Musical Hats and the other games, and after his first reassurance she had not asked any more questions about the phone call. She had acquiesced in the suggestion that the children should sleep at the bungalow. Was it possible that Reg was right? He gnawed at his lip, feeling less frightened but full of indecision. Then he switched off the bedside lamp and crept out of the room.

Dennis insisted on carrying Paula over the threshold of Linnet Cottage.

'I have to admit things improved this evening,' he said breathlessly, going straight through to the bedroom and depositing her on the bed. 'Nice meal, good company, those kids are fairly decently behaved—'

'The baby is so . . . so *gorgeous*!' she said. 'And did you see Adam give Gemma a kiss? Wasn't that the sweetest thing you ever saw? Oh Chiv . . . darling Chiv . . . can we have another baby after this one? Maybe this one will be twins. Wouldn't that be the most wonderful thing in the world?'

'Darling. You really are drunk, aren't you? But

I love you just the same. And I do understand about this nesting instinct thing. And I want you to have a good time – I promise I won't be jealous any more – though you do seem to be keen on Mark Jepson . . .' Dennis was undressing her as he spoke, throwing her woolly hat into a corner of the room and pulling off her thick sweater as if he were peeling a banana. 'Tell me you don't like him, Polly. Just tell me that – even if it's not true.'

She giggled helplessly. 'I'll tell you that if you'll let us stay for New Year!'

'Oh God, Polly! What are we going to do all week? Play in that bloody mud every day? I can't bear it!' Her boots hit the floor with a clunk and he started on her jeans.

She said, 'Well then. I am very keen on Mark Jepson. If he were here now he would get me some hot milk to drink—'

'We haven't got any milk!'

'Yes, we have. Ivy gave us some so that I could make mince pies. And I'm going to do that tomorrow. And then Mark says we can go to the pantomime in Weston. And then he'll take us out in his boat. And then—'

'Mark, Mark, Mark! You're not keen on him – I know that! I know you love me! But I want you to tell me . . . go on, tell me.' He tickled her and she gave a little scream.

'I might . . . I *will* . . . Just promise me we can stay here till New Year. Go on – promise.'

'OK, OK, I promise! I'll be a good boy and go to the pantomime and out in the boat. Now say it!' He fumbled helplessly with the zip on her jeans.

'Not enough, Chiv. Get me some hot milk like Mark would. Then I will. Honestly.' She kissed him and then deliberately turned her face away. He lifted his head to stare down at her. Her mouth was pursed with a kind of sweet stubbornness which he found irresistible. He groaned and climbed off the bed and she rewarded him with a murmured, 'Dear Chiv,' and a swift removal of her jeans.

He smiled as he fiddled about in the kitchen. Ever since that nightmare experience on the sledge, he had appreciated her more than ever. She was so full of life and vivacity. No wonder his parents had taken to her; they knew she would have to be very special to put up with him. He paused, fridge door open, and thought about what she had said back in the bungalow . . . Was he really not 'nice'? Paula was drunk, that was certain, but they said the truth came out when people were drunk. He knew his parents had always spoiled him, but did that make him not 'nice'? He slopped milk into a saucepan and then had to find a cloth to mop up the mess, during which time the rest of it boiled over onto the hob and smelled terrible. He swore and poured what was left into a mug. It was skinny as well as smelly. He turned everything off and carried the mug into the bedroom.

'I've done it, Polly. I'm sorry it's not much but everything seems to be against me in this place. I'm afraid I've made a bit of a mess . . .'

There was no reply and when he looked at the bed he saw she had kicked her jeans onto the floor, rolled herself into the duvet and was fast asleep.

Ivy couldn't stop talking. 'I told Holly everything. I promised I would and after the children were asleep we went into the kitchen and had a cup of coffee and – and I just did.'

'I told Reg.' Ted shivered. The night air was cold and the damp penetrated his anorak and chilled his bones.

'Holly said you would deal with it and you have, Ted! Tell me again what you said. I wish I'd heard you. No-one has stood up to Stanley before. They say that about bullies, don't they? Holly said he was a bully and if only we could stand up to him, he'd just crumple. And you did and he has!'

Ted shivered again. It was wonderful that Ivy was not suggesting packing up and going back – just like Reg Jepson had said – but in other ways Reg was quite wrong.

'I can't really remember what I said now.'

'You told him that he must do what he feels he has to do.' She took his arm and hugged it to her. 'I can just hear you saying it, Ted! Not angrily. Just saying it straight out, like you do. And I'm so glad that everyone knows your real name now. I didn't like you being called Stanley. It's the most horrible name in the whole world. And Ted is the best name in the whole world.'

'Oh Ivy.' He squeezed her arm. 'Not everyone knows. The window-cleaning ladies don't know. Neither does the young couple or that artist and his daughter.'

'Oh yes, she knows. She came in to say good-night when I was telling Holly and I asked her to stay and listen. She's very, very nice. I thought how nice she was this afternoon, in that wetsuit, giving everyone rides on the sledge. Oh Ted.' Ivy stopped in the middle of the drive and looked around her wonderingly. 'Oh Ted . . . I am so happy. I have never been so happy in my life before. I like all the people here, don't you?'

'Yes. Yes, I do.'

'And it's wonderful to be alone with you like this. Holly knew we needed some time together. To talk and decide what to do. And you've decided what to do, my dear, dear Ted. So we can just be together.'

He wondered what she meant by that and he looked down at her and saw in the misty light of the moon that her face was as wide and open as a child's. There was no fear, no introversion; she was like one of that artist's ghastly paintings . . . completely vulnerable.

With that thought came fear again. He had not asked Stanley where he was. Supposing, just supposing, he had been in that pub – the Lantern – at the top of the drive? Or using a mobile. Supposing he was now sitting on the verandah at Magpie Cottage waiting for them?

She lifted her face to his. 'Ted. I want us to be together. Properly together. I feel that we are married. As if we have always been married. I'm not frightened any more – you are not Stanley. You are stronger and better than Stanley ever could be. You would never try to hurt me.'

He made a sound of protest and she quickly put up her hands and cupped his face.

'I didn't think you would, my darling. That never entered my head. But I thought that when you touched me it would remind me of . . . him. And it would spoil it. But now . . . now I know that nothing about you reminds me of him. Nothing. You are Ted Harris. You don't have to prove anything to anyone, you are simply yourself, and you know who you are.'

'Oh Ivy . . . I wish I was like that. I wish I was courageous and—'

Her laugh was incredulous. 'You are the most courageous human being I have ever met!' she said. And she drew down his head and kissed him on the mouth.

Much, much later, when they had slept and woken and slept again, he lay on his back and stared at the window and knew that he could conquer the world.

Nine

Ted did not tell Ivy about Stanley's deadline but all the next morning he could almost hear the hard voice: 'If you're not home by tomorrow afternoon, I'm coming for you.'

Mark and Holly brought the children down at ten thirty, washed and fed and ready for anything.

'Why is it called Boxing Day, Daddy?' Gemma asked, hanging Regina over one shoulder like Holly did when she was winding Giles. She thumped the doll's back. 'Come on, Regina. Bring it up now.' Adam made a loud burping noise and after an astonished moment everyone collapsed with laughter.

Ted said, 'I don't really know, Gemma, but what about asking the boys if they'll let you have the boxes from their cars? Then I think, with a bit of this and a bit of that, you might make them into a very nice cot for Regina.'

'And it would be really and truly a boxy day!' Gemma laughed again with delight and the children gathered around the table while Ivy made the inevitable tea. Mark looked meaningfully at Ted and wandered into the living room.

'Reg told us . . . Ivy had already given Holly most of the picture. You don't mind too much, Ted? Us knowing, I mean.'

Ted said frankly, 'I'm relieved. I didn't like being Stanley Edwards.'

'No. I shouldn't think Stanley Edwards likes it much.' Mark went to the window and peered along the beach. 'Reg says that he has threatened to come here if you don't go home. Is that right?'

'Yes. But I haven't said anything to Ivy. We're so happy, Mark. I don't want to spoil anything.'

Mark turned from the window, smiling, guessing at what must have happened between these two isolated people last night. 'Funny you should say that. Holly said almost those same words to me.' Not that he and Holly had been able to do more than kiss. Yet her kiss had been infinitely tender and she had looked at Giles asleep in their bed, made a face and whispered, 'We don't need anything else, do we, my love? It's so perfect, Mark. So wonderful. I'm frightened that something will happen to spoil it.' He had reassured her and they had held hands across Giles's curled form all night long.

Ted was suddenly embarrassed. 'It was good of you to take the children like that. It made . . . a difference.'

'Would you like us to have them this afternoon? I don't think he'll turn up here but just in case?'

'Thanks, Mark. I suggested to Ivy that we take the children to Cheddar today. Let them run wild.'

Mark nodded. 'Know what you mean. Well, listen. When you get back, come to us for a bit of high tea. Just beans on toast or something.'

'It would be nice.' Ted looked doubtful. 'What about Holly and May? They did such a lot yesterday.'

'Holly is going to take it easy today. Arthur and May are taking Reg to the Lantern for a couple of hours and she's going to lie down. Feels a bit queasy actually.' Mark grinned. 'I'll get the tea. How's that?'

'If you're sure . . . then I can pop down here while they're eating and make sure . . . you know.'

'I'll come with you.'

Ted stammered his thanks. He wondered later whether he ought to deal with this by himself. That would be fine if he knew what he was dealing with and what to do. And then he wondered whether he was just running away from the whole problem by driving them up to the Mendips and then taking them to tea at the bungalow. Would the real solution be to return home by himself and face up to Stanley? But then what would happen? Would he have to hit him? He could not imagine hitting anyone, not even Stanley Edwards.

Ivy poured tea and said in a low voice, 'I'll never be able to thank you, Holly.'

'You don't have to. We love having the children.' Holly looked at them as they worked together at the table. 'They get on so well, Ivy. They really are a family, aren't they?'

Ivy gave a small, wistful smile. 'It seems like it. If only they were.'

'They will be. *You* will be. You'll have to work through it. Get hold of someone decent from social services and tell them everything. It'll take ages but eventually you'll get there.'

Ivy nodded determinedly. 'Of course we will. Ted will make it happen.'

'You too. You must be strong to have put up with it all these years.'

'Ah . . . it was weakness to put up with it, Holly. That's the trouble. That's been my trouble all along. I've sort of . . . gone along with a lot of things which haven't been right. When I lost Marilyn – our daughter – it was because Stanley pushed me down the stairs. So why did I stay then . . . let myself get pregnant again and again? That wasn't strength, that was weakness.'

Holly watched as Gemma put her doll into one of the shoeboxes and covered her with two paper hankies. Then she said quietly and slowly,

'Yes . . . I've been weak in that way too. And now I've got to live with it.'

Ivy looked at her sharply. 'You're pregnant,' she said. 'I wondered . . . once or twice, I've wondered.' She put a tentative hand on Holly's arm. 'That's wonderful, surely? Mark will be delighted.'

Holly stared at the tiny birdlike woman, younger than herself, who had known so much pain and suffering. She had intended to keep her secret to herself for always, but somehow she found herself saying, 'It's not Mark's. That's the trouble, Ivy.'

Ivy said, 'Someone raped you? Like Stanley raped me? And you went along with it too?'

Holly felt her eyes begin to fill. Ivy seemed to know and understand so much.

'Yes.'

Ivy said urgently, 'Don't tell Mark. It will be harder for him than for you – if I told Ted half of what had happened, he wouldn't be able to bear it.'

Holly said, 'I know. But . . . it's so awful. I've been beastly for ages. To him. Somehow . . . I don't know . . . blaming him for everything. It's as if this has happened to show me what a fool I've been.'

Ivy guided the two of them away from the children.

'What are you going to do?'

Holly sighed. 'I think I must have an abortion.

I did wonder . . . a friend of mine passed off her twins as belonging to her husband. They didn't. It seems to have worked very well. I thought it might be an option for me. But the circumstances were so different. It was almost like this modern surrogacy thing. No . . . I must see my doctor in the New Year. Organize something.'

'Can you go and see . . . the man? Talk to him?'

'Oh no! Oh Ivy, I never want to see him again!'

'It's just that . . . if he agreed to see it as a surrogacy arrangement, perhaps it could work.'

'Never. He often gets drunk and then he talks. He couldn't keep it to himself.' Holly glanced over her shoulder. 'Ivy, I'm sorry. I shouldn't have lumbered you when you've got so much on your mind.' She turned towards the living room. 'We'd better go. Perhaps we'll see you later.'

Ivy knew that the moment of intimacy was over and might prove an embarrassment in the future. She said quickly, 'It's good for me to know that other people have problems.' She followed Holly into the other room where the two men were – rather surprisingly – shaking hands. 'Please talk to me again. If you like.'

'Yes. All right.' Holly beamed at Ted. 'Thank you for letting us borrow your family. And we're all so glad you're not Stanley.'

Ted looked at the two women, so different yet so alike. His Ivy came up to Holly's shoulder and she was spare and dun-coloured. Holly was like a daffodil, tall and beautiful and blond and blue-eyed. A bit like Marilyn Monroe. But she too felt her happiness was fragile and had said as much to her husband; just like Ivy.

He laughed suddenly and everyone looked a question. 'Just a thought,' he said apologetically. 'Holly and Ivy. Christmassy.'

Dennis insisted that Paula should spend Boxing Day morning making it up to him for what he called her defection of the night before. She giggled and told him that defection meant going over to the other side and he told her it also meant sleeping on duty which, in the good old days, meant the firing squad.

'I must have tea first,' she stipulated. 'Feeling distinctly under the weather.'

'I'll get it. I didn't burn all the milk last night.' He brought the tea in on a tray with one of Ivy's mince pies. She shuddered. 'It's your own fault,' he said. 'All that mucking about in mud yesterday afternoon – you've probably got the flu or something awful.'

'That did me good,' she said. 'This is something else.'

'You've got a hangover.' He took the cup from her and kissed her. 'Poor baby. You're not used to them. I know all about hangovers. Put yourself in the hands of Dr Chiverton and he will make you all better.'

'No, Chiv! Not yet. Tea . . .'

But it was too late. The cup was on the floor and there was no holding Dennis. Paula did her best but her heart wasn't in it. She was cold and she desperately needed a hot drink. She tried not to think of Mark Jepson putting her feet up and switching on the fire full blast.

'Oh Polly Chiverton, I love you . . .'

'I love you too, darling.' Maybe a bit of dry toast would help too. It would have to be dry because they didn't have any butter. Though she had a feeling Ivy had given her some margarine to make the mince pies . . . or was it lard?

She gasped, 'Oh Chiv. I want to make those mince pies today.'

'All right, baby . . . all right.'

'And we could go for a walk. Not far. Just a gentle stroll . . .' She gripped his shoulders hard and made a sound.

He panted, 'I know, I know, sweetheart.'

She almost called Mark's name and then changed it swiftly. 'Oh Chiv . . . oh Chiv . . .' And he was kissing her eyes and for some crazy reason she was weeping and trying to think of mince pies.

'It's all right, Paula.' He was a bit worried. 'It's all right. Cry away, my darling. My God, you don't usually go this far!'

'I love you!' She almost shouted the words and he laughed and cradled her.

'Sweetheart, it's OK! I love you too. You don't have to convince me.'

But it was herself she was trying to convince. 'Kiss me, Chiv.' She held onto his head and dragged him to her and he obeyed, still laughing. And then she kissed him back and they did their usual things slowly and voluptuously and gradually it was all right. He lay breathless by her side.

'I didn't expect that. You're sex-crazed, that's what you are.' She smiled at him and he went on, 'It's being pregnant, isn't it? Last night you were on about wanting more children. I can see where all this is leading!'

She laughed obediently but then her eyes filled up again and he propped himself on one elbow and stared down at her, really concerned.

'What is it? Tell me, my love.'

She did not know what to tell him but she knew there was something. She blurted the first words that came into her head. 'I want your mother. I want Helen.'

'But, love – you know we can't tell them yet. We're going to break it to them in the New Year. Remember?' He was suddenly talking to her as if she were an invalid to be humoured.

She took on the role. 'I want Helen,' she said childishly. 'I want another woman to talk to. I want a mother!' And it was true. She had always wanted a mother and she had one now and she needed her.

Dennis said, 'Listen. I'll make fresh tea and

some toast and I'll switch on the fire and we'll be parents. You and me. How does that sound?'

She considered it and nodded. Perhaps that was what this awful yearning was all about. Just the old nest-making thing again.

They sat either side of the fire with a tray on the floor between them. The toast was hard and shattered into pieces when she spread it with Ivy's marge but she picked up each piece daintily and tucked it into her mouth and then swilled the lot down with gorgeously hot tea.

Dennis said, 'I've left plenty of marge for the mince pies. And while you're doing them I'll pop up to the pub and buy Reg a drink. Is that all right with you?'

It wasn't; not really. She said, 'Of course. You've done your duty here.'

He thought she was joking and said, 'It was a pleasure, ma'am, no duty, I do assure you.' He leaped up and came over to her and kissed her and the next minute they were both on the rug in front of the fire. She did all she could to make him stay and help her with the mince pies but once it was over he lifted her back onto the chair and stood straight.

'Anything you want while I'm up there?'

'Nowhere will be open.'

'If the little shop is open I'd better try for some milk, hadn't I?'

She said stolidly, 'And bread. And butter. And marmalade. And cereal. And something for supper. Eggs and bacon will do. And some fruit. And a few nuts. And chocolate—'

'The old girls gave you chocolate for your Christmas present!' he said triumphantly. 'Gotcha!'

He was gone in a flurry of laughter and she sat very still and stared at the wreck of spilt tea and toast crumbs on the tray. And then she hoisted herself upright and began to collect things together to make mince pies.

The 'girls' in Seagull Cottage breakfasted very late. Mavis was fully dressed in her golfing trews; Bernice and Pansy wore dressing gowns. Bernice's was tailored alpaca, Pansy's a flowered Viyella.

Bernice said, 'Well, this is marvellous. I slept almost ten hours. Haven't done that since I was a teenager. Who wants bacon?'

Pansy nodded vigorously then said, 'I woke at eight when Mavis went out, but then I slept again. What time is it now?'

'Almost ten.' Bernice lit the grill over three rashers of smoked back bacon. 'I've done you some too, Mavis, is that all right?'

'Yes. Thank you.' Mavis peered through the window. 'Golly, it's raining cats and dogs now. What on earth shall we do with ourselves all day?'

The other two looked at her in surprise. Pansy said, 'You were the one who said how romantic everything is . . . We'll just revel in being romantic, I suppose.'

Bernice turned the bacon expertly. 'Didn't you enjoy your swim this morning, Mavis?'

'They didn't turn up,' Mavis said. 'I went down in my costume too. Hung about for ages. I was absolutely frozen.'

'You muggins. Why didn't you knock them up?' Bernice frowned across the kitchen. 'Cree probably had a hangover and it would have done him good to have a dip.'

Mavis fiddled with the jar of marmalade. 'Actually, I did. I knocked and there was no reply, so I looked through the window. They don't pull the curtains across that big window. No privacy at all.'

Bernice and Pansy exchanged glances. Pansy said, 'Well . . . no. That's part of the freedom thing, isn't it? You know, they're open to the whole world.'

Mavis did not pick up on that; her mouth became small and tight. She said, 'They were fast asleep in bed. Sprawled around . . . they looked terrible.'

Bernice took hot plates from the oven and put out bacon and tomatoes. 'But that's the point, surely? They don't care. If people queued up to look at them in bed, that's all right with them.'

Mavis said, 'There was just me. And I didn't like it.' She drew a plate towards her. 'After all, if she's his daughter—'

'But you know she's not! You yourself told us that they slept together so therefore she must be his model!' Pansy was exasperated. 'Honestly, Mavis, you can't have it all ways. That's how he is. You've got to accept that. If you did decide to . . . you know, do it . . . with him . . . well, you'd also have to accept that you wouldn't be the only one!'

Mavis cut her bacon and chewed it unappreciatively. 'There are limits, Pansy. Obviously when I realized they were a couple I assumed that they were not father and daughter. But yesterday one or two things were said . . . Reg said things which I overheard . . . and I cannot assume – anything – any more.' She took a deep breath. 'Girls . . . I am pretty certain that they are father and daughter, and I know for a fact that they are also a couple. That – that's—'

'Incestuous,' Bernice supplied.

They were all silent, digesting this fact with their breakfasts. Then Bernice spoke again. 'Girls, I suggest we go out today. We can offer to take Reg out to lunch, have a look at the sales, get back just before dark.'

Mavis said, 'Wouldn't it be a better idea to talk to Cree and Cass? Find out where we stand?'

Pansy gave a cry of protest and Bernice said very sharply, 'Don't be absurd, Mavis! It's none of our business – they're both consenting adults, for Pete's sake! And I think it would be good not to see them for a while. You don't want

224

either of them to think you're hanging about waiting on them, Mavis. This place is all very well – romantic, nice people, et cetera – but it's also claustrophobic.' She gathered up the plates resolutely. 'No more arguing. We're going out for the day.'

Pansy and Mavis knew that when Bernice spoke like that there was no arguing, no discussion. In any case they knew that she was right. Mavis did something she wouldn't have dreamed of doing two days ago: she took a piece of bread and wiped around her plate.

'That was delicious, Bernie dear. Thank you.' She stood up. 'I'll wash up while you two shower and dress. And perhaps I'd better change. I'm not really dressed for shopping.'

'Perhaps that would be best,' Bernice said. And she did something unexpected too; she put an arm across Mavis's chunky-knit shoulders and kissed the lobe of her ear.

They were so determined to be exclusive that they hardly noticed Paula Chiverton striding ahead of the car as they drove slowly towards Reg's bungalow. When they did, Pansy had the grace to wind down her window and offer the girl a lift. They all noticed that she looked flushed in spite of the rain.

She said, 'Where are you going?'

'Probably Weston. To the sales and to have some lunch. We're hoping that Reg will come with us.'

Paula scuffed her walking boots on the drive. 'I'm muddy. But if you don't mind.' She scrambled in by Pansy. 'I was going up to the bungalow to have a word with Mark. But I'd love to go to Weston. Don't get me wrong, I love it here, but just for today it would be nice to get away.'

Bernice and Mavis looked at each other in the mirror. Reg was one thing, Paula Chiverton another. But Pansy didn't mind in the least.

'Exactly how we feel!' she beamed. 'Will your husband mind you popping off with us like this?'

'He's gone to the pub. He won't mind. He probably won't be back till it's dark anyway.'

Pansy's beaming smile diminished a little. She recalled how her ex-husband, Luigi, had disappeared for long periods.

They stopped at the bungalow and May told them that Reg and Arthur had gone to the Lantern and Mark and Holly were down at Magpie Cottage. Not a bit disappointed, they drove on into Weston, parked the car and split up. Bernice and Mavis went shopping and Pansy and Paula decided to walk along the front. They promised to meet for lunch at one thirty.

Paula said, 'I haven't got a penny on me. Can you lend me a fiver, Pansy? I'm so sorry. I could have run back to Linnet and got my purse.'

'My dear girl . . . no problem.' Pansy giggled. 'Tell you what, it's such awful weather, let's go into the first café we come to and have coffee

226

and buns. I can tell you about Luigi and you can tell me about your Dennis.'

'That would be wonderful. I haven't really eaten today. It could be that.'

'Could be what? Aren't you feeling very well?'

'It's a hangover. Dennis knows about hang-overs and he diagnosed a hangover.' They both laughed. Paula said, 'I'm famished actually. One of the reasons I was going to the bungalow was that Mark would have made me a hot drink. He's so kind like that.'

'Come on then, we'll buy one instead.' Pansy led the way into a beachside restaurant. 'This is nice. A view of the sea.' She settled herself, keeping an eye on Paula who made no attempt to unbutton her jacket or straighten her rain-soaked hair. She said, 'Mark is very protective, isn't he? My husband used to leave me on my own a lot of the time and we had a neighbour . . . he was the same. So kind to me that Luigi thought . . . imagined . . .'

Paula said, 'Oh, nothing like that. Honestly. But yes, he is protective. He popped in on Christmas Eve and he sort of . . . told me how to make it homely and pretty . . . and then Ivy gave me some margarine and flour and mince-meat and told me how to make mince pies.' She smiled rather wanly. 'I'm not very domesti-cated.'

'None of us are at first.' Pansy patted

the small, blue-veined hand. 'It's quite a slow process.'

'It can't be for me. Because of the baby.'

'True.' Pansy looked past Paula's head. 'I wonder if it would have worked for us if we'd had a baby.'

'It doesn't always, does it?' Paula too stared at something invisible. 'We didn't get married till I was pregnant. It might have been better if we hadn't really. I think Dennis might feel a bit . . . trapped.'

'Rubbish!' Pansy sat up and tried to sound like Bernice. 'Rubbish – you mustn't even think that! My goodness, he so obviously adores you! When he thought you were going to fall off that blessed sledge, he nearly went crazy.'

'Did he?' Paula sounded pleased. 'Yes, he did. And of course he loves me.' She thought of the two of them that morning and giggled. 'Of course he does.'

Pansy said, 'Here's the waitress. What would you like? Coffee and cakes? Yes, please. And can the cakes be quite substantial? We're very hungry.'

Cass turned down Cree's offer of lunch at the Lantern because she thought it better to avoid Reg for a while, but when Cree had gone and it turned out that Mavis, Pansy and Bernice had also gone, she changed her mind. There was nothing to do at Wren – or Christopher as Cree insisted on calling it – and after she had been for a walk along the shore and discovered that the Edwards family had also disappeared and then so had Paula and Dennis Chiverton, she began to get the unpleasant feeling of being left out of something exciting. Besides, she had to admit that she wanted to see Reg again. She wanted to sit by him and hold his hand and talk about things Cree never wanted to hear: her unsuccessful love affairs, her life in America with her mother and her mother's boyfriends, the impossibility of ever making something special and good just for herself. She wanted him to tell her again that she was beautiful. She didn't want any more talk of 'bargains' or 'deals'. But she wanted to know that someone on this earth thought she was wonderful.

But when she went into the lounge bar of the Lantern, Reg appeared to be having an argument with Dennis Chiverton and, apart from waving to her from his wheelchair, he ignored her almost completely. She went to the bar and ordered herself a gin and tonic. Cree and Arthur Long were sitting by the window and she went over and held out her hand.

'Money,' she said tersely.

Cree rolled his eyes. 'You're getting expensive, Cass. Even for a kept woman.'

It was a joke but he had used it once too often and for two pins she could have hit him across the face. Instead, she leaned down and kissed him very deliberately and saw awareness leap into his blue eyes.

'What the hell was that for?' he asked hoarsely.

'I'm trying to earn my keep,' she said.

'How low can you sink?' He fumbled for change. 'You can tell it's the morning after the night before. All was sweetness and light yesterday. Now Dennis has left Paula on her own, Reg is giving him what for, and you're behaving like a slut just to punish me.'

'Right.'

He put a hand on her arm. 'Are you all right, Cass?'

'Much you care,' she replied and went back to pay for her drink and then to draw up a chair next to Reg.

He was obviously running out of words. 'I know I've said that three times already – though it's not for you to remind me – and I would like to say it another three times and another after that! She's pregnant. There's no food in the cottage and you've left her on her own and buggered off up here! It's not good enough and you're a damned fool.'

Arthur Long's voice came from the other corner. 'Already told him all that, Reg. I thought he was going to turn over a new leaf.'

'I turned it over all right.' Dennis sounded as cocky as ever but he had put down his half-drunk glass of beer. 'You old codgers don't know a thing about it, do you? We love each other. But we don't have to live in each other's pockets to prove it. She's down there making mince pies as happy as a sandboy. And I've come in for a swift pint and to get some food from the shop. Then when I get back it's reunion time. That's how it should be. And that's how it is.'

Reg breathed deeply. 'I hope you're right, my son. After what she said last night, I must admit I've got a few doubts. But if you say so—'

'And I do.'

'—then obviously that's good enough. Now drink up and get down to the bungalow. The shop's closed, but Mark will let you have some stuff. Milk, bread, butter and cheese. There's tins of food too. Don't be shy, just ask.'

Dennis was not shy but the thought of asking Mark was not attractive. He finished his drink and went round the back of the shop in case anyone was there. They weren't and he continued down the drive to the bungalow where Mark and Holly and May were having a scratch lunch at the kitchen table. Holly filled four bags and could have managed a fifth but Dennis stopped her.

'Can't carry another thing. It's really good of you. Let me pay you.'

'Certainly not.' Mark picked up two of the bags. 'Come on, I'll help you down with these. I was wondering how Paula was this morning.'

'She's fine. Had a hangover at first but that soon went.' Dennis could not think of a way of getting rid of Mark so he walked ahead of him. Mark was bumbling on in an indulgent-old-uncle way about Paula having a bit too much to drink last night, and for two pins Dennis could have told him that he'd had enough of all the oldies at the holiday village and he could keep his rotten groceries and his rottener sympathy and stick them where the sun never shone.

He found his key and put it in the door, only to discover that the door was not locked. And that was when he smelt the terrible smell. Something was burning; the place was on fire; he had always known it was not safe, probably never even seen a health and safety inspector. He burst into the living room.

'Paula!' he bawled. 'Paula – Polly – oh my God, Polly, where are you?' Mark was close behind him. 'The bloody place is on fire!' Dennis yelled. 'Where are the fire extinguishers?'

Mark dumped his bags and went through into the kitchen. The sides of the oven were leaking acrid smoke.

'It's all right,' he called back. 'She's put something in the oven and it's burning. Don't panic!'

Dennis pushed in behind him. 'Oh my God, it's the mince pies! She's put them in the oven and forgotten them. That's typical – she's absolutely hopeless.'

Mark switched off the oven then opened the door. The tray of mince pies was a blackened mess. He covered his mouth with a tea towel, and with another towel he picked up the tray and put it in the sink. Hissing steam rose to the ceiling.

'What a shame,' he said regretfully. 'She'll be so disappointed.'

'She'll be more than disappointed when I've finished with her!' Dennis said grimly, not knowing what he meant any more, so worried and relieved, resentful and angry was he. 'Where the hell can she have got to?'

'Well . . . she's not at the pub. She's not at the bungalow—'

'Full marks for stating the obvious!'

'So she's either taking a walk or she's called in at Seagull Cottage. I know Ivy and Ted have taken the children out today so she won't be at Magpie.'

Dennis immediately turned and left the cottage and after a second's hesitation Mark followed him. He was quite certain that Dennis Chiverton was no wife beater, but the way he had spoken just now boded ill for Paula and it would do her no harm to have a third person around.

Magpie was obviously empty and by the time they had gone over to Seagull and looked down into St Margaret's Bay, Dennis's mood had changed.

'Where on earth could she be?' He was glad of Mark's company now. He knew from yesterday, when she had whirled around on that sledge, that if he was on his own he would begin to imagine the worst. He frowned at Mark. 'I know she's scatty but she wouldn't have left those mince pies. She was desperate to make them. The nesting thing, you know.' His frown deepened. 'And the door wasn't locked either. She wouldn't have forgotten to lock the door, would she?'

Mark suddenly remembered Stanley Edwards's threat to turn up here this afternoon. He bit his lip. Surely the man wasn't crazy enough to take Paula hostage? Or was he? He sounded mad and mad people were . . . well, mad.

He said, 'I think we should go back to the bungalow and ring the police.'

Dennis gave a yelp. 'The police? My God, man, you yourself said she'd probably gone for a walk! She could have got as far as Clevedon and be having a cup of tea on the front there.'

'Yes, but . . .' Mark bit his lip again. 'Look, let's go back to the bungalow and ask Holly what she thinks. Another woman . . . you know.'

'Yes.' Dennis grabbed at the straw. 'Yes, you're right. Holly will probably know how Paula's mind works. When she dropped in on Christmas Eve I thought how alike they were.' He started back up the drive. 'I just wish my parents lived closer. Sometimes I don't understand Polly. This morning she suddenly said she wanted my mother!' He knew he was babbling but could not stop. 'She never knew her own mother. Terrible, isn't it? She thought she would be able to put my mother into that slot. But of course we've hardly seen anything of them because of this baby thing. They're rather stiff-necked, you know . . .'

'They'll have to know sooner or later. Perhaps it might be an idea to invite them down for a day.'

'This is supposed to be our honeymoon,' Dennis said. And then suddenly, 'But you can't have a honeymoon on your own.'

Mark nearly told him that he should have thought of that before but Dennis was suddenly looking much older and rather sad. So he said nothing.

Bernice said accusingly, 'You're not eating much, Paula. Is there something wrong with that fish? Tell me if there is and I'll send it back immediately.'

'No. Not at all. I have to admit I am feeling rather strange. I don't think I could put up with many hangovers. I didn't realize they were quite so awful.'

'D'you feel sick, dear?' Mavis enquired.

'I do a bit. In fact, I think I'll have to leave you a moment.' She suited action to word and hurried across the restaurant bent almost double.

'Oh my God,' Bernice moaned. 'Some lunch this is turning out to be.'

Pansy finished her fish and wiped her mouth with her napkin. 'Might as well confess, Bernie,' she said. 'We had coffee and cakes earlier. Not much earlier either. The poor child was starving then.'

Bernice looked relieved. 'That's all right then. Once she gets rid of it, she'll be better. Now what about dessert? Fresh fruit salad all round, I think, don't you?'

'If you say so, Bernie.' The other two spoke in unison.

They ordered and the fruit salad came and still there was no sign of Paula. Twice Pansy said she had better go and see if she was all right and twice Bernice stopped her. When she did so a third time, Bernice stood up.

'I will go,' she said. 'You'll probably give her a bar of chocolate and start the whole thing off again.'

She marched across to the cloakroom. Inside the luxurious powder room lined with mirrors and dressing tables there was no sign of Paula. She went through into the toilet area and called the girl's name.

'Bernice? I'm in here. The door's not locked.'

Bernice pushed at the one closed door distastefully. The view inside was not reassuring. Paula was huddled on the lavatory seat; her underclothes appeared to be very bloodstained.

She looked up from her knees; her face was greenish white, her eyes enormous, her hair sticky with sweat.

She gave a slight smile. 'I think I might have lost our baby,' she said. And started to cry.

Ten

Bernice drove behind the ambulance and Pansy and Mavis sat inside it each holding one of Paula's hands. None of them had had any experience of miscarriages so they were all terrified and trying to reassure themselves.

Bernice muttered to herself the whole way along the front, 'She's going to be all right, she's going to be all right.' Her jaws were clamped so that the words came through menacingly. She forced them apart, consciously relaxing her iron grip on the steering wheel, and said loudly, 'Of course she's going to be all right.' Then her muscles tightened up again as the ambulance circled a mini roundabout and entered the hospital grounds.

Pansy said, 'Don't worry, Paula. It doesn't mean a thing these days. I think they'll keep you in bed for a bit and then you'll be back to normal.'

Mavis, who could not stand the sight of blood, kept her eyes determinedly above waist level and murmured like a Greek chorus, 'Of course, of course.'

Paula said, 'It doesn't matter. Not really. I don't think Dennis was particularly keen. It was just . . .' She sobbed. 'I was beginning to enjoy it. I really was. I didn't have a mother so I wanted to *be* one. And anyway' – she held onto the anchoring hands grimly – 'I'm *frightened*!'

'We're here, darling.' Pansy felt particularly close to Paula after their illicit coffee and cakes. 'Bernice is behind us in the car. We won't leave you.'

Mavis said, 'They probably won't let us stay with her all the time, Pansy. After all, we're not relatives.'

Pansy said, 'I shall tell them I'm her aunt. I'm not leaving her and that's that.'

Paula's eyes filled gratefully and after that outright declaration she could hardly say that she would have preferred someone who knew something about being pregnant. Ivy Edwards perhaps. But Ivy had had so many pregnancies probably they stopped being special after a bit. And then she knew who she wanted.

'Listen, in case I do get whipped away, will you ring this number for me? As soon as you can.' She recited Helen's number in Leeds without difficulty. 'It's my mother-in-law. And father-in-law too. Ask them if they can come down.'

Mavis smiled with relief and released her hand to find pen and paper. 'Of course we will, Paula.

239

How lovely that you get on so well with them.'
She scribbled the number. 'And we'll ring
Reg's bungalow too and leave a message for
Dennis.'

Paula closed her eyes. Dennis would be furious
so she stopped thinking about Dennis and
thought about Mark instead.

Mark and Dennis got back to the bungalow as
Reg's old clock was striking three. It was raining
and overcast and would be dark in an hour.
Dennis, who had been so startled at the idea of
ringing the police, was now all for it. Mark
wanted to wait until the Edwardses got back
from their outing so that he could check with
Ted about how much to tell the authorities.
Holly, just getting up from her afternoon rest,
could not make head or tail of their story for a
while. Dennis had reached the gibbering stage
and Mark did not want to confide his private
fears about the dreadful and probably crazy
Stanley Edwards.

'It's all right.' Holly held up a hand. 'She's
gone for a walk, it's obvious. She'd had enough
of making the mince pies so she slipped out for
a breath of air—'

'Left the door open, pies burning,' Dennis
jabbered.

'She forgot them. She intended to be five
minutes and she's run into someone and gone
into another cottage—'

'No-one about. Pub. Everyone,' Dennis went on.

'OK.' Holly persuaded him into a chair. 'Let's look at the worst scenario. She's slipped and broken her ankle. And she's waiting for us to find her. Which we will do. Quite easily because she won't have gone towards St Margaret's Bay – too many steps – so we know she's on the Clevedon path which is quite muddy in places—'

'Tide coming in.' Dennis tried to stand up. And the phone rang.

Cass said, 'Would you like a walk before it gets dark? I could wheel the chair quite a long way down the coast path. There's a view of the pier if we take the top road.'

Reg said, 'You want to get back to your cottage, put your feet up for five minutes before Cree comes in.'

She glanced across the bar to where Cree and Arthur Long were discussing cricket. 'He won't be home till they throw him out,' she said. 'Come on, let's have a walk. You'll love it. It's raining and rain is so good for you.'

They both laughed and she wrapped him up like a mummy and pulled down his woollen hat so that his nose stuck out like Punch's. She tramped along the coast road pushing the chair until they came to a viewing point and there, suspended in mist, was Clevedon's Victorian pier, delicately ethereal.

'Took 'em a long time to get that put right,' Reg said. 'But they've done a good job, haven't they?'

'Sure have.' She crouched by the chair. 'Can you remember it when they had bathing machines?'

'Not quite. I can remember running trips round the bay in my father's old boat. Just before the war, that was. That's what got me started on the holiday idea.' He laughed. 'I liked being with people who were having a good time. When the war was over I bought my first chalet with my demob money.'

She wiped a drip from her nose with her glove and leaned over to do the same for him. 'Wish you'd got it in sunny Spain,' she said.

He laughed again. 'I'd had enough sun in the desert. I longed – really longed – for a day like this.'

'Yes, maybe then. But surely not now?'

'Why not?' He looked at her. His eyebrows and lashes were beaded with rain. He said, 'I'm happy, Cass. That's what counts. Being happy. And if we were in sunny Spain right now, I couldn't be happier.'

She stared at him and then could not look away. For a long moment they shared something that might have been labelled epiphany. She said shakily, 'You're such a silly old fool, Reg.'

He smiled slightly. 'Yes.'

She said, 'Dammit all, so am I. Happy, I mean.

I didn't recognize it. But that's what it is. Christ, Reg! I'm happy! D'you hear me? I'm happy!' She stood up suddenly and flung her arms in the air and shouted at the top of her voice, 'I'm happy!'

He couldn't stop laughing. All the way down to the footpath he laughed, sometimes hiccoughing loudly as the chair went over a stone. Now and then she would give him an extra shove and scream at the top of her voice, 'Whoopeee! We're happy!'

By the time they had turned right and ploughed past Magpie Cottage it was almost dark, but she still insisted on shunting him through the little grove of trees to the top of St Margaret's Bay.

'I want you to see where we swim, Reg.'

'I know. I've swum there before. With Maude and May. And then the boys.'

'The boys?'

'May's twin boys. Mark came once but they ducked him and he didn't come again until he brought Holly down.'

Cass said, 'You've got so much to tell me, Reg. Don't let's go back to the bungalow. I'll make you some tea at Christopher Wren.'

'Holly will worry. She does worry about me.'

'I know. But she won't realize you're not at the pub. Cree and Arthur could tell her but they're well and truly stuck in.' She whirled the chair round towards the wide windows of the studio cottage. 'We've got the whole evening to ourselves, Reg.' She giggled. 'Practically an illicit weekend!'

It was a pity Dennis had had the lunchtime drinking session as he was still incoherent when he held Paula to him and told her it didn't matter, nothing mattered so long as she was all right.

The doctor wanted her to stay in overnight and she was glad. She felt perfectly calm now and the thought of going back with the weeping Dennis was unsettling. Besides which, he wanted to take her straight back to the flat.

'It's that place, Polly,' he said, kissing her frantically, her eyes, her ears, the tip of her nose. 'It must be damp. And all that ridiculous business on the sledge, and then drinking too much . . . Oh my God, my darling, I can't live without you, you must get better.'

'Of course I shall get better, Dennis,' she said, leaning away from him onto the pillows. 'The doctor says it would have happened whatever I had done. And Mavis says it's nature's way. Bernice says next time it will be quite all right. And the doctor said that too.'

'And what did Pansy contribute to all this advice?' he asked sarcastically.

'She said of course you wouldn't be angry because you love me too much.'

He was all instant contrition. 'Oh darling Poll. Oh my love, my little love. She's right – she couldn't be righter. When I thought . . . Mark will tell you . . . I nearly went crazy.'

'Mark was with you?'

'We looked for you together. He wanted to call the police.'

'The police? Oh, I'm glad it didn't get that far.'

'He and Holly want you to go back to the bungalow so that they can look after you but I said we'd go straight back home.'

'No.' Paula sat up straight in the bed. 'No, I don't want to go back yet. The doctor says I'll be quite all right tomorrow. It was only three months. I want to stay in the bungalow with Mark and Holly and see the New Year in there.'

He made a conscious effort not to argue with her; she would change her mind by the morning. He let Bernice show him where the hospital shop was and went to buy grapes and flowers; Mark took his place by the side of the bed.

He said, 'Paula, I am so sorry. So very sorry.' All the way here he had imagined what it would be like to be expecting a baby and then to lose it. 'I don't know what to say.'

He was the first person to grieve at her loss; everyone else had told her that she would be all right and there would be other babies. Her eyes filled easily.

He took her hand. 'I don't know anything about it, Paula, but one thing I do know is . . . well . . . you've been pregnant. It wasn't a waste of time. You were going to have a baby.' He put his face into her line of vision and tried to smile. 'I'd give such a lot for Holly to be able to say that, Paula.'

She stared at him through her tears; it was exactly what she wanted to hear. It gave the whole thing a dignity that somehow she had lost when she sat on that toilet seat in the hotel. She whispered, 'Oh Mark. Only you could have said that. Thank you. Thank you so much.'

He shook his head modestly and said something about stating facts, then he laughed to cover his embarrassment and so did she.

She said, 'D'you know, when we arrived and Holly popped in to see us, I thought for a wonderful moment that she was pregnant too. It would have been such fun to share everything with her.'

He blinked. 'What made you think that?'

'I can't remember now. Oh, I know. Dennis had some ginger wine and he practically forced her to have a glass and she brought it up.' She sighed. 'It was probably off or something, knowing Dennis. But then you brought me home and told me about decorating the place and making it a home . . .' Her eyes filled again. 'Mark, please don't let's lose touch. After New Year and everything, come and see us now and then. Will you? Say you will!'

'I will,' he said solemnly. And then laughed again.

*   *   *

When Ted and Ivy arrived at the bungalow, tired but happy, looking forward to beans on toast and telling Reg and everyone about climbing Jacob's Ladder to the very top, they found Holly and May alone in front of the fire. Holly told them briefly about what had happened.

'We'll soon rustle up something to eat,' she said to the children. 'Uncle Reg and Uncle Arthur are still at the pub. I don't know whether Mr Evans and his daughter will want to have tea with us. In any case we'll have ours first, shall we?'

'We're starving,' Tom said frankly. And did not seem surprised when Adam echoed him. 'Starving.' And then Gemma said, 'Starving.'

They all trooped into the kitchen and May said, 'We've just phoned the hospital and they're keeping Paula in overnight. Which probably means that Mark and Dennis will hang on. Mark drove Dennis down.'

'What about the window-cleaning ladies?' Ivy asked and then had to explain about Gemma's joke.

'I don't know. Sounds as if they were wonderful. Looking after her, getting her into the emergency room. You wouldn't think they'd be able to cope, would you?'

Ivy spread her hands to the fire. 'Mrs Smythe seems very capable. She would have made sure Paula was well looked after. I'm sorry about the mince pies. She was so keen to make a batch herself.'

'Shows the state of mind she was in.'

'Yes.' Ivy glanced at Ted. 'And we've been having such a happy time.'

May puffed a laugh. 'Well, don't sound so guilty about it! You've had your share of grief by what Holly was telling me.' She too looked at Ted. 'You don't mind me knowing? Holly thought it was important. In case the real Stanley Edwards turns up.'

'I don't mind. I'd prefer you all to know,' Ted said. He was feeling slightly dismayed at the realization that Mark would not be around to go with him to Magpie and check for any signs of Stanley Edwards. But only slightly. While the children were having tea, he would go down himself. Light the fire and do the hot-water bottles. Ivy had already told the boys that they would be sleeping in the other room with Gemma and Giles. Adam had smiled and made a sound which could have been 'Good'. Tom had just grinned. It was difficult to know how much Tom understood; he was only ten after all. Ted found himself grinning just like Tom. It was a dream come true; he and Ivy, a married couple, in a proper double bed. No-one could take that away from them now; not even Stanley Edwards.

Ivy went into the kitchen and cut bread while Tom and Adam laid the table and Gemma carefully folded the remaining decorated serviettes from yesterday. Giles sat in his high chair and banged a wooden spoon on the tray.

Holly said, 'Adam's talking.'

And Ivy nodded, smiling. They both listened hard and, at intervals between Gemma relating how she had lost count of the steps of Jacob's Ladder and Tom's disbelief that she could count at all, Adam inserted single words. 'Steep,' he suggested when she said each step was too high. Then 'eighty-nine' when she was counting.

'Tell Holly how difficult it was for Giles,' Ivy suggested, putting a bottle of sauce in the middle of the table.

Tom snorted. 'He was on Ted's back. Dad's back, I mean.'

Holly laughed obediently and then said that lots of children called their parents by their names these days. Tom snorted again but much louder and said, 'What do you think about that then, Ivy?' Adam laughed so much he almost fell off his chair.

Ivy made a face. 'I don't like my name, that's the trouble. Ivy. It's awful.'

Tom made other suggestions. 'Gladys? Gert? Ermyntrude?' Adam and Gemma clutched each other and Giles's drumming increased.

Ivy looked at Holly and saw the yearning behind the wide smile. Ivy spoke beneath the racket. 'Try not to worry. Do what you have to do and don't think about it. It's the only way.'

Holly nodded and widened her smile until she

felt her face must crack. She had done a pregnancy test earlier. It had been positive.

Reg and Cass lay side by side on the bed. The big window reflected the room darkly; the coal-effect electric fire, the small table drawn up by it containing the remains of their tea, an untidy pile of clothes.

Reg spoke in a low voice. 'I thought I was happy before.' He reached for Cass's hand. 'My dear girl. You are wonderful. Wonderful.'

She clutched the hand. 'Oh Reg . . . I didn't want it to get heavy. But . . . dammit, I think I love you!'

'I don't have to think about it. It's not sudden for me. I have been falling in love with you for the past three or four years. But I never thought . . . this.' He turned his head and looked at her. 'To be honest, Cass, I didn't think I could. You made it possible.'

'Yes.' She too looked at him and they shared another of their moments. She said, 'It was rather clever of me, wasn't it?' She tried to laugh. 'What you don't realize is, Reg Jepson, I haven't done that for years. Literally years. Not since New York in 'ninety-four.'

He too tried to laugh. 'It's like riding a bicycle,' he said.

'Oh Reg.' They both stopped laughing and she leaned over and kissed him. 'How can this be happening? We're not in the least suited.

And you've got this new hip and should be resting—'

'What am I doing now?'

'And I'm a hopeless case, unwanted daughter of a man who won't really try to do any decent work any more.' She propped herself on an elbow and looked down into the still handsome face. 'I can't leave him, Reg. You know that, don't you? He's absolutely helpless. Since his last mistress went and he sent for me, he's got worse.'

'I know.' He smiled. 'I refuse to think past the new millennium. I refuse to think past this evening.' He put out his hand and ran his fingers over her shoulder and down her arm. 'You remind me of those paintings of women in Italian galleries. You are so abundant, so generous—'

'You mean overweight and promiscuous.'

'Don't joke, Cass. You're being rude about the woman I love and I can't bear it.' He cupped her face and sighed deeply. 'D'you know what I hate about this?'

She was dismayed. 'Is there anything you hate? I thought you said—'

'It's that I've now got to ask you to help me get dressed.'

'You didn't mind asking me to help you get undressed!' She swung her legs off the bed and reached towards the pile of clothes. 'Why should you hate that so much?'

'It makes me dependent. And I want to look after you for a change.'

She helped him expertly. 'This is just another way of making love,' she said, buttoning his shirt. 'Think of it that way and it makes it all right.'

'All right.' He leaned forward and picked up her bra. 'Now let me help you.'

She laughed. It took much longer than if she had done it herself, but she knew that probably this evening was all they would have and she did not try to take over from him. Even so, she was glad when they were both fully clothed. She could imagine what Cree would have said if he had stumbled in earlier.

She turned on her knees and kissed Reg lingeringly.

'Let's have another cup of tea and then I'll take you home,' she whispered.

'That sounded like a last goodbye,' he whispered back.

Ted did exactly as he had planned. He checked the cottage thoroughly, even looking under the beds and in the cupboards; he laid and lit the fire and placed logs carefully so that by the time the family arrived it would be a glowing mass; he boiled the kettle several times and filled four hot-water bottles, putting them in both bunks and both camp beds. Tom could sleep on the top bunk and keep an eye on Giles

252

from there; Adam could have one of the camp beds and watch from below. They were good boys. Ted felt a glow when Tom called him Dad. Not that he minded being called Ted either. It showed that Tom accepted him in all kinds of ways. It might be more difficult for Tom and Adam to accept him as their mother's new husband but Ted had noticed today that Ivy had told them one or two stories about the old days when she and Ted had gone out together. They had accepted those all right.

He grinned as he looked in on what was now their room. Some time this morning before Holly brought the children home, Ivy had managed to lay out her toilet things on the dressing table, flanked on either side by a slender vase containing some of the berried twigs they had picked. Her nightdress was neatly folded on her pillow next to his pyjamas. He thought of the hundreds and thousands and probably millions of couples who took that sort of thing for granted. He never would. It would always be special and an honour for him to share a bedroom with Ivy. He went into the room and carefully turned down both sides of the bed. Then he drew the curtains.

It was very dark outside; still raining, clouds obscuring moon and stars. Not the sort of night for Stanley Edwards to lurk about and try to terrify his wife and children into submission. Ted had gloried in the rain all day for that very reason. Nevertheless, as he went round pulling all the curtains he looked out just in case. And when he finally locked up to go back to the bungalow and pick up Ivy and the children, he took a little walk along the shingled beach, sniffing for the scent of a fire, studying the faint outline of the shore for any sign of a tent. There was nothing. As he said to Ivy when they walked back all together, 'I've really enjoyed the rain today. But now . . . it's not a night to be out and about, is it?'

She knew what he meant all right but it was as if she didn't care any more. She walked slightly behind him so that she could keep an eye on Giles in his canvas seat and just kept laughing at Gemma and Tom who were still supplying her with alternative forenames.

'Wilhelmina,' Tom said.

'Window cleaner!' shrieked Gemma.

And suddenly Adam said contentedly, 'Mum.'

In twos and threes everyone arrived back at the bungalow to 'report in', as Bernice put it. The three 'girls' were unusually quiet. They told their tale to Reg and Cass who were suitably shocked and concerned, then to Cree and Arthur who were less so because they were well insulated with most of the food and drink the Lantern could offer, and then they got back into their car and went home for another early night. It was eight o'clock before Dennis and Mark drove up. Mark showed Dennis the guest room and supplied him with some pyjamas. Dennis had a bath and went straight to bed. He hadn't eaten since the brittle toast of that morning. He felt ill and strangely frightened. He clutched his pillow and thought of Paula and cried himself to sleep. Mark then helped Reg into bed and noted that he was very quiet.

'Feeling a bit under the weather, Nunc?' he enquired.

'I feel better than I've felt for years, Mark.'

'Good. Good.' Mark wondered how much the old man had had to drink. 'Are you hungry, Nunc? I could bring you in a sandwich.'

'I've not long had tea and toast, thanks, old man.'

'Good.' Mark said goodnight and closed the door. He had not realized the Ship's Lantern did teas. Reg was so sensible; he wasn't supposed to drink while he was on medication, and obviously he hadn't. Mark went into the kitchen and confided these conclusions to Holly. She smiled and nodded.

'He's pretty good, isn't he? And he's so enjoyed it. When does he have to go back into hospital?'

'Not until after the New Year. They want to keep that ward closed if possible.' He slipped his arms around her waist and kissed the back of her neck. 'Is that all right?'

'Oh yes.' She turned and gave him a full-blown

kiss on the mouth. They held each other for a while.

'What a day. Are you all right, my love?' she whispered.

'I'm absolutely all right. It's awful for Paula and Dennis, particularly Paula, but somehow it seems to make what we've got even more precious.'

'I know.' She smiled at him. 'That's how I feel – often and often.'

'It's worked, hasn't it? Coming here. Doing an Uncle Reg-type Christmas.'

'Oh, it has.' And she thought that if it hadn't been for Hugo Venables she would not have come. She and Mark might even have split up. 'Don't go.' She hugged him to her. 'Just hold me for a little longer.'

He held her.

The staff at the hospital had asked Dennis to leave at eight o'clock, but they could not turn away Helen and Walter Chiverton who had driven all the way from Leeds to see their daughter-in-law. The single ward was darkened but Paula was still propped on pillows looking at her hands, quiet at last and thinking of what had happened.

Helen stood at the bottom of the bed. She had taken Mavis's call at three o'clock that afternoon and Mavis had pulled no punches.

'We were having lunch . . . a very nice hotel.

She seemed fine, though she'd said several times she felt odd. Anyway, I'm so sorry, Mrs Chiverton . . . it's a miscarriage. You must have been so looking forward to your first grandchild and I hate to be the one to tell you. She insisted. She wanted you to know even before she phoned Dennis. And she would love to see you. It's Boxing Day and a long long drive, but if you could possibly . . . ?'

Helen had said, 'Ah. We did wonder.' She looked across the room at Walter. They'd had people in for drinks and they were both looking forward to a peaceful afternoon by the fire. She said, 'We'll leave within the hour and go straight to the hospital.'

And that's what they had done. Walter looked a bit haggard but Helen was as immaculate as ever, her abundant, carefully tinted hair in a tidy French pleat, her camel-hair coat and silk scarf casually impeccable. Paula looked at her and started to cry.

'I'm sorry . . . I'm so sorry,' she sobbed. 'I wanted to tell you but we thought – you might be hurt. Or offended. And now I want you to know. Because it was a baby . . . it was a *baby*, Helen! And I can't ever forget that we had a baby, even if – if – I couldn't do it properly. I was a mother and Dennis was a father and you were a grandmother and Walter was – was—'

She could say no more because she was enfolded in Helen's sweet-smelling coat. She breathed in the outside air mixed with eau de Cologne and clear soap.

Helen was whispering in her ear. She listened.

'Darling, don't put it all in the past. You *are* a mother and Dennis *is* a father and Grandad and me . . . we're' – she breathed a laugh – 'we're Grandad and Grandma! No-one can take that away, can they?' When Paula gripped her hand, she kissed the top of her head. 'Listen, Paula. You've done nothing wrong. It's happened, that's all. There's got to be a reason. Be patient and you'll understand later. Or maybe not.' She held the girl to her. 'Sometimes, darling, we never do understand. Perhaps that's where it's necessary to operate on blind faith. What do you think?'

'Yes. Oh yes.' It was as if Helen was taking all the pain away, all the guilt of the past few months, all the foolish deceit. Paula tucked her head inside the camel coat and discovered a cashmere sweater that felt like silk against her cheek. She said, 'I mustn't muck up your clothes, Helen. You look so good. I am so pleased to see you.' She noticed Walter on the other side of the bed. 'You too, Walter. I've spoiled your Christmas yet here you are consoling me . . .'

He smiled and covered one of her hands with his. 'Where's Dennis – why isn't he with you?'

'He was. They threw him out at eight o'clock. He's going to sleep at the Jepsons' bungalow tonight. Mark will look after him.'

Walter sat on the edge of the bed. 'Tell us about the Jepsons and Mark. And then we must leave you in peace and we'll come back tomorrow.'

'Oh, how lovely.' They settled her on the pillows again and she lay back and looked at them both. In a minute she would tell them about everyone at the holiday village. She would describe the mud-sledging and the Christmas dinner and how she had made mince pies according to Ivy Edwards's instructions.

She sat bolt upright in the bed.

'Helen. Walter. I didn't switch off the oven! The mince pies will be burned to a crisp!'

Everyone slept well that night. Dennis imagined he would weep all night for Paula and their lost baby, but after that first outburst he slept like the dead. Holly and Mark held each other all night long; Holly did not wake feeling sick and when the first grey light showed around the edges of the curtain she stayed where she was, smiling into the half light, feeling a strange sense of optimism which was completely unfounded. Reg dropped off with a smile on his face, as well he might, and May and Arthur slept what Arthur called the sleep of the righteous – as well they might too. The 'girls' were exhausted, their minds in a turmoil. They creamed their faces, did things with their hair and then fell into their separate beds. Cree had drunk too much and had not been able to take in all that had happened to everyone else. He said to Cass, 'Somehow . . . all this . . . is making me frightened.' And she said, 'Come on. Nothing awful is going to happen. You haven't eaten anything. Have some toast and I'll massage your feet and then you'll sleep really well.' Cass was always right. She slept too, one hand reassuringly on Cree's shoulder, her dreams all of another man who was just as unsuitable and just as old.

Ted Harris had imagined he would wake at every little sound throughout that night, but he held Ivy in his arms, waited for her to sleep and then joined her. When the light filtered through into their bedroom, he slipped out to make her some tea and peered through the curtains. The sun broke through a cloud and flashed on the windows of Linnet Cottage, which he knew was empty. Just for a moment it looked as if someone had switched on a light in the kitchen over there. He shook his head, impatient with himself, and filled the kettle.

Eleven

The next three days passed peacefully enough, and after the first shock of seeing his parents Dennis was forced to admit they weren't the old codgers he had always supposed. He couldn't get over the fact that Paula had always known it.

'All very well you sending for them like that,' he said to her the next day when she had arrived back at the bungalow in their BMW. 'What if they'd called you a hussy? Or let you see that you had tricked me into marriage!' It was one of his typically jocular remarks but even as he said it he realized that it was not appropriate.

He said quickly, 'Polly. Darling. I'm sorry. Not just for saying that stupid thing just then, but for being a selfish pig.' He took her in his arms. 'Listen, honeybunny, I'm going to turn over a new leaf. D'you hear me? I'm not going up to the pub any more. We're going to stay together and do what you want to do for a change.' They had taken over the guest room in the bungalow

and he laid her tenderly on one of the twin beds
and looked doubtful. 'What would you like to do,
sweetheart? I mean, what can you do – did the
doctor give you any advice?'

'I can do what I can do,' she said, stretching
luxuriously, for the first time in her life
delighted to have a bed to herself. 'And I don't
want to tie you to my apron strings, Chiv.
You must go up to the Lantern with the others
when they go. And take Dad. He would like
that. Mother will be here with me. And Holly.
And May.' She smiled beatifically. 'Oh, it will be
lovely, Chiv. The doctor says I'll have mood
swings and be really unhappy sometimes, but not
to worry because then I'll be all right again.' She
let him take her hand and hold it to his face. 'I
did feel so unhappy about our baby, Chiv. But
now I don't . . . not any more. Mother talked to
me and I felt all right.' She smiled. 'In fact,
darling, I feel rather guilty for being pampered
like this. And actually enjoying it.'

'Oh, Polly.' He kissed her small hand. 'You
haven't had much pampering since we got
married, have you?'

She stroked his hair with her spare hand
and said roguishly, 'I've had plenty of loving
though!'

He caught that hand too and cupped them
both around his face. 'I could love you now, my
darling. If it's permitted.'

She said rather too quickly, 'No. Not for a

while. I just want to . . . you know . . . be. Just *be*. Can you understand that, Chiv?'

'I can understand anything. Just to have you here . . . it's wonderful. Polly, twice I've thought I might lose you. And I've been so frightened.'

'Poor baby.' She spoke indulgently and when he continued to kiss her hands and then work his way to the inside of her elbows and beyond, she closed her eyes. 'Chiv, I'm so tired. Would you mind if I just went to sleep for an hour or two?'

'Oh Polly!' He was instantly contrite. 'Of course I wouldn't mind. I'll go and collect the rest of our stuff from Linnet Cottage, shall I?'

'That would be nice.' She was almost asleep and smiling. But half an hour later, when Helen came in with tea, she was sitting up reading a Harry Potter book left on the bedside table by Tom the night before.

The 'girls' came over on two of those three evenings and taught Paula to play bridge. On Wednesday evening, the family from Magpie came for tea as well and organized a riotous game which entailed a lot of cards being slapped onto the table to the cry of 'Donkey!' Pansy sat one side of Reg and Cass the other. The three of them seemed to take it in turns to be the Donkey; Bernice accused them of not concentrating. Cree said, 'For heaven's sake,

Bernice! It's a game.' And Bernice looked him in the eye and said, 'Oh I know that, Cree. I'm glad you do too.' And Mavis laughed and said, 'At last! I knew you'd understand eventually, Bernie darling. A game – a glorious game. That's what life should be!' And then was thoroughly taken aback when Cree congratulated her, held her to him and kissed her on the mouth. Afterwards she said to Pansy, 'I don't know whether I liked it, Pansy dear. You know . . . a proper kiss. St John was always so fastidious and I've never . . . well, not like that anyway.'

Pansy, who would always love her Luigi, nodded wisely. 'It's like I said before, Mavis. I'm very, very fond of Reg and I admire him a great deal, but I couldn't . . . go all the way.'

Mavis flung up her hands. 'Oh no!' she agreed.

They both nodded and Pansy said hesitantly, 'Actually, Mavis, I'd like to talk to you some time. About Reg. Not in front of Bernice.'

Mavis opened her eyes wide and then nodded again. 'All right, dear. I understand.'

Ted and Ivy were deeply and idyllically in love. Everything they did and said seemed to have special significance for them. There had been no more phone calls or messages of any kind from Stanley and they had made the last four days a completely magical honeymoon. On Monday night, after spending nearly all day with the sledge on the outgoing tide, Ted had mentioned the wasted years behind them and Ivy had shaken her head.

'Nothing is ever wasted, Ted. We would never have been so much in love if we hadn't both been locked into loveless marriages.'

'Yes, but when we used to go to the pictures and sit in the back row—'

'That was attraction . . . friendship . . . almost kinship. This – now – is something so special, Ted.'

'It would have grown into this.' He kissed her. 'What I'm trying to say, Ivy love, is that we mustn't waste any more. However difficult and painful it is, we've got to fight to stay together with our children.'

'Oh yes . . . oh yes.' She held him, revelling in his wide shoulders and chest, marvelling at his sheer solidity. She said joyously, 'You're alive and you're here! And so am I!'

'So are you, oh so are you!' His hold was tender and very careful. She seemed to him terrifyingly fragile. She was no smaller than Paula Chiverton but she had none of the younger girl's strength. When she was asleep, he whispered into the dark, 'Keep her safe. Please keep her safe.' Every morning when he got the tea he looked through the dark kitchen window towards Linnet Cottage, but there was never any light there. He told himself that Stanley had decided to drop the whole thing and go back to Wales.

Reg wanted to go into Bristol on Thursday to see his solicitor and he was asking Pansy whether she would like to come and have a look round the shops.

'We'll take a taxi,' he said. 'I won't be long in Queen Square. Then we can take another taxi through to Broadmead and shop to your heart's content.'

Cass frowned slightly. 'Is that a good idea, Reg? It sounds very tiring. Let me come with you and I can drive you, wheel you into the solicitor's and then we can come straight back.'

Reg smiled. 'I thought Pansy could do with a change. We haven't seen much of each other this holiday.' He wriggled his eyebrows meaningfully at Cass but she did not pick up the message and subsided into her chair clutching her cards to her. Reg turned back to Pansy. 'I won't keep you long in the solicitor's. Need a witness, that's all.' He dropped his voice on the last words and Cass leaned further away.

Holly kept her eyes on her cards. There was time to make an appointment with Dr Lanercost if she phoned early tomorrow. She glanced up at Ivy and said, 'Actually, I wouldn't mind going into town with you, Reg. If that would be all right.'

Mark looked up from his cards, surprised. 'You need some shopping? We did that order for the New Year stuff.' He glanced around the table. 'We thought perhaps a buffet until eleven? Then we can have fireworks on the beach.'

Mavis clutched her cards ecstatically. 'What fun! Paula will be well enough to come down by then.'

Paula smiled. The doctor had been right: she was either very content or strangely unhappy and disconnected in some way. Helen and Walter could usually help, but they were going home tomorrow for their own millennium party. She was already feeling very disconnected indeed.

Holly said, 'I would like a few more fireworks. For the children. Sparklers and so on.'

Mark smiled. 'Fine. I'll drive you. That way I can help Nunc in and out of the wheelchair.'

Holly looked over at Ivy for help; Ivy made an enormous moue of disappointment. 'Oh Mark! You promised the boys you would take them fishing tomorrow!'

Holly followed up swiftly. 'Darling, we can manage. I'll drive. Please don't worry.' She glanced at Reg. 'You won't be long, Reg?'

'I've made an appointment for eleven. Perhaps half an hour? Old Protheroe is a bit of a windbag but I wouldn't think even he could stretch it much more than that.'

Mark smiled. 'You'll be longer than that getting the blessed fireworks!' But he raised no objections to taking the boys out.

Walter put his cards surreptitiously on the

table and nudged Tom who nudged Adam who nudged Gemma. Eventually Cass was left as the donkey. She managed a laugh as they all screamed at her, but she bowed out of the next game and went to help Holly and Ivy make cocoa and cut sandwiches. She had a feeling that she wasn't really wanted in the kitchen either, so she wandered through the hall door and stood under the porch looking across the roofs of Seagull and Wren towards the lights of Wales which seemed to waver. She blinked hard and the lights steadied so she knew she was crying and was furious with herself. 'Damn you, Reg Jepson!' she muttered. 'You're no better than all the others. But I'll lay odds that Pansy Pansetti won't take you to bed like I did!'

From the other room came a burst of laughter and then Cree's unmistakable boom. 'You're a cheat, Reg!'

She whispered, 'Yes. That's what you are, Reg.' She thought of spending the rest of her life with Cree and decided that it wouldn't be so bad after all. They had crazy good times like swimming in midwinter and going for pub crawls throughout Birmingham eating the peanuts and pork scratchings left on bars, talking to anyone and everyone. The good times far outweighed the bad ones, surely? So why on earth was she still crying? She turned to go to the bathroom and wash her face. From the direction of Magpie Cottage she saw a light. She blinked again and it was gone. 'Damn fool,' she muttered. 'Pull yourself together and stop whingeing like a child!'

In the kitchen Ivy said quietly, 'I can't tell you what to do, Holly. All I know is that I've lived all my life with secrets. And now there are no more secrets. And it's wonderful.'

Holly stacked cheese sandwiches on a plate and piled packets of crisps into a bread basket. She too spoke almost in a whisper. 'I can't tell him, Ivy. I just can't. I feel terrible about it. Maybe afterwards . . . it won't seem such an awful thing to do. I might be able to forget that I was ever pregnant.'

'You did the test?' Ivy knew it already. She sighed. 'I don't think it will be quite as straightforward as you think. Don't they counsel you or something?'

'My doctor is pretty good. He saw me through the IVF treatment. I think he'll just arrange an appointment at the clinic and . . . oh God.'

Ivy said quickly, 'Try not to dwell on it.' She picked up a tray. 'Why is Reg seeing his solicitor, I wonder? Is he feeling rotten?'

Holly opened the door for her and they both saw Cass heading for the bathroom. 'I think he's making a good recovery actually. That's one thing – he's so enjoyed this whole Christmas. That is great. Really great.' She followed Ivy with a tray of drinks. 'He's probably writing a codicil to make sure we go on running the village!' She half smiled. 'D'you know, at one time that would have infuriated me. Now . . . things change so much, Ivy.'

Ivy nodded. 'Don't they just.'

That night Adam found a note beneath his duvet. He knew immediately who it was from and just for a moment he thought of showing it to Tom. But then he didn't. He took it into the bathroom and, as if the sound would cover his terror, he flushed the lavatory before he read it. It was printed. It said, 'You were always my favourite. I can make you talk again. From your devoted father.' Adam waited until the cistern refilled and then pulled the flush again and watched the note whirl down the lavatory pan. Then he cleaned his teeth. When everyone was asleep he crept into the kitchen and took the bread knife from the drawer and put it under his pillow.

It was awful saying goodbye to Helen and Walter. Paula and Dennis were going to stay with them at Easter; it was all arranged. Even so, Easter seemed a long way away and Paula wondered how on earth she was going to manage in the Bristol flat until then. Helen felt it too. 'You are the daughter we never had,' she said, hugging Paula to her. 'Please take care of yourself. Promise.'

'I promise.' But Paula broke down at the last. 'You are the mother I never had . . .'

Walter said bracingly, 'Come on, you're making each other worse. Walk with us to the car and then go into the Lantern and have a pre-lunch drink on us. How does that sound?'

'Brilliant!' Dennis said. 'Come on, Polly.'

But Paula could not bear the thought of seeing Cree and Cass sparring with each other. May and Arthur too. She said, 'I'll stay here. Make some lunch for when you get back. I don't want to watch the car drive off.'

She kissed Helen and turned away immediately into the kitchen. Helen called, 'See you at Easter!' and she called back, 'Oh lovely!' And that was that.

She was leaning over the sink when Mark came in. He started to tell her that the boys had not wanted to come fishing after all and then realized that the sounds she was making were nothing to do with a coughing fit. He was his usual sympathetic self. She listened to him telling her about the chemical reactions happening in her body and thought how lucky Holly was. Dennis would have been kissing her frantically by now, licking her tears, probably edging her towards the bedroom. Mark pulled a sheet off the paper towel and held it towards her.

'Come on, Paula. By the time you go up to Leeds at Easter, you'll be pregnant again and

271

you and Helen can go shopping for baby clothes. You've got so much to look forward to. So much . . .' His voice trailed off because she turned from the sink and almost threw herself at him. He was forced to hold her otherwise she would have fallen down, but he was not forced to rest his head on top of her curly mop as if she were a child. 'What's all this about?' he asked rhetorically. 'Come on now. Nothing is as bad as this, surely?'

And then she started to babble and once started she could not seem to stop herself.

'I don't think I love Dennis any more. He doesn't know how to be – be – be—' she hiccoughed and then said, '*tender*! That's what it is . . . he doesn't know how to be tender.' She hiccoughed again and clung to his shirt-front. 'I think I love you, Mark. Yes, I do. I love you quite desperately. I'm jealous because Holly is expecting and I'm not. But I don't want to have Dennis's baby – not again. I want yours. Oh Mark, I'm so sorry, but I do love you so. Kiss me. Just hold me for a while and kiss me. That will be enough, I promise. I won't be a nuisance. Just kiss me, Mark . . .' She stopped clutching his shirt and slid her hands up his chest to his head. He was still dealing with her outburst, trying to tell her that Holly and he could not have children, trying to tell her that she would love Dennis again for his down-to-earth humour. When her mouth met his he felt a sense of shocked outrage because he had kissed few women and no-one save Holly for twelve years. And then, even as he was drawing away from her, something happened; the shock remained, the outrage disappeared. She was so fervent, it was as if with the sheer passion of that one kiss she strove to make herself part of him. This was nothing like the slow and appreciative love-making he shared with Holly; this was crazy, futile, all-consuming. She held his ears; she almost pulled them off; her mouth moved from his and then returned avidly; her hands scraped upwards to his hair and she hung onto it. It was agonizing; like a series of electric shocks. When she pulled away and looked at him he bent again and kissed her of his own accord and they reeled against the kitchen table and then she was lying on it and he was kissing her throat and then her eyes and she was making desperate little noises and kissing him back and biting his ear . . . and then the front door banged.

They leaped apart, one each side of the kitchen table. Someone went into the lounge and then across the hall and into the guest room. Mark and Paula were panting wildly; Mark forced himself upright and pulled at his shirt then ran his hands through his hair. Paula closed her eyes and controlled her breathing. The kitchen door swung open and Dennis came in.

'Oh there you are. I couldn't go into that pub,

Poll. Not without you. Came straight back.' He stopped speaking and looked at Mark. 'Anything wrong? You both look a bit worried.'

Mark shook his head, unable to speak. Paula gave a small laugh. 'Oh look, we've upset all that salt. Isn't that supposed to be unlucky?'

A salt cellar lay on its side on the table; there was salt everywhere. Dennis took a pinch of salt and threw it over his left shoulder.

'There. Now don't say I never take any notice of you! Pure superstition but if it makes you feel better . . .' He took another pinch and another and started to sing some ditty about doing anything for true love. Mark stared at him, not believing that he didn't sense the tension in the room. Then, incredibly, Paula started to laugh. She staggered over to Dennis and put her hands on his shoulders and they went into a semblance of dancing.

'You're mad,' she told him, interrupting his trilling. 'Mark has just told me I love you for your down-to-earth humour.' She stopped the singing with a kiss and then flung back her head. 'He's right. I do love you for being a clown! Take me – take me now!' She was joking of course. Mark told himself that even as Dennis, roaring like a mad bull, picked her up bodily and carried her through into the guest room. But joking or not, it was obvious what was happening on one of the single beds and he stood outside and felt a moment of terrible, pure jealousy and anger. He wanted to hammer on the door and say it was too soon and it might harm her and didn't either of them have a bit of sense. But Mark was almost another generation and he did none of those things. Instead he went back to the kitchen and made some tea and felt un-utterably miserable and guilty.

Reg was tired. He was so tired he had to make a conscious effort to speak, opening his mouth first of all, shaping the words with tongue, lips and teeth, forcing sound from throat to the outside world. He was so thankful to see Mark he would not let go of his hand, even when Mark had gently helped him under the duvet and adjusted the pillows.

'Girls . . . so good,' he panted. 'Not strong enough.'

'You've overdone it, Nunc. Would you like some tea and a painkiller?'

Reg moved his head in negation. 'Must rest.' But he did not release his nephew. After a period of crouching over the bed, Mark sat on Maude's side and let his thoughts drift inevitably back to Paula and that scene in the kitchen when he had so nearly . . . He squeezed his eyes shut. If Dennis had not come back then, what would have happened? He loved *Holly*. He *loved* Holly.

Reg made a sound and Mark leaned closer.

'Need to talk to you. Explain.'

'Tomorrow, Nunc. Not now.'

'Now. Want you to do something.' Reg summoned the ghost of a grin. 'Sacred trust really. Not sure about sacred. Secret. Secret trust. You will, won't you, Mark? You've always been . . . good. You are a good man, Mark.' His voice grew stronger and he opened his eyes.

'Of course, Nunc. Whatever.' Mark couldn't care less. He wondered if he would ever be able to forget Paula Chiverton.

Reg took a long and trembling breath then slowly and clearly he said, 'The twins . . . May's twins. I am their father. I can't leave them anything officially. Arthur would know – I think he suspects now but he would know for sure. So you must see to them, Mark.' He tried for a grin again and said, 'Your inheritance, my boy. You never got on with them, did you? Now you're stuck with them. Sorry, old man. Sorry.'

Mark wondered why he wasn't stunned by this piece of news. Reg and May Long. Maybe on the kitchen table. Oh God.

He said, 'Don't be sorry. It's – it's – well, a sort of privilege, Nunc. Have you got anything in mind?'

'Old Protheroe sorted it out and wrote it down. Just for your eyes, Mark.' He sighed. 'I said you were a good man. Thanks.'

'Listen, you're really bushed. Let me get you a brandy.'

'Yes. Maybe . . . in a minute. Something else.

I've left a tidy sum for Cass Evans. I want her to be independent. Be able to choose what she does. Probably not until Cree pops his clogs. But then . . . She's a wonderful woman, Mark. You won't mind?'

'Good God, Nunc. We're talking about your money.'

'Yes, but it's yours too. You've probably been banking on it all these years.'

Mark was genuinely surprised. 'We've never talked about it – never considered it.'

Reg tried another smile. 'I think poor Holly was scared to death I might insist on you running the village.'

'At one time. Perhaps.' Mark too grinned. 'She's changed, Nunc. She's happy here.'

'Dear girl. She's beautiful. She reminds me of Maude.'

Mark thought that anyone less like Maude would be hard to find but he said nothing.

Reg went on slowly. 'Of course, the village is yours. But there's no conditions. If you want to sell it for building, you might well find yourself a millionaire. It's up to you, the two of you. I've had my fun here. No regrets whatsoever.'

Now Mark was stunned. He stared at the old man and wondered how on earth he had accumulated such wealth. Yet, if he and Holly sat down and worked it out, they would have realized. The village was sited on prime building land with services already laid on.

Mark found his voice at last. 'Nunc, shall we leave all this till tomorrow? I doubt whether I've got a job to go back to – Holly certainly hasn't. We'll stay here and keep going as long as we possibly can. How does that sound?'

Reg's eyes were closed again but the smile was definitely in place. 'Like having a cake and eating it,' he murmured. 'I was always good at that.'

Tom was furious with Adam for backing out of the fishing trip. He sulked around the kitchen while the others made pastry at the table, and when his mother asked him to help Ted bring in some wood for the fire he went into his room and slammed the door. Adam followed him contritely.

'I don't get it!' Tom said from the top bunk, looking down on his younger brother with dislike. 'Hanging onto me like a baby! I could have gone by myself, but oh no, Adam acts all daft and doesn't want to be left!' He waited while Adam scuffed about below him then he said, 'Very handy not being able to say a word, isn't it, little bro? Everyone thinks you're so sweet, kissing Gemma, looking after her . . . Makes me want to puke!'

Adam looked up with new eyes and said very clearly, 'Jealous!'

Tom stared down in disbelief then he swung himself off the bunk. 'You – you little fraud! I'm not jealous! And you're not' – he struggled with his desire to shock – 'a dumb stupid moron!'

Adam stood his ground but it was as if the blood in his face drained away; it was not just white, it was translucent. He stared at Tom and he was silent again.

Tom said, 'I didn't mean it . . . sorry. Sorry, Adam. I don't know why I said that.' He shook his head. 'Say something – anything – like you've been doing this week . . . Please say something.' Adam was not just silent, he appeared turned to stone. Tom wanted to take him by the shoulders and shake life into him. He said, 'Listen, maybe I'm jealous. Oh God, maybe I'm like our father, jealous all the time, wanting to hurt you into talking.' He took a step away from his brother. 'I always thought . . . I would make you talk. But the words you've been saying have been for Ted and Gemma and Giles. Except that one. "Jealous".' He turned and got back onto the bunk. 'Leave me alone for a bit, Adam. Sorry, but I have to be by myself.'

Adam blinked and seemed to relax a little; colour came back into his face. He looked at Tom's humped back, opened his mouth and forced out a word. 'Cold.'

'It's OK.' Tom spoke gently as if to Gemma. 'I'm warm enough. Go back into the kitchen.'

Adam looked around the bedroom. Gemma's new teddy was propped on her pillow next to a sketchbook and crayons. He picked up the sketchbook and started to write. And then he went into the kitchen.

At any other time Mark would have been able to tell Holly some of what Reg had told him, but not that afternoon. Holly herself was very quiet; she made tea for all of them and then stayed in the kitchen preparing the evening meal. Cree Evans called for Arthur, and Mark decided to join them for a drink at the Lantern. May sat at the kitchen table making a list for the next day's buffet. Reg slept peacefully and there was no sign of Dennis and Paula. Holly made sounds of assent as May read out her list but did not add any suggestions.

May eventually looked up. 'Is something wrong, Holly? I thought you'd want to get some sausages for the children. Or something.'

Holly looked up from a bowl of potatoes. 'I wasn't thinking properly. Yes, sausages would be nice. I've noticed Tom likes sausages.'

'Anything else?' May wrote 'sausages' then crossed it out and replaced it with 'chipolatas'; she thought it looked better.

'No, I don't think so.'

'You're not with us tonight, my dear. Is something wrong?'

'Nothing at all. I was just remembering what you told me last week about keeping secrets. D'you remember?'

'I'm not likely to forget. And d'you know, it's

working out for me, Holly. I look at Cree now and all his shenanigans with the window-cleaning ladies, and I wonder what on earth I got into such a tizz about. And I don't feel guilty about Reg either because I was reading in the paper about surrogate parenting and I thought . . . well, what was our little arrangement if it wasn't just that?'

Holly smiled at last. 'Too true, May. And I reckon that's exactly how Arthur would see it too.'

May said swiftly, 'Except that he'll never know. You're not suggesting I should tell him, are you, Holly? Because I won't. I couldn't risk that. Him and me . . . we're a pair. And he loves his boys. And they are his boys. Nothing must come between us.'

'Of course I wouldn't suggest that. Everyone is different. Look at Ivy . . . you can't imagine Ivy keeping anything from Ted, can you? And that works fine because Ted is so . . . under-standing.'

'Well, so is Arthur. But it's too late now, Holly. If I'd told him right at the beginning . . . but I didn't. And for all these long years he has had two sons. I can't do anything to spoil that, can I?'

'No. Certainly not.' Holly cut a potato in half and then stared at her thumb where a bead of blood showed bright red. 'But it proves Ivy is right. Everything out in the open, as it happens – that's the best way.'

May sighed and went to the fridge to begin checking on the list. 'I don't know, I'm sure. Life is so complicated, Holly. Even simple, ordinary lives like ours are never straightforward. I suppose everyone has to do what they think is right at the time.' She grinned over her shoulder. 'That's my excuse and I'm sticking to it!'

Holly mustered another smile and nodded. She had come to her decision.

She waited until after dinner and then suggested an early night on the grounds that tomorrow would be so hectic. She was surprised when Mark said he thought he would go for a walk by the sea.

'Don't let me keep you up, Holly.' His smile was infinitely gentle. 'I feel a bit . . . confused.'

'How much did you have up at the Lantern?' she asked without thinking.

He flushed, almost annoyed. 'Not enough to be fuddled, I do assure you.'

It was so unlike him; she was immediately apprehensive. Could he possibly have guessed something? If so then the sooner she told him, the better. Anyway, she had to tell him. There was no way round it.

'Carry on then,' she said as equably as she could. 'I might join you later.'

He left without a backward glance and she wondered if he had even heard her. She got her coat and followed only a few yards behind him, and when he reached the flat beach in front of

Magpie she caught up with him and put her hand through his arm.

'I've had to run to catch you!' She was breathless but not with running. 'Are you escaping from demons?'

It was a strange thing to say and he looked round at her sharply and then slowed right down.

'Sorry.' He kicked at the shingle. 'Can't go very fast on the pebbles anyway.' He bent and picked up a flat stone and skimmed it across the glassy surface of the sea. It meant that he freed himself from her hand. The stone ricocheted along the line of moonlight and then disappeared. They both stood and watched where it had gone.

She said, 'I have to talk to you, Mark. It – it's serious.'

He went on staring at the water and the moonlight. 'Can't it wait? There's such a lot to be doing at the moment. Let's promise each other a good talk on . . . oh, I don't know . . . January the second in the year two thousand.'

'Mark, stop it. We're here, together, now. And what I have to say is long overdue.'

He drew a breath and let it go in a long sigh. 'I can probably guess, can't I? You know about Reg's will and you don't want to stay here for the rest of your life and this is the time to split up.'

She was shocked. 'Of course not! I don't know a thing about Reg's will – I don't care! And I love you, Mark. I don't want to split up – it's the last thing . . .' Suddenly her voice choked on a sob. 'But, yes, I suppose it might come to that.'

'I thought so.' He sounded suddenly bitter. 'It's been such a good Christmas I let myself imagine that things were how they had been. You say you love me. I don't think you've loved me for a long time, Holly. Do you remember when we came here first and swam and then washed each other?'

'Of course I do! And I felt – I felt it was like that again on Christmas morning when we got in the sea with Cree and Cass and Mavis. Mark—' She held his arm and forced him to face her. 'You've got to believe that I love you! Otherwise what I am going to tell you will destroy us both.'

He said nothing, simply stood there facing her, apparently not seeing her.

She bit her lip; she had rehearsed this so often but it was not going as she had planned. She spoke quietly and quickly, trying to get it over with.

'The night of the party. When you were called to the hospital to see Reg. It was raining. Hugo drove me home. He'd had too much to drink and he drove badly and by the time we got on the Downs I was terrified. I thought if I stayed perfectly still he would get the message. But he didn't.' She looked into his face for some reaction; there was none. She went on desperately, 'I was so glad to see you, Mark. I knew then that nothing else mattered to me. Just you. I didn't care where we lived or what we did or whether we had children or . . . anything. When you told me that you were going to take over the holiday village, it was like an escape for me. I didn't have to go back to the office. I could run away. I ran away with my husband.' She tried for a laugh. And then sobered. 'But you can't run away, can you? It doesn't work like that. I did a test. A pregnancy test. It was positive. So I went to see Dr Lanercost this morning. And he is booking me in for an abortion.'

She stopped speaking and waited. Mark's eyes focused on her at last. A strand of blond hair blew suddenly across her face and she pushed it behind one ear.

He said, 'Are you saying you are pregnant?'

'Yes.'

'By Hugo Venables?'

'Yes.' The hair blew across again and she moved it and felt its dampness.

'He raped you in the car on the night of the party?'

'Not really . . . raped.'

'You didn't hit him or try to get out of the car?'

She heard herself say, 'It was raining.'

'So you are pregnant by another man because it was raining?'

'Mark! Please!'

285

'You thought he would stop because you put up no resistance. I haven't heard that one before.'

'Mark!'

'How did he manage to undress you, Holly? Where did you put your legs? I know he's got a big car but . . .' He took a step away from her and seemed to study her. She began to sob. He did not soften. He kept asking her questions: personal, awful questions. She was so ashamed she covered her face with both hands. He asked her how often it had happened before. Was that how she had got the precious partnership? Where might it have happened – always in the car or maybe across the desk in Hugo's office? He stopped speaking then and turned abruptly away from her. She ran crunchingly over the pebbles and took his arm.

'Please, Mark! I'm having an abortion! I had to tell you—'

He shook her off angrily. 'Why didn't you just have the baby? Say nothing. Pass it off as mine, just as May has passed her twins off as her husband's.'

She gasped. 'How did you know? I thought of doing that . . . but then I couldn't. I looked at Ivy and Ted . . . so much between them but nothing secret, nothing kept back. And I have never seen anyone so happy.'

He doubled his pace. 'There are certain things . . .' He swallowed audibly, almost choking, and then added, 'This is something I did not want to know.'

She gave up trying to follow him and stood at the top of the shingle beach, her shoulders sagging with despair.

'Mark, you can't just . . . go! You can't just . . . hate me!'

'I don't hate you.' He paused momentarily. 'I hate myself . . . everything!' And he broke into a run.

He was almost level with Magpie Cottage when the door opened and Ivy appeared with Ted close behind. Ivy ran to the gate; she did not see Mark. She looked wildly at the sea and then she let out an enormous cry like an animal.

'Tom! Oh God – come back, Tom! Tom, where are you?'

Ted, close behind, gathered her up but she appeared to be fighting him off. He lifted her bodily and began to take her back to the house. She started to scream. Adam and Gemma appeared in the doorway. Gemma was weeping, and somewhere in the background Giles was wailing. It was pandemonium.

Mark's voice cut through the racket.

'What the hell is the matter? Ted, put her down, for God's sake!'

Ted turned and Ivy struggled free and ran to Mark.

'He's gone! Tom has gone! He went into his

room this afternoon and we all thought he was sulking.'

Ted said, 'He'll be walking along the beach like I said, Ivy. He'll be back before you can say—'

Very clearly, Adam spoke above Gemma's sobs.

'*He*'s got him. *He*'s taken him away. He was going to take me but Tom was on his own. So he took Tom instead.'

Gemma was quiet; they all looked at Adam.

'It's my fault,' he said. 'I made Tom cross. He thinks he's like our father. So he probably went with him without making a fuss.'

Ivy's voice was shrill and uneven. 'Do you mean your father has taken Tom away with him somewhere and you knew about it?'

'He left a note. Under my duvet. I tore it up and flushed it down the loo.'

Mark crouched before the small boy. 'What did it say?'

'It said he would come for me and make me talk again.'

'And you think he's taken Tom instead?'

'Yes.'

Gemma started to cry again. Holly appeared out of the darkness and took her hand.

'Let's go in by the fire and decide what to do,' she said.

Twelve

Ted wanted Gemma to go to bed but she hung on grimly to Adam and Adam said, 'Giles is too young but Gemma . . . we're a family.' He looked at Ted. 'Please, Ted.' None of them could quite believe it was Adam who was speaking, using whole sentences, showing a maturity none of them had envisaged. There was no way they could have refused him anything, so Gemma sat on Holly's lap and Mark made tea and Ivy sat silent and white-faced with Ted holding her hand and rubbing her shoulders occasionally.

Holly said, 'How do you know so much, Adam? Did you see your father?'

'No.' Adam cleared his throat; already his underused voice was cracking. 'But I know Tom. We're . . .' He waved his hands helplessly. 'We're connected, you see. That's why he was angry with me. He thought I was – was – pulling out the plug.'

Holly glanced at Ivy, who said woodenly, 'For the last year, Tom has spoken for Adam. He knows what he wants to say and he says it for him.'

Holly glanced at Mark and then Ted but neither of them commented on this, so she said carefully, 'So Tom thought you were disconnecting yourself and he was angry with you.'

Mark put six mugs on the table and started to pour milk into them. 'You didn't want to come fishing with me,' he said, speaking in the same expressionless tone as Ivy. 'And you didn't want Tom to go either.'

Adam nodded miserably. 'If I'd gone, none of this would have happened because Tom wouldn't have gone into his room by himself.' He gave a dry sob. 'I wanted us to stay together all the time. But I didn't think it mattered inside the house. I thought we were safe inside the house.'

Holly said quickly, 'Giles. Is Giles all right?'

Ted spoke at last. 'He's gone back to sleep. It was when I put Giles to bed that I realized Tom wasn't there. The duvet was humped so I didn't get it at first . . . Oh God.'

Mark poured the tea and thought that if the boys had come fishing with him, the scene with Paula would never have happened.

Ivy said, 'He's got what he wants. He won't come back again.'

Gemma whimpered. 'I'm frightened.'

Holly put her spare arm around Adam and drew them both tightly to her. 'We're all frightened, darling. We're going to have to think what to do.'

'Like the dragon-slayer in my book?'

'Just like that. Exactly like that.'

Mark passed her a mug of tea and thought what a wonderful mother she would be. She could be. His eyes were hot.

He said, 'Listen. We've got to phone the police. There's no way round it. I know that both of you wanted to keep officialdom out of your dilemma but this is something that only they can deal with.'

Ted nodded. Ivy said, 'If he takes him back home . . . unless he harms him . . . what can they do?'

Adam said, 'I was trying to explain to you. Tom hasn't been *taken*. He's gone. I wrote him a note and it's not there any more so he read it. And that's when he decided to go.' He looked round at them and saw they were all staring at him. He turned his head into Holly's shoulder.

'It's all right, Adam.' Ted left Ivy and came round the table. 'It's all right, old man. We know that you are talking to us because it's so important that we know everything. And we know it's difficult. But go on . . . please go on . . . when you can.'

There was a long silence; Ted gently stroked Adam's silky hair and after a moment Gemma put out a tiny hand and stroked as well. Adam turned his head slightly so that he could speak.

'There was a note under my duvet like I told you. From Dad. Saying he would come for me and make me talk again. So I tried to keep us together. I was so frightened Dad was coming for me. When Tom was angry with me, he thought it was because he was getting like Dad. I couldn't explain so I wrote it down on Gemma's sketch pad. And I think – I *know* – that Tom saw Dad and went out to him and made a bargain with him. He would go wherever Dad wanted him to go, so long as Dad left me and Mum alone.' He looked over at Ivy. 'See . . . it was his way of not being like Dad. Of being like you, Mum. And Ted.' And then he started to cry and Ted lifted him and held him tightly.

Mark said slowly, 'This is going to be tricky when we get the police in.'

Ivy was crying quietly, watching Ted and her son. She said, 'He doesn't even need to hide, does he? He could be in one of the empty cottages . . . bed and breakfast . . . anywhere. He's not breaking the law.'

Gemma started to cry again in sympathy and Holly held her closer and rocked her until the sobs turned to hiccoughs. Ted said, 'She'll be asleep soon.' He sat down with Adam on his lap. 'As a matter of fact, I've thought there was a light in Linnet. Several times.'

Mark said, 'Of course! Everything is switched

on over there. Paula and Dennis probably left food in the fridge. I'll go over now – have a look.'

Ivy put out a hand. 'Please, Mark, don't do that. If he's there – wherever he is – let him think he's won. That way Tom will be safe.'

'If I go over there, Ivy, it will be your husband who won't be safe.' Mark had found an outlet for his anger. 'I'll make sure I bring Tom back with me and Stanley disappears.'

Ivy said, 'Ted would do the same. I know that. But it won't do. Can't you see that would give him grounds to get custody of the boys?'

Ted said slowly, 'Ivy's right, Mark. I don't like it, but that's how it would be. Obviously Stanley made no complaint about . . . the incident which landed him in hospital. But if it came to . . . officialdom, as you call it . . . he would bring that up as well. Two physical attacks . . . It wouldn't sound good, would it?'

Holly said, 'Isn't there anything we can do? Do we just go to bed and forget it?'

Ivy's voice seemed to be getting smaller. 'We'll sit up with the children of course. But . . . you two . . . you must go back to the bungalow. Yes.'

Ted cleared his throat gently. 'Ivy . . . dear Ivy. You know we cannot do that. He expects us to do that – it's the submission thing again. We're not going to do what he expects, are we?'

Her eyes filled with tears again and she looked at him. 'No, Ted.'

He glanced at Adam and saw that he was fast asleep so he stretched out a hand towards her.

'Listen, my dearest. First of all we have to let everyone know what has happened. Not counting Reg and the children that will make' – he did a swift calculation – 'five of us men to search the village. And if – when – we find the two of them, perhaps we can talk. Persuade Stanley to get some help . . . be sensible.' He cradled Adam again. 'You and Holly should go up to the bungalow with the children to be with May and Paula. Cass Evans can go in with the window-cleaning ladies.' He smiled gently at her. 'How does that sound?'

'Oh Ted.' Her mouth worked uncontrollably. 'You're so . . . wonderful.'

They tried to be methodical, switching everything off and packing a few essentials for the children, and then they all trooped up the drive to the bungalow like a column of refugees; which was exactly how they felt. It was another moonless night with a sea mist encapsulating each of them damply. They gave Linnet Cottage a wide berth – 'until we're ready', Ted had told them – and shut the door of Magpie and locked it carefully.

Mark muttered to Holly, 'How one man can hold us all to ransom like this, I do not know.'

She said sadly, 'It's all too easy, isn't it? When that man is holding the trump card.'

He thought she was thinking too of Hugo

Venables and he dropped behind her. He shifted Adam's dead weight further onto his shoulder and hoped he would be the one to find Stanley Edwards. All his life he had been peaceable: no reason to be anything else. He knew he was peaceable no longer; he planned what he would do to Stanley Edwards.

Ted felt the same as Mark: he had been frightened and subdued for so long, and now the time had come to act. Like Gemma said, he had to kill the dragon.

It took some time to raise Dennis and Paula and then to explain everything to them with May and Arthur aghast in the background. Holly and Ivy put the children in the double room.

'We'll sit up,' Holly said. 'No hope of sleep anyway.'

So the four women sat around the kitchen table, Paula and May drinking tea, Holly and Ivy unable to face any more. Paula kept asking questions, incredulous that so much could have happened without her knowing.

'It makes me feel rather . . . I don't know . . . small,' she confessed. 'I thought the whole world was revolving around me and the baby and then not the baby and – and' – she glanced at Holly – 'whether I still loved Dennis and why he wasn't tender and caring like Mark and having Helen and Walter for parents . . . Oh Ivy, I wish I'd known what hell you were going through.'

Ivy shook her head. 'It's not been like that. I

thought I'd left the hell somewhere else. I've been so happy – so very happy.' She gave a small, tight smile. 'Now I feel like you do. As if somehow I've been dodging the whole thing. Ostrich. Sand. You know.' She looked across the table at Holly. 'What I said to you about secrets. It's as if I kept this particular secret from myself too! I should have faced it years ago before he tried to throttle Adam . . . before Tom hit him.'

Paula made a sound of horror and May glanced across at Holly. 'Some secrets have to be kept,' she said. 'There's no sense in spreading them because they spread unhappiness too.' She put her hand over Ivy's. 'Perhaps yours was like that, Ivy. You thought if you kept it all to yourself it wouldn't infect anyone else.'

Ivy said nothing and after a while she stood up and went to check on the children while Holly looked in briefly on Reg.

Some time in the early hours Mark came in to tell them what was happening.

'Mavis is with Cass in Christopher Wren,' he reported. 'That way there are two cottages he won't use. We know Magpie is sealed. We've searched Linnet and the two spare ones – Robin and Sparrow. Dennis has taken Bernice's car and is driving along the top in one direction, while Ted is going in the other. There's a possibility they might try to hitch a lift – Ted says Stanley hasn't got a car and he can't drive anyway.'

Ivy said, 'He might have had a long start, Mark.'

'Yes.' He sighed. 'I'm sorry, Ivy. It looks as though they made straight for home. I'll drive you back tomorrow.' He pulled his woollen hat back on. 'I'm going to walk along the beach again. Around the next point there's a cave. If they're trying to walk to Clevedon they might have holed up there for the rest of the night.'

Paula said, 'In that case, why don't you wait for the morning like they will?'

He did not look at her. 'Because I can't, that's why,' he said briefly and turned immediately. 'Don't expect me for some time. It's dark down there.'

Holly looked after him and then back at Paula. 'He's tired and anxious,' she apologized.

Paula nodded and said unexpectedly, 'He thinks I'm silly and shallow and immature. That's how I'm feeling too.'

Morning was a long time coming. When the mist began to pale at eight o'clock the women assembled a breakfast for the children and Holly took tea in to Reg. At eight thirty the men returned. Cree went straight into Reg's room with a mug of tea and a round of dry bread.

Reg was awake. He said, 'I thought you looked pretty good for your years. But not today.'

Cree said, 'I'm too old for this game, Reg, that's for certain. But I have to admit it's good for the soul. It's been like living one of my nightmares and finding that in the end there's not a lot to be feared except fear itself.'

'Who said that?'

'Me,' replied Cree and they both managed to laugh.

Arthur sat at the table with his head hanging and May fed him bits of crustless toast and sips of tea and then ushered him into their bedroom.

'I'm bushed, old girl,' he confessed as she tucked him into bed. 'In case I don't wake up again, give me a kiss.'

She sobbed as she put her lips to his forehead. She said, 'Don't you dare talk like that. If you ever leave me, I'll never speak to you again.'

'If I've stuck it this long . . .' He grinned and lifted his mouth to hers. He said, 'You know I still love you, don't you?'

'Of course. Silly old fool. I love you too.'

'Good. Don't ever forget that.'

She looked at him closely, but he said no more and after a moment closed his eyes. 'You never would talk things out, would you?' she whispered. And to her shocked amazement he murmured back, 'What's yours is mine. Is that enough talking for you?'

She straightened and stood for a long time watching him sleeping and then snoring. She wondered whether she would dare to ask him what he had meant. Did he know . . . and if so, how long had he known?

*   *   *

Ted had driven as far as Bristol without encountering one hitch-hiker. On the way back he had stopped at every garage and shop to enquire for a man and a young boy. At seven thirty on the morning of New Year's Eve he had not come up with one sighting. He went down to Magpie to change his clothes and to try desperately to make a plan.

Dennis decided to stay up until Mark returned. Paula would not go to bed without him so he cradled her head on his shoulder and she smiled sleepily up at him. She thought it was such a *tender* thing to do.

Holly and Ivy made more tea, washed up, laid the table with cereal for the children who slept blissfully on, and kept glancing at the clock. Mark came in at nine, breathless. He had run from the beach.

'The boat's gone. Our boat. It was there when I started to search towards Clevedon but when I came back – just now – it had gone.'

Ted, coming in behind him, felt terror and relief at the same time. At least they knew that Stanley Edwards was still in the area. But the fact that he was out in a boat was not good.

Ivy said, 'He can't swim. Why would he take the boat?' Her eyes were unnaturally wide. Ted thought in agony that he was going to lose both of them, Tom and Ivy.

He said, 'Perhaps it was Tom's idea. He can

299

swim. Perhaps he thought he could jump out and swim to the shore . . .'

Mark said, 'That wasn't a part of Tom's plan, was it?'

Ted said quickly, 'No, but he could have changed his mind. Through the night.' He looked at Ivy, 'I don't mean that Stanley might have hurt him, love. But it's just possible they went back to Magpie – we left in such a hurry that I don't know whether some of the mess is ours or theirs. And if Tom slept in his own bunk, he had plenty of time to think it through properly. And change his mind about the bargain.'

Mark said, 'My God. That's possible, isn't it? Stanley must have had a key to get in when he placed that note under Adam's duvet! So while we were searching everywhere else . . .' He bit his lip. 'He's more devious than I thought.'

Dennis said tentatively, 'Shouldn't we go down to the shore? Call the coastguards or something?'

Ted said, 'Stay with the kids, Ivy. We'll let you know the minute we see them.'

Ivy said, 'I can't—'

And Paula immediately said, 'I'll stay. May and Arthur are here. And Reg and Cree. I'll see to the breakfast. Go on, all of you. Go!'

The five of them poured out of the kitchen door into the mist. Cass and the other women were coming up drive and turned with them.

Holly explained on the way down to the beach. Cass turned right and said something over her shoulder. The others stumbled on past Magpie and down to the shingle. Visibility was no more than twenty yards; Ivy sobbed aloud.

They split up and ranged up and down the beach, staring helplessly into the mist. At one point Cree joined them.

'There's nothing for it,' he said. 'We shall have to ring for help. Neither of them know about the sea and the currents are desperate in this area.'

Ivy said, 'I'll do it – I'll go back now—'

Mark said sharply, 'Wait!' He was looking behind him. 'The sun is going to break through,' he said. 'See how the mist is pearling already?'

They all turned and stared. The sun was coming up invisibly behind the holiday village and Magpie, Linnet and Reg's bungalow were plain to see. They waited, standing very still as if one movement might arrest the sun, and then a single beam shot from the direction of the Lantern and highlighted the beach. They could see the grey-glass sea glittering a hundred yards out. Within fifteen minutes it was a glorious morning; the mist had gone and the air was sharp and cold.

And there was no sign of a boat anywhere.

Ivy phoned the coastguards and bathed Giles and Gemma and got them dressed. Adam scrambled into jeans and sweatshirt and left the bungalow without eating or drinking. He fetched the red plastic sledge from outside Magpie Cottage and stationed himself at the edge of the shining mud. Cass arrived, looking ridiculous in the wetsuit she had borrowed from Reg. Over her shoulder was a coil of rope. 'Good lad,' she said to Adam. 'Between us we'll be there as soon as we see them.' Adam gave her a watery smile.

'He's in danger,' he said. 'Tom's in danger. I can tell.'

'Where the hell are the coastguards . . . the helicopter?' Mark asked. 'It must be half an hour since Ivy phoned!'

'It's New Year's Eve, Mark.' Ted hunkered by Adam. 'Try to find out where they are, Adam. Think about Tom. What can he see?'

There was a long silence broken only by the lapping water. Mavis started to cry and Pansy joined her; Bernice told them sharply to shut up.

Adam let his breath go in a gasp. 'Steps. That's all. Steps.'

'St Margaret's Bay.' Cree was already starting back up the beach at a shambling trot. 'You know, Mavis. The steps going down to the bay.'

Everyone began to move off. Mark said, 'They'll drift round here, the current runs that way when the tide is ebbing. I'll stay.'

Ted knew a moment of complete uncertainty. Adam said, 'I'll stay with you,' and the moment went. 'Me too,' Ted said.

Cass said, 'Take the rope. If I can see them, I'll swim behind. Do what I can.'

The three of them, Adam, Mark and Ted, watched the others scrambling up to the cottage and then disappearing across the drive towards Seagull and Wren. Then they turned and resumed their own watch.

They were an unlikely trio; the boy was undersized, shivering in spite of the sun, holding the rope of his sledge; the two men were almost the same height and normally wore the same mild facial expression, but Ted, the younger one, seemed somehow to be curving his body towards the horizon like a question mark. He was thinking: I've got to get rid of him . . . I've got to drown him so that he can never hurt Ivy again . . . I've got to do it . . . Can I do it?

Mark was standing solidly, squarely, on the shingle like an obelisk, still and menacing. He thought: I'll get the boy in first, then I'll go back and I'll kill him. I want to kill him. I want to hit and hurt him and then . . . then I will feel better.

Suddenly, without a word, Adam launched the sledge onto the mud and ran after it, landing prone and driving it forward with his own impetus. It slid inexorably towards the receding water.

Ted called after him and he turned his head under one frantically paddling arm and hissed, 'I can hear them. I can hear Dad. He's laughing.'

Neither man could hear, but they did not

argue. Ted fiddled with his belt and got rid of his trousers; Mark did the same. Gingerly they entered the water.

On the other side of the little headland, in St Margaret's Bay, Cass was already in the water; she had seen the boat a few minutes before and lowered herself in from the rocks beneath the steps. She began to swim quietly out into the sea, keeping as close as she could to the small headland. Above her, the sun sparkled on the big studio window of Wren Cottage. The others, grouped around the top of the steps, kept very still and quiet, eyes fixed on the small boat. Stanley Edwards evidently did not see them or Cass. But they could see him and they could see that Tom, in the stern of the boat, was tied hand and foot and gagged as well. Even as they all registered this with sick horror, Stanley laughed.

Cass heard it too. She tightened her lips and regulated her breathing. Already she was planning to overturn the boat. If Stanley drowned then that would be on her conscience for ever, but she told herself she had not got much to show for her life and this would free Ivy and Ted and the children. She must do it. She stretched her body along the water, head well down. She wondered how long it would be before he saw her. The cold was penetrating the ancient wetsuit; if he threw Tom into the water she would have to get him very quickly.

The watchers at the top of the steps turned

and began to hurry back to the beach. Holly was audibly sobbing but Ivy did not make a sound. Her eyes stared from her white face; she wondered what other unspeakable things Stanley had done to his son through that long and awful night.

Immediately the boat cleared the headland and came into the wide stretches of the bay, Stanley spotted Ted and Mark swimming towards him. He actually laughed again and then waved to them. Mark trod water, staring incredulously, and then realized that Tom was bound and gagged. He gave a strangled shout. Ted kept swimming; he knew that once he stopped he would be done for.

Stanley yelled, 'Don't come any nearer! If you do I'll chuck Tom in! D'you hear me, you bloody great idiots? Did you think you could get the better of me?'

Mark shouted, 'Untie him! You're a coward – frightened of a kid! Untie him!'

Stanley rocked with laughter. 'He came to me of his own free will. I could have kept him – taken him home – he would have come, no trouble. But I want them all back. All of them. D'you hear me? I want my family back! And if I've got to use up this one to do it, then so be it!'

Mark swam two more strokes and then trod water again. He was still too far away.

He shouted, 'You'll spend the rest of your life in prison – is that what you want?'

'You don't know the half of it, do you! You think you're some bloody knight in shining armour. But my family have been stolen from me – how would *you* like that? If someone took your wife . . . how would *you* like that?' The sharp, extended Welsh vowels seemed to echo across the water mockingly. Mark thought of Hugo Venables and wondered just who it was he wanted to kill.

Ted, rearing up desperately to get a decent breath of air, suddenly saw Cass gliding around the headland and making for the open sea. He saw what she was doing. If Stanley kept talking to Mark she would get behind him. But Mark was no longer talking and no longer swimming.

Ted shouted, 'Who do you think you are then, Stanley? The model father? Is that why you tried to throttle one son and are now threatening to drown the other?'

The effort of shouting this little speech exhausted Ted; he had to fight the water to stay above it. But it kept Stanley's attention and he lifted an oar and waved it furiously at Ted's thatch of wet hair.

'I'm going to kill you, Ted Harris! D'you hear me? Come any further and I dump the kid and then you'll get it. That's a promise!'

Ted looked across the stretch of water at the raised oar; it was strangely like the tail of a dragon. And the dragon wanted to kill him. A ripple ridged the icy sea over his head and he gulped water and then kicked out; when he surfaced he had decreased the stretch between them by at least two yards. He kicked again and reared up in the water. Beyond the boat Cass's head appeared for a moment and then submerged again. He knew exactly what she was going to do. She would tip the boat and then it would be up to Mark to get hold of Tom and it would be up to him, Ted, to keep Stanley away from Tom. And that would mean he had to kill him.

And then everything seemed to happen at once. Mark and Ted saw Cass's large and capable hand on the edge of the little fishing boat and realized in the same instant that she would be pulling it towards her and away from them. With one accord they launched themselves forward, ignoring Stanley's screaming threats. At the same time, with a sudden roar that shattered the winter calm, a helicopter rose from above St Margaret's headland. Stanley Edwards, on his feet and still waving the oar aggressively, looked up at it, twisted round and fell into the water. And Tom, reacting instantly to the enormous diversion, stood up in the stern, turned towards Ted and launched himself out of the boat almost into Ted's waiting arms. The two of them sank like stones, Ted holding Tom and kicking fiercely. Close to them, Mark hesitated, stunned by the noise and the sudden turn of events. Cass, unexpectedly relieved of the weight in the boat, found it upturned over her head. She dived from beneath it and just for one instant felt a hand on one of her ancient flippers. And then it was gone and she was surfacing to see Mark pushing Ted as far out of the water as he could. Clinging to Ted, Tom breathed fiercely through his nostrils. Cass swam behind him and began to rip off the gag. Once free of that, Tom put his head into Ted's neck and began to cry.

'Ah, my dear, dear boy. You're safe now. Ted's got you . . .'

Cass felt frantically for his hands but the knots, soaked in sea water, refused to budge. 'Take them in, Mark. Can't move the knots. Take them in. I'll look for Stanley.'

Mark heaved the two heads onto his chest and began to paddle back to the shore. Holly was there, with Bernice and Cree, and willing hands pulled them in. Ivy was weeping at last. The three of them, she and Tom and Ted, sat on the shingle, muddy and wet, and held one another for a long time while the others watched anxiously as Mark swam out again to Cass.

Above them, the coastguards in the helicopter had spotted Stanley and were winching a man down to bring him out. Cass righted the boat and she and Mark hung onto it and watched. Stanley appeared to be unconscious. The pilot used his loudspeaker to tell those in the sea and on the shore that they were taking the 'victim' to hospital. Was an ambulance needed for the survivors? Cass waved that they were all right. It was a relief when the helicopter veered off towards Bristol.

Cass looked at Mark. 'If he hadn't gone overboard when he did, I intended to tip him out,' she said soberly.

Mark nodded. He was freezing and felt ill and frustrated. 'So did I,' he said.

Cass began to shove the boat towards the shore. 'Ted must have intended the same.' She kicked with her flippers. 'How awful. Three of us. He didn't stand a chance, did he?'

Mark remembered that Reg had wanted Cass to be independent . . . free. Reg had said she was a wonderful woman. He tried to put a hand over hers as it gripped the boat. 'Remember, we didn't do it. It was the shock of seeing the helicopter. Nothing to do with us.'

She said, 'Oh God, Mark. You're blue. Come on, back to dry land and hot baths and drinks and food . . .' She tried to laugh and found that her facial muscles were stiff.

They knew there would be repercussions: police interviews, lots of questions. As yet they didn't know if Stanley had survived. But for the moment they could do nothing but feel utter thankfulness for getting Tom back. Reg had switched on every heater there was and Paula had opened a dozen cans of soup and made a pile of toast. The bathroom was in demand for the next hour and then, wrapped in blankets, the four who had been in the sea were thoroughly spoiled by the others. Just for the moment problems were forgotten or laid aside. 'It's like the war,' Pansy said ecstatically. 'All that community spirit and whatnot.'

'What would you know about the war, you child, you?' Cree boomed.

And Bernice said soberly, 'Pansy has had to fight a war too, you know, Cree.'

He slid an arm around her waist and held her to his side for a moment. 'Haven't we all, beautiful Bernice? Haven't we all?'

Dennis spooned soup into Tom's mouth. 'My God, you're a hero, Tom. D'you know that? What does it feel like?'

'Cold,' Tom said, still shivering, but grinning at Adam, thinking how they would talk about this in the days to come and make it into an adventure; because Adam was talking properly now. And Ted had come to the rescue just as Tom had told his father he would, and Ted was here to stay too. When Stanley had seen Ted's stuff around the chalet, it was as if he realized that Ted wasn't frightened of him. That had seemed to push his father past all reasoning; that was when he had tied Tom up and pushed the awful old hanky into his mouth.

Tom looked across at his mother, cuddling Giles and smiling and smiling. He put one thumb up at her and she returned the gesture.

Dennis said, 'I hope Paula and me have a boy. Just like you or Adam.'

Adam chipped in. 'If it's a girl, it might be like Gemma. If you're lucky.'

Dennis laughed and clapped him on the back. Gemma smiled at everyone like Ivy and experimented with the new word. 'Hero . . . hero. Tom is a hero.'

Mavis said, 'What a blessing it's all turned out as it has! My goodness, girls, when we decided to come down here for Christmas, little did we think . . .'

Reg moved his wheelchair closer to Cass and echoed, 'Little did we think . . . eh, Cass?'

She looked at Mavis and then at Reg. She was glad she had not had to kill another human being but still she had a very definite feeling that problems weren't solved quite so easily as everyone appeared to think.

She said, 'Are you all right, Reg?'

Cree, leaning over the wheelchair, said, 'He wasn't. I thought he might peg out on me earlier. But he's got a second wind, the old reprobate!'

Reg put a hand out to each of them. 'I'm all right. I think I've been – always – a truly happy man. Can't say more than that, can I?'

Before either of them could think of a reply to that, Holly said loudly, 'Has anyone seen Mark? His blanket's here, but he's not!'

'Bathroom?' asked Reg.

'I've looked. Everywhere.'

May appeared from the kitchen carrying more mugs of hot chocolate.

'Mark's popped off to get those sparklers you mentioned, Holly. You know, for the children. He said you forgot them yesterday.'

Holly looked at her blankly. And Tom said, 'I'd forgotten it was New Year's Eve. And it's only one o'clock! We can still have a bonfire and fireworks at midnight, can't we? Can't we, Ted? Can't we, Mum?'

'We'll go home and rest first,' Ivy decreed. 'See how we feel later.'

The party broke up gradually. Cass stayed close to Reg; Cree and Bernice wandered off together. Ted gathered up his family and shepherded them down to Magpie Cottage . . . his family, his very own family. Arthur took May, Holly, Pansy and Mavis up to the Lantern for lunch. The holiday village was quiet again.

Thirteen

Mark knew he was driving badly and tried to calm himself down by cutting off various avenues of thought which inevitably led to unacceptable images. Unfortunately, the images had a way of appearing out of the blue, unconnected with any logical thoughts. For instance, he was working out where to go for some children's fireworks when he saw, with terrible vividness, the inside of the Venableses' car parked on the Downs in pouring rain. He managed to cut that one off before it went any further, but it was almost immediately superseded by the ghastly memory of himself and Paula on the kitchen table. If Dennis had not arrived home then, would he have torn off her clothes and made love to her? Was it possible that he could have done such a thing to a young girl who had so recently had a miscarriage? It would have been criminal. He groaned aloud and forced himself to recall the events of that morning and to wonder whether the terrible Stanley Edwards was dead or alive.

Mark almost offered a prayer that the man was dead, and then some remnant of his Sunday school days obliterated that too. And anyway, was Stanley Edwards the evil-doer they had all believed him to be? Would he actually have killed his own son?

'Oh God . . .' Mark groaned again and sped through amber traffic lights. 'I wanted to kill him myself – he represented wickedness and I thought by killing him I would be killing that bit of Hugo bloody Venables.'

A car passed him and flashed its brake-lights angrily; he wondered why but did not check his dashboard. He knew that he must pull himself together but did not know how. He negotiated the long hill down to the Cumberland Basin with exaggerated care. Fireworks. He had come to buy fireworks, which were probably unobtainable at this late date. He had come because he could no longer sustain the awfulness of being under the same roof with Holly and Paula. He had come to get away from Reg and his over-whelming benevolence . . . He had wanted to drive as fast as he could even if it meant going into a tree.

He said aloud, 'I'll go to the flat and have a drink. And then I'll call on Hugo Venables.'

Of course. That was what he had intended to do all the time. He knew that he could not let Holly have an abortion; he knew that she would have the baby and he would love it as his own.

Just as Arthur had loved the Terrible Twins. It was the only thing he could do because he loved Holly and surely he understood how it must have happened because hadn't he nearly – so nearly – gone the same way with Paula? So he would have to forgive and forget. It would be hard at first but gradually, because he loved Holly, it would be all right. There was no other way. She would be such a wonderful mother and he thought – he knew – he could be a pretty good father. They were both civilized people . . . There was no other way.

But first . . . first some kind of justice had to be seen to be done. First, he had to beat Hugo Venables into a pulp.

The bungalow was empty and Cass wheeled Reg into his room and leaned down to take off his shoes.

He said, 'Cass, darling girl . . . I can't make love to you. Forgive me, this whole thing . . . too much.'

She smiled up at him. 'I know. We'll rest together, my dear. The two of us. I'm not going to leave you, Reg. You tried to push me away yesterday. I'm not going to be pushed away. I love you. That's that.'

'I love you too.' He levered himself gingerly onto Maude's side of the bed and leaned back on the pillows with a sigh. 'I wouldn't push you away ever – why do you say things like that?'

315

She tucked him in expertly and came round to his side of the bed.

'You and that Pansy. Taking her to Bristol. What do you expect me to think?'

He breathed a chuckle. 'Pansy Pansetti. You must be mad.'

She made herself comfortable and then took his head onto her shoulder. 'I know that you probably made love to the three of them when you were on the cruise together. I couldn't care less because I wasn't there. If I had been . . .'

'I wish you had been. Ah . . . I do wish you had been.' He turned his head into her neck and inhaled the scent of her luxuriously. Then he said, 'I needed her for a witness. Codicil to my will. I hoped that Mavis would find a clear field with Cree.'

'Cree's not interested in Mavis. Nor she in him. Not seriously.'

He sighed. 'I know. It's Bernice, isn't it?'

'Bernice Smythe?' She considered, staring at the ceiling. 'Could be. Yes. That would explain one or two things.'

'Have they . . . ? I mean, how serious is it?'

She laughed. 'I don't know. Bernice is so proper. I can't imagine . . .'

He said slowly, 'Bernice is very deep. Very, very vulnerable. She adored her husband and when he died she thought there would be no-one else. When she discovered that her feelings were still there, she was horrified.'

Cass turned her head and stared into his eyes. 'You taught her about her suppressed feelings. Did you? Yes . . . of course. I've seen the way she doesn't look at you!' She smiled and then kissed him. 'Oh Reg. You wanted a flirtation and it turned into something else?'

'Maybe.' He lifted his head for another kiss. Then he lay back. 'Cass, I can't do anything any more. I'm so damned tired all the time. But could you talk to Cree? It will be just another flirtation for him too, but for her . . . I don't know how she would survive it.'

'Are you serious?'

'Perfectly. I've seen another woman fall in love with your father. It's taken her twenty-five years to get over it. And Bernice is much more complicated, much more passionate.'

Cass said, 'Wow!'

'Yes.'

'You're a bloody complicated man yourself, Reg Jepson. You say you love me, but I know the love of your life was your Maude. And now, it seems, Bernice Smythe had a slice of it too! How many others?'

He smiled with his eyes closed. 'I'm on Maude's side of the bed, Cass. That's because I'm half Maude . . . and some of me is Bernice too. Maybe others. Remember you fell in love with me because I am what those others have made me.'

She stared at his face. Then she kissed his

closed eyes and lay back down on the pillows. 'I suppose I'm the same,' she sighed. 'Oh Reg . . . I wish we were younger and had more time.'

'I'm not going anywhere,' he whispered back. And they fell asleep.

Dennis and Paula walked along the small beach of St Margaret's Bay. Already the mist was returning with the tide and they stood and watched it, holding each other close and then closer with a kind of delicious terror.

'Not much chance of describing this week as boring,' Dennis commented. 'I'm half expecting Ivy's awful husband to appear out of that mist again at any minute!'

Paula shivered and he opened his coat and sheltered her inside it.

'I'm glad I didn't see him,' she said. 'Especially when he fell into the sea . . .' She shivered again. 'If he dies, that's two deaths. The baby and him. And they say these things go in threes, Chiv. Do you think there will be another one?'

'Of course not. Idiot child.' He kissed her fondly. 'God, Polly. I feel I've lived a whole life this week. I've been sort of reborn. The one enormous thing I've learned is that . . . I'm nothing without you. I can't live without you.' He was kissing her frantically as he spoke, little, desperate kisses all over her face. She spluttered and laughed helplessly. 'No, seriously, my darling. You must tell me that you will never leave me. Promise me, Polly. Now. Please. Promise me.'

She promised and kissed him back and for a while they were incoherent. And then she said, 'One of the things about the miscarriage . . .' She stopped speaking and kissed him again.

He lifted his head. 'Go on. What?'

'I was so frightened you'd be angry that I sort of pushed you away somehow.'

'I know. It was awful.' He tucked her curly head beneath his chin. 'I'm glad you're so close to my parents, but I felt they were . . . ousting me.'

'Yes. It was because I just wanted to be loved.'

He made a sound in his throat. 'Did you think I didn't love you? God—'

'I thought it was just sex for us. That's fine because it's how we show our love – I know all that, Chiv. But they were giving me support . . . understanding . . . I don't know. I'm not sure any more.' She remembered how good it had been with Mark at first. His sheer tenderness. And how that had escalated into sex on the kitchen table.

She said, 'It was so wonderful when you'd said goodbye to them and you didn't go to the pub but came straight back to me. I knew then.'

'My God. You were wonderful.' He spoke huskily, also remembering. 'I've never known you like that . . . passionate . . . and yet so *com*passionate. I fell in love with you all over again. I do that every five minutes. It's the most amazing thing.'

She was silent, peering from beneath his jacket at the creeping mist. After a while she murmured, 'It would have been nice to have done what everyone here seems to do. Swim in the sea. But maybe . . . maybe we're expecting another baby, so shall we give it a miss?'

He laughed and hugged her again. 'All right. Just this once.' They kissed yet again and then he said seriously, 'It would be a bit soon, wouldn't it, Polly?'

'Yes. But this is a magic place, remember.'

'I know.' He turned her and they began to walk back to the steps. 'Let's go back to our cottage now, shall we? Mark stocked us up with groceries on Boxing Day. We could have a late lunch and then lie in front of the fire and talk until it's time for the evening do.'

'Just talk?' she teased.

'What's wrong with that?' he teased back.

They laughed and ran back up the steps.

Cree stood in the big window and watched them as they took the steps two at a time.

'Christ, they're young,' he commented.

Bernice was making tea and smiled as she found cups and saucers. 'You sound envious. You don't do so badly for an eighty-year-old.'

He turned, eyebrows shooting to his hairline.

'Seventy-eight if you don't mind, young Bernie! And most people think I'm still in my sixties!'

Her smile exploded into laughter. 'That was a test, Cree Evans, and you failed!' She poured the tea black and strong. 'I thought you were vain and, by golly, I was right. As if two years matter!' She carried the cups over to him and sat on a low chair previously occupied by Mavis on Christmas Eve. It crossed her mind that that particular night seemed a lifetime away now: they had all been vastly different people then.

He drew up his stool and sat down opposite her so that his knees just touched hers. She moved sideways and drew her tweed skirt down and then stroked it carefully into position.

He said, 'Dammit, Bernice! That is one of your more irritating habits. For God's sake, stop it!'

She smiled, well pleased. 'What? Avoiding nasty old men touching me up?'

He really was furious. 'I am not a nasty old man! And I am certainly not trying to touch you up – not in that sense anyway. I wanted to make contact. That's all. In a world that is bloody well disappearing much too fast, I wanted to make contact with someone I respect.' He breathed deeply and stared at her raised brows and curved mouth. 'Yes, respect! Is that too difficult for you to understand? If I didn't respect you I would have ignored old Reg's warnings and you'd be on that bed with that damned tweed skirt on the floor!'

He continued to breathe heavily and she continued to smile as she very gently sipped her tea.

'I do apologize that there is no milk,' she said. 'I did sniff it and it had obviously gone off.'

He exploded again. 'That's another thing! The way you smell all the bloody food we keep in the fridge. It hasn't killed Cass or me yet.' He took a mouthful of tea and spluttered as it burned his tongue. 'For God's sake!' he yelled at the top of his voice. 'You're trying to scald me now!'

This was too much for her and she started to laugh. Tears streamed down her face. She had to put her cup on the floor and hold her sides. He watched her and began, reluctantly, to smile. When she calmed down, he said, 'The habit I was referring to in the bloody first place was the one where you smooth your clothes. I've never seen you stand up without smoothing down your skirt. When you put your coat on, you flick your shoulders as if you expect them to be covered in dandruff. You are forever smoothing or flicking. It's absolutely infuriating.'

She was genuinely surprised. 'Do I really? And it gets on your nerves?'

He said levelly, 'It does.'

She was silent, gazing at her skirt. Then she said, 'You're right. I'm only just holding back from smoothing my skirt right now. How – how awful.'

He visibly swallowed. 'Actually . . . it's not awful, Bernice. It – it's really very, very sexy.'

She was shocked. 'That's worse! Much worse!'

'It's obviously subconscious,' he hastened to say. 'I mean, you're probably feeling embarrassed or something.' He sipped his tea cautiously and added, 'I mean, it's not as if you're caressing your own body or anything.' He swallowed again. 'Oh my God. I shouldn't have said that, should I?'

'I don't know. Do you think . . . could it possibly be a sort of . . .'

'Masturbation?'

'Oh, you really are a nasty old man!' She jumped up and kicked over her tea. 'Now look what you've made me do!' She went for a cloth and rubbed at the stained carpet. 'That's dreadful – a dreadful thing to say – or think.'

He got on his knees and tried to help her. 'It's not what I think! You seemed to be searching for a word and I just supplied . . .'

'Exactly. You supplied what that cesspit you call a mind dredged up!'

'Bernice, stop. Just for a second. We can be honest with each other. All right, it might sound to others as if we hurl insults all the time, but it's our way of being honest and . . . sort of flirting. Isn't it?'

She stopped scrubbing with the cloth and sat

still, all the feisty ripostes in the world gone from her.

At last she said, 'I don't know any more. We seem to have gone past that now.' She looked at him; her eyes were almost navy blue. She said slowly, 'Do you sleep with your daughter?'

He gestured behind him. 'You can see there's only one bed.'

She sighed. 'All right. Do you make love to your daughter?'

'No.' He thought of Cass and the way she sometimes made him feel. He said again, 'No.'

She went on looking at him for a long time then said flatly, 'I don't get it.'

He took a deep breath. 'OK. Well, I don't know whether you can take this. I am totally unaffected by women. I see them as models – or not as models – and that is all. But there are occasions when Cass . . . oh God . . . when Cass excites me. How far that would go, I don't know. She makes sure it goes nowhere.'

'That's sick.'

'I know. But Cass is so good to me, Bernice. One of the reasons she sleeps with me is because I get night terrors.' He hung his head and sighed. 'Sounds so pat when I put it like that. Night terrors. I've tried to do myself in before now.'

'Why?'

'It's something to do with eternity. I can't take it.'

'What does Cass do?'

'She holds me. She makes tea. She tells me not to be a silly old fool. She – she's *there*!'

'Are you telling me you can't cope without Cass?'

'I suppose I am.'

'What's in it for her?'

'Nothing. Not even job satisfaction because she'd like me to do some decent portraits and I'm frightened to try that too. I'd fail, you see, and I can't stand failing. Besides, we'd starve.'

'Poor Cass.'

'Yes. Poor Cass.'

Very slowly she levered herself back onto the model's chair. She pulled her skirt over her knees and stroked it once then quickly clasped her hands together and put them on her lap. He stayed on his knees on the floor.

She said quietly, 'My turn, I think.'

'Bernie – you don't have to – it's not like that.'

She appeared not to hear him and said over his words, 'My husband's name was Robert. We ran a business together. Antiques. He was the expert, I was the saleswoman. I'm bossy – the other girls will have mentioned that, I daresay. I'm the one that does the organizing. Drives the car. Decides where we eat and when. I've always been good at admin. Robert told me that and was quite happy for me to run everything. I mean everything. The shop, our lives . . . the only decision I remember him making was that we shouldn't have a family.' She held up a hand as Cree made a sound of protest. 'I didn't mind. I really didn't. I adored him, you see. He was everything to me. I ran the business for him and did everything at home . . . ironed his shirts . . . he liked starched collars and cuffs and good cuff links. He was immaculate. Always.' She smiled slightly. 'Perhaps that's why I'm constantly grooming myself!'

He said, 'Oh Bernie. I am so sorry.'

'Don't be silly. Neither of us need apologize to the other. At least that has been made clear today.' She unfastened her hands and reached out for a second to touch his wiry hair. 'It's good to be honest, Cree. Even when we've been sparring . . . we've been honest.'

'True, true.' He wanted to grab her hand and press it to his face but he did not. Instead he hung onto the edge of her chair and looked up at her and was very conscious of his paint-stained torn shirt and his awful old jeans. As far as he could remember he had never owned a cuff link.

She said, 'I thought I might die of grief when he was killed. A car accident.' She stared out of the window and down into St Margaret's Bay where the tide was beginning to ooze in. She said, 'Then the police told me . . . he was drunk. He'd got drunk with someone called Marilyn Friedman. She had an antique shop in Brighton.

He'd been there all weekend. Brighton is the place for that, isn't it?'

He drew in his breath sharply. 'Oh God. Bernie . . .'

'Don't be sorry for me. It stiffened my spine . . . knowing he'd been unfaithful. There were quite a few women at the funeral – women I didn't know and who didn't know each other. I wanted to ask them things. Personal, embarrassing things. So that I could find out if he found them . . . better . . . than me. But of course I couldn't do that. So I'll never know why he went elsewhere. How I failed him. Whether I was too bossy. If I didn't starch his shirts just the way he liked them. Or whether . . . it was just the sex part.'

He said hoarsely, 'Don't you think it was he who failed you?'

'But it doesn't mean so much to men, does it?' She turned and looked at him appealingly. 'I mean – if you'd managed to get Mavis into bed, it wouldn't have meant much to you, would it? You'd just go on to the next one and it wouldn't cross your mind that maybe Mavis's heart was broken.'

'Oh Bernie . . .' He sat back on his heels and dropped his head onto his chest.

She said, 'What? It's true. Go on, admit it.'

He made a sound and shook his head and she turned back to the window and said sadly, 'There's nothing to be done about it, Cree. A lot of women are like me. All their eggs in one basket.'

He said in a strangled voice. 'May. May Long.'

'What about May?'

'I thought that was just an affair. And it wasn't. Not for her. She said her heart was broken.'

She lifted her brows again. 'May? When was this?'

'Twenty-five years ago. Maybe more.' He shook his head again. 'I'd forgotten about it till now. She and her Arthur are so settled, such a couple, I'd pushed it right away. But it happened.'

'What since then?'

'Nothing. No-one. Models come and models go. Until Cass.' He sighed. 'When the – the panic attacks began, I wrote to her. She came straight away.'

'We're back to Cass. Full circle.' She stood up and stretched mightily. Then looked down at him. 'Come on, old man. Stand up. You look ridiculous down there on your knees.'

He said, 'I can't. I'm stuck. Can you help me, Bernie?'

She started to laugh as she took his hands and hauled him to his feet and then she was in his arms and he was kissing her and she stopped laughing and quite suddenly she sobbed and held him close and kissed him back.

* * *

Mark parked the car just outside the garage allocated to the flat. He switched off and sat still, trying to pull himself together. No point in putting the car away. He would have to drive up to Redland where the Venableses lived. But first he had to stop shaking and concentrate his mind on his driving.

He got out of the car slowly like an old man and fumbled with the bunch of keys. And then he climbed the stairs to the flat and went into the living room and thought of how happy he had been when Holly had so suddenly had a change of heart back in November and they had planned to organize Christmas at Reg's holiday village.

And now he knew why.

He looked around. The room was overly neat; Holly had cleaned it thoroughly before they left two weeks ago. No books, no papers, no knitting. Every surface was gleaming. He had no idea why the neatness angered him further, but it did. Perhaps everything would anger him from now on. Perhaps he would not be fit to be a father. Perhaps he would always have to exercise this enormous self-control in everything he did with Holly. Perhaps . . . perhaps. Everything, every last little thing, was so hypothetical and had been for all his married life. He should never have relied on his mother for money; he should have given the garage an ultimatum; he should have agreed to adopt a baby years ago. And he should never have allowed Holly to work with that slimeball Venables.

He was shaking again so he made tea and drank it with powdered milk and felt sick. He went into the bathroom and was sick. Then he sat in the chair by the desk and picked up the phone and dialled Reg's number and then listened to the recorded message and the bleeps and wondered if Stanley Edwards had made a miraculous recovery and gone back to finish what he had started.

He said roughly, 'Message for Holly. I'm at the flat. Thinking. But I don't need to think. Not really. Don't do anything, Holly. Please. This baby needs good parents and we'll be good parents. We'll make sure of it. Cancel the appointment. Do it as soon as you get in. I'll be back in good time for the buffet.' He was going to send his love and then he did not. He left the flat as slowly as he had entered it, locked the door carefully and got into the car.

When he drew up outside the Redland house, there were noises of jollification coming from the garden. Was there some kind of party going on? The clock on the dashboard said one fifty and he checked it incredulously with his own watch. It had been twelve thirty when he left the bungalow and he felt he had lived a lifetime since then. There hadn't been much traffic and he knew he had driven like a lunatic. So . . . the party was a lunch party and would not be over for a while. He couldn't wait that long.

He left the car in the road and crunched across the gravel past two other cars to the back door. The garden, bleak and muddy, ran down to a stream and some children were down there all togged up in wellingtons and ancient anoraks. It was yet another drawback. He had planned on getting Venables into the garden and knocking him flat out there. But he knew if he hesitated he would most definitely be lost; already the thought of landing his fist in somebody's face was becoming more and more difficult.

He rapped sharply on the back door and almost immediately it opened and Dinah Venables stood there.

'Oh – sorry – I thought it was one of the children.' She had a tea towel in one hand and she dried her hands on it as she stared at him. 'Good Lord. It's Holly's husband, isn't it? We met at the party, didn't we?'

'Yes. That's why I'm here.' And it was. Of course it was. It wouldn't have happened if there hadn't been a party.

'Well, come in! We've been expecting to hear from you. Hugo will be glad to see you – he's been hoping Holly would change her mind about resigning. He's phoned your flat I don't know how many times. It was your uncle, wasn't it? We guessed you'd get in touch as soon as you could.' She pulled the door wide and stepped back. 'Do come in.'

He did not remember her being like this; she'd always been a bit superior with Holly and he'd got her down as an overbearing wife. And he hadn't wanted to go in, but it was so damp and she'd got the door open . . . He put his foot over the threshold and stood inside the warm kitchen.

'I just wanted a word. And you've obviously got guests.'

She smiled. 'The children. Yes. They belong to Hugo's brother and my two sisters. We have them nearly every weekend in the school holidays. It helps me come to terms with . . . well, you know. Childlessness.'

He was having to readjust a lot of preconceptions: the warm, homely kitchen full of food remains; the children having fun in the water; upturned wellingtons drying on the radiators . . . He said, 'Sorry, I didn't know.'

She laughed and shrugged, not a bit embarrassed. 'I thought it was the joke of the office. You know, poor old Hugo firing blanks. He says I'm lucky because I can always hand the family back at the end of the holidays. But he misses them as much as I do. Silly old fool.' She put the towel down and looked at him. 'You're as white as a sheet, Mr Jepson.'

'Please call me Mark.' He tried to produce a smile. 'It's raw out there.'

'I know. The children will be blue when they come in for tea. But they can't keep away from water, can they? Let me make you a cup of tea—'

'No, really. I have to get back. Fireworks and so on.'

She nodded and led the way through the door into a wide Victorian hall. 'We're going to insist on the children having a rest soon. We're taking them into the city to see the display later.' She paused outside a door. 'He's retired to the study. That means he's a bit the worse for his lunchtime wine. Treat him gently.' She grinned but he did not smile back. His mind was reeling.

Hugo was indeed asleep in an armchair pulled close to a log-effect electric fire. The room was dark and claustrophobic. Team photographs hung on the walls and the two armchairs were overstuffed leather. Just for a moment, before Dinah woke him, Hugo's collapsed face made him look the archetypal roué. And in that moment Mark felt a pang of pity.

'Christ almighty!' Hugo woke with a deliberate flurry, sitting up, waving his legs, adopting instantly his role of overgrown schoolboy. 'If it isn't Holly's very own Mark!' He made to leap up but fell back in the chair. 'No slur intended, old man – definitely not!' He held out his hand. 'Forgive me . . . post-prandial nap. Bloody kids all over the place . . .'

'I'll have to keep an eye on the bloody kids,'

Dinah said in a voice of steel. 'Offer Mark a drink, won't you, Hugo? Unless you've emptied all the bottles yourself.' This was the Dinah described to him by Holly. Almost tough and definitely unforgiving.

Hugo turned his head with difficulty to watch the door closing and then levered himself up. 'She's been on the vinegar as per usual,' he commented, going to the sideboard. 'I have all the kids here every weekend just to keep her happy.' He lifted a bottle and his eyebrows at the same time. Mark shook his head. 'Sure? Driving of course. Bloody nuisance.' He tipped the contents of the bottle into a glass and began to look happier. 'Well. Sit down and tell all, old man. I was a bit fed up with your wife leaving me in the lurch like she did. But I knew something pretty cosmic must have happened. So. What was it?' He took a gulp of his drink.

Mark said tersely, 'My uncle needed help at his place on the coast—'

'The ghastly run-down holiday village?' Hugo laughed loudly. 'Holly has told me about it in the past. Thought you were going to give it a miss this year.'

'We've had the best Christmas of our lives, actually.' Mark held onto the back of a chair. The room was much too hot and the over-furnished effect made it stifling. It was a Victorian study-cum-snug. A declaration of masculinity.

He said, 'I haven't come here to make excuses

to you. Holly has left the firm and you know why. That's why I'm here.'

Realization dawned and the folds of Hugo's face degenerated again. He put the glass down on the sideboard and gripped the back of the other chair. They stood facing each other.

'Look here, old man.' Hugo tried to inject some bluster into his voice, failed, cleared his throat and started again. 'Be reasonable, Mark. For God's sake, what have I got to look forward to? The only good thing about being Hugo Venables is that he can have a bit of fun without any after-effects.' He stopped speaking because Mark's indrawn gasp was nearly a yell.

Mark let the breath go and stared across the two chairs. Somewhere at the back of his mind, an enormous bubble of elation was being born. But he could only deal with one thing at a time.

He said levelly, 'You raped my wife, Venables. Because you thought everything was safe and superficial, you raped her. It was superficial for you, but not for her. It never is for the victim.'

Hugo took one hand off the chair and held it up. 'Now hang on there, Mark. Just listen for a moment. There were no victims around that night! I have known Holly longer than you. I have fancied her ever since I took her on. I'm not saying I love her, but I am very fond of her – very fond indeed. And I respect her too. Did you know I made her a partner in the firm?'

'And then demanded payment?'

335

'Not payment. I thought she might want to show her gratitude . . . Anyway, what are we talking about? Holly knew the score. You weren't there and I don't know what she's told you, but she knew exactly what was happening. And to call it rape is . . . dammit, it's funny!' He tried to laugh, throwing back his head and then righting it quickly and gripping the chair harder. 'For God's sake, Mark, I'm in no condition for this conversation. Take my word for it, rape was not on the agenda.'

Mark drew another breath. 'You are an insensitive, drunken lout! You used my wife to feed that enormous ego. But at the same time, you are pathetic. I hope I'll never see you again. This is how I shall remember you. In your pseudo-Sherlock Holmes study when you could be down in that brook with your nephews and nieces. You really are pathetic!'

He turned and left the airless room, went down the hall, past the startled Dinah and out into the fresh air. Hugo came after him, gibbering something about staying friends and filling everyone in on the true picture. Dinah's voice screeched, 'For Pete's sake, Hugo! You've got no shoes on!' The children looked round and one of them began to scramble up the bank. The others followed. Mark had got as far as the first car parked on the gravel when Hugo's hand clamped on his shoulder.

'I absolutely insist—' he began.

Mark turned and looked into the crumpled face of someone who was about to burst into tears. The children were in sight. There was only one thing for it. He made a fist of his right hand and brought it up from his hip until it connected with Hugo's jaw. There was nothing to it really. He did not enjoy the sound it made but Hugo's startled expression balanced out any horror and when he staggered back against the car, his hand to his jaw, he was still able to speak.

'You absolute swine!' he said, and his voice squeaked with outrage.

The children gathered around him. Dinah was behind them, grinning all over her face.

'Are you all right, Uncle Hu?' one of the girls said. And a boy asked urgently, 'Shall we call the police?'

'I'm all right.' He looked past them at Mark. 'Clear off!' he yelled fiercely.

Dinah directed her grin at Mark. 'Thanks, Mark. Regards to Holly. Happy New Year!'

The bubble of elation was going to explode at any moment. He grinned back. 'Same to you all!' he said and went down the drive, got into his car and switched on the engine. He thought he would shout with joy but suddenly he was crying. He drove around the corner somehow, parked again and put his head on the steering wheel.

'My dear Holly,' he wept. 'My dearest dear.'

And then he trumpeted into his handkerchief and glanced at his watch. He could be back at

337

the bungalow in half an hour. Just gone three. Plenty of time to call into one or two shops for sparklers. It would still only be about four o'clock when he got back. He could help put up the tables again and start getting the food out for the buffet.

Fourteen

Mavis woke from her afternoon nap and turned indolently towards her travelling clock on the bedside table. She couldn't read the figures and realized it was getting dark. Probably four o'clock. And Bernice would be up and doing before anyone else and might bring a cup of tea. It would be marvellous to sit up against the pillows and drink a cup of tea and gossip about everyone.

She stretched under the covers, pointing her toes like a ballerina and then stopping quickly before she got the cramp. She felt as content as a cat lying there, warm and full of good things with even better things to anticipate. If they could stay here exactly as they were for the rest of their lives, she would be quite happy. She had become a new woman by posing for Cree Evans and that had come to an end when she was beginning to tire of it anyway. But the newness, the feeling of freedom, had stayed with her. She lay there revelling in it, whatever it was, enjoying

339

being Mavis Gentry probably for the first time in her life.

That thought was quite a shock and she turned on her back, crooked her knees and slowly pushed herself up onto the pillows. Had she really never been happy with Mavis Gentry before? Surely . . . surely the boredom she had felt had been nothing to do with being Mavis Gentry? And if it had been, exactly what had changed?

She reclined there, thinking hard, but could find no answers. Mavis Gentry pre-Christmas and Mavis Gentry post-Christmas were one and the same person. They had to be. But they weren't.

Frowning with concentration, she found herself sliding her legs out of bed and feeling for her slippers, then padding across the hall and into the kitchen and putting on the kettle. Then laying a tray with three cups and saucers. Then taking all that off the tray and searching for a traycloth before relaying it.

She carried the three steaming cups into Bernice's room and found it empty. Then she went into Pansy's room.

Pansy woke with a smile. She hadn't changed; she was always smiling.

'Oh how lovely! How just lovely,' she greeted Mavis and the tray. 'I've had the most marvellous nap and everything that has happened seems to be clicking into place now. That awful man and those dear children and poor little frightened Ivy and wonderful manly Ted . . .' She sat up and ran her hands through her hair and Mavis realized that she hadn't been doing that to her own hair for ages now. She probably looked a wreck. But she didn't care. And *that* was something different about her – that she didn't care how she looked.

She said, 'Bernie's not in her room. I thought she'd want a nap too. It's been a busy time.'

'A busy time but a wonderful time.' Pansy took her cup and inhaled the steam, closing her eyes ecstatically. 'Oh Mavis . . . I do love you.'

Mavis looked surprised. 'Because I've brought you in a cup of tea?' she asked.

'No. Yes. Of course. But for everything that goes with that.' She looked through the tea-steam and her eyes were swimming. 'I know I'm a silly, sentimental old fool, but this holiday . . . it's sort of cemented us together. Don't you think that?'

'Yes. No.' Mavis laughed. 'Sorry, I'm not copy-catting. But yes, we have been particularly close, haven't we? But also . . . we've been free.'

'Oh, you and your free thing!' Pansy sipped and then put cup and saucer on her table. 'You'd better not say too much about that in front of Bernie on the way home. It irritates her.'

'Does it?' Mavis was genuinely surprised. 'I didn't realize . . . but that's over. That little bit of craziness. I can just imagine what an idiot I must have looked to you two.' She laughed. 'I know now that Cree is a hopeless case. Probably if it weren't for Cass, he'd be in a loony bin!'

'Oh, he's not that bad.' Pansy glanced at Mavis. 'You do realize, don't you, that that's where Bernie is now? With Cree Evans?'

Mavis laughed again. 'You say that very . . . portentously!'

'That's how I mean it.' Pansy picked up her tea, well pleased with the effect she had caused.

'They went for a walk, that's all.'

'And they're not back yet. They didn't come to the Lantern with us for lunch, so they would have been walking for three hours. In this weather. Not very likely, is it?'

Mavis stared. 'But – but – what about Cass?'

Pansy shrugged. 'Different relationships? You know him better than me.'

Mavis sipped her tea and considered. 'No, I don't. But that doesn't matter. Oh dear. Will Bernie be all right, d'you think?'

'She's not like us. Let's face it, Mavis dear, we were both dumped. It's put us off men . . . in that way. She was . . . loved. Right up to the end.'

Mavis nodded. 'Yes. All right. I accept what you are saying, though . . . of course you didn't know St John, so . . . but yes. And I know that about Bernice. I know she is quite a – a—'

'Passionate woman?'

'Yes. A passionate woman. What I meant

342

was . . . will he dump her? I mean – break her heart again?'

'I don't know.' Pansy drained her cup and put it back on the saucer. 'I don't think there's much we can do about it. Be there for her later, perhaps.'

Mavis passed over Bernice's cup and saucer. 'Oh Pansy, what a lovely thing to say. Here. Have her cup of tea. A sort of symbolic chalice.'

Pansy burst out laughing. 'That Cree man has got a lot to answer for!' she said. 'You're getting distinctly flowery in your old age, Mavis!'

'Yes. Well.' Mavis went to the window and stared at the little copse dark against the skyline. 'I was wondering how this place had changed me. So it's made me flowery, has it?'

'It's changed us all, Mavis dear. It's made us realize that we love each other. It's all right, I'm not turning gay. But I do love you and Bernie. And I'm not ashamed to tell you, so there!'

Mavis turned, smiling. 'Thank you, Pansy. I feel the same way.' She gathered up the cups. 'Let's get dressed and see if we can help Holly up at the bungalow.' She went to the door. 'Oh, I know what I wanted to tell you. I think there's something going on between Reg and Cass. What have you got to say to that?'

Pansy sighed. 'You might have changed in some ways, Mavis, but not in others.'

Mavis was unabashed. She took the tray back to the kitchen and called over her shoulder,

'I think Paula and Dennis are all right now too.'

Pansy thought of Paula in that hospital bed, all eyes and frizzy hair. That was how she must have looked when she was Paula's age. She sighed. 'I hope so,' she said.

Ted had made up the fire in the living room and brought all the duvets and blankets in from the bedrooms to make a huge nest. They all got into it, the children in the middle and Ted and Ivy on the outside, their bodies curved protectively. 'You all right, Tom?' he asked, feeling the boy's feet, wrapping another blanket around him.

Tom's eyes were already closed. 'You've asked me that a hundred times already. I'm quite all right.' He managed a smile. 'Thank you for saving me, Ted.'

'We all saved you, my son,' Ted murmured. He too was exhausted. Adam was already asleep, as were Gemma and Giles.

Ivy whispered, 'Are the doors locked?'

'Yes. And I've pushed the table and chairs against them. Don't worry.'

She said, 'I love you. You were wonderful.'

'I love you too. And you are wonderful.' He opened his eyes to look across at her. 'Our ducklings.' He smiled. 'Oh Ivy . . . I think it's going to be all right.'

But she was already asleep. And then so was he.

*　　*　　*

Holly managed an hour's nap when she got back from the Lantern and then woke with a jerk as May came in with some tea at three o'clock. May was smiling sentimentally.

'There's a message for you on the answering machine,' she said. 'It's from Mark and he's OK.'

Holly felt all the misery of the day sweep back into her mind. She pushed herself up in the bed with some difficulty; all her limbs ached with tiredness.

She said, 'Is he coming back?'

'Yes. He'll be here – with fireworks – as soon as he can.' May sat on the end of the bed. 'Drink your tea and then go and listen to him. I don't think you'll mind me hearing what he has to say, but I don't expect you'll want anyone else to hear it.'

Holly could imagine. She took the tea gratefully and let the steam warm her face. She remembered Mark's anger and frustration last night. She had hoped some of it had been used up in the sea this morning but that was obviously too much to hope for.

'You were right, May. Some secrets are best kept.'

'Well, I'm not so sure about that any more. I've got a feeling Arthur has known for some time about the boys.'

Holly looked over her cup. 'Has he said anything?'

'Not directly. But I know him very well!' May smiled again. 'What he has said is . . . quite wonderful. Yes, actually that's what it is. Quite wonderful.'

Holly forced a grin. 'My God. You're falling in love with your own husband, aren't you?'

'Am I?' May looked surprised. 'Perhaps I am. I haven't thought he was wonderful for an awfully long time.' She stood up. 'I'll take him in a cup of tea and tell him.'

'Tell him what? That he's wonderful?'

'Yes. And that I love him!' May turned in the doorway. 'You've talked me round. No more secrets.' She closed the door behind her then immediately opened it. 'Go and listen to Mark. Now!'

When May came out of her bedroom an hour later, Holly was still sitting by the telephone in the hall, her head bent and tears coursing down her cheeks.

May put an arm around the bowed shoulders. 'Come on. You must have known it was what he would do. He's so like Reg. No way on earth would he have let you have an abortion.'

'He can't do this. I don't want anyone else's baby . . . only his.' Holly scrubbed at her eyes and looked at May. 'I'm sorry, May, but I can't do this. It's not just for Mark. It's for me. I don't want Hugo Venables's child – I don't!'

May hugged the golden head to her shoulder

and looked through the glass of the door. A car was coming down the drive.

She said urgently, 'Listen, love. Leave it all for now. Let's get the cold collations out on the table and then have our baths and get ready for this evening. We're all tired. Think about it tomorrow. Eh? A new year.'

'I don't know whether I can cope, May. I feel terrible. I'm so sorry but I can't face anyone. I'm so ashamed . . .'

The car had pulled up outside the bungalow. One person got out and started up the path. May said hurriedly, 'I'll have to go, Holly. Bathroom.' She pulled away abruptly and Holly almost fell off the chair. And then the front door opened and Mark was there.

He saw Holly sitting by the telephone and wanted to gather her up and take her to their room and tell her the wonderful news . . . He saw she had been crying for some time. She looked drowned in her own tears. He felt her grief as his own, knew her bewilderment and ultimately her bitter shame. They had to deal with that first . . . and together. He was glad he had hit Hugo; he had done it for Holly.

He closed the door gently and leaned against it.

He said, 'Darling. I'm so sorry. Those things I said last night. I didn't mean them. I was angry with myself.' He stopped speaking and drew a deep breath. He had to tell her about Hugo. He had to get Hugo out of the way.

'Holly, my love. It's all right. I promise you it's all right. I went to see him. Venables. He has no idea – stupid idiot – of what he has done. He thought it was just a casual . . . I don't know – *embrace*. I know it's going to take time for you to forget all that, love. But eventually you will. I promise you will. Simply because he's such a fool. If it meant nothing to him, then one day it will mean nothing to you.'

She began to weep again and he knelt by her and held her to him. She clutched at him almost frantically.

'I thought you must have left me.' It was difficult to decipher her words. 'I'm so glad to see you. And what you said . . . the message you left. Oh Mark. I cannot have his child. I simply cannot do it, darling.'

'All right. All right, Holly. You won't.'

She took a deep, shuddering breath and then leaned her weight fully on him. 'Thank God. I thought you would feel bound to be . . . quixotic. When did you realize it was impossible?'

He leaned back so that he could see into her face. Her eyes were swollen and red. She looked tired and ill. He thought he had never seen her so beautiful.

He whispered, 'It wouldn't have been impossible, my love. Because of us. But it simply doesn't arise any more . . . Listen, Holly, my darling Holly. He can't have children. That's why he thinks it's all right to do . . . what he did.'

He smoothed her hair from her eyes and tried to smile. 'But . . . oh Holly, it seems . . . we *can* have children. This baby is ours. It's our baby, Holly. We've started our family!'

She was very still, staring at him. At last she said, 'You mean . . . this baby isn't his?'

'That's exactly what I mean. He knows he can't father a child – he knew it at the time. That's why it was just a game to him. He didn't mean to hurt you.'

'Then . . . then what you just said . . . about starting our family . . .'

'Yes.' He freed one hand and fished a handkerchief from his pocket. Gently he began to dry her face. 'It's our baby, Holly.'

She was silent for a long time, staring at him. At last she breathed, 'Darling. I know we're tired and over-emotional but . . . I can't believe it, Mark. It's so wonderful I can't believe it.'

'I know. I was the same. I thought I was going to cheer with delight all the way home. But it took me that time to assimilate the . . . the *fact*. The actual fact that we are expecting a baby.'

'What happened? You saw him – you said you saw him?'

'I saw him. But I saw Dinah first. It was Dinah who told me Hugo is infertile. She was quite decent about him actually. She's almost nice till she's with him.'

He finished dabbing her face while he told her disjointedly about the children playing in the brook and the kitchen smelling of food and the awful, overheated, overfull study. She listened as if her life depended on understanding every word. Then she put her hand on his cheek and traced the bone down to his chin. She said, 'Do you know what I will never forget? That before you knew the baby was yours, you wanted to keep it.' She hiccoughed a little laugh. 'Thank you for phoning. I wouldn't have known otherwise.'

He stood up and drew her with him. 'I need some tea. Hot and sweet. And it looks as if you do too. And then can we have just one hour's sleep?'

'Yes . . . oh yes.'

Bernice joined Mavis and Pansy in the kitchen of the bungalow. No-one else seemed to be about and all the bedroom doors were shut.

'Let's get started,' Pansy said, spreading bread rolls over the kitchen table. 'We'll butter these, shall we? And leave them open for people to fill them as they wish?'

'Sounds a good idea.' Mavis smiled at Bernice. 'Is that all right with you, Bernie?'

'Of course.' Bernice fetched a knife from the cutlery drawer and glanced at the other two, who were both looking at her. 'Why wouldn't it be?' she added sharply.

'No reason.' But Mavis smiled warmly and uncharacteristically.

'Is anything the matter?' Bernice asked.

'It's just . . . Pansy and I were talking. After we'd had our naps. And we thought how much we love each other.' Mavis smiled again. 'And that includes you, of course.'

Bernice said, 'How nice.' She sat down and began to split rolls.

Silence reigned for a long minute then Pansy said, 'Aren't you tired, dear?'

Bernice glanced up. 'No. And please don't call me dear. Or is that part of the love-in?'

Pansy spread butter on one half of a roll and surveyed it. 'Sorry, Bernie. I feel oddly . . . protective towards you.' She looked very pink. 'Don't laugh at us, Bernie. After all that's happened, we feel part of something . . . quite special.'

'Sorry. Sorry, girls.' Bernice smiled at last. 'Perhaps I am tired. I should have cut short that walk and come and had a nap with you two.'

'Oh no.' Mavis piled buttered rolls into a basket. 'We didn't mean that. We are together. Of course. But we're also free.'

Pansy said, 'I thought I told you not to start that kind of talk with Bernice!'

Bernice laughed easily. 'Don't worry. I know exactly what Mavis means. But actually, girls, I wish I had stayed with you. I think I behaved rather foolishly this afternoon.'

Mavis and Pansy glanced at each other

nervously but it seemed that Bernice was not going to make any confessions.

'Never mind. We're together now and we shall all be together tonight.' She grinned. 'It's going to be fun. We must make it fun for those children. They've had a rotten experience.' She sighed. 'What a day.'

'And what a night,' Mavis agreed. 'Sitting up all the time waiting for that ghastly man to break in . . .'

'Has anyone heard anything from the hospital?'

'No, still nothing.'

'And what a week.' Pansy fetched a huge container of sausages from the freezer and began to arrange them on a baking tray. 'Poor Paula.'

'They'll be all right,' Bernice said. She set her mouth in a straight line. 'And so shall we.'

'Let's take Reg a cup of tea,' Pansy said. 'Then we can put up the trestle table and start laying everything out.' She filled the kettle. 'Isn't it nice to be able to help out Holly and May?'

They pottered around in the kitchen thoroughly enjoying themselves. There was more room than in their chalet and they worked well together. 'We ought to move in together, really,' Pansy said. 'You know, buy somewhere large enough so that we can have our own bits but share a kitchen.'

'It wouldn't work,' Bernice said definitely. 'We'd lose our friendship. I'm sure of it.'

They wheeled the trolley carefully across the hall and tapped on Reg's door. When there was no reply Mavis eased the door open and then stood very still. The others looked over her shoulder. Reg was fast asleep in the crook of Cass's elbow and she had dropped off with her cheek against his head. Mavis closed the door very carefully and turned to the others. They were both pictures of astonishment. Mavis whispered triumphantly, 'I told you so!' and Pansy whispered back, 'I know. But it's so . . . unlikely.'

Bernice said, 'You didn't say anything to me. I wish you had. It makes . . . quite a difference.'

'How?' the other two said in unison.

'I didn't want to come between Cass and her father. They're interdependent. But if she and Reg . . . I mean, that's what we've just seen, isn't it? Cass and Reg? Together?'

'Oh yes,' said Mavis.

'Then that means Cree will be on his own. And I don't think he can manage on his own.'

'And you would . . . ?' Pansy's big blue eyes were nearly popping out.

'I think I would, girls. I know it's crazy and mad. But I think I would.'

Mavis said, 'That's what I meant about being free. Not stuck in any groove in any way. If it's crazy and mad, well, it doesn't matter. Does it?'

'No.' Pansy held onto the trolley and kept staring at Bernice.

Mavis said, 'He *needs* you! You'll be able to persuade him to do proper portraits, not misshapen women with odd arms and legs and breasts and everything.'

'But you'll have to pay for everything,' Pansy said. 'He hasn't got a bean.'

'But he'd be worth investing in. Wouldn't he?' It was so obvious that Bernice needed reassurance and the other two both put an arm around her.

Mavis came out with absolutely the right thing: 'Robert would want you to do it,' she said.

Bernice said, 'Oh *girls*! You're right. I do love you.'

Reg's bedroom door opened and Cass stood there looking like the wreck of the *Hesperus*.

'We can hear the tea trolley shaking like a leaf,' she announced. 'We're both dying for some tea before it gets cold.'

'I'll fetch another cup,' Pansy said.

Cass said, 'Get four. Let's all have tea sitting on Reg's bed. There's plenty of room because Maude was a large lady.'

The phone started to ring and Cass picked it up. She said yes and thank you a couple of times and replaced the receiver.

'That was the police. Stanley Edwards was dead on arrival at the hospital. And the police will want to interview all of us after the holiday. So we have to stay put.'

They stared at each other silently. It was

Bernice who said slowly, 'What is this going to do to Ivy? And the children?'

Mavis put a hand to her throat. 'They'll work through it.'

Pansy nodded. 'They've got Ted.'

Cass took charge of the trolley and spoke briskly. 'It's what we all wanted, isn't it? To set them all free? Supposing he'd lived?'

They all considered that possibility and shivered.

It was eleven o'clock before they all gathered on the beach outside Magpie Cottage. The party had started at nine and the children, refreshed from their long sleep, had done complete justice to the food and then everyone had settled down with coloured paper, scissors and glue and tried to make themselves some kind of fancy dress. They looked a motley crew as they went about the business of sorting the fireworks in the lee of a rock. Mark was supposed to be Robin Hood in a green tissue hat with a fringed newspaper feather; Arthur and Cree glittered with kitchen foil as beings from outer space; Reg had a stuffed parrot on his shoulder and was limping around his wheelchair with sticks; Ted and Dennis had done their best as tramp and scarecrow respectively; Gemma had decorated her doll, Regina, with paper flowers and the boys were wearing masks and calling themselves Batman and Robin. The women had resorted to

355

flowers in their hair and summer skirts and were either country dancers or hula-hula girls. What they lacked in finesse they made up for in enthusiasm as they collected wood for the fire, rolled newspapers for spills, relit the candles that guttered out in the mist and encouraged the boys to pile pebbles around the site of the fire to protect it.

At half-past eleven the knotted newspaper was lit beneath the kindling and, after a frantic ten minutes of feeding more dry twigs into the pile, the flames took hold and they all sat or squatted around. Reg had long since collapsed into his wheelchair and directed operations like the conductor of an orchestra, using his walking sticks as batons.

'Firework display ready?' he called into the darkness.

'Aye aye, sir.' Mark came into the ring of light and made a mock salute, which delighted the two boys. Ted appeared bearing more wood which he fed into the flames. Dennis came behind Paula and slid his arms around her waist.

'You made me jump.' She turned within his grasp and kissed him. 'Oh Chiv . . . admit to me – go on, admit it – that coming here was the best thing we ever did!'

'In spite of the baby?' he tested her.

'Because of the baby. It was a special place before, but now . . . now it's very special.'

'Yes. You're right.' He kissed her. 'You're so right. My wonderful Polly.'

'I hope Ted and Ivy feel the same. I'd hate it if all that business with that horrible man had put them off coming again. I'd like to meet them every year.'

'You hit it off with Ivy, don't you? I can understand you liking Holly. I'm rather surprised about Ivy.'

She rubbed her nose against his. 'She's so wise, Chiv. D'you know what she said to me? She said we ought to give the baby a name. What d'you think?'

'Well . . . OK. But we don't know whether it would have been a boy or a girl, do we?'

'No, but I think it was a girl. I *feel* it was a girl.'

He said again, 'Yes. OK.' He kissed her left eye. He would have gone along with anything she said; twins, even.

'And I thought . . . darling, how about Denise? After you.'

He felt a rush of tears; they were becoming familiar to him; he had done a lot of crying in the last few days.

'Oh Polly. Oh *Polly*.'

'I know, my love. I know. There. It's all right.'

'Oh it is. Oh it is, Poll. I love you so much.'

'And I love you too.' She had chosen the name because some time during the long night she had realized that Dennis would always be like a child to her and she would have to look to his parents for strength and support. But she still loved him and always would. She looked over his shoulder at Mark Jepson and felt a small pang of remorse for using him to shake herself out of her depression. But then Mark leaned over Holly and kissed her too and the remorse went. After all, the passion Mark had kindled had been so easily and readily turned towards Dennis and it had obviously worked the same way for Mark. She put her mouth to her husband's ear and whispered, 'I know I'm crazy to tell you this, but I think – it's just another feeling I've got – that when we sort of went mad yesterday afternoon, we started another baby.'

He stopped weeping, aghast. 'Poll! Not yet! We shouldn't have done all that so soon . . . my God, it's less than a week since the miscarriage!'

She giggled into his neck. 'I know. I'm a scarlet woman, Chiv. But then you knew that when you married me!'

He looked down at her. She was so damned pretty with her curly hair and heart-shaped face. He started to laugh. Laughter, tears . . . what was the difference?

With some difficulty Reg manoeuvred his wheelchair away from the lights of the fire and lanterns. Beyond them the sea shifted with reflections and the tiny waves flopped onto the shingle and tried in vain to suck it back into the depths. He knew he was blessed with a contented nature but the last few days had offered him such heights of happiness he could scarcely believe in them. He thought of Cass yelling into the mist that she was happy as if she was wresting happiness from the very air around her. And that was how it had been. Snatched. They had both come upon it unexpectedly and taken it. The Garden of Eden. Eve . . . the forbidden apple. He felt filled with the glory of Adam who must surely have said that it was worth it . . . my Garden for one apple.

From the darkness of the rocks Cree's voice spoke. 'OK, Arthur? I think that does it. A match to this fuse and one by one they should ignite.'

Reg looked across the fire to where Bernice was cavorting with Mavis and Pansy. He had never seen her like this; she had been happy on the cruise but not like this, not excited, not foolish. Of course they had all been under a terrific strain for the past twenty-four hours but that did not account for Bernice's childishly high spirits.

He said into the darkness, 'I want a word with you, Cree. Pull the chair back out of the firelight, can you? Just for a moment.'

Cree did as he was bid and then crouched by his old friend. He said tiredly, 'OK. So you were right. I've gone too far. I'm crazily in love with her. And she feels the same way about me. And you're right, she's like a volcano and terribly vulnerable and if I'd listened to you she wouldn't be hurt.'

Reg turned his head and studied his friend. He said, 'She doesn't look very hurt at the moment, old man.'

'She's used to putting up a front, let's face it. Oh God, Reg. She's wonderful. If we'd met years ago . . . I want to lie at her feet. Have you looked at her hands? Really looked at them? They're pale blue and you can see the veins and the bones and the nail beds . . . Her neck is long and it supports a head that is damned near classical in shape!'

'So you think her body is great?' Reg asked dryly.

'I know what you're saying. Lust. But, Reg, that's important. I haven't been able to lust after anyone for ages.' He almost laughed at Reg's expression. Then said, 'But it's not only lust, old man. She is a whole human being. She knows what she's doing. She doesn't blunder around like most of us do. She eats a breakfast and a lunch and a supper. I mean – proper meals, old man! And she knows that I can paint. She says it so calmly. "You can do anything you want to, Cree. You're a painter. You don't have to abide by any rules." She meant it, Reg. She believes in me!'

'Other people have told you that, Cree. Cass, for instance.'

'Yes. I know. That's the trouble, Reg. Cass.' He sighed. 'Of course she's told me she believes in me. But she doesn't . . . transfer that belief into *me*.' Cree lifted one giant paw and stabbed at his own chest.

'So you don't believe in her?'

'Christ, I don't know. She's so wonderful, is my little Cass . . .' To hear Cass described as little made Reg smile but Cree did not see that in the darkness. 'She sits up with me sometimes, Reg. I've never told you that, have I? When I get my black dogs – you know, the ones that sit on your shoulder and won't let you sleep . . . she keeps vigil with me then, Reg. Not many daughters would do that, would they?'

'Not many daughters would share your bed, put up with your shiftless ways, trawl around the pubs looking for freebies . . . You must realize, Cree, that Bernice would never do that. Your bed, yes. Nothing else.'

'That's just it, old man. She wouldn't do it and she wouldn't let me do it! She won't allow any black dogs anywhere in the vicinity and she'd make sure I ate three meals a day so that I didn't need to trawl the pubs. She knows what she's doing, Reg, and she would know what I was doing too! Can you imagine anything so totally relaxing?'

Reg started to laugh and Cree stopped staring at Bernice cavorting around the fire and looked at Reg reproachfully.

'All right. So she's got money to make all that happen. But I promise you that the money is a bonus, not a necessity. She'd get by on anything

Social Services handed out. She'd work . . . clean windows, scrub floors. I'm thankful she doesn't have to. Is that selfish, Reg?' He didn't wait for an answer. 'All right,' he said yet again. 'So that means I would have to obey her rules. I know it sounds crazy, and most men would hate it, wouldn't they? Not me. Not now.' He thumped the arm of the chair. 'But after saying all that . . . dammit, we can't be together! Neither of us can do that to Cass. And she wouldn't agree to a *ménage à trois*.'

'Wouldn't she?' Reg was genuinely surprised.

'I meant Bernice.'

'Ah. Quite. Yes.' Reg controlled his sniggers with difficulty. 'Well. All this is very interesting. Very interesting indeed. But not quite what I intended to talk about.'

Cree raised his brows. 'I thought you were going to give me a wigging for seducing Bernice—'

'You seduced her?' Reg interrupted delightedly.

'It wasn't difficult. But she was very surprised. She thought she was in control. She thought it was still a flirtation. But then . . . all that business with Ivy's crazy husband . . . made us a bit more serious, I suppose. And she knew what she was doing.' He drew a deep breath. 'My God.'

Reg said quickly, 'No details, old man. Please. And I won't burden you with any either. Very briefly, Cree, I've written Cass into my will. I want her to be free to do her own thing. Travel. Buy a home. Whatever. I was going to ask you to let her go, but it seems there's no need.'

'You mean . . . Cass?' Cree's knees were stiffening and he stood up slowly and leaned over, rubbing them. 'I don't get it, old man. You were going to tell me that you wanted me to let Cass go?'

'In essence, yes. I think she would have stayed with you, money or no money. Seen you out. But let's face it, Cree, you've got the strength and stamina of someone ten or twenty years your junior. I wouldn't be surprised if you made it to your hundredth birthday. She could be seventy before she's free. And I didn't want that.' Reg smiled. 'I was going to appeal to your better nature!'

Cree put his palms on his knees and leaned over them. He said slowly, 'You've never thought much of me since that business with May Long, have you, Reg? I didn't realize that until now.'

'Make Bernice Smythe happy and you'll redeem that over and over again,' Reg said steadily.

Cree swallowed. Then he said, 'You've always put every woman you've ever met up on a pedestal, Reg. And they're not like that. If you'd seen half of what I've seen—'

'They're just human beings. Like us. We're precious. You silly old fool, Cree Evans. You've got a gift. You could record our preciousness. And you don't. For God's sake, use all the extra years you've got doing just that! That's what will make Bernice happy!'

Cree did not move. He seemed to be considering every word Reg said. When he spoke his voice was so quiet Reg could barely hear him.

'You mean that, Reg, don't you? Every damned word.'

'Every damned word.'

'All right, old man. That's what I'll do.'

'Promise?'

'Of course. My oath on it. I don't make idle promises.'

'And keep an eye on Cass. Let her go but let her know where her home is.'

'You'll do that too.'

Reg said heartily, 'I certainly will.'

Mark yelled, 'Sixty seconds to go! Fifty-nine, fifty-eight, fifty-seven . . .'

Everyone took up the chant, Gemma just behind. Giles yelped his joy and held his fist in the air. Between them Ivy and Ted held him high.

'Midnight!' everyone shouted. And Arthur put a taper to the fuse. A rocket soared into the air. 'Happy New Year!'

Cree shoved the wheelchair towards the fire and they all held hands and sang with a will. The fireworks leaped and sizzled. The children held sparklers aloft. Pansy wept and said, 'Oh my

God, I feel like history! Two thousand! Is it possible?'

Bernice hugged her. 'It is! It's like Mavis says – we're free and anything is possible when you're free!'

Mavis poured champagne and Cass passed around the glasses. Mavis said, 'If you're at a loose end, my dear, you can live with me. I think we'd get on really well.'

Cass said, 'Oh Mavis! You are kind! But what on earth would you do with someone like me?'

'Swim,' Mavis said. 'There are perfectly good swimming baths just down the road and you could teach me.'

Cass screamed with laughter. 'The whole point of our swims, dear Mavis, is that they are crazy and cold and – very slightly – dangerous! We're sharing the element with eels and crabs and other species . . .'

Mavis felt as if she were running and getting nowhere. She said desperately, 'All right, we'll travel. We'll swim in the Aegean. And the wine-dark sea . . .'

Cass sobered and said, 'Mavis, I love you. Let's do that.'

Pansy, slurping champagne as if it were lemonade, said, 'May I come?'

'Of course! Anyone can come!' Cass held her glass aloft. 'Here's to the new millennium and new everything!'

Reg smiled quietly and lifted his glass. As the fireworks spluttered in the sky and showered silver stars into the sea, Holly and Mark came and sat either side of him on the shingle.

'Nunc,' Mark began. 'We've got something to tell you . . .'

Fifteen

Bernice said it should have ended there. They should all have packed up on New Year's Day and left for home and thought about everything and then come to decisions in the cold light of the new millennium. Too much had happened too soon; they were really all strangers, and to be making promises to keep in touch and meet up every Christmas . . . it was so rash.

However, the fact was that they could not leave until the police had interviewed them, and after a long lie-in most of them met up at the Ship's Lantern for a sandwich lunch and an exchange of the kind of promises Bernice had foreseen.

It was an amazing day. The sea lay calmly at the bottom of their little holiday village, pearly and inviting, though in fact no-one got into it; the sun seemed higher in the sky than it had been yesterday, in December, and the sky itself was bright blue and cloudless. And the air had changed overnight from a damp and gentle mist into an elixir that tingled in the nostrils and bellowed the lungs into action. The first of January was indeed beautiful.

The girls were the first to arrive at the pub. Pansy wore her red dress; it was highly unsuitable but she was still in a party mood. Mavis wore her chunky sweater and checked trousers because, although she hadn't had a swim for two days now, the outfit made her feel outdoorsy and active. Bernice was in her usual tweeds but somehow latterly they had changed; or perhaps it was just Bernice who had changed. She looked rather dashing and sexy. She and Cree had managed a long talk while they were clearing up the fireworks last night. There was nothing to stop them being together any more. And they were ecstatic about it. Bernice felt beautiful and Cree felt masterful. He wanted her to spend the rest of the night with him in his Christopher Wren chalet but Bernice was strangely reluctant. She wasn't certain whether she wished to come so completely out of the closet just yet.

'We can't do that to Cass,' she protested, though she had already seen Cass pushing the wheelchair up the rise towards the bungalow and would have laid odds on Cass staying there all night.

'Perhaps not,' he agreed. He wanted to talk to Cass anyway. Just to make absolutely certain she knew what she was doing.

So they went their separate ways and Bernice found a familiarity, a kind of solace, in being with Mavis and Pansy again and talking over everything that had happened. Pansy said, 'It's been lovely and wonderful and everything, but I think we've had enough now. I shall be quite glad to get home. I've booked an aromatherapy massage for next Wednesday and my hair needs doing too.' And Mavis said, 'I want to book a course of swimming lessons.' That was when Bernice said what a shame it was they couldn't leave after breakfast.

But they couldn't, so on New Year's Day they sat at the bar of the Lantern and ordered their gin and tonics. 'No ice, just a slice,' Pansy giggled as usual.

Mavis said, 'We'd better keep it to one. After all, we've had no breakfast and we don't want to be tiddly when the police get here.'

Bernice said, 'We could have had lunch in Evesham and been home in time to unpack and have a cup of tea in front of the television.'

'We shall miss each other.' Pansy looked sad but Mavis said bracingly, 'We'll be meeting up every day. And we shall see all the others next year. Maybe we could ask Ted and Ivy to bring the children over for a day. Some time.'

Bernice said nothing.

Ted and Ivy arrived at that moment, smiling as usual and dressed as they always dressed, in woollen hats, anoraks, jeans and an assortment of gloves and scarves. The boys asked immediately if they could go out on the terrace and Gemma of course went with them. Ted settled Giles in one of the bucket chairs where he sat like a small Buddha surveying everything with obvious enjoyment.

Ivy said tentatively, 'Is it wrong to feel happy? I mean – Stanley is dead and he was my husband for twelve years. And here I am with Ted and Gemma and Giles as if we've always been together. It's crazy!'

Pansy and Mavis were vociferous with their reassurance and Bernice added something about being in the right place at last. Ted's eyes were suspiciously bright as he put his arm around Ivy's narrow shoulders.

'They're right, my love. And it's such a lovely day, all the mist and fog gone. It's so good to be alive.'

'It is.' She wanted to be reassured. She pecked Ted's cheek and smiled. 'It really is. The air is like wine.'

Bernice asked whether they would like a drink. They opted for coffee. 'We didn't bother with breakfast,' Ivy confided. 'We ate such a lot last night and we thought if we're having lunch here . . .'

'Chips and things,' Ted agreed. 'Someone might be carsick later.'

Dennis and Paula came next. They looked like two sleepy children in the middle of a three-legged race, definitely joined at the hip. Bernice glanced at them occasionally and thought that some things should be kept for the privacy of one's own room, though their public display of affection seemed to please everyone else. Ted kept smiling at Ivy and Ivy said audibly, 'Aren't they sweet?' But for some unknown reason they made Bernice wish that she and Cree had been a little less wholehearted in their own love-making. Thank God it had been conducted in the privacy of Wren Cottage. Then Bernice remembered the big studio windows and swallowed convulsively.

Cree shambled in at that moment looking unkempt and not very clean. He grinned at the group around the table, chucked Giles under the chin and put a hand on Bernice's shoulder as he made for the bar. For a terrible moment she thought he might slide his hand down her tweed lapels and her whole body became rigid. But then he didn't. Perhaps he was having second thoughts too.

'What a wonderful day, Cree,' Paula sang out from the crook of Dennis's arm.

Ted said, 'Air like wine.'

Ivy said, 'Who would have thought it after all the mist and fog of the past few days?'

She and Ted kept that going until Cree joined them with his large whisky. He almost fell into a chair next to Bernice and told them unceremoniously to pipe down. 'Bit of a hangover,' he added by way of apology. 'Had a rotten night after I rather overdid the nightcaps.'

Bernice said, 'Then why don't you have black coffee now?'

'Hair of the dog,' he retorted. He tossed back his whisky and looked at her reproachfully. 'No sign of Cass,' he added.

She shrugged. 'She's a big girl now.'

He looked surprised. 'I didn't have you down for that kind of cat-comment,' he observed. 'Come and buy me another drink and I might overlook it.'

He lumbered out of his chair and Bernice sat still and mortified. She had simply meant that Cass was old enough to make up her own mind, but any kind of explanation now would make it too important. She held the arms of her chair as if she expected to be dragged out of it.

Ivy said, 'Let's go and see what the boys are cooking up out there. Looks as though Adam and Gemma are doing physical jerks or something!'

Ted hoisted Giles onto his shoulder and they wandered towards the patio doors. Mavis joined them and then so did Pansy. Dennis and Paula were locked in another embrace and did not miss anyone.

Cree threw himself back into the chair next to Bernice and frowned over his fresh whisky. He had needed Cass last night to fend off the inevitable visit from his black dog, but he had also wanted to talk to her. A fatherly talk. Surely he should be doing – saying – something? And she should be saying something back; explaining her feelings perhaps? Cree did not know what to make of it all. It was obvious to him that Reg was very fond of Cass and if he was leaving her a nice little nest egg that was fine. Of course. But how fond was he? And how fond was Cass of Reg? The thought of them sleeping together was quite shocking; he reminded himself that he had made passionate – even violent – love with Bernice Smythe and that after his talk with Reg last night he fully expected to be doing so for the rest of his life. Bernice was considerably younger than he was, probably twenty years or so. But Cass . . . Cass was still his daughter. And Reg was his contemporary. Almost. He forced himself to recall in some detail all that he and Bernice had got up to only yesterday afternoon . . . and behind the rocks last night, come to that. If Cass and Reg . . . somehow that wasn't right. Not his little Cass. And not his friend, Reg.

He frowned, swilled a mouthful of whisky around his tongue and swallowed it gratefully. His empty gaze settled on Paula and Dennis Chiverton. Christ, they were so intertwined he couldn't tell where Dennis ended and Paula began. He wondered what they did in the privacy of their quarters if they were getting this far in the lounge bar of the bloody Ship's Lantern.

Bernice spoke suddenly from his side as if she could read his mind. 'You know, Cree Evans, you're not always a very nice person, are you?'

'Can I help it if they want to go so public?' he protested righteously. 'If they were older it would be downright disgusting!'

She felt herself heat up and knew that her face was bright red. 'How much older?' she asked.

He focused on her. 'Sorry.' He grinned and leaned across to her. 'Sorry.' He kissed her and managed to slop some whisky onto her jacket. 'Sorry,' he repeated more urgently. 'Oh Bernie – sorry – sorry – I love you, I love you—'

She snapped, 'For God's sake, Cree. You're drunk!'

'No, I'm not drunk. I'm exhausted because I was on my own last night and I needed you and you weren't there.'

'Don't be ridiculous!' She dabbed frantically at her jacket with a flimsy handkerchief.

He tried to repeat the word 'ridiculous' and made a mess of it. 'Bernie,' he said despairingly. 'Don't you love me any more?'

'Of course I love you!' she said irritably. 'But not overwhelmingly just at the moment.'

Fleetingly he wondered how she would be about holding his head when he woke in the night and making him tea laced with brandy and telling him that eternity was here and now so how could that possibly scare him.

He said in a carefully jocular voice, 'Does that

mean you've changed your mind about coming to live with me and look after me in my old age?'

She did not answer immediately; she was making an absolute meal of cleaning her jacket. He studied her and found that she was as beautiful as a woman could be. She seemed to be sparkling this morning. Her dark eyes snapped with life – or maybe irritability – and she wore diamond studs in her ears that caught the morning sun and almost blinded him. She smelled of some kind of perfume and her thick, thick hair was twisted and pushed behind her ears. He remembered how it had felt in his hands yesterday afternoon and wondered if it was possible for a man to swoon with passion like an Edwardian lady.

She left the cleaning and glanced at him, then smiled unwillingly because he looked so ardent.

'When you put it like that . . .' she said.

But he couldn't pretend humour any longer and whispered, 'Let's go back to the chalet, Bernice.'

It put her right off. 'I want my lunch,' she said flatly. 'We didn't bother with breakfast and I like my food at set times. Then we should wait together for the police.'

'They might not come today. It's a public holiday after all.'

'They'll come,' she said confidently. 'I hope it'll be soon because the girls and I would like to get off during the afternoon.'

375

'You're going?' He was aghast. 'You can't leave me, Bernie! You know it's all right with Cass. And you said if it was all right with Cass you would stay and we would live together. Bernie . . . please.'

She took his arm warningly; Paula almost surfaced at his raised tone.

'I know it's all right with Cass.' She smiled at him and he blinked helplessly. 'I'm not sure whether it's still all right with you.'

He clutched at her hands, anguished. 'Bernice . . . I love you.'

'I know. But you're still so dependent on Cass.' She bit her lip. 'Cree, I can't just become another Cass. I can't do that.'

'I don't want that! What makes you think I want you to be Cass? Do you imagine Cass and I do the kind of things you and I did yesterday?'

'Please, Cree. Paula will hear you.'

'I don't bloody care. I can understand why they're behaving like they are in front of all of us. They're making a statement. They're saying—'

'I don't want to hear what they're saying, thank you, Cree.'

'Then come back to Wren. Now. Let's make a private statement of our own.'

'Don't be ridiculous—'

That word again. He swallowed it somehow.

'I've already said,' Bernice continued, 'we have

to wait for the police and then the girls and I are leaving.'

He was aghast again and she held up a hand. 'Please. Let's just leave it at that. I have to take the girls home. I am the driver.' She looked at his face and said slowly as if to a child, 'They don't drive, Cree.'

'Oh God. They must do. Nobody doesn't drive in this day and age.'

She said, 'Well, they don't.' She glanced at him again and saw that he was near to tears. She said quickly, 'Listen, Cree. We can't do anything in a hurry. You need time, so does Cass. And I certainly do. If you're coming to live in my house there will be certain alterations to be made. And I shall have to introduce you into conversation.'

'Warn all your friends that you are cohabiting with a mad artist?'

'Yes. Exactly.'

He looked at her; he knew that any second now he would blub. Like a great overgrown schoolboy he would break down and sob. He said carefully, 'Bernie. I don't want to live in your house. I want you to come and live in my flat. I won't need to introduce you into any conversation because nobody has much to do with me. So you can come straight away.'

She was very still, looking at him, seeing the tears properly now. She said, 'You want me to give up . . . everything? My home, my friends, my theatre trips, my music club, my poetry circle—'

'Yes. I thought it was what you wanted too.'

She looked away from him with some difficulty. On the other side of the window in the chill sunshine Tom and Adam had made the terrace into a sailing ship. The chairs and tables were piled into a corner for the winter and in their angles were cabins and a wheelhouse. They had mounted a paper napkin on an upturned table leg for a flag. Tom and Gemma were going through frantic motions of hoisting the mainsail; Adam was grappling with a recalcitrant wheel. They had created a separate and personal world and she thought that if they could do it then surely she could too.

She spoke with some difficulty. 'I don't know. I'm sixty, Cree. A creature of habit. You're asking a lot.'

'You did say . . . yesterday . . . you would live with me and inspire me to do wonderful paintings of people and places and – everything – the world—' He knew he was gabbling. 'You did say . . . you did, Bernie.'

'I know. I would have said anything yesterday.'

'And not today?'

'I think we need time, Cree. As I said just now—'

'I heard what you said. Christ, Bernie. It sounded like no.'

'Why should I have to move? Why can't it be you?'

He was miserable knowing logically she was right.

'I don't know.' He felt something run down his face; dammit, he was crying. He said, 'Bernie. I love you. Don't say no. Just don't say no.'

She was exasperated. 'I haven't said no. Not once have I said no. For goodness' sake, Cree. This is just a decision to be made, not a drama.'

He was almost desperate. He said, 'Come back to the chalet. Come on.' He half stood up. 'Now. Come back now. Then I'll be certain that you still love me.'

'Cree. I've already told you. Not before lunch.'

He straightened and then released her hands. The others came in from the terrace, saying that in spite of the sunshine it was cold. Behind him, Dennis surfaced and said, 'They're ages coming up from the bungalow. Shall we order our food now? I'm starving.'

Cree said loudly, 'Yes, let's have our lunch. All right, Bernice? All right, girls?'

Everyone nodded. Ivy settled the children around the table again. Ted bounced Giles on his knee. Paula sat where she was, smiling idiotically, one hand on her abdomen. She was so sure . . . so certain.

Pansy said, 'Are you all right, Bernie? What are you going to have?'

'I'll order my own,' Bernice said, making for the bar and the menus.

The police had in fact gone to the bungalow and talked to Holly and Mark. It was not so much an interview as an exchange of facts: Stanley Edwards had discharged himself from hospital over a week ago and when approached by a nurse had knocked her to the ground and sprinted off. The crew of the helicopter had seen Tom in the boat, bound and gagged. Obviously they had no idea that the three swimmers were approaching the rowing boat with murderous intentions: as far as they were concerned, they were heroic rescuers.

Mark was succinct. 'I don't know any previous details of course,' he said. 'But Mrs Edwards and her younger son, Adam, had both suffered at his hands before they came here. Mr Harris is an old friend of the family and brought them away with him to give them a break. It would seem that the husband – Stanley Edwards – followed them here and was willing to use any means to get them back.'

The detective nodded. 'If it hadn't been for Mr Harris we gather the boy might well have lost his life.'

Holly nodded as she passed coffee cups. 'He's very good with both boys. And Ivy is the same with his two children.'

The police seemed to think that would do for

now. 'It may well be – later on – that the Social Services will need to drop in on them. But as far as we are concerned, that's it.' He lifted his cup. 'Happy New Year to you.'

Mark grinned and nodded. 'Will you want a word with them? We're supposed to be meeting at the pub on the main road for a spot of lunch. They'll be there already, I expect.'

'We've got what we came for. The background story. Now we'll get in contact with the Midlands and tie it in with anything they know.'

They drifted off just as May and Arthur emerged from their room. Like Holly and Mark, they were obviously very happy with life. Mark reported on what had happened and May kissed Holly and said, 'So that's it. The end of the story.'

Holly smiled beatifically. 'Yes. And we're all going to live happily ever after – all right?'

'Definitely.' Arthur put some bread in the toaster and stared through the window. 'Now that the police thing is out of the way, I wouldn't mind making tracks this afternoon, May. How would you feel about breaking up the party?'

'Yes. Fine.' She stood close to him and said in a low voice, 'I shall want to say goodbye to Reg first.'

'Of course. Of course, old girl.' Arthur turned. 'When are you taking him back to hospital, Mark?'

'Tomorrow. The ward's reopening.' Mark

picked up Holly's hand and held it. 'What are we going to do, darling? Are we going to close up here and go back to the flat?'

She shook her head helplessly.

May came to sit at the table too. 'Listen. Why don't you two stay on here? Reg would just love to think of you living in the bungalow and keeping it warm for when he gets back. You could start spring-cleaning the chalets, Mark. New curtains, Holly – we were saying one or two of the chalets could do with new curtains, weren't we? Plenty for both of you to do. Think about it.'

Holly said slowly, 'I can't see us back at the flat somehow. Can you, Mark?'

His grin seemed to stretch wider still. 'I don't mind. We're together. That's all that matters.'

She lifted his hand with hers and put them against her face. 'You're right, of course.'

May said, 'That still leaves Reg in the lurch. Let's take him in a cup of tea and tell him you're staying.'

Holly laughed. 'All right. Come on.' She stood up. 'You two had better stay on as well. That would please him even more.'

Arthur made a face but nodded. May was delighted by the idea. She would enjoy passing on a million tips to Holly. Then she glanced at Arthur, saw his expression and said immediately, 'I don't think so, my dear. Arthur has probably got a meeting of the club and I think one of the boys will be getting some leave soon.' She smiled at her husband. 'Besides, it will be nice for you to be on your own for a bit.' He took her hand and squeezed it. 'For us too,' she added.

They put tea and toast on the trolley and made a ceremony about wheeling it up to the door and knocking before opening it. And then they froze in their tracks as they took in the tableau before them.

Cass was sitting high on the pillows, cradling Reg against her shoulder. Tears were streaming down her face. It was quite evident that Reg was dead.

So no-one went home for another week because the undertakers were busy and the crematorium was busy and Reg's funeral could not be arranged until the following Friday. They gathered in the bungalow and tried to come to terms with this catastrophic end to the holiday.

'No point in us going home and then coming back,' Pansy said, speaking for everyone. 'Besides . . . I don't feel like leaving Reg. Not now.'

Paula nodded. 'We can stay, can't we, Chiv? Term doesn't start for ages.'

Dennis nodded too. 'I wonder if the parents would come down for the funeral. They fell for Reg, didn't they? Well . . . we all did.'

Paula hugged him. 'Oh darling, you are marvellous! Of course we did. And of course they did too. We should all be together at a time like this.'

Ted looked at Ivy. 'We'd like to stay too. But there's my job . . .'

Ivy said, 'We've got till next Thursday, haven't we? Could you ask for some annual leave perhaps?'

'Please, Dad,' Adam said urgently. 'Please say yes.'

Gemma started to cry and Tom said, 'We can't go . . .'

'I'll do that. I'll take the day off at least. It'll be all right.' Ted was not as confident as he sounded; he had taken time off when Louise left last year and then when Giles had croup. But once he and Ivy were established he would not need to ask for any more favours.

Cree clapped him on the shoulder. 'Of course it will, old man. You and Ivy and the kids . . . Reg thought the world of you. It was almost as if he worked it so that you'd come down together.' He glanced worriedly at Cass. 'No problem for us. Cass and me. We can stay as long as we're needed.'

Arthur, still stunned, said, 'I'll phone the boys tonight. See if they can make it.'

May, who had held up very well till then, felt her bottom lip become unmanageable. 'Oh Art . . .' she said. And he took her in his arms.

Mark and Holly came in from the kitchen with the inevitable tea. They had done their weeping and felt very close to each other and to Reg. There was obviously no question of them going back to the flat now. Holly sat cross-legged by the children and asked them whether they would like to come to the funeral.

'I know you didn't want to go to . . . the other one.' Stanley Edwards had been cremated just three days before and the boys had opted to stay with Gemma and Giles at the bungalow. 'This will be different. We'll make it cheerful,' she promised. 'Like seeing him off on a train.' She looked round at Ted and Ivy. 'What do you think?'

Ivy said, 'If the boys would like to—'

'Me too,' said Gemma. 'And Regina of course.'

'We won't go without Gemma,' Tom said, looking at Ted.

'If it's all right with everyone else, then we'll go together,' Ted said.

Holly smiled. 'That's good. Now, how about each one of you choosing a hymn. Your favourite.'

' "Away In A Manger",' Gemma said instantly.

'That's a carol,' Adam pointed out.

'I think Reg would love that. We'll have it. What about you two?'

The boys hesitated, almost embarrassed. Then Tom said, ' "Onward, Christian Soldiers",' and Adam said he would think about it.

It was a strange six days; they told one another they must not grieve because Reg had had a

385

wonderful time and then just gone to sleep in the arms of someone he loved very much. But they did grieve. And they were oddly at a loose end. As Bernice said, 'It's such an anticlimax. Sorry, Reg, wherever you are, but it jolly well is!' They missed his benevolent presence more than they would have believed possible. Pansy and Mavis made no more efforts to dress up; Dennis and Paula felt that their rediscovered passion for each other was now unseemly and sat separately on Reg's three-seater sofa when they were at the bungalow, not quite knowing what to do with their hands; the children told the adults that Reg was in heaven and they mustn't cry, but every now and then Gemma clutched Regina and burst into sobs and then Adam wept with her and Tom had to stare very hard out of the window.

But it was Cass who worried all of them. Cass the competent was suddenly incapable of even the smallest task. She made tea and forgot the teabags, she cut bread and butter and nearly sliced off her thumb and she could not hold a conversation for longer than a single exchange. She moved back in with her father but their roles were reversed now. It was Cree who held her as she lay staring dry-eyed at the opposite wall, and when he found her one night standing by the window looking at the frosty stars as they climbed above the sea it was he who said, 'It's all right, honey. He's not all cold and lost out there.

He's with us – Christ, I can hear him laughing! Can't you?'

She said steadily, 'A week ago – ten days – I thought he was a dirty old man. And now . . . I don't think I can live without him. Cree, what am I going to do? Where can I go? I'm no use to anyone any more!'

He held her fiercely. Just for a second he thought of Bernice, then he said in his strongest voice, 'You stay at home, where you belong, my dearest daughter. With your ancient father. Only he's going to make things a bit easier now.'

Cass remembered how Reg had said that he wanted her to travel and meet people and enjoy life. At last she started to cry.

On the Wednesday, Helen and Walter Chiverton arrived from Leeds. They were laden with food and gifts. 'We didn't bring Christmas presents for any of you before because we didn't know you. And Dennis told us that this is a celebration of Mr Jepson's life and celebrations always mean food.' Helen unloaded things for the freezer. 'Who has never had caviare? And what about Fandango ice cream with chocolate dip? Oh, and here are some crackers and sweets.'

'Don't forget the torches,' said Walter.

'Torches?' queried Tom and Adam in unison.

'It's a game we used to play when we were younger. A bit like hare and hounds except that it has to be played in the dark and you signal each other with torches. We thought that when we get back from church and everyone has gone, we ought to play a game. Your Uncle Reg would like that, wouldn't he?'

The children had not played much in the last four days and Gemma nodded vigorously. 'But he's not Uncle Reg. He's just Reg. Like my doll,' she explained. She said, 'Would you like to come down to the beach this afternoon and see us mud-sledge?'

Ted was still away but Ivy nodded. 'If Mark and Dennis will come and help I really don't see why not.'

Mark was keen. 'Thanks for bringing us back to life,' he said to Walter that afternoon as he donned Cass's wetsuit and slid around in an incoming tide.

Walter said, 'Well, somehow you've all managed to have a wonderful time in spite of all the things that have happened. I think your uncle would want you to go on doing that.'

'I suppose there have been a few catastrophes.'

Walter listed them. 'Our Paula lost the baby. A madman was drowned and almost drowned one of the children. And now . . . this.'

'I see what you mean.' Mark made a wry face. 'But you don't know about all the good things. Quite a few of those as well.'

Walter watched him swing the sledge in a huge arc around the bay. He wanted to tell this nice young man about their own good fortune: they had found a daughter. But it sounded sentimental so he did not.

The church was well filled. Reg had collected an army of friends locally and the death had been published in the Bristol paper so his cronies from the Ancient Order of Whelks were there too. His solicitor, John Protheroe, sat behind a pillar. The two soldiers who were in the back row joined May and Arthur outside afterwards to admire the flowers. They did not stay. Arthur said, 'We'll see you next week anyway. Thanks for making the effort.' They both cuffed Mark as they left and Mark cowered as usual. Holly looked from them to May and thought of all that had gone on here in the past and felt that strange sensation described as a goose walking over a grave. Mark, glancing at her, said, 'Are you all right, Holly?'

She took his arm as they walked up the path to the gate of the cemetery. 'Mark . . . I don't think I want to stay here always.'

He said comfortably, 'Then we won't.'

'It's what Reg wanted.'

He smiled down at her. 'Darling. Reg wanted us to be happy.'

'But it's a job. In fact two jobs. And we haven't got jobs any more, darling.'

He opened the door of the car and tucked her inside. 'Let's talk about it tonight. I think we can work something out.'

He opened the back door for May and Arthur and they drove sedately back to the bungalow and yet another of their buffet meals. May thought how marvellous it would be when she and Arthur could sit in front of the fire with a tray each and watch the news while they ate their supper. And even Paula wanted to get back to the Bristol flat now and try out the recipes given to her by Ivy. Helen and Walter drank a cup of tea apiece and got on the road, after many promises to meet up again in the summer.

Bernice could not wait to leave: she remembered how much she had wanted to go on New Year's Day. If only she had . . . if only Reg hadn't died . . . things might have been so different. But everything had gone wrong and Cass was back with Cree and all passion was spent. Her grandmother had had some saying about cold porridge. This porridge was very cold indeed. She had a quiet word with Pansy and Mavis and they left as soon as they decently could.

'We'll see you all in the summer,' they promised. And Mavis said to Cass, 'I'm going to learn to swim. We'll have before-breakfast dips every day! How does that sound?'

'I don't know,' Cass said helplessly. She had visibly lost weight and in one of Bernice's black dresses she looked like an Italian peasant woman in need of a good plate of spaghetti.

Cree sat hunched over his knees, hands dangling between them. He did not look up when Bernice said goodbye or when May passed him more tea. His hair, off-white and stiff with salt, curled over the collar of his jacket. He had driven home during the week in a last-minute effort to find his old uniform to wear to Reg's funeral. It had long gone and would not have fitted him anyway. Its loss was somehow the last straw. He could not comfort Cass's grief any more because his own had overwhelmed him.

Mark came and sat by him.

'It'll get better,' he said quietly. 'For both of you. Reg has left her some money so life will be easier.'

'He's taken too much with him, Mark.' The old man looked up and grinned wryly. 'I was going to do some decent work again, did you know that?' He shrugged. 'Not any more.'

'Why not? It would give him a hell of a kick to know you were going to try.'

'He's taken all that with him. All that . . . youth and endeavour and excitement and en- thusiasm . . . oh Christ, you know what I mean.'

'I think I do. But he hasn't. He's sort of kicked us in the solar plexus and we're winded. But that's all. He hasn't taken a thing. In fact . . .' Mark leaned down so that he could look into the empty blue eyes. 'He's left us far more than money. All those feelings and ideas . . . that's his legacy.' He frowned. 'I don't want you to forget that, Cree. Because if you throw that away, you're insulting him. And you were supposed to be his friend. I gather you were pretty close in the army?'

Cree said dully, 'He was my batman. He saved my life actually. A couple of times.'

Mark did not show his surprise. He said, 'What for? So that you could paint rubbish? Or so that you could do something halfway decent?'

'Oh God. Oh Mark. I need to cry. I'll have to go.'

Mark said urgently, 'Stay a few days longer. The studio is there.'

'I want to get Cass away.'

'Just tonight then.'

'All right. Walk Cass down when she's had enough, will you?'

'Of course.' Mark went to the door with him and watched him stumble down the drive and thought of that time a week ago when he had listened to him falling about in the trees and cursing loudly. So much had happened . . .

The solicitor stood up as if to leave and then reached down for his briefcase.

'I think perhaps now is the time to read Mr Jepson's will. Is that all right with everyone here?' He smiled at their surprise. 'In many ways Reg was old-fashioned and this was the way he wanted it. Everyone concerned is here, and it won't take long, so perhaps you can gather round.'

Ted said quickly, 'We'll go and leave you

in peace. It's all right to stay another night at Magpie Cottage, is it, Mark?'

'Please do. Holly and I would appreciate that.'

The solicitor put out a hand. 'Actually if you are Mr Edward Harris, then the will does concern you. And your partner, incidentally. Mrs Ivy Edwards?'

Ivy nodded, clutching Giles, looking very apprehensive. Everyone's surprise increased. Cass began to cry again and Holly sat by her and held her in her arms.

The solicitor said, 'It won't take long, I do assure you, Miss Evans.' He made a space on the table and took out a clutch of papers. 'The will is in the form of a letter to you all. Reg came into my office on the Thursday before he died and gave me the original of this letter.' He held up the top sheet of paper. 'He signed it in the presence of Mrs Pansetti and myself, which makes it a legal document, but of course it is very informal. I've had copies made for each one of you. If you would prefer to read your copies privately, then I will go no further.'

They looked at each other, not knowing what to say.

Holly cleared her throat and said quietly, 'Is there anything in the letter that might embarrass anyone?'

'I don't think so. And it is unsentimental. I think it might help Miss Evans.'

'What do you think, Cass?' Holly bent her

head to where Cass was almost crouching within the crook of her arm.

She looked up momentarily; her face was colourless and drowned.

'I don't care,' she said hoarsely.

The solicitor glanced around at the others, who all nodded or shrugged.

'Very well. Please stop me at any time if you would prefer to change your minds.' He continued in exactly the same tone of voice to read from the page in his hand. ' "Dear friends, Seems strange I won't be there when you read this. Or perhaps I will. Who knows. Anyway, no more of that. I'm writing mainly for my nephew Mark and his wife Holly; my friend's daughter, Cassandra Evans, known as Cass; Toby and David Long, sons of my friends Arthur and May Long, and Mr Edward Harris and Mrs Ivy Edwards who have been staying at the village for two weeks over this Christmas and New Year. But to all of my friends this is a chance to say thank you. And that is what I am saying. Thank you. I am no good with words but all I can say is, my life has been good; I would not want to change anything in it. Thank you.

' "To Mark and Holly I leave the holiday village. Sell it and buy your dream house. Live in it and watch all those sunsets. I don't mind which you do. Just be happy. I am leaving you a lump sum too, to keep you going until it all happens.

' "To Cass I leave half of whatever is in the bank. It will be a decent sum, Cass, because the village has always given Maude and me a good living and we were able to save. You and me . . . we talked about travel among other things, didn't we? I always fancied Italy. Go there for me, Cass. Soak up the sunshine and look at some proper paintings! But whatever you do is all right with me. I would like you to spend it on yourself though.

' "To Toby and David. You don't know me very well and when you were small and spent holidays in the village, you created havoc! But because of your mother and father, Maude and I looked on you as our family. I want you to have a percentage of what is left from my savings. When you come out of the army it will set you up in your own homes if that is what you want.

' "Finally, Ted and Ivy. You will soon be married and I know that together you can tackle anything. But if you want to move away from where all that awful business happened, then perhaps this small legacy will help. Protheroe will work it all out, of course, but it should be enough to set up home somewhere new and keep you afloat until Ted gets another job. It is strange that when you first wrote to me and booked Magpie Cottage for Christmas, I knew that it was going to be a special time: I was not surprised to find that Stanley was no longer with Ivy but I was very glad. May you be happy.

' "May you all be happy. Cree, if you don't start painting seriously again, I shall come and haunt you. Bernice, if you don't go looking for happiness again then I shall do the same to you. Mavis and Pansy, enjoy everything. Go to Italy with Cass, learn how to swim, shout into the wind! Dennis and Paula . . . you will be all right, no need to haunt you! And dear May and Arthur, you've not been left out – you know that.

' "I think it's safe to say that I will see you all soon." '

The solicitor looked up. 'That's it. Our accountant has worked out the specific amounts of the bequests and I have them here. They are substantial.' He glanced around. 'I will leave the copies of Reg's letter on the table for you to collect. And if you want to ask me anything, please feel you can. Now or later – my telephone number is on my card and you each have one.'

This time they kept their eyes down. Cass had stopped weeping and stared at her locked hands, seeing something quite different. Holly was having obvious difficulty in restraining tears and hiccoughed quietly. Mark held her against his side and put his forehead against her hair. Ted stood like a ramrod, rigid with surprise. It was Ivy who broke the silence.

'Oh . . . how wonderful. What a dear, dear man.'

And Holly turned her face into Mark's shirt and sobbed uncontrollably.

* * *

That night Cass did not sleep. She stared into the half-darkness and thought about the rest of her life and the enormous sum of money mentioned by the solicitor. At six o'clock the next morning she slid out of bed and went to stand by the big studio window. Lights pricked the darkness over in Wales and strung a line across the river where the new bridge linked the two countries. She was determined not to start crying again but she shivered in the cold and clutched at the window latch to keep her balance.

Cree came up behind her and put his arms around her and held her tightly against his barrel chest.

'Nothing to be frightened of, Cass,' he said steadily.

She gasped a laugh. 'Hark at you! Of all people!'

'That's why I'm the one to be able to tell you.' He tightened his grip. 'You told me you felt awkward because he was my friend and he'd left me out. But you were wrong.'

'Oh I know. He expected me to share. Obviously. What's ours is ours.'

'No, I didn't mean that at all. In fact, I'm surprised he didn't tell you to make me stand on my own two feet!' He laughed gently. 'Maybe that's what he meant about my painting. Yes, he probably did. But I meant something completely

397

different. Reg left me something infinitely precious and he knew he was doing it. He left me . . . well, a kind of faith, I suppose.' He laughed again and kissed the top of her head. 'I can't be frightened of eternity now, can I, Cass? Not when he's going to be there wearing his Father Christmas stuff.' He shook her gently. 'Did I ever tell you he saved my life in the war?'

She managed a return laugh. 'Yes. Several times.'

'He's done it again, Cass. Saved my life. If I'm not scared, of course I can paint. Properly. Bugger the money. You're all right and I'll always be all right. So I can paint what I want to paint. Do you see, love? D'you understand?'

She was silent, staring out at the invisible sea and the lights and the sheer awfulness of eternity.

She whispered, 'I'm glad. But it's worked the other way for me. I'm so frightened, Cree. So very frightened. He's given me what he sees as freedom and I don't want it. I don't want the responsibility of having to be happy for his sake. Can *you* understand that?'

'Of course. Of course, sweetheart. And he understood that being with me, looking after me, thinking of me before yourself . . . that was a breeding ground for dependence and – ultimately – fear. That was why he mentioned travel. Italy. Cass, they'll love you there. I did some work in Florence years ago. You must go to

Florence . . .' He stopped speaking because she was shaking so badly.

She said, 'Will you come with me, Cree? You'd love it too.'

He almost shook her. 'Haven't you been listening? No, I will not come with you, idiot child! The cage door is open, Cass. For God's sake – fly!'

She turned into him and wept again and he held her until the storm was over. Then he lifted her and put her back on the bed.

'You're absolutely exhausted. Go to sleep. I'm going to potter about – you'll feel quite safe – and we'll have a sort of brunch when you wake.'

She clutched the sheets and blankets around her and lay on her side watching him. For some time she did not know what he was up to over in the corner where she and Mavis had posed a lifetime ago. And then she realized he was preparing a canvas and paints.

She mumbled, 'Too dark.'

And he looked over at her, almost surprised that anyone was with him, then he said, 'I want to paint the dark. Make it a friend.'

She whispered, 'A friend . . . I wish Mavis was here. No more swimming . . .' and she was asleep.

Ted and Ivy could not get over it.

'It – it's like a book,' Ivy said. 'A happy ending. A proper, old-fashioned happy ending!'

Ted said, 'We wouldn't have forgotten him anyway. Ever. But now . . .'

Adam said, 'Is it a lot of money, Dad?'

'It's enough for us to move house.'

'Let's move down here,' Tom said. 'It would be like moving close to Reg if we moved down here.'

'Reg,' Gemma said sleepily, clutching her doll.

'Not much work down here, Tom.' Ted looked round at them all. He had a big family to support now. 'I need a decent job.'

'Could you set up on your own, Dad? Maybe buy a shop with a flat over the top. My friend at school, his dad keeps a shop.'

Ted knew he was not the sort to be self-employed. He needed a weekly wage so that he could make a budget. Cutting your coat according to your cloth was how he always put it.

He said, 'It's a bit risky, old man.'

Giles, asleep in Ted's arms, made a gurgling sound and threw up a fist. They all laughed. Adam said contentedly, 'It wouldn't have mattered really, would it? If he hadn't left us anything, it wouldn't have mattered. It's just so nice to be a proper family. That's what he gave us.'

Ivy hugged him. 'And he's started you talking again,' she said.

'We must all talk,' Ted said solemnly. 'Decide what to do. It must be a family decision. We'll go into it properly tomorrow.'

They all smiled.

Gemma said, 'Shall we have a cup of tea?'

And they laughed.

Holly could not stop walking around the bungalow. Mark begged her to come and sit down and relax with a cocoa before bed, but after five minutes in the chair she was up again and wandering from room to room.

'It's so empty,' she said. 'Do you realize we're here by ourselves?'

'Of course I do. But we don't have to stay, love. Not if it's giving you the creeps.'

'It's not. Not at all. But I have to get used to it, Mark. We're living here now, not just staying. It's home.'

He said, 'It need not be, Holly love. We've read the letter a dozen times. He meant what he – dear old Nunc. He's quite happy for us to sell up and move on. We can take our time – find a place in the country where you can set up a kiln and a wheel and I can have a market garden.'

She paused and looked down at him, clasping her hands under her chin.

'I know. I know. It would be wonderful, Mark. But we can't. Not really. Can we? This is Reg's own holiday village . . .' She enunciated each word distinctly. 'We can't ever sell it, Mark.'

'No. I feel the same way.' He sighed deeply. 'I've had an idea. Was going to talk it over tomorrow with you but if you're going to keep walking all night perhaps I'd better tell you now.'

She managed a wry grin and sat down next to him.

He held her to him and said slowly, 'How about if we put a manager in here . . . someone who needs a big bungalow for a large family . . . who is totally honest . . . who would enjoy every minute of it . . .'

He paused and she breathed, 'Ted. And Ivy. Tom, Adam, Gemma and Giles.' She screwed her head round and peered up at him. 'Would they?'

'I haven't got the faintest. But I'm pretty certain they will want to move right away from the Midlands. Which means Ted won't have any work.'

She continued to stare at him, then she said, 'Mark Jepson, you are not only a genius, you are also a second generation Father Christmas!'

Nine days after the funeral, on a particularly dreary Sunday when it was getting dark, Mavis's doorbell played its usual tune and the three 'window-cleaning ladies' put down their teacups almost in unison and two of them spoke to Mavis.

'Who can that be?'

They were all suffering from a bad bout of anticlimax and had assembled at Mavis's house because she always kept a supply of cake and Earl Grey.

Bernice felt both dreary and angry. Once again she had made a complete fool of herself. It hadn't mattered with Reg, who was discreet and infinitely kind and sensitive. But Cree Evans was another kettle of fish altogether. She wondered whether he had confided in Cass and, if he had, how it would have been done. And if he'd kept his counsel so far, how long before he went into a pub, got drunk and started to boast of his latest conquest. And then she would remember that conquest and her heart would ache and she would become utterly dreary again.

Mavis, so full of plans to learn to swim and exercise and maybe take up painting, was wondering where all that Christmas energy had gone to. She was so tired – no wonder, of course, because she couldn't sleep any more – and her hair had gone absolutely flat and she looked about ninety. Suddenly she was asking herself whether her life was worth living.

Pansy had been exhorting them both to do some voluntary work.

'Girls, we've got to be useful,' she said. 'We've got to – to – what is it they say? We've got to *make a difference*! So that when we die our – our absence is noted—'

'Shut up, Pansy,' Bernice said briefly.

Mavis said, 'What do you suggest? Working in the charity shop in the precinct?'

'Why not?' Pansy said. 'Though it does smell rather . . .'

Bernice looked at them bleakly and knew that they would be an asset to any charity shop; they would pitch in, get to know regular customers. And she would not.

Mavis said longingly, 'I wondered about spending the winter and spring somewhere . . . not too warm but warmer than here. And interesting. Where we could be – sort of—'

'Free?' Bernice queried, intending to sound ironic and hearing her own voice shake pathetically.

And that was when the doorbell rang.

Cass stood in the porch looking like a drowned rat, although Cree's ancient car was parked in the drive.

She waved her hands. 'I went to Bernice's address. And then Pansy's.' She tried to smile. 'It's sod's law that I'd find you in the last house!'

'Is that how you got so wet?' But Mavis didn't care. She was so pleased to see Cass that she threw her arms around her and gave her a huge kiss. 'Life was looking pretty grim. And now you're here we'll all cheer up.'

Cass gave an upside-down smile and followed Mavis into the sitting room. While the other two exclaimed and took her mac and pushed a chair close to the fire, she took in the sheer cosiness of Mavis's house. The thickness of the carpets, the squashy, comfortable armchairs and matching sofa, the knick-knacks on every surface, the gas fire that looked exactly like burning logs . . . Her heart sank.

She said yes to the tea and no to the cakes and smiled at the barrage of questions. 'Yes, we're back home. I thought perhaps Holly would have phoned you.'

'I phoned her to say we were all safely in our nests,' Mavis said. 'She told me that the solicitor had read the will and that she and Mark would be staying in the village.'

'When was that?'

'Friday evening. The day of the funeral.'

'And that's all she told you?'

'Yes.' Mavis was agog. 'Why? What's happened, Cass? We're so pleased to see you but why are you here?'

'I couldn't stand it any longer.' Cass tried to smile and her face went out of control. 'I suppose I've run away.'

They stared at her. She got out a soggy handkerchief and mopped her face. Mavis passed her a tissue.

Eventually Bernice said quietly and sensibly, 'Start at the beginning and tell us everything, Cass.'

Cass rolled the tissue between her palms and threw it at the fire and Mavis leaped forward and retrieved it.

'It's only a gas fire,' she apologized.

Cass seemed to be cheered by the little

incident. She smiled properly and said, 'I need you, Mavis. I want you to come with me to Italy. I need to go to Italy, you see – it's what Reg wanted me to do. And I'm frightened. I'm frightened all the time and I'm clinging to Cree and he says I mustn't do that. Reg has opened the cage door and I must fly away. Will you fly with me?'

They stared at her. Bernice said, 'Go on.'

'Reg left me a lot of money. He said I could use it any way I liked. But I know he wants me to travel.' She looked around the room. 'I'm a fool. I couldn't ask you to leave the comfort of your home and just . . . take to the road.'

Pansy said, 'We do it quite often, actually. We like travelling. Don't we, girls?' She took one of Cass's hands in hers. 'We were just wondering what we could do now . . . It's so dull after what has happened. Perhaps this is it.'

Bernice cleared her throat. 'Why Italy?' she asked.

'He said I should look at proper paintings.' Cass looked down at Pansy's hand; it was soft and manicured. 'It's a lot of money. I thought Cree would come. But he won't. He says that's not what Reg wanted at all. He wanted me to be . . . free.'

Mavis murmured, 'Free. Oh yes.'

Pansy said, 'It's ideal. We'll come. Won't we, girls?'

Mavis murmured again, 'Oh yes.'

Bernice remained silent.

Cass started to weep. 'I can't leave him, you see. He – he's so vulnerable. And he's cancelled that commission he was working on. And he's burned the stuff he did down at Wren Cottage. And he's trying and struggling – he didn't go to bed at all last night. He wants to paint . . . .' She looked up. 'Bernice, he wants to paint you!'

Bernice looked across at the drowned face of Cass Evans and her own eyes began to fill. She wanted to come back with a retort about not undressing for anyone, let alone Cree Evans, but she did not. The tears spilled down her cheeks.

Cass said, 'It's not only the painting, Bernice. He needs you. He says he doesn't need anyone and I'm to go, even if he has to throw me out and lock the door . . . Of course he wouldn't do that.' She blinked and said sharply, 'You do know how kind he is, don't you? He's thoughtless and selfish and Reg was angry with him for something he'd done – or hadn't done – years ago. But, you see, he has got a talent and people with a talent are sort of . . . slaves to that talent. It doesn't mean they are *selfish* . . . not really. They're just protecting the talent.'

Somehow Bernice found a voice. 'I know that,' she said.

Mavis passed another tissue and Bernice blew her nose fiercely.

Cass said, 'I've got a copy of Reg's letter here.

Please read it. There's messages for all three of you.'

She lay back in the armchair and closed her eyes while the others crouched over the letter. The heat from the fire soaked into her limbs. She wondered whether she would ever be able to control this stupid weeping.

Bernice said, 'He wants you to go with Cass to Italy . . . look. Here.'

Pansy said slowly, 'And he wants you to look for happiness. Oh Bernie . . . you know what that means.'

Bernice took another tissue and pressed it to her face.

Mavis said, 'I'm so pleased about Ted and Ivy. That is a generous gesture. He was a generous and wonderful man, was Reg Jepson.'

'Who are Toby and David?' Pansy asked.

Cass said without thinking, 'His sons.' She corrected herself. 'Well, May and Arthur's sons. But Reg and Maude always looked on them as theirs too.'

Mavis said slowly, 'Ah. I see.' And Pansy said, 'I'm glad. Really glad.'

Cass said, 'Mark and Holly have offered Ted and Ivy the job of managing the holiday village. They would live in the bungalow.'

'Will they do it?'

'They're delighted. They can sell their own homes and with the legacy they will have a good nest egg for the children.'

'What about Mark and Holly?'

'They're house-hunting. Having a wonderful time. They want somewhere with more room for the baby, a smallholding with a barn where Holly can have a pottery.'

'Is she all right? Is the baby all right?'

'Yes, everything's fine.'

'I didn't know Holly was interested in making pots.'

'No-one did.'

The questions ceased at last and the women looked at each other. It was Pansy who spoke for them all.

'We went to the holiday village because Reg asked us. And we had the best time of our lives. And now he wants us to go with Cass to Italy. Well, that's easy. I'd love to go back there anyway. I might even look up Luigi.'

Mavis nodded. 'That's settled. We'll swim in the Adriatic, Cass. You can teach me.' She took a breath and looked at Bernice. 'Now. What are you going to do, Bernie? Come with us? Or go to Cree?'

Bernice said in a low voice, 'I haven't got much choice, have I? Cass has already said she can't leave her father alone.'

Suddenly Cass seemed to regain some of her old strength. She leaned forward and fixed Bernice with a stare. 'Oh no you don't. No-one's pushing you anywhere. If you go and live with Cree it must be because you want to do just that!'

Bernice's dark eyes opened wide with surprise. 'But you said you couldn't leave him alone—'

'I don't care what I said! He's in love with you and if you're not in love with him then it's no good. Cancel everything!'

Bernice did not look at the other two; her colour deepened. 'But he won't come and live here! He wants me to go there. It's all on his terms! It's not fair, Cass.'

'Go somewhere else then. You've got cash. Use it. Take him to Brittany. There's a little artists' colony inland . . . you could get a studio for a song. The weather is better than here.'

'My friends—' Bernice bleated.

'You make new ones. Together.' There was a pause. 'Or . . .' Cass shrugged. 'Or you don't. You stay in your comfortable house with your comfortable friends and you . . . what *do* you do exactly, Bernice?'

Bernice said slowly, 'I stagnate. What did you say about making a difference, Pansy? Well, I don't make a difference to anyone. And if I went and lived with Cree I would make quite a difference to him.'

Cass smiled. 'Promise?'

Mavis said enthusiastically, 'You could set him free, Bernie. So that he can use his talent!'

Bernice tried to smile but still could not. She said hesitantly, 'I suppose that is what love does, isn't it? It sets you free.'

Cass got up and hugged her damply. 'Oh

Bernice. No wonder he loves you. You've got it so right!'

Three months later, when the daffodils bloomed in drifts all the way down to the beach and Ted was painting Seagull Cottage, Dennis and Paula Chiverton came for the day and caught up on all the news.

'I can't believe that Bernice Smythe is living in sin with that old Cree man!' Paula said incredulously. 'I didn't suspect a thing – did you, Chiv?'

'No. But I didn't clue in to the Cass and Reg relationship until the day he died,' Dennis said. 'And I thought you and Ted were an old married couple, Ivy, until your husband turned up.'

'My husband is Ted now,' Ivy said proudly. 'We were married the day we moved in here. Ted calls the bungalow Honeymoon House.'

'Oh, that's just wonderful. And I'm pregnant!' Paula threw her arms wide. 'I thought I was while we were still down here. Well, I wasn't then, but I took a test last night and I am! Isn't that marvellous?'

Ivy was genuinely pleased. 'Congratulations to you both. May I tell Holly? She usually rings at weekends.'

'Tell everyone! We're so pleased.'

'And this time we're not going mud-sledging or overdoing anything,' Dennis said warningly.

'We're going to stay with Walter and Helen,'

Paula confided. 'Dennis has to do a thesis and it will take all the summer, so we're going to live with them. But we thought we'd drop in here first and see when the others have booked their holiday. Then we can book ours.'

Ivy took a large red book from the bureau drawer. 'The first guests came in nineteen fifty,' she said, showing them the original bookings. 'So this year is rather special. A golden jubilee.'

'Last year was special too,' Paula recalled.

Dennis put his arms around her; they were as demonstrative as ever.

'Every time we come here is going to be special,' he announced.

A car drew up and Tom, Adam and Gemma emerged from it and ran up to the front door. 'Can we help Dad?' Adam asked, bursting in on them.

'He said we could,' Tom put in.

Ivy said placidly, 'Say hello to Dennis and Paula. Then change your clothes. Then you can go.'

The children recited obediently, 'Hello, Dennis. Hello, Paula.' And left.

Ivy laughed. 'It's such a marvellous place to bring up children,' she said.

She went outside to wave goodbye to the friend who had dropped off the children, who was turning her car at the bottom of the drive.

Dennis hugged Paula to him. 'You're right.